D1927877

Looking Glass Portal
Swimming Kangaroo Books, January 2007

Swimming Kangaroo Books
Arlington, Texas

ISBN: Paperback 1-934041-18-1
MS Reader 1-934041-17-3
Other formats available: Mobi, PDF, HTML (no ISBN's are assigned)

LCCN: 2006940765

Looking Glass Portal © 2007 Larriane Barnard
ALL RIGHTS RESERVED. This book may not be reproduced in whole or in part without permission.

Warning: The unauthorized reproduction or distribution of this copyrighted work is illegal. Criminal copyright infringement, including infringement without monetary gain, is investigated by the FBI and is punishable by up to 5 years in federal prison and a fine of $250,000.

This book is a work of fiction and any resemblance to persons, living or dead, or events is purely coincidental. They are productions of the author's imagination and used fictitiously.

Cover art by Berin Uriegas

Swimming Kangaroo Books

Dive into a good book! Come visit us at

http://www.swimmingkangaroo.com

for a unique reading experience.

I

The staple gun popped, sinking the metal bracket into the fence post and pinning the twisted strands of barbwire. Done was the last post, the last piece of wire, and the last staple needed to repair a short section of a long line of fence, but it would only be good for a time. Tomorrow or the next week, or next month another post would rot or another staple would rust through to loosen another strand of wire or two, or three. The job of finding and tightening those loose wires or felled posts was endless. When the man doing it was in pain, it seemed all the more futile. He wondered again what the hell he was doing as he straightened, the simple movement causing him to grimace and flinch.

"I ought to give it up, Boss," he said to the big, bay gelding that was ground reined and waiting for him.

He crossed to the horse, whose ears pricked up to listen. Garrett Maniam chuckled softly. He dropped the staple gun into a pouch on his tool belt and unfastened the belt from his narrow hips to put in his saddlebags.

"But you and I know I lack good sense."

His shadow stretched out in front of him when he turned from the horse. The dark shape mocked him with no indication in the silhouette of the weakness eating away at his strongly built body. The only reason he was still working at even so minimal a job was because his condition wasn't visible. The first time any employer knew of the constant pain in what appeared to be a strong back and muscular legs or saw those legs crumble uselessly under him, for no matter how brief a time, Garrett would be fired. Six feet plus of solid muscle at one hundred and ninety pounds, he still looked fit and strong at what Garrett called the way wrong side of forty, though he knew the years of constant pain had etched lines in his face to make him look older. The body, however strong, was useless when the lower half suddenly went numb and lifeless. No employer wanted a possible liability like that around.

With a rock for a seat Garrett stretched his right leg out to dig into the thigh pocket of his chaps for a cigarette and matches. The first heavy draw of smoke was held in his lungs as he flipped the match out but not away. Years of habit had him hold the match to cool first while his slate blue eyes stared out over the hills of scrub oak and juniper of the high mountain desert. He exhaled slowly, pushed the worn and stained hat back from his brown, gray-streaked hair, and leaned forward with his elbows on his knees. A nerve played in jerks along the edge of his strong jaw before he spoke to the horse again.

"Been thinking, Boss, I ought to take that pistol out and strap it on my hip." The horse nickered at him. "Could be anytime," he went on conversationally. "Hate to be caught down on the ground where I couldn't do anything about it."

He drew deeply and the smoke drifted out of his thin lips. Garrett didn't expect anyone to grieve over his death. He'd made sure during the last twelve years of his life that there was no one to care, no one but the horse that stood a few feet away.

Boss moved closer to Garrett, knowing the man was through working. Being of a herd nature, the horse sought companionship. Garrett, a man with natural herding instincts as well, had forced himself to be a loner. Over the years the bond between animal and man had grown strong.

The horse played at the rolled-up sleeve of Garrett's faded denim work shirt with his upper lip. The attention drew Garrett away from his pensive thoughts and brought a full smile to his lips. "You're damn near worthless," he told Boss with an affectionate slap on the neck. "And quit slobbering on my shirt."

Boss sucked in air, swelled his chest. A neighing followed, complete with a spray of saliva while Boss swung his head up and down in acknowledgement of the conversation. Garrett stood quickly to avoid what he knew was coming. When Garrett grabbed for the saddle horn to keep from falling the horse understood the sudden need to stand still and steady. The quick movement had caused an onslaught of intense pain through Garrett's back and down his legs, taking his breath away. He hung there waiting for normal breathing to return and the pain to lessen.

"It's getting bad," he gasped when the horse turned his head to nuzzle at his shoulder. His jaw clinched while he pulled up and got his legs back under him. He was covered in sweat as he put his full weight back on his legs. The pain told him his legs weren't at the stage of giving out completely, not if he lessened the strain, and he eased down to the rock. With his breathing almost back to normal, he talked with a sardonic half-smile.

"What am I going to do with you, huh? You're too old to make a decent cowpony." He gave a short, bitter laugh. "No one wants a cripple in a wheelchair and a broken down old horse. Think there's going to be a miracle come along and save us?" Boss snorted and shook his head. Garrett laughed again. "Me neither. So what do you think? I can just turn you loose out here and bang." He imitated pulling the trigger with his finger pointed at his temple. "No more problems."

Boss tossed and shook his head, making Garrett smile crookedly at him. "Okay, I'm not quite ready to give it up, but I don't know why." He stood and grimaced, caught and held his breath briefly. "There isn't anything around the corner up here I haven't already seen, and I'm not going anywhere else."

He looked for the cigarette he had dropped and crushed it out with the high heel of his riding boot. Just as his hand closed on the nearest rein, Boss threw his head and backed, yanking Garrett off his feet. The smell hit Garrett as he landed on his knees. It was like nothing he had ever smelled before, and as a working cowboy he had smelled some of the worst. The odor was like something between a skunk and a rotted carcass. The stench drove Boss wild, and made Garrett sick. He held his breath and crawled in a desperate attempt for the reins.

"No, Boss!" he cried out.

The fence with its flesh tearing barbs was behind them, but Boss was too panicked to see it as he whirled and lunged. Garrett got one foot under him only to go down when something hit him in the back. He saw Boss hit the wire as he fell. He saw the wire snap and whip as the ground rushed up to slam him in the face. He heard Boss's screams of pain and terror. His own terror began.

Garrett couldn't move.

The source of the smell was like nothing he had ever seen in fact or fiction, and it wasn't dead. A man, almost as wide as he was tall and about four feet in height, stood before him. He had the face of a Neanderthal and was dressed in furs. The stench from him gagged Garrett as the creature flipped him to his back. Garrett's stomach heaved, and he felt as though he would vomit while he lay flat on his back unable to move with the foul-smelling creature leaning over him and grunting like a pig.

Garrett's mind fractured as the smell nearly suffocated him. One part of his mind thought he would vomit and drown in his own puke, which was an absurd worry when a few minutes before he had been calmly contemplating blowing his own brains out. The other part of his mind screamed in an effort to will the pig-grunting man to hear and help Boss. Neither part of Garrett's mind understood why he couldn't move. He couldn't even close his eyes and, to judge from what followed, that was just how the pig-man wanted him.

The creature dragged Garrett by his hair to the rock where he had sat moments before and propped him against it like a floppy, rag doll. The thing backed off and grunted while blunt, square-shaped hands dug through its fur covering to pull out a slim, narrow box. What looked to be no more than a spot of light shot out, and a rapid succession of grunts followed as the thing leaned down to lift Garrett's arm for him to see what it had done.

"This can't be real," Garrett thought. He must be delirious, or in the grip of a nightmare. No spot of light could punch through flesh and bone leaving his arm hanging, bloodlessly, attached below the elbow by only a thin string of flesh. That was something straight out of Star Wars, and he wasn't in any movie. It couldn't be real. He had to wake up. Boss's screams were real. They had fallen. That had to be what had happened. He was unconscious, and Boss was hurt. He had to wake up.

The thing stepped back, pointed the box, and a second spot of light shot out. The same succession of grunts sounded as it moved back. Garrett decided it had to be a sick laugh as the thing grabbed him by the hair and pushed his head down to see the bigger hole neatly punched through the right side of his chest.

"Let me wake up!" Garrett's mind screamed as his head fell back, and the thing moved off again. *"I've got to help Boss!"*

The thing jumped, squealed, and shoved its hands into the fur wrappings. Its stance changed to defensive, as stiff and as straight as its height would allow.

A girl, as beautiful as the man was ugly, moved into Garrett's line of vision. Corn-silk hair hung down to her waist, and a full billowing gown of pure white covered her from her neck to the ground. She floated rather than walked toward the creature, holding out her hand. The thing protested the obvious demand with squeals and grunts. The girl sang. It wasn't words, but musical notes that alternated with the sounds the thing made until it gave her the box it had so quickly hidden.

When she turned to face him, Garrett wanted to smile. She was a woman actually, not a girl, probably in her early twenties, and her eyes were the color of wild Bachelor Buttons, a brilliant blue violet. She was a dream as lovely as the creature was grotesque, but more importantly, she only looked to where Boss screamed and thrashed for the tormenting sounds to stop. *Thank you,* Garrett thought, knowing without seeing that she had helped Boss. *Thank you,* he thought again, when she sank down beside him and with a brush of her hand closed his eyes.

###

He floated. There were sounds, soft and hushed, singing and soft whistles. Nothing disturbed him until the light came on.

"You can understand me?"

Garrett blinked against the bright blue light. He thought he was waking up in a hospital, and a nurse was talking to him. "The light is too bright," he murmured weakly.

A hand moved to shadow his face. His eyes followed up a white shrouded arm to blue-violet eyes. "You can understand me?" she asked again.

He understood what she said but nothing else. A patch of bright, blue light covered his body. There was only darkness beyond it and her.

"I must question you," she told him. "Were you upon your beast of burden when you were attacked?"

She spoke English, and Garrett stared. Her words didn't move with her mouth. It was as though he were watching a dubbed movie.

He answered in a weak whisper, confused and in shock. "I thought he was a man at first, not some kind of animal,"

"The Karoz is a male humanoid of a primitive race," she told him crisply. "Were you upon your—?"

"Humanoid?" His characteristic sardonic smile twisted his lips even as weak as he was. "If I'm not delirious, I've got to be crazy."

"Delirium is from fever of which you have none. However, your vessel of life is weak. The time of questions must be short. Were you upon your beast of burden when you were attacked?"

The question seemed important though Garrett couldn't understand why any question, either in dream or craziness, would be. "No," he said and closed his eyes. "I was on the ground when that ape thing came at us. Boss..." His eyes popped back open. "Is Boss suffering?"

"Boss is your beast of burden?"

"Yes, is he suffering?" He struggled to get up, but the only thing he could move was his head.

"No, and do not exert yourself."

He gave up, too dazed then to panic. "I could hear him screaming, but I couldn't move. Can't move...must have hit my head...damn I'm tired."

"You are weak."

Garrett gave her a slight smile and told her faintly, "Lady, if any of this was real, I'd be dying or dead."

"You are not dead," she informed him dispassionately, "but you will die without treatment. With treatment you will live, but you cannot return. Do you choose treatment?"

"Sure," he told her with a crooked grin. There was no treatment for a four-inch hole through the chest.

She dropped her hand, and the light hit him in the eyes. He squeezed them shut in reflex and opened them in small slits, just enough to watch. She moved away and became no more than a light shadow in the darkness of the room. A larger shadow loomed in front of her. Its height so exceeded hers that the top of her head barely reached its chest.

"I do not believe, Midradina," said a soft male voice, "that he comprehended the significance of your last question."

Garrett's eyes closed, but he continued to listen.

"The choice of death," she answered indifferently, "over life is always present."

"What of the Karoz? He did not mistake the man as part of the animal as he claims. In my opinion he is guilty of all charges. What will be his punishment?"

"He will be forbidden five hunts."

"That seems very little for what he has done." The voice sighed heavily. "What of this one? Is he to be punished for a crime he has not committed? Discuss it with the Thornns. They have made it too simple." His voice rose in agitation. "How has this happened? No hunter was to go to any inhabited planet. For the Karoz—one of the worst— to go is unforgivable, and to have such a weapon."

Garrett drifted into sleep and missed the answer.

###

Whatever hovered over Garrett was not human. He knew it the instant he woke. He knew he was awake even though he couldn't open his eyes, and he still could not move. However, whatever it was hovering over him didn't cause alarm. If it wanted to harm him, it would have already done so. The presence he sensed wasn't what caused a rapid growing panic; it was the fact that he couldn't move. He fought to move and failed no matter how hard he tried. He had feared partial paralysis. Now he was totally trapped inside a useless body. Nothing responded, not his arms, legs, hands, or even his eyelids. The doctors had told him everything to expect, but they hadn't told him this. He had to be dreaming, and his fear must be manifesting itself in grotesque exaggeration.

"You must calm yourself," a familiar, feminine voice told him.

The effort he put into moving his head caused it to snap a few inches off the table, but nothing else moved. The same blue light from before shrank down to his shoulders. His eyes popped open only to squeeze shut against the brilliance of the light, and he dropped his head back to the table.

"Damn it," he muttered and took deep breaths to quell the building panic attack. "I'm still not awake."

Midradina corrected him coolly. "You are awake."

In a squinted effort to see her, he responded, "Then why can't I move?"

"The field holds you immobile. It is necessary for the treatment."

"Treatment? Oh, yeah." He gave her a disbelieving grin. "Lady, there isn't any treatment for something like that anymore than there's a sawed-off monster to do it."

"Not in your world," she agreed pragmatically.

Garrett grinned. "Sure, that explains it."

She shielded his eyes to explain further. "Your world is many thousands of your units of measure away. You are on a Thornn research vessel."

"In a galaxy far, far away?" he quipped.

"Yes."

With a bemused smile Garrett half-shook his head. "In the way of miracles, that wasn't what I had in mind."

"Your words translate; their meaning does not."

"We're in the same predicament then."

"You do not comprehend what I have told you?"

"I comprehend. I just don't believe it."

"Your Earthling technology is inferior."

Garrett's eyes narrowed to study her. The lady didn't like him. That thought amused him. If he was going to dream of a beautiful, young woman to provide a miraculous cure, he should have made her like him.

"You will," she continued in a condescending tone, "come to accept the reality of your situation, as the treatment is irreversible."

"Your words translate, lady," he taunted, "the meaning did not."

"When you accepted treatment, the yayantz acted," she told him coolly. "Bonding and transformation of you body's injuries have begun. Until it is complete and bonding is severed you may not damage yourself in any way."

"You still ain't making sense." ..." he drawled out, teasing her while thinking this was a crazy way to dream his back was going to heal.

Annoyance flashed in her eyes. Garrett grinned at seeing it. That puzzled her, drawing her arched brows down until they nearly met.

Since it was only a dream, Garrett began to entertain himself and continued in his best imitation of an illiterate cowboy. "I ain't got no notion of what a yaya is, and I cain't make head ner tails of bonding and transformation."

"The yayantz, Earthling, are—"

"Name's Garrett Maniam," he interrupted. "Just call me Garrett."

"The yayantz are creatures you have never seen before," she said stiffly. "Their appearance may alarm you, which is why the room has been kept dark until you have been prepared."

With a flick of her hand the room lit, softening the brilliance of the blue light. Garrett's eyes adjusted to see gray, bare steel walls in a high-ceilinged room. A creature like none he had ever seen floated from a far corner. Its head appeared to be no more than two huge multi-faceted eyes, like those of a bee. A furry, round body extended from behind the head with six spider-like legs, each with a three-fingered hand. The wings, less than half the size of its body, moved in a silent blur at the speed of a hummingbird's.

"I bet they said that would never fly," he commented in fascination. "Does it have a mouth?"

"It does not bite," she countered, making Garrett suspect she had expected, if not terror, at least a startled reaction. "The yayantz produce an organic substance which when placed in a wound bonds with the surrounding flesh, and transformation to the host form begins."

"How?"

Midradina gave an impatient sigh. "Each cell of the molding will enclose a host cell and alter itself to the host pattern. Those two cells divide—you are aware a complete form pattern is within each cell?"

Garrett ignored the question and the even more obvious arrogance. "That sounds cannibalistic."

She sighed again. With a look from her the yayantz moved closer and stretched out one spidery arm. The hand slipped under Garrett's head and raised it, higher than Garrett could on his own. He didn't like what he saw. To begin with he was laid out on a gray metal table, stark naked, with his flesh a disturbing blue color from the light. What had been a hole in his chest was now something colored a sickening shade of green. The same substance formed a bridge that joined the two pieces of his arm with the substitute of flesh and bone in both areas formed to the shape of what was missing.

From her description, it sounded to him like the stuff, the molding, as she called it, was eating off him in some way. It looked like meat rotting within his flesh. The edges of his wounds were no longer clearly defined as the edges of the molding glimmered with the same shade of blue as the rest of his body. Looking at it, all Garrett could think of was that he wanted to wake up. It may be fun to tease the haughty young woman, but nothing else was in the least bit amusing.

The yayantz decided when he had looked enough. Garrett's head was lowered as carefully as it had been raised. The yayantz withdrew its arm, but it did not move away, instead hovering half in the light and half out. As it looked at him, Garrett studied it, amazed at how detailed his imagination was, and decided to not be upset, not even over the sickly green molding. He was only dreaming, and he would just enjoy it as though he were watching a movie.

Each of the yayantz's legs was three feet long. The body, including its head with the protruding eyes, was no more than a foot in length. The blur of its wings covered about half a foot in area. It had an ominous look to it, but there wasn't anything threatening in its manner. Its touch was gentle and by the woman's words, it was a healer, but, as gruesome as other parts of his dream had been, Garrett wondered if a vicious stinger wasn't hidden somewhere in that furry tail-end. Despite the thought, he grinned. What a wacky dream, not like any he had ever had before, and it was cheaper than going to the theater.

"Hi," he said to it.

"The yayantz do not communicate by speech or sound," she informed him. "They are, however, sensitive to your feelings while in bonding."

"Which is why you don't care if I damage myself until after?" he asked with a mocking grin.

"It would be unfortunate if you were to regret your decision," she told him. "A valuable resource would have been wasted."

"Not me, lady, I've always been curious about what's around the next corner. Got me a feeling there's lots of corners in this place." He abruptly changed the subject. "What's his name?"

"They do not have names."

"How do you tell them apart?"

"It is not necessary. One is the same as the other." She looked at the yayantz and nodded. "You must rest now. The yayantz grows weary."

In an instant the light shone in his eyes. His head, eyes, and voice were as frozen as the rest of his body. He could feel the gentle touch from the yayantz closing his mouth and his eyes in preparation for a sleep he did not want. In taunting the woman he'd gotten sidetracked from the many questions he wanted answered, but he did sleep.

When he woke the third time and was again allowed control of his head, he asked, "How long do I have to be like this?"

"Four of your days," she answered. "Your vessel of life can not tolerate the influence of the field any longer."

"How long have I been here?"

"One of your days."

"Lady, I don't—"

"I am Midradina, Emissary of the Thornns. You will address me as such," she told him with her chin at a haughty lift.

"Just as soon as you address me as Garrett," he countered shortly, "I'll address you as Middy-whatever."

"I am—"

"I really don't give a damn what you are," he told her with a crooked grin. "I didn't ask for any of this, and I'm already tired of being spread out stark naked like a corpse in a morgue and being manipulated like a doll by a giant bug. I'm not in any army, and I'm not going to be bossed around by a snooty beauty with her nose in the air."

"Thank him for the compliment," came from the shadows.

Garrett recognized that voice from the first time he had awoke—or dreamed he had. Its owner stepped up beside her. Garrett looked up and up the front of a deep, red robe, over a chest-length white beard, to a well aged face.

"Do not be absurd," she retorted, making the man chuckle. "As usual I fail to grasp the source of your amusement."

"Because, Middy-whatever, an appreciation for humor, the Thornns failed to teach you. Better it may be with him I speak."

"As you wish," she stated indifferently and moved away.

He chuckled again as a chair with a high, gray back slid across the floor to him.

"Did you move that?" Garrett asked while he studied the wrinkled parchment face.

"Telekinesis my power within is not." There was merriment in the man's eyes and crowfeet wrinkles around those eyes to show humor was there often. There was also a look of great wisdom. "Eight feet and six am I in your unit of measure; the first of some answers this of questions have you? Mystaleah am I, the Ancient called by many. Now my face studied you have, see you what you like?"

Although Garrett had some difficultly following the strange speech pattern, he answered truthfully. "Yes."

"Well this is. Also see what like I. Your custom it is, believe I, hands to grasp in greeting friendly. For a time pleasure forego we must as alone the yayantz may the blue light enter without paralysis to some and pain to many. Their nervous system quite different is than of humanoid. Another answers this of your questions?"

"Kind of figured that," he murmured.

Mystaleah chuckled deeply. "Much comprehend you, man called Garrett. Offense you have taken to an arrogant air, mocking to pretend ignorance. Successful you be. Weak of mind believes she you, but remember pretender are all, if pretend think they must be."

"What does she pretend?"

"To one only refer I did not. A warning give I. What will see you and what hear you may not be as seems." He lifted a hand to rub his eye, "Important most what feel you."

Garrett got distracted. Mystaleah's hand was long and slender with only two fingers and a thumb. He was not an oversized human as Garrett had assumed. His dream was definitely being influenced by his watching of too many episodes of Star Trek.

"Ah," Mystaleah drew out slowly. He held his hand closer so Garrett could see it more clearly. "The form of my hand your feelings have altered?"

Garrett looked back into his eyes. "You'd make one hell of a basketball player."

"Basketball? A brief description, please."

"Two teams match up to see who can throw a ball through a high hoop the most."

"A game, a sport, yes?"

"You're speaking English!" Garrett exclaimed. That was why Midradina's mouth hadn't moved with her words. "That's what she meant when she asked if I could understand her. What did she do, and how do you—?"

He didn't finish. The blue light flashed across his head, freezing all movement. An instant later the yayantz hovered over him, closing his eyes. He could hear, but he couldn't do anything else.

"Excited you have I," Mystaleah said softly. "Forbidden it is. Too delicate is your healing." His robes rustled as he moved to his feet. "Later come I."

What excited him wasn't Mystaleah. Mystaleah had just warned him, told him what he saw and heard may not be what it seemed. Midradina had attached or implanted something to translate their language into his while not distorting other sounds. They had done something to him without his knowledge or permission. His life wasn't his own, not even his own body. Something alien had been planted in him to devour him a cell at a time. He had no way of knowing if it was transforming itself to him or him to it. He only knew that while it was happening he was a prisoner.

The panic built until his sense of the ridiculous popped up. It was silly to get worked into a panic over something that wasn't real. He promised himself that when the wild dream was finally over, he would never read another science fiction book or watch another science fiction movie. His fascination with both had to be the source of this crazy dream or— a new idea occurred to him— maybe he actually was crazy. Maybe the fear of what his real future held had pushed him over the edge, and he'd slipped into some kind of illusion to escape from it. Whether he was asleep, unconscious, or walking around mad as a hatter, what was happening to him wasn't real. It couldn't be.

###

Damned if it didn't seem real. He couldn't recall ever seeing or reading of such characters though he supposed they could be composites of ones he had encountered in books or movies. Mystaleah could be an over-sized Merlin, but he couldn't think of anything he had ever seen that came close to the appearance of the yayantz.

Mystaleah told him, "Thoughts your on my words are not."

"Nope," Garrett admitted. "I'm fascinated by them though. I've always known I have a good imagination, but I'm surprising myself, not all pleasantly."

Puzzled at first, Mystaleah smiled. He steepled his six fingers under his chin and leaned back in his chair. "All see, hear, and feel you, decided created you has your mind. But possible all is not? A philosopher has said conceive what a mind can, so achieve can."

Not quite a direct quote, but close enough. "Yeah," Garrett agreed, "and another one said, my mind's made up, don't confuse me with facts." He started in a joking manner, but his crooked smile faded.

Mystaleah's smile faded as well. His face and eyes grew solemn as he leaned forward to speak, and what he said next put his lips out of sync with his words. His voice had lost the musical quality and become mechanical. "What I say to you now, I say in my own language. Though I know English well my mind must search for the words, and I wish no mistakes. You asked if I am capable of moving things without touching. Is it a common practice of your world?"

"Only in fiction."

"Yes, and here you will see many things, creatures, and technologies which may be very similar to what is fiction on your world. I believe minds of higher orders are linked to receive impressions over vast distances. While it is an idea on one world it may be real on another, or limited from completion by technology on one world while in use on another more advanced. But I will not tire you now with my theories. You spoke of things unpleasant. The attack of the Karoz was, as was the suffering of your Boss, yes? What other things are disturbing?"

"Besides the obvious?" Garrett asked mockingly.

"May I touch you?"

"I can't do anything to stop you," he said with tightness in his voice.

"Any resistance from you, and the yayantz would push me away."

"Why?"

"They have given much of themselves on your behalf. As a creature void of emotions, it is governed by an instinct of survival. When you have pain in the wounds it has treated, it has pain until the transformation is complete, but it has no tolerance for pain. For you a pain that is no more than annoying would be agonizing for it. We are not insensitive to your feelings, but your pain would be extreme and cripple them without the light and any stress to you will delay the process. To hasten the process and eliminate—"

"I get the picture. I'm an asshole."

"This did not translate."

"I'm an ungrateful—"

"No, no, no," Mystaleah cried. "Do not think so of yourself even when you grow impatient." He smiled again, but with sadness. "It is as you said, you did not ask for this. You have reason to be angry with the Thornns. The responsibility for this lies solely with them. We can not alter the necessary manipulation until you leave the field, but whatever else we may do to ease your transition, we will."

"Can you get them to stop turning my head off?"

"I will speak of it to Midradina. You have been covered, and I have spoken to her of her manner toward you, though I doubt it will alter. You spoke also of the molding with distaste. If I may touch you, I wish for you to see how it progresses."

"Sure," he answered glibly. What Mystaleah said made so much sense he was beginning to wonder if it all wasn't true.

They knew immediately Mystaleah was not to touch Garrett. The yayantz moved so fast to hover protectively over Garrett's body, it seemed to materialize in the air.

Mystaleah did not challenge the creature but drew his hand back from Garrett's head and commented, "It seems exceptionally protective of you."

"Okay, watchdog," Garrett told it. "I'm getting tired anyway, but do me a favor and leave that light off my head."

"It does not understand you, Garrett," Mystaleah told him. "It communicates telepathically with Midradina only through a device the Thornns created for her. Neither have I ever been able to detect it as capable of reason, its actions being instinct only."

One small hand reached out and lifted Garrett's head to enable him to see his own body as Mystaleah had been about to do. From the waist down a sheet covered him. As a concession to his modesty the gesture was a little after the fact, but still comforting. So were the green spots in his flesh. They were smaller than they had been before and were infused with purple lines.

"Primary bonding," Mystaleah explained, "will be complete in twelve more of your hours."

"It's all going to be healed in four days?" he asked in dazed wonder.

"No, it will be primary only. Your body can not sustain the light for the required length of time for complete transformation."

"If it's not complete, what happens to the yayantz?"

"You will take great care to prevent it any discomfort," Mystaleah answered with perception. "It is extremely fortunate there were no unexposed injuries to complicate things. The yayantz can only treat open wounds."

Garrett was instantly angry. "How long will the yayantz hurt because the Thornns ordered it to help me?"

"Your pain will be of tenderness, much like you would have from a bruise," Mystaleah started to explain.

"Tenderness for me but excruciating to it," Garrett retorted.

"First you must understand, they were not ordered to do this, but were compelled by their nature. Also as protection for themselves, they have the ability to draw pain from one another to lessen the suffering and—"

"So instead of one, I'm causing pain for several?"

"It was necessary. You would not have survived without the yayantz."

"They should have let me die."

Mystaleah cried, "Do not say such a thing."

"You—"

The blue light silenced him. He got angry, and the yayantz reminded him to be calm. He was forced to think instead of verbalizing his frustration. He hadn't dreamed of a miraculous cure for his back. The yayantz could treat only open wounds. Because he believed there was no treatment for what the Karoz had done, his flippant answer had locked two lives into a body that wasn't worth saving. The yayantz's capabilities were being totally wasted. In the month or two the doctors predicted the body they worked so hard to save would be useless, dead from the waist down. What a cruel joke.

In the next moment Garrett mentally laughed. It was a joke, on him, some screwy trick of his mind.

###

Garrett had no concept of time. The only break in monotony was when Mystaleah came to visit. Over the course of his visits, he told Garrett much about the Thornn culture.

The Thornn had begun their search of the stars many centuries before. Because it was against their nature to kill any living being, the ship was designed to provide accommodations for the specimens taken for study. They had long ago abandoned the taking of specimens since creatures living on the ship did not age, and therefore quarters became limited. The specimens had been divided into three groups—passive, aggressive, and the intermediate—also referred to as scholars, hunters, and the liaisons. If it was within a being's nature to kill, for whatever the reason, he was deemed a hunter. Mystaleah disagreed with this policy. Many choose to be hunters for reasons other than wanting to kill because hunters were allowed to leave the ship to spend short periods of time on various planets.

"I do not believe there will be a choice for you," Mystaleah said.

"I don't enjoy killing, Mysty."

Mysty quirked his eyebrow over his new name, but stayed on the subject. "I did not think this would be so, Garrett, but I believe you will need the hunt. You are a man of intelligence, absorbing knowledge easily, yet in your time of machines of land, air, and water, you traveled on an animal. I sense in you a need for the earth, sky, and wind. The hunt will provide these while you need never kill, except perhaps to protect yourself. You must understand many among the hunters enjoy not the hunt, but the kill."

"What you're telling me is that the only deaths on this ship come from the hunters' violence?"

"If you go among them, not the scholars," Mystaleah said with a slight nod, "always must you be on your guard and never must you show a weakness."

"No Mr. Nice Guy?" Garrett asked with his crooked smile.

"The meaning of your words did not translate, but I think I comprehend. You must, at all times, be hard and unfeeling, showing only strength. As long as they do not sense the gentler qualities of your nature, they will be less apt to challenge you, forcing you to defend yourself."

"That's pretty heavy stuff," Garrett quipped.

"That is good. Your lips smile while your words sting or confuse. You use many words in unfamiliar ways and words of which the meaning does not translate clearly. It will cause them to be unsure of you."

"How do the words translate?" Garrett asked when reminded of something he had forgotten from earlier.

"For now, translators lie in each of your ears. Before you join the others they will be implanted—"

"No!"

The kindly wizard was startled by Garrett's forceful rejection. The yayantz flew forward to hover over him.

"It is a simple procedure. There will be no pain or discomfort," Mysty explained.

"I'll pass," he told Mysty. To the yayantz Garrett said, "It's okay, Bud, I'm cool."

"Without it you will be as a deaf man."

"I'm doing okay now,"

"It must be done," Mysty insisted.

"If he keeps pushing, Bud, I'm going to get excited again. I'm really going to get excited, if he tries burying something in my head."

"It is a simple implant."

"Not in me," Garrett said coldly.

"Why?"

Garrett tried to shrug. He wasn't sure why the idea was so repugnant. It just was. His whole being rebelled against the idea.

"Perhaps you will reconsider at a later date when you feel more in control of your circumstances."

"He thinks," Garrett told Bud, "I'm being childish."

"You mock. You are annoyed with me?"

"No, but I'm getting tired. You've given me a lot to think about all at once."

"I will go."

"I think he's mad at me," Garrett said of the yayantz.

Mysty chuckled. "The yayantz have no emotions, nor do they have gender. They are neither male nor female."

"Hermaphrodite?"

"No, they simply have no reproductive systems."

"Then where do baby yayas come from?"

"They do not," Mysty answered with a smile as he left.

"Hey, Bud," Garrett asked when they were alone, "are you mad at me?"

One spindly arm reached out to touch Garrett's cheek lightly before it returned to its shelf in the corner.

###

It didn't take long to figure out when it was the end of the fourth day. Mysty was beside him, discussing Earth, a favorite subject of his, when four yayantz appeared. Garrett could not help feeling overwhelmed by them. He had gotten used to Bud, but 'his' yayantz stayed on his corner shelf as the other four lined up to hover over Garrett. They lifted him straight up off the table.

The sheet was rolled up towards his waist while loose fitting pants were worked up his legs and tied with a drawstring at his waist. At the same time black patches were applied, one each over the bonding in his chest, front and back. A sheet of the same black substance was wrapped completely around his left arm from his wrist to his elbow.

The blue light went out, and Garrett was lowered to the table to sit on the side. For the first time since he had been attacked by the Karoz, Garrett could move again as eighteen hands slipped away from him. One yayantz stayed, steadying him with one hand to each shoulder. Without its support Garrett would have fallen head first off the table.

"You have dizziness?" Midradina asked as she came in.

"Oh, yeah," Garrett answered with feeling and reached for his head.

The yayantz blocked his arm with one of its free legs while two legs supported Garrett's head. Things stopped swimming.

"You are not to move," Midradina informed him. "They wish to gauge sensitivity before allowing exertion."

Garrett relaxed to let the yayantz support him, but twisted his head enough to see to the corner. "How you doing, Bud?" he asked.

"Has it not been explained to you," Midradina asked, "they do not communicate?"

Garrett ignored her and watched Bud. With its legs folded under it to form a nest for its body, Bud didn't look to be in any discomfort. But then Garrett wasn't either. Aside from the dizziness, he felt fine. Even when the yayantz moved his arm and twisted his body, he felt no pain, and Bud remained serenely in his corner.

"Close your hand tightly," Midradina ordered.

Garrett felt a twinge of tenderness in his arm. Bud withered. One leg contracted violently, tipping its body sideways. Garrett flipped his hand open. "Maybe you better turn that light back on."

"Your vessel of life can no longer tolerate it," Midradina told him indifferently.

"It can not be done, Garrett," Mysty explained further. "Damage would occur to your organs from disuse and death would soon follow. Already there are dangers that must be watched for. Nor can you go any longer without substance and fluid. With the shields, if you practice caution, the yayantz will not suffer."

Most of what he said went right through Garrett's head. "I won't move a muscle," he promised. Bud was again nestled placidly in his corner.

"You must move to stimulate your body functions," Midradina told him tersely. "Must the simplest of things be explained to you?"

"Your bedside manner stinks, lady," Garrett told her rudely.

"Garrett, please," Mysty implored. "Please, be patient."

"I'm stimulating my body functions," Garrett tossed back.

"Yes," Midradina said coolly, "your pulse and breathing have accelerated."

Garrett was out of breath and had a dull ache in the left side of his chest. He looked at Bud. Instead of one yayantz there were three, their legs entwined around each other.

"They disperse the pain amongst them," Mysty explained. "Unless you are injured again in the bonded areas before total transformation, there will be none of the great pain for them you fear."

The fifth yayantz crowded Midradina aside. It carried a gray, cone-shaped container and joined the one hovering in front of Garrett. One of its hands replaced the other one's hand on his right shoulder and together the two yayantz held the strange cup to his lips. He wasn't given time to see or smell what it was before liquid filled his mouth. There was neither smell nor taste, but with one swallow warmth spread out through his body.

"Any nausea?" Mysty asked.

"No, what is it?"

"It is essence to accelerate healing," Midradina supplied. "Also your vessel of life has been dormant for four days. The organs must be stimulated back to their normal functions."

"Already said—" Garrett started to point out tersely.

Another mouthful shut off his words. Behind the first wave of warmth was limpness and nausea. "Getting sick," he murmured sleepily.

"It seems," Mysty said with a chuckle, "he has had enough."

Garrett wanted to ask a question. He forgot what it was when he saw the thing on the front of Mysty's robe. Like a black, huge, hairy spider, it climbed—one tiny hand over the other—to Mysty's shoulder.

While the creature curled two sets of six legs around Mysty's neck in a high collar, he said in embarrassment, "It is what you would call a pet."

Not any kind of pet he had ever seen, Garrett thought as he drifted into sleep. All the pets he'd ever had had four legs with paws, not hands. They'd walked on those paws, not climbed or flew. No, Bud wasn't a pet. Garrett had to remember that Bud was a creature without emotions, an 'it', not a he or she. Nevertheless, he sure missed the little bug when he woke in his new surroundings.

II

The new room was smaller and with a much lower ceiling. Bare walls were the same gray color as those in the yayantz room, and the only furnishing was the narrow gray bed he laid on. In solitude he had more than enough time to examine the coverings the yayantz had placed over his wounds. Not much time was needed.

They were made of a black glossy substance resembling thin leather, but in looks only. Leather didn't seal itself the way the seam in the arm guard did, and both chest and arm guards had formed to him like a second skin. He couldn't so much as get a fingernail under them. Other than that there wasn't much to examining them. The same was true of the translators that snuggled up against the back of each ear in a flat crescent shape. Like the guards on his chest and arm, they adhered in some way, and like the guards they didn't offer much to keep his mind occupied.

Nothing in the bare room was interesting, and he was afraid to move to explore what might be behind the two doors. Not for his own sake, but for Bud's. No one had told him if it was safe to move, a fact that chafed at him while he poked at the gray spongy material of the mattress. He hated needing permission to do anything more than the inactivity itself. It angered him that no one was there to ask. When someone did come in, a scarlet-skinned man with matching hair, wearing what looked like a set of white pajamas, Garrett nearly screamed at him.

"Can I get up?"

"Yes, yes, of course, yes," the man answered with a flutter of his thin hands and lips out of sync with his words.

His whole body fluttered. He turned sideways, astonishing Garrett with how thin he was. He looked normal from the front, but from the side he looked like he had been flattened by a steamroller. At that moment Garrett didn't care what he looked like; all he wanted to do was move. He swung his feet to the floor, shot up, and immediately fell to his knees.

The scarlet man went into a frenzy. "Too fast, too fast," he tittered. "Too, too fast." The more he talked the higher his voice rose, and the more his body trembled. "Too weak, too, too weak. Must get up, up."

"Give me a minute," Garrett gasped out.

"No. No."

With strength unexpected for one with his nearly two-dimensional body, the scarlet man lifted Garrett and deposited him back on the bed. Garrett appreciated the speed with which he completed the action. The touch of the scarlet man's hands burned Garrett's skin.

The scarlet man wrung his hands and moaned, "Oh dear, oh dear, it will be angry, very, very."

From the door Midradina said, "It will not be angry with you, Esten."

"Oh, good," he sighed, "good, good."

"Have you examined him?"

"No, no, too fast, too fast, fell, fell."

"Fell, fell," Garrett mimicked in panting frustration. There hadn't been any pain, but the simple move left him in a struggle for air.

"Yes, yes," Esten answered back. "Must be more careful, must, must."

Midradina cut in with, "Will you examine him now?"

"No, no, not now." He moved out the door with undulating waves of his body.

"Sorry," Garrett said glumly.

"For falling or for distressing Esten so badly?" she asked.

"He does seem to distress easily," Garrett countered dryly, "like he's afraid of falling off the tree." He really didn't feel like baiting her and asked, "How's Bud?"

"The yayantz are fine," she said in terse correction. "We have yet to discern how you are."

"I'm okay, but I'm bored. Could I have a book or something instead of just being entombed in here?"

"The only book we have in English is a dictionary with few pictures. I doubt it would hold your interest."

She drew it out of him. "How about a coloring book?" he asked sweetly. "I should be able to handle that."

"As for being entombed," Her voice rose slightly as she attempted to ignore his taunt, "once you gain strength, you may leave this room and begin to familiarize yourself with your new surroundings."

"Oh, goodie, goodie."

Garrett saw the flicker in her eyes when she turned away and knew he had annoyed her. He didn't feel any satisfaction over it. He would rather have her there insulting him, than be alone. Arguing with her occupied his mind. At least he could move, if he did so carefully. He had made it as far as sitting on the edge of the bed before Esten returned.

"Oh, dear, dear," he began as soon as he saw what Garrett was doing.

"I'm being careful," Garrett assured him, "not too fast."

"Good, good, I may touch you? I may?"

"What for?" Garrett didn't like the idea. The last time the scarlet man's touch hadn't actually burned enough to do more than leave a few red marks, but it had been uncomfortable.

"To examine, examine, I must touch, touch. My temperature is higher, higher."

"I know."

"Oh, dear, dear, forgot, forgot. Burn, did, did?"

"No," Garrett lied. He didn't want to start him off in a fit again.

"Careful now, careful, careful, must touch," he chattered and shook his hands vigorously.

"Go ahead." If it was too warm, he could always pull away.

His hands had cooled, but touching sent Esten into another series of spasms. "No pulse, none, none," he cried with his fingertips pressed to Garrett's elbow.

"Try my wrist," Garrett told him torn between exasperation and amusement. As the scarlet fingers slid down, he guided. "Other side—there."

Esten sighed in relief and rolled his eyes until the pink-tinged whites disappeared. When the orange-shaded iris came back into view, he asked, "Ninety-seven per a unit of your measure that is good, good?"

"It's okay," he said, wondering what kind of doctor first couldn't find a pulse and then didn't know what it should be?

Esten folded practically in half, dropped on the bed beside Garrett, and unfolded to sit. "Scholars never get sick, never, never. How can I treat you, treat, treat, when not know humans?"

"Don't worry too much about it," Garrett told him. He had gotten an answer to his unasked question, which only made him wonder why a doctor who didn't know anything about humans had been sent to examine him. "As long as I eat, drink, and pass it off, I'll be all right."

With another sigh Esten folded his hands in his lap. "Oh, good, good. Yantz make me nervous, do, do. Eat now, now?"

"Sure." He puzzled over why Esten would be made nervous by the yantz while he stored away the shortened name. There had been that business earlier too of him being afraid of making 'it' angry, but Esten was easily made nervous, a fact that was proven a moment later when Esten took a hold of Garrett's arm, and Garrett jumped.

"Oh, no, no, burn, burn," Esten cried and shot to his feet, fluttering.

"You just startled me," Garrett said, not adding that he had jumped because Esten's touch was so hot.

"Forgot, forgot," Esten cried in a near weep and shook his hands furiously. "Not now, not now, help you, help you walk."

His hands were cool when he helped Garrett to his feet, a fact that, along with Esten's strength, fascinated Garrett. The man had to be all muscle. There wasn't any room in that body for bone or anything else as far as Garrett could see including stomach, lungs, or heart. He didn't think the scarlet man had much of a brain either, scholar or not.

They went through a door that opened by itself to another gray room, almost as bare as the first. There was a bench along one wall and a table with two stools along another. The table was a pole with a circular top. The stools were a smaller version of the table. All of them were made of the same gray material as the walls, floors, and ceiling.

After he deposited Garrett on the bench, Esten went to one wall where a two-foot by two-foot panel opened in a way Garrett couldn't see, and he returned with a glass, also made of the same gray substance. Garrett half expected the contents to be gray as well. Since it was clear and odorless, he assumed it was water and being thirsty; he drank it quickly, which put Esten into another fluttering fit.

"Slow, slow, too fast, too fast, fast."

His warning was too late. The liquid hit Garrett's stomach and exploded. He hadn't been so miserably full since gorging the last time he'd had Thanksgiving dinner at his grandmother's many years before. The difference was that his stomach was in no condition to deal with it. Garrett staggered up, one hand to his stomach and one to his mouth. Fortunately he didn't have to explain the problem. Esten half-carried him back the way they had come. A door opened in the corner of the first room. The furnishings and room were as gray as everything else, but it had what Garrett could recognize as a toilet. The bowl of what looked like an oversized mushroom caught the thick globs of gelatin-like stuff his stomach heaved up.

Garrett was exhausted, on his knees with Esten's support at the shoulders. Hell, he hadn't been in very good shape to start with. His whole body trembled with weakness as Esten helped him to his feet. The scarlet man turned him, and Garrett got a glimpse of his image in a mirror. He was as gray as the walls, except for his eyes, which were so hollowed and sunken they looked black. A scrubby growth of beard covered his face.

"I look like hell," he groaned just as his legs folded up under him. "Feel like it too."

"Bad, bad," Esten wailed and picked Garrett up in his arms.

He deposited Garrett back on the bed and walked off in a flutter, repeating the same words over and over. When he came back, he had the gray glass. Garrett shook his head. He didn't want to repeat the bathroom routine.

Esten insisted, "Must, must, slow, sip, sip."

To get rid of him Garrett took one careful sip and handed the glass back. "I'd rather have just plain water."

Esten's objective seemed to be to please. He disappeared for a few seconds, barely enough time for Garrett to close his eyes, and returned, gray glass in one hand; a three-foot round disk in the other and a pole tucked under his arm. Garrett recognized it as the table from the other room. Esten stuck the pole on the floor and dropped the disk on top. Somehow it stayed in place. Garrett promised himself he'd investigate how when he woke up.

###

The first day out of the light and out of the yantz's hands hadn't gone well, but from there things improved, physically at least. The colorless, odorless liquid was called substance, a substitute for food. With nourishment Garrett's strength rebuilt steadily. Their equivalent to a shave, cream smeared on and splashed off with water, improved his appearance, as did the return of some color to his face. The blackness faded from around his eyes. As far as pain went, there wasn't any. He experienced a twinge once in a while if he moved too fast, never without guilt over the pain he might be causing Bud. Aside from being weak his recovery rate was fine. The emotional and mental aspects of his situation were what he had problems with.

The room had nothing to offer that could occupy his mind. He spent ten minutes looking over the table to discover how it had stayed upright. The rough ends of the pipe post adhered to the smooth surface of the tabletop and floor. In another ten minutes he learned that all the furnishings were constructed the same way, a rough surface adhering to a smooth surface like metal Velcro. The joints on the bed and bench were as easy to pull apart as they were to put together.

Once he finished examining those his boredom was only relieved by visits from Esten and games the scarlet man brought with him. Some of the games were so childish they were insulting, and Esten alternately amused or annoyed the hell out of him, depending on Garrett's level of restlessness. Hiding his reactions was also wearing on his nerves as was the fact that he couldn't get out of those two rooms.

Esten could walk towards any of the three doors at any time, any speed, and from any direction, and they opened for him. Garrett tried everything including shoving and kicking at the doors. The damned things would not open for him. He'd just traded one type of prison for another as far as he could see, and all Esten would tell him when he asked about getting out was, "not yet, yet." None of it put him in a very good mood for Midradina's next visit.

Garrett rose from the bench out of habit when she entered. He ended in a mocking bow. "Welcome to my comfy quarters," he told her with a sardonic smile. "With a few dollies and a couple of what-knots, it'll soon be just like home."

"These are not your quarters," she told him curtly. "They are only temporary."

"Ah, gee, and after I went to so much trouble to decorate. I call it early monastery. How do you like it?"

She looked around the barren room and back at Garrett. He grinned at her and asked, "It's that little touch of color that really sets it off, don't you think?"

"Why do you insist on speaking like an idiot?" she asked him tersely.

"Who? Me?"

"You know proper English. To use it would cause fewer complications in communication."

"Proper English? Boy, howdy, that's a tough one." He dropped back down on the bench and lounged on one elbow. "Guess I missed out too much on schooling."

"You are quite capable of complex reasoning, deduction, and comprehension," she retorted.

The games Esten had brought took on an entirely different meaning. "Just a little thickheaded and gullible," he answered tonelessly. "So how did I do, teach? Didn't get no F's, I reckon, but got me a sawbuck says there weren't no A's either."

"Your colloquial vernaculars are most confusing."

Garrett chuckled and deliberately misunderstood. "There you go, calling me an idiot again."

She pressed two fingers to her forehead and closed her eyes briefly. The gesture almost drew regret from Garrett for baiting her—almost. He still didn't like the idea of being tested and evaluated like a lab rat.

"Figure me to be a disappointing specimen?" he asked. Was that all he was to them?

"You are not a specimen." Her hand dropped to her side as she gazed coolly at him. "That practice was abandoned long ago."

"Then why did you bring me here?"

"I have found myself asking that very question."

He gave her that twisted smile. "Iffen you wanted yourself a lap dog, ya shouldn't've picked a man. Old Boss would'a been better than me. Little big, but he'd have laid right in yar lap fer a ear scratching, if he could'a got away with it."

"A lap dog is…?"

"Cute and cuddly, follows you around just waiting for a pat on the head."

"I thought it would be derogatory." She pressed two fingers to her forehead again. "And old Boss?"

"Best horse I ever had. Ya know, iffen ya don't let me outta har purdy soon, I'm gonna get rowdy."

She gazed at him with narrowed eyes for a moment. "You have obviously recovered to a sufficient degree. Your introduction will begin now. It will be up to you as to what speed it progresses from this point onward."

Garrett had the nagging suspicion that was exactly what she had come for. It reminded him of Mysty's advice to be patient. "Did I jump the gun?"

"I do not know, Earthling, nor care," she said. "When you deliberately antagonize me I barely understand half of your words. I have too many duties and too little time for such trivial matters as your indoctrination."

"And we were just getting to know one another."

"An experience we shall both be saved."

"Come back anytime," Garrett called out as she left. "I really enjoy our stimulating conversations."

Esten walked in with a wheezing, fat man. Garrett's suspicion as to why Midradina had come was confirmed. His impatience had turned what should have been a simple matter into an unpleasant contest of wills. He'd feel like an ass, if he hadn't just found out about the testing.

The fat scholar didn't bother with any polite formalities. Before Garrett could even stand, he let him know his studies had been interrupted and ended with, "You will address me as Vizron. We are far in advance of your primitive culture, but once you've grasped the concept of written words and reading—if possible—you may serve in menial capacities."

Garrett sat back down and did a little mental teeth gashing while Esten went into the flutters. "No, no, you misunderstand. She did not say, could not, only English, only, only, English."

Vizron wheezed, "He came from an uncivilized era, pre-machinery."

"Machinery?" Garrett asked brightly, ready for some devilment.

"You know what motorized travel is?"

"A horseless carriage? Sure, Smelly, noisy things that scare the horses. Never will catch on."

"You are mistaken, not right, right," Esten told Vizron.

"Nonsense," Vizron told Esten in dismissal and asked Garrett, "Yours is a warring world. Have you been a soldier?"

Garrett's expression hardened as too many memories flooded through his mind, not of killing but of the deaths of too many friends.

"You have. You have killed," Vizron said with satisfaction.

"No, no," Esten cried, "say it is not so, say, say."

"It is," Vizron wheezed arrogantly. "I can see it in his eyes. I can feel the violence in him. A violent man, primitive, he will never do for here."

"You got that much right," Garrett told him coldly.

"He will, will," Esten argued and quaked to the point that Garrett wondered how he stayed on his feet.

"He has killed. He has to go to the hunters," Vizron decreed.

Esten wailed and wrung his hands. "Oh, no, no."

"Take it easy, Esten," Garrett told him. "You're going to shake yourself apart."

"You do not understand, no, no. They are savages, are, are." He turned to his companion. "It will be a waste, waste. He is intelligent, is, is and kind, kind and gentle."

"It is the law," Vizron stated firmly. "Come with me, Earthling."

"No, no!" Esten cried.

"Do not be hysterical," Vizron ordered coldly.

Esten clasped his hands together to plead with Garrett. "Say you will stay, please, please, please, say, say."

Garrett was dumfounded both by Esten's description of him and agitation on his behalf. "Look, Esten…" he began.

"Please, please."

"He can not stay," Vizron stated emphatically.

Esten gave up. He folded down on the bench and did not unfold as he sat there quaking.

"Are you okay?" Garrett asked.

"You are gone now," Esten moaned, "gone, gone."

"This way," Vizron ordered.

Garrett wanted to punch the fat man, and it must have shown. Vizron stepped back and drew his head into his multi-layered chins when Garrett stood.

"Just show the way," Garrett told him. He hesitated a moment to tell Esten, "Thank you, Esten, for all you did for me."

"It was nothing, nothing."

Pretty much right, Garrett thought, but Esten had kept him from going stir crazy, even if he had just been doing what he was ordered to do. Just because the scarlet man said some nice things and went into a frenzy over the idea of Garrett's going to the hunter section was no reason to feel weighted down with gratitude. Esten went into frenzies easily and had long before Garrett had had any chance to be kind, kind.

After leaving Esten behind Garrett taunted the fat snob. The man asked questions despite his low opinion of Garrett. Garrett responded with absurd 17th and 18th century answers instead of those from the century he lived in. But Garrett soon tired of the game. He tired period. Infuriatingly, the fat, wheezing guide didn't. The further they walked, the more winded Garrett became. Fatso had wheezed standing still, but the exercise had no ill effect upon him. He talked and walked while Garrett panted and struggled to move his leaded legs. To his relief, he at last saw a break in the bleak, gray corridor. Parched, panting, and drenched in sweat from the exertion, Garrett's only concern was to get to the bench along one wall before he fell.

"Wait here," Vizron told him.

"Sure, just tell me where the water is."

No one answered. Garrett swore. He was alone again, shut into a barren room. The door he'd come through wouldn't open, and there were no other doors along the blank walls. If his legs hadn't been so weak, he would have taken the bench apart to use on the door. He did get as far as jerking one bench leg free before he dropped to the floor in exhaustion. He had just exchanged one cage for another, one less accommodating. Even worse, he had walked passively into it.

###

Just because Garrett couldn't catch his breath didn't mean he sat passively. He was a fighter. Fighting was what had put him back on his feet twelve years before when the doctors had told him he would never walk again. With the same determination he'd had then, he was ready and waiting with a bench leg in his hands. Another one leaned against the door as an alarm in case he went to sleep.

He shouldn't have warned the arrogant beauty about causing trouble. He wouldn't again, he promised himself, while he sat there with his hands and bench leg draped over his knees and his body shaking with chills. The shaking was another result of his stupidity. He had pushed too hard to get something better when all he got was something worse. They played with him, made him promises while they treated him as a research specimen and observed his reactions. He swore the only further research they would get from him would be if they did an autopsy.

A black shape suddenly appeared, startling him out of his angry musings. Halfway to his feet he realized it was the strange little creature Mysty had called a pet, and it seemed more scared than he had been startled. It scurried to the furthest corner to huddle and shake. Two of its legs wrapped over the end that faced Garrett, and the other four disappeared under its body.

Garrett looked around the room for some opening he had missed as he settled back down on the floor. There wasn't any, but he knew, even as furious as he had been, he couldn't have missed the black blob if it had been in the gray room before. "Where the hell did you come from?" he gasped.

The two front legs shifted. Two solid black eyes, soft and liquid, stared at him.

"How did you get in here?"

The bench leg was still in position against the door. No one had opened it while he slept. Even if the pipe had fallen and not wakened him, it couldn't have been put back in place if the door was closed from the outside. He looked at the creature's miniature hands and shook his head to dismiss the possibility that it had. He brushed at his burning forehead with his arm and mumbled, "I must be hallucinating. Although why I would conjure you up, what you're supposed to signify, I don't know."

The thing quit shaking. Its front arms folded down to rest its chin, if it had a chin under all that fur.

"Something warm?" Garrett mused. "Something soft and cuddly? Huh? Are you any of those things?" The thing bobbed up and down twice. "Sure you are. You're... Mysty's pet. Old friendly Mysty..., he wouldn't have...a pet that wasn't all...soft and cuddly." He laid his head back against the wall and closed his eyes to ramble and suck in air between words. "Old friendly Mysty...just couldn't keep from visiting me in my new cage..."

He dozed off and woke to something black in front of him. It didn't startle him as badly as before. He only jerked at finding those black eyes barely a foot away from his own. Mysty's pet scrambled backwards until it returned to the far corner.

"Well, stop...sneaking up on...me," Garrett gasped out. "If you're going...to spy on...least make a noise...I know you're there." He had to stop for a couple of seconds to suck in some air. "Stop shaking, I'm not going...hurt you. Now Middy-whatever..." He had to stop for a couple of breaths again. "...I would like...wring her neck." Right along with that fat scholar's, but he didn't waste his breath to say it.

He started to chuckle with gasps for air in-between at the thought of Vizron. He was willing to bet that arrogant ass had gone straight back to his studies to figure out how they had gotten their information so screwed up after the twisted information Garrett had given him.

"The air," he told the pet between gasps. His fingertips were blue under the nails, and he figured his lips were as well. "They're suffocating—"

The wall across from him slid open. Midradina, with a yantz behind her, rushed in a few feet. The pipe fell from the door opposite him. Vizron rushed in through the door with a tray in his hands. The wall to the other side of Garrett slid open, but nothing entered. It, a huge it, dropped down on one knee to peer inside.

"Stay," Midradina ordered as Vizron turned to run.

Vizron trembled, and as much as Garrett derived a perverse pleasure from seeing the man's fear, the creature kneeling where the wall had been was more fascinating. He wasn't human, unless he was afflicted with some grotesque deformity that made the skin of his monstrous form lumpy, leathery, and hairless. He was also too tall to be human, at least ten feet.

"You will explain," Midradina demanded, "why you placed the Earthling in the connecting chamber without water or substance, knowing of his condition."

"I...I was bringing—" Vizron stammered.

"How long later?"

"I was...my studies...I was..."

"You have no studies for a space of ten times the time you have caused him to suffer."

"Midradina," he sobbed, "you can not."

"I have. Go to your quarters."

Vizron left weeping like a child who had just lost his one and only toy. The door slid shut, and Midradina turned to the huge creature that held Garrett's attention. "Mord?" she questioned.

"He's a sick one," a high, whiny voice answered, the words out of synch with the mouth movement. "Better hand him out to me. Easier than me trying to get in."

The voice confused Garrett. He thought the high sound had to have come from something else. He looked to the yantz hovering behind Midradina's shoulder. They didn't talk. That left the pet, but he couldn't see it anywhere.

"Where did it go?" he asked of no one in particular and then laughed wildly. "Hell," he gasped out, "it wasn't…here, not unless…can walk through walls."

"Hurry," the whine urged, "he is delirious."

"Halluci…nating," Garrett corrected between gasps. He pushed up to his feet, staggered, and without wanting to, sat back down. His legs wouldn't hold him.

Midradina moved towards him. Garrett pushed with his feet, away from her coming at him in front and the giant reaching for him at the side.

"Use the yantz," the whine urged.

"The bayantz may not touch him. You know this."

"Then call a ya."

"They can not leave their sanctuary."

"Do something," the whine ordered. "If he goes into convulsions, I could lose him."

Garrett still looked for the pet. "How did…get out?" he asked for the puzzle seemed very important.

"What do you speak of?" she asked.

"Mysty's pet."

Midradina folded her hands together and turned to face him. "The animal you speak of does not walk through walls. It is a chameleon."

"Does it…have a…name?"

Mord answered, hunched over to ease his bulk in further. "Glemm."

Garrett discovered if he whispered he could talk easier. "Everyone should have a name," he told her soberly. "Even without a sex…should have…a name…identity."

Midradina held his attention while Mord inched his way in on his hands and knees. She told Garrett, "I regret this has happened. I was away when you made the choice so quickly. I was unaware until a few minutes ago."

"Being…nice?" Garrett asked suspiciously.

She stiffened visibly. "It was never my intention for you to suffer either in mind or body. I do not intend to be cruel. You are very strange to us, as strange as we are to you. Never has a stranger come among us. We are inexperienced with the difficulties. Nothing like this will happen again, I give you my pledge. For now, you must let Mord help you."

No, he didn't trust them. When a huge hand closed on his ankle, Garrett had every intention of kicking the lumpy, distorted face behind it. He would have, if he hadn't passed out.

###

"Has the inferior Earthling taught the exalted Midra a lesson?"

Mysty's voice came to Garrett from what seemed a very far distance, but he couldn't get his eyes to open to see where they were.

"Yes," she answered tartly. "One of which I was already aware. I gave myself some of the freedom you so constantly urge on me, and this has happened. Had the yantz not warned me, the Earthling might well have died, because I was not here to see to communications."

"Give the skill to others."

"It is not mine to give."

In an exasperated tone, Mysty changed arguments. "It was not caused by your neglect but the very things against which I argue."

"Old arguments for which we always find the same answers."

Mysty's voice changed to a plea. "Do not put him with the hunters, Dina. Leave him here with Mord and me with freedom to roam the planets."

"It is forbidden," she answered bluntly. "Speak no more of it."

There was a brief silence during which Garrett drifted back into sleep. The sharpness of her voice brought him back to a semi-conscious level to listen in detachment.

"Is his condition so severe?"

Garrett forced his eyes open, but couldn't see what she talked about. He saw briefly, as his focus drifted in and out, a white wall lined with white cabinets and counters. Hospital he told himself and let his eyes close. Maybe now the crazy dreams would stop.

They didn't.

The whine answered her with, "I take no chances with a man in high fever and only one lung."

"He has two lungs," she retorted.

"Only one to function or did the yantz not inform you the shields paralyze the lung, for their protection, no doubt."

"The shields," she corrected tersely, "are to prevent delicate tissues from rupturing and to neutralize the nerve endings against pain until the transformation is complete."

"And the arm?"

"The same, as well as a support structure until the bones and muscles have completely formed. Adaptations were necessary. His vessel of life was unable to tolerate the field the required length of time for complete transformation."

"How long is it to take, and what may I expect?"

"A month."

The whine rose to a shriek. "A month? None of the hunters have taken a month to heal even without the yantz treatment."

Her voice rose as well, "And how many were you unable to treat and watch die?"

Mysty interceded quickly. "The wounds were gruesome, Mord."

Mord's voice dropped an octave. "I have seen many gruesome wounds, some inflicted by the Karoz club, but never from two blows to those areas that would take that long to heal."

"These will," she told him and added in warning, "The yantz come."

Garrett forced open his eyes to see a multi-faceted set hanging over him just as a tiny hand slid under his head. A second hand held the cone-shaped cup to his lips. In his paranoia, he took some comfort in knowing what to expect from the yantz's odorless, tasteless liquid. The warmth spread out through his body to take the discomfort away. The floating sensation followed, though it didn't take him immediately to sleep as it had before. He still heard the voices around him.

Mord sounded professionally jealous. "Why did they not come immediately, if he is their patient?"

"Time was needed to prepare the essence. He was not expected to have a need for it again. There would not have been, had I— "

"The cause was not your fault," Mysty interrupted her with.

The previous argument began over. Garrett only caught bits and pieces as he drifted in and out of sleep, until finally the essence took him into quiet escape.

###

Garrett arms flew out, and his hands thudded onto a smooth hard surface when he woke. He quickly twisted them to press his palms against his new prison.

"It is not a cage," Mysty said quickly. He leaned over the transparent dome covering Garrett. Glemm was on his shoulder, its arms wrapped around his neck. "It is a hood to enable Mord to control your oxygen level."

With his hands pressed against the clear sides Garrett's suspicions grew. That Mysty used the term "cage" so soon after he had used it when talking to Glemm in a bare room could be a simple coincidence. It could also be that he had been observed as they continued to test him.

"I was looking forward to your arrival here," Mysty continued. "I expected you would choose the hunters, but not before you had seen both for comparison."

Garrett shrugged indifferently. "You guys got your wires crossed on that one. I wasn't given a choice."

Midradina made her presence known as she glided into his view. "What?" she demanded.

"Vizron," Mysty exclaimed. "Garrett, I do not know what that imbecile said to you, but you have the choice as I told you. I will take you myself through the scholar section."

She said, "I will."

"Just call it D.O.R and forget it," Garrett told them indifferently.

"What is that?"

"Figure it out for yourself, lady. Meanwhile get out of here and leave me alone."

"That is advisable," Mord whined. "He is very weak."

"Not his tongue." She turned to Mysty. "I will speak to you."

Mord loomed over Garrett after they left, and he wasn't happy. "Now Earthling I speak to you. I have watched your pulse and breathing rise in anger. For the anger, I do not blame you. That you direct your sharp tongue to Dina, I do. What happened was not of her doing. She is but one. She can not do all or be responsible for all, though she strives to." He tapped the side of the table hard enough to make it vibrate. "I am not a passive scholar. You talk so to her again, and I will punish though I may have to set your bones after."

"Now," the deformed giant went on, "for yourself you must understand the yayantz treatment is deceiving. You were fatally wounded. You have not been healed as you may believe, but are being healed. You have seen your flesh turn pink again and think it is so, while beneath the organ and structures are still incomplete. They are outlines, shells of what will be, and most importantly the loss of them is still a shock to the body. You do not feel pain; that is deceiving as well. It is good for you, preventing more shock, but imperative for the yantz while bad for you that you did not know. Now you may sleep."

Jackass, Garrett thought, as the giant moved away.

###

Mysty smiled self-consciously when he saw Garrett was awake and watching him. "It is at times a great nuisance." He pulled at the thin black arms wrapped around his neck. "Either I can not get free of it, or I can not find it for days."

Garrett's eyes wandered off. He ignored Mysty as he drew his chair closer. Mysty continued to talk, despite the fact that his words and company was very obviously not welcomed.

"Just as when it was closed in with you. I hope it caused you no displeasure. It is a shy creature, nearly always hidden, yet curious as well to cause itself distraction and oft times tripping your feet."

Garrett wanted to know if he would get a straight answer. "How did it get in there?"

"It had to have been with you when you went in. It has not the abilities, fortunately, to open doors."

With all he could stand of its suffocating attention, Mysty forced Glemm from him. Glemm disappeared. The only place Garrett could see it was where its hands and arms slipped away from Mysty. His curiosity got the better of him, and he bumped his head on the top of the dome to see where it had gone. Mysty pointed to a spot where Glemm couldn't be seen, but neither could the joint where the wall met the floor, a spot that moved rapidly out of sight.

"I became aware of it missing right after they had taken you away," Mysty told him as Garrett dropped his head back down and looked away. "It must have followed into the scholar section and could not return. Only Dina can open the doors between the sections."

"To keep the big, bad hunters away from the precious scholars?" Garrett asked with no effort to hide his anger.

Mysty nodded with a smile and switched to his poetic English. "For their protection," he agreed. "With lacking one in the patience possesses you, Vizron, fear I, damaged quickly would have been, such odious things to you said he."

Garrett was determined to shut himself away from Mysty. He didn't want to like him anymore or trust him, even if an explanation of Glemm's behavior had removed some of his doubts. An antiquated word like odious caught his attention. If he hadn't been so set on not responding, he would have asked what century of Earth they had studied and how Mysty had learned English.

Mysty edged a little closer. "Partially yours the blame is. Such a titter was he over information given duties his were forgotten with haste to correlate. Were not so that but minutes would have been your wait."

"How long was it?"

"Ten of your hours," Mysty told him sadly. He leaned forward. "I may touch you?"

"Sure," he retorted. He thought Mysty had forgotten the plastic shell around him. However, the three-digit hand passed easily through the shell. Garrett jerked his arm away. "How did you do that?"

"Anyone can."

"I can't."

"You are the patient."

"Prisoner!" Garrett corrected hatefully.

"Garrett, no, not as you mean." He twisted as Mord ambled into the room. "Can you not the dome remove?" he pleaded.

With a glance at a monitor board at the head of the table, Mord leaned down to Garrett. "You are in a state of temper again, I see." His mouth was in sync with his words, and his voice was not so much a whine.

Garrett smiled at him. "So break my bones," he dared and added to his meager base of knowledge. Mord spoke English.

"Unnecessary," he answered. He touched a spot on the board. The dome dissolved, andGarrett gasped for air.

"Mord!" Mysty exclaimed in alarm.

Mord held Mysty down with one hand and pressed a thin, blue mask over Garrett's mouth and nose with the other. It looked like a paper painter's mask, only it stuck in place. "See you now, Earthling, the difference between the air of a room and that under pressure."

"You..." Garrett panted under the mask, "...son-of-a-bitch."

Mysty relaxed as Garrett's breathing leveled. "I believe that an insult to be."

"You got it."

"I am correct?" Mysty questioned.

"Right on."

"Curious," Mysty observed to Mord. "It is much like a new language we learn."

"I wasn't having trouble breathing like that before," Garrett said in accusation.

Mord told him, "You were before in rooms with raised oxygen levels to allow you freedom and to accommodate your damaged lung."

"Esten...," Mysty explained quickly, "...a higher level can sustain comfortably than a human. Chosen why was he for you to care."

Garrett smiled wryly and murmured, "She paid me back in spades." She had held her head because she was dizzy in the high oxygen level, not because of a headache or fatigue. "She really won that round."

Mysty's mouth went out of sync. "I am not sure I understand your meaning, but if you believe your difficulties were of Midradina's design, they were not. Because of your premature decision you walked in corridors and were placed in a room that had not been prepared for you. It was your decision. You did not challenge Vizron's declaration. You said not that you had killed, but that Vizron was correct in his opinion you would not do there."

"Sounds like you've been busy," Garrett said tartly.

"Dina has. If a choice had been denied unfairly, you would have been given the opportunity again." Mysty straightened his back. "I believe the air has adjusted."

"Yes." Mord moved sluggishly to remove the mask from Garrett's face. His mouth went out of sync with his words and back to a whine. "It is now at a level for you. Your body will have no additional need, if there is no excessive exertion."

Garret wasn't overly grateful and asked sarcastically, "Is sitting up excessive?"

"No, and I am sure you would prefer it for the introductions."

III

Two men were brought in and introduced. Garrett was fascinated by the one called the Freet, who quite obviously had little or no interest in Garrett. He could have been a model in stature and dress to any number of Great Plains Indians. He was tall, maybe an inch over Garrett's own height, proudly erect, stoic, and with a well muscled body displayed admirably by being bare from the waist up except for leather bands around each upper arm. Another strap of leather encircled his forehead to hold his shoulder length hair close around a strong-featured face with an aquiline nose. Only his coloring didn't coincide with an American Indian image. There was no copper sheen to his skin, his hair was a medium shade of brown, and his eyes were hazel green. Knee length moccasins were wrapped tight around his calves over loose pants. Only a loincloth was needed to complete the costume making Garrett wonder if the Freet wasn't really an Earthling.

"Your customary greeting must be forgotten here," Midradina told Garrett. "To some to be touched is offensive, an instant challenge to battle. From others there could be unintentional injury caused."

"From Flame it would be intentional," the second man, the Gunian, said with a sneer. "What is your customary greeting?"

That one took an instant dislike to Garrett. Correction, the Gunian disliked him before he ever saw him. His tawny colored eyes were filled with animosity the second he walked in the door. It intensified as he looked over the yantz shields. He didn't like Garrett to start with, really didn't like the shields, and he was sizing Garrett up as a future enemy. To judge by the compact body under the popular pajama style clothes, even though Garrett had several inches on him, Garrett would lose. The weight he had lost during his illness was too evident just as was his weakness. As far as Garrett was concerned battle lines had already been drawn with the fair-haired man. There was only one way to respond to that attitude. Garrett smiled at him and said, "I'd offer my hand."

"A passive gesture," the Gunian retorted.

"Only if yours was empty," Garrett answered with a flip of his eyebrows.

The Gunian's golden eyes dilated in interest. "You are of a warring culture?"

"Off and on," Garrett answered dryly. He judged from the Gunian's reaction that he was from a warring culture.

"What—?"

"Not now," Midradina interrupted the Gunian's question. "Freet?" She received no response and raised her voice. "Freet?"

The Freet still did not answer or turn his stony gaze in her direction. The Gunian sneered. "He has never learned what he is."

"He knows well what he is," she answered. "He cares not what we call him, when it is not what he calls himself."

"What does he call himself?"

"No one has ever learned. Mord have you a vocal translator?"

"In the drawer," Mord told her.

Midradina moved to an adjacent wall. Garrett twisted to see why she was doing it herself. Neither Mord nor Mysty had contributed to the conversation nor had they moved. Mord had gone so far as to let her know she could fetch for herself. But then neither seemed very perky. Dizzy, no doubt, from the high oxygen content of the air adjusted for his benefit, and Garrett wasn't sure if he appreciated their consideration.

Midradina returned with a gray—what other color would it be—disk about the size of a fifty-cent piece. She held it out to him. "You must speak into this when you wish to speak to the Freet. He has no permanent translator."

"Oh? Why is that?" he asked caustically. Mysty had acted as if there was no choice in that matter.

"His flesh rejects it."

"Lucky him," he retorted. He put the disk to his mouth. "Hey, Chief, what's bumping. Taken any good scalps lately?"

He heard what he said in English, the translator broadcast it in what was gibberish to him, and he heard it back in English again almost instantly in a weird and distracting echo.

"That is forbidden," Midradina exclaimed and then altered her voice to cold. "You, Earthling, will be well schooled in the rules of the hunt and the punishments for breaking them."

"I can't wait," he answered just as coldly. "Five hunts wasn't it for paralyzing..."

"Wait in the hall," she told the other two men quickly and waved them away.

"...and making..." Garrett went on and noticed the Gunian held back to listen until the yantz started towards him.

"Silence," she told Garrett.

"Go to hell, lady," he countered as the door closed.

"Garrett, please?" Mysty implored.

"Why didn't you want them to hear what happened?" he demanded.

"The weapon is forbidden." She left through a different door than the men had, telling Mysty, "You will explain."

Garrett twisted on the table to look at Mysty. He and Mord both were putting a mask to their faces, green when his had been blue. "If you don't want me giving anything away, you better let me in on it."

Mysty sighed. "We had hoped as you recovered from the shock, you had not remembered. You did not mention your wounds again."

"What about his wounds?" Mord asked.

"From a weapon of awesome power," Mysty explained. "It melted away flesh and bone."

"What?" the huge man shrieked. "How?"

"The Karoz has always had it. It has taken him this long to learn how to operate it. He called it a litch."

"If the others know of this— "

"They do not," Mysty said quickly. "The others will not go near him for the stench, and Dina has taken it from him."

Mord rose clumsily to his feet. "Whoever would have thought of the Karoz having such a thing?"

"He knew no more than it was a weapon."

"If he has shown it to any of the others— "

"He has not, nor has he the mind to reproduce it." Mysty turned to Garrett. "That is why it is imperative you do not tell of this weapon, not a word of how it appeared or what it did."

"Keep them pregnant and barefoot?" Garrett queried sarcastically.

"If that means ignorant, yes. You do not know what such a weapon in the hands of the hunters can mean."

"You got that wrong."

"Yes," Mysty said sadly. "Yes, you know better than any. It is because of that weapon you are here."

The litch hadn't been the only problem. Something had gone way wrong with him even before the Karoz had pulled the litch out. All he asked though was, "So how did someone as primitive as the Karoz get a hold of something like that?"

"In trade before he was taken."

"From his next door neighbor?" Garrett retorted.

"Oh, no, on his planet where there were those of other races of more advancement, perhaps an inter-stellar trading port. We speculate, as the yantz have never seen such a weapon before. It is frighteningly deadly."

Garrett scoffed and pushed off the table to his feet. "Yeah and if she hadn't stopped him, he'd have finished me."

"Is that what you wish for?" Mysty asked with a start.

"It sure as hell would have made it a whole lot easier for everyone."

###

The next set of gray rooms, identical the one he had left behind, was obviously to be his permanent quarters. His own clothes, minus his mangled shirt, were on the bench in the first room. He wasn't given time to explore or change clothes before his two guides took him, in pajama pants and bare feet, to the common room. Garrett was disappointed in the occupants scattered about on the benches along each side of long tables in a mess-hall style room.

A dozen or so stole glances at him and whispered to the ones near them. Leather, hides, and furs were the most common type of clothing on those who didn't wear pajamas. Some wore a crude cloth either wrapped or hanging around them, but they all looked more or less human. Some were tall, some short, some had more than a normal amount of hair, body and facial, some had none. Their skin color ranged from pale tan to green. A lot had exaggerated features, but all had two eyes, two ears, one head, two legs, and two arms. Not a single pair of antennas, three eyes, or four arms in the place.

"Breaking me in gentle?" Garrett queried.

"That did not translate," the Gunian told him. "What is breaking gentle?"

"Showing me new things slow, so I don't spook?" he asked patiently.

The Freet stepped closer to Garrett's other side and said softly, "No stare. Many straight look be challenge."

Gunian snarled, "They are not as stupid as to challenge. All know your protected status."

Garrett was tired of the contemptible treatment, but he smiled as he said, "You're really starting to put my teeth on edge, Gun, old boy."

"What does this mean?" Gunian asked.

"Forget it. A man could get plum wore out explaining everything to you," he answered in a very deliberate insinuation that Gunian was stupid.

"You are very brave while you wear the yantz shields," Gunian hissed. "Later when you do not have them to protect you, will— "

"Why does he?" one sitting at a nearby table shouted.

"Yes," another cried. "Why is he given what we are denied?"

"Do not worry, Earthling," Gunian told him. "None will attack you while you hide behind the female's skirt."

"I'm not hiding behind anything, you scum bucket," Garrett told him coldly. "You want to dance with me, and these things scare you, you'll be the first to know when they come off."

"I do not dance."

"We'll just see how high you can jump."

The last words sounded exceptionally loud since the room had suddenly become silent. Into the silence Midradina spoke as she glided into the room with a yantz behind her shoulder. "I see it has not taken you long to create a disturbance."

Garrett spun, ready to do battle, but he wasn't the one she was after. It was the Gunian she spoke to.

"Now that you have incited them to near riot," she went on, "you may quiet them, before they begin to fight amongst themselves."

"Answer their questions," Gunian returned smugly. "That will quiet them."

The onslaught Garrett expected didn't come. With the exception of the Gunian and the Freet, everyone in the room was very careful not to look in her direction.

Gunian was furious. "Cowards," he shouted. "It does not attack for words."

The 'it' he referred to was obviously the yantz. As he thought about it, Garrett remembered it had not been with her in the scholar section and was not always with her in the intermediate. He was going to have to start paying more attention to things like that. He was going to have to start paying attention to everything. If these men were afraid of it, he could see why Esten had been. He just didn't know why.

Gunian stood his ground. "Why has this Earthling received such favor? Why has he received the yantz treatment denied to us?"

"Need I explain again why he was brought onboard, or what you already know of the yantz as to why he was treated?"

"You do to me," Garrett said tightly. He didn't like what he was hearing.

Midradina's eyes shifted towards him for a moment and away to listen to the Gunian.

"That does not explain why you have called for guides for him," Gunian retorted. "None of us were given guides to make our way easier."

"The guides are for the protection of the yantz," Midradina told him in easy dismissal. "None of you have ever known of the yantz shields before."

"Now we know. No more guides are needed."

Garrett would give her one thing, she was a diplomat. Whatever Gunian knew of the yantz had lost the argument long ago. The confrontation had degenerated to trivia. Gunian argued on principle to save face, but she allowed him a tolerable exit.

She turned to the rest of the room and asked, "What say you here? Have all three hundred heard of the shields and know the newcomer who wears them?" No one answered. "Do I hear objection to guides?" Again there was no answer. She turned back to the Gunian. "Only you object. Perhaps it is because you do not care for the position. You may resign."

"I do. I will not coddle a weakling."

"Hey," Garrett called out and gave vent to some of his anger as Gunian walked off, "don't forget our date."

"I do not forget, Earthling." The Gunian dropped down at a table and twisted to put his back to them.

"Translator," Midradina told Garrett.

"I don't have it," he answered belligerently. She had put him in one hell of a position and hadn't even warned him of it.

"In your quarters?"

Garrett shrugged. He didn't know where it was and didn't care. He wanted to get out of there and have time to think, but he knew if he left too soon, it would be interpreted as cowardice.

"I must speak with the Freet," she told him.

He glanced at the Freet. He hadn't moved, but Garrett suspected if anything had started he would have—to be well out of the way.

Annoyed and showing it in the sharpness in his voice Garrett told her, "Then go get it."

After a brief and sharp catch of her breath she told him, "Only you can open your door."

She had given the Gunian an honorable way out and then him. Garrett accepted because there were a few things he wanted to ask. "Come on, Chief," he said with a wave of hand. "She wants to talk to you."

Garrett didn't look back to see who or what followed. He made it to the first corner and knew which way to turn, but by the second he was winded and disorientated. One gray hall looked the same as the other.

"Right," Freet whispered in Garrett's ear, surprising him. He'd had no idea the Freet was so close behind him.

He couldn't blame anyone else for his lack of awareness. He had walked too fast, put too much of a strain on his lung until he was so light-headed he could barely think. He turned some of his anger on the Freet. "You sneaking—"

"Be still," Midradina ordered in a whisper and held a mask out to him. He glared at her, not taking for the mask even though his breathing was labored. "Do not be foolish. You have done much to establish yourself. Do not destroy it by allowing any to see how vulnerable you are."

"Does it matter?" He snatched the mask from her hand and pointed with the other at the Freet. "He sees."

"He is different. Use the mask before you faint and the Freet is forced to carry you."

Garrett shoved the mask against his face, spun, and staggered. Two strong hands caught him at the shoulders and set him up straight. "Excuse, no permission," Freet said and backed away.

Freet may have saved him from a fall, but Garrett wasn't grateful. "Like you give a shit," he panted and leaned against the wall.

He was sure Freet didn't care. He might have bluffed enough in the common room to establish himself as a hard-ass, but he knew he hadn't fooled the Freet. The Freet knew how weak he was.

"You have not been insulted," she whispered. "Why do you stare so?"

"Sizing up the opposition," Garrett muttered.

"You are the same size and not opponents." She pointed the way for him. When he refused to move, she added, "Do not challenge me now. The only secure place for a private conversation is in your quarters."

"And you sure don't want to put your yantz in jeopardy."

"Do you?" she asked softly.

The softened tone of the question caught Garrett's attention more than the question. She had promised he would never suffer again. The Freet following at his heels was a guarantee. She also told him he had done much to establish himself, knowing it had all been a bluff, just as he suspected much of her performance had been.

"You'd do well in poker, lady," he told her and shoved away from the wall.

###

With a truce of sorts between them, Garrett fell in behind her and the yantz. With the mask to ease his breathing, he was able to leave his mind free to study the woman.

Her floor-length gown reached up her neck to her chin and was cuffed at the wrists. It hung from her, bell-like, from gathers across a yoke at her shoulders. Garrett wondered how much of her bulk was actually her or the things she carried under the gown such as the mask she had produced for him. He was musing over how she was built when she stopped and faced him.

With her palm out flat on the door, she told him, "You must open the door."

"Sure," he told her with a sardonic nod, "but I haven't been having much luck at that."

"This door will open at your thought command."

Thought command? Garrett stared at the door. The way Esten had opened the doors from any direction, the speed of thought made sense, but thought command?

"You must think open," she told him.

Garrett thought the single word. The door slid open. He wasn't given any time to marvel over it. Freet stepped inside, and she told Garrett, "Guests must enter first." She and the yantz moved inside. "The door will close automatically as soon as you pass. None will then seek to harm you as they could not escape and would slowly starve to death. Nothing within will operate except for you."

After meeting Gunian and the few others Garrett could see the reason for the precaution. He questioned her as he stepped inside, and the door slid shut behind him. "You just set that thing through your hand?"

"Yes," she answered without hesitation.

"And you can still open it?" he asked, just as she had opened the door in his temporary quarters.

"Yes again. The Freet also has command, a precautionary measure to be removed at a later date."

He knew he wouldn't be the one to decide when. Garrett grunted derisively and asked, "He opened it the first time so the Gunian wouldn't know I couldn't?"

"Yes."

"Why? What makes him different?"

"He is a hunter who does not hunt, but he has killed," she warned. "The others learned long ago to leave him be."

"I'll bet they did," Garrett looked at the man who stood like a statue. "I damned sure wouldn't want to tangle with him." He looked back at her. "You ready to tell me why you didn't give me any warning over how they were going to feel about the yantz treating me?"

She gave him a blank look for a moment and then asked, "Mystaleah did not?"

"No, he did not," he retorted, not that he remembered anyway. "Just why won't they treat hunters?"

"The hunters chose their life," she said haughtily and produced a stack of masks from beneath a fold of her gown. "You must have at least one with you at all times. Prevent, if possible, the others from seeing them for they will know them for what they are." The other hand held a small cylinder as big around as her little finger and a half inch long. "This is an audio translator for the Freet. There is less distortion than with the vocal translator and translates all languages."

She handed Garrett the masks and turned to Freet. She motioned for him to take the translator and waited for him to hold it to his ear. "The Gunian has resigned."

"I'll bet he figured that out on his own," Garrett muttered and tossed the masks to the bench.

"Do you stay now that you have seen the feelings towards him?"

The Freet's eyes shifted towards Garrett, but did not look directly at him. "Four hunts," he stated.

"You're paying him?" Garrett questioned in delight.

"Why does that thought amuse you?" she asked.

To not be suspicious of Freet's motives was amusing and a relief. His help made a lot more sense if he was being paid though Garrett didn't explain. "Maybe you should have offered the Gunian five hunts."

"Perhaps I did not offer him anything," she said stiffly.

"A little manipulation, Princess?" he asked mockingly. "Did you get what you wanted out of him?"

"What I expected."

Why that made her mad, he didn't know, but their truce was definitely broken. She left before he could ask the rest of the questions brought up by the meeting in the common room. All he got before she sailed out the door was a curt order to heed the Freet's warnings.

"Damn it," Garrett exclaimed.

The Freet squatted in the corner.

"Are you going to become a piece of furniture?" Garrett asked, irritated quickly over being ignored. "Cat got your tongue? Or are you one of her pets like the yantz?" The Freet didn't have his hand to his ear. "You're worse to talk to than Glemm. At least it looked at me."

He squatted in front of Freet and tapped his own ear. Although Freet didn't look at him, he raised his hand to his ear. Garrett could either bait Freet or use him for a source of information. He picked one subject from all those jumping around in his head.

"Why is everyone afraid of the yantz?" Garrett asked.

"Killers."

"They're healers," he exclaimed incredulously.

"Sometime heal, sometime kill."

Garrett shifted in an attempt to catch Freet's eyes. "What times kill?"

"Threat to Midradina."

That gave Garrett a slight chill. He had wondered if the yantz didn't have a stinger hidden the first time he'd seen one. He asked, "How? Beat you to death with their wings?"

The Freet stood. Garrett followed. "You more like the Indians than you look? You figure your eyes to be windows to your soul, and I'll steal it looking into them?"

"No." Freet looked directly into Garrett's eyes. "You no think. Some do. No want touch eyes, no force."

"Okay," Garrett said calmly while he fought off a chill. He had cold eyes that Freet did. "So how do they kill?"

"With claws like knifes." His hand rose with a double-edged knife in it. "Slash to death."

Garrett supposed that producing the knife was a warning. He tucked away its existence and the way Freet handled it for the time being and didn't believe what Freet said. He had felt the hands of the yantz. They were soft and didn't even have nails, let alone claws. "Have you seen them, these claws?"

"No."

"Has anyone?"

"One."

"Maybe he was a plant," Garrett suggested.

"Be Trego, no plant."

Garrett didn't explain what he'd meant. If Midradina supported her disciple with well-placed fables, he wasn't going to upset it. After exposure to the group, he knew how badly discipline was needed.

"I'm going to lie down. Come back later." Garrett reached for his chaps with the closest hand to them, his left. His fingers closed, but their weight pulled through his fingers when he tried to lift them. His inability to hold so light a weight shocked him. He absently took notice of the vocal translator on the bench, took the chaps with his right hand, and walked to the bedroom. The door shut behind him, something he barely noticed as Garrett pondered the state of his healing.

###

Garrett was furious. Not only did it hurt, it was humiliating especially when Freet said from the other side of the wall, "Think open."

"I'll kick the damned thing in," Garrett retorted and gave the door a kick for emphasis. He didn't care to explain that he had thought "Open," or he wouldn't have walked into the door. His kick didn't move the door. A section of the wall moved instead. It scooted a quarter of an inch out of line with the adjacent sections.

"Easier," Freet said, "think open."

"Anyone ever tell you you're an ass?" Garrett stared hard at the door. The outer door had opened easily before, but it took three tries to open the inner one. When it did, he saw the outer door was open as well.

"Which one did I open?" he asked wearily.

Freet stared back at him from where he squatted. Garrett tapped his ear. Freet turned both arms from where they dangled over his knees to show Garrett empty hands. Garrett wasn't sure if he was telling him to go to hell or that he had lost the translator. It really didn't matter. He had a question to ask, and Freet was getting paid to put up with him. He grabbed the vocal translator.

"Which door—?" Hearing the translations following so close together they almost, but not quite, sounded simultaneous gave Garrett an idea. "We could use this thing to-"

Freet stood, and the earplug fell from his clothes to the floor. "No that." He retrieved his and held it to his ear.

"Yeah, Chief, but we can use this one to learn each other's language."

"No try. Four hunts no long a time."

"Oh, now you've cut me to the quick. You sound like you're anxious to lose my company.

"Is so," he told him bluntly. "What question?"

"Chief, I think we ought to have a man to man talk. No more pussyfooting around. I want to know exactly where I stand with you."

"Brief."

"Now be straight, don't worry about hurting my feelings."

Freet dropped his hand and gave Garrett a cold stare that made Garrett wish he hadn't pressed to be looked at directly. The Freet had a way of dissecting him with those bleak eyes of his.

"Okay, strictly business." Freet didn't replace the earplug. Garrett used the vocal one and spoke slowly to hear each translated word before the translator in his ear caught it. "Which door did—?"

Freet raised the plug to his ear. Garrett tossed his on the bench. Freet made it clear their association was to be business only, although Garrett was a little suspicious of the answer he received about the doors. Freet told him he had thought too hard and opened both doors. That didn't make sense. True, he didn't know anything more about thought control than what he'd read about in fiction, but still the explanation didn't seem right. How could someone think too hard? He hadn't had any problem opening the outer door the first time. The strength of his thoughts shouldn't have anything to do with it, but when he concentrated as hard as he could, each time he tried to open the inner door, the outer door opened along with it. He tried not to concentrate as hard, and only the outer door opened.

"Think too little," Freet told him from the corner where he sat on his haunches.

"Where's the—?" He pointed to his own ear. Freet raised his hand to his. "Don't lose that again."

Freet tossed it to him. "You keep, no lose."

"I don't have any pockets in this get up. Where would I keep it?" He looked at his own pants on the bench and half-shook his head. "Dumb." There was no reason for him not to wear his own clothes, except for one. He didn't want to strip down in front of Freet, but to get into the privacy of the bedroom he had to conquer the door.

Freet's explanation still didn't make sense to him. He hadn't forcibly thought the outer door open when he had opened it the first time. He was doing everything the same way and—and that was it. Garrett changed tactics. He didn't think of the outer door or how he had opened it. He looked at the inner door and thought the single word. The inner door opened; the outer stayed shut.

"Better," Freet told him tonelessly. "Practice make faster."

"You know, Chief," Garrett said thoughtfully, "either you aren't very bright or you just played me."

"You have translator," Freet reminded him.

"Yeah and as long as I smile...," which he did, "...you won't know if I'm calling you a son-of-a-bitch or God."

IV

Freet became an annoyance, real fast. He wouldn't leave. Garrett told him to several times, by vocal and audio translator and hand motions. He simply repeated "I stay" and shut the outer door each time Garrett opened it. With his restlessness growing, Garrett wanted to pace. He did not want it to be where that stone-hewn man could watch or hear. He decided if Freet wouldn't leave he would brave the thinner air outside his quarters to walk the halls. He anticipated Freet wouldn't let him go alone. He did not anticipate Freet would not let him go at all. The new plan seemed to be out of sight, out of trouble. However, staying in his quarters all the time made Garrett claustrophobic. He finally went to the bedroom, shut the door, and paced. That didn't help matters any.

Logic told him he was being irrational. Another part of his brain told him he had just traded cells again and jailers. He was still being tested. They had given him the additional ability to open the door out of the cage, but they had put a guard in place to keep him from doing so. He still could not go as he pleased, not even into the bare, gray corridor. The tension built up until he shot through the bedroom door. He was prepared to knock Freet down if he had to, as long as he got out of those two rooms.

Freet didn't try to stop him. Garrett hit the hall at a fast pace, slowing as his breathing increased. As he slowed, Freet came up beside him. Without a word or glance, he held out a mask, something Garrett had forgotten in his panicked rush to get out.

He snatched the mask out of Freet's hand. "You'd make a great nursemaid."

"You have translator."

He didn't. He had forgotten it just as he had forgotten the mask, but the sense of panic subsided. At the slower pace and with the mask, his breathing steadied as well. Good thing considering what happened next.

"Others come," Freet warned unnecessarily.

Garrett had already crumpled the mask into a ball in his hand to hide it.

In a voice that only carried a few inches, Freet told him, "No look straight at. No greet. No block. Move I do."

Freet moved towards the approaching two without a break in their pace. They were of the Neanderthal variety dressed in thick furs, but taller by two and a half feet than the Karoz, and slimmer, although by no means skinny. They looked to be more intelligent than the Karoz, and if the small, pitch-black eyes in their wrinkled faces were any indication, they were mean. Those eyes, more than their size, made Garrett uneasy. They blatantly scrutinized him when he'd been told not to look directly at them.

A bare six feet from them Freet stepped to the side to stand against the wall. Garrett stepped in unison with him. The two men passed with plenty of distance between them. As soon as they passed, Freet stepped back out and walked at the same pace. "No look back. No stop."

The other two men stopped with their voices rising from a low murmur to an angry rumble.

"Go right. No fight me what do."

"What's—?"

"No talk."

A door swung open, and Freet shoved Garrett into a cylinder-shaped cubbyhole with barely enough room for the two of them.

Freet pulled the door shut and pressed a fingertip to Garrett's lips for silence. It pushed Garrett's head back against the smooth, cold surface. With forced bravado, Garrett raised his arms over his head to unfold the mask. While he fought claustrophobia, he pushed Freet's finger back far enough to slip the mask under, then returned Freet's finger. The narrow-eyed look Freet gave him helped fight down the growing sense of being suffocated.

"Think down," Freet ordered.

Elevator, Garrett assumed, and thought *down.* The floor disappeared from under him. He grabbed frantically, as any normal human being would who suddenly found himself standing on air. His right hand found a hold cut into the smooth wall. It took that long for him to realize he wasn't falling. He had dropped until his arm was fully extended, but the weight of his body hanging from his arm was next to nothing. He floated in a tube.

Freet looked up from several feet below him and drifted slowly further away.

With his heart still doing ninety miles an hour and panting for air, Garrett let go of his handhold. *Down,* he thought, *down slowly, please.* Whatever kind of gravity device controlled the tube obeyed him. Once he realized he was in control, he rather enjoyed the ride. The next time, he promised himself, he would. He wouldn't have his heart in his throat from an unwarned introduction to it, and he wouldn't knock his mask off in a mad scramble to catch something. Fortunately the mask was waiting for him at the bottom.

"Cute," he gasped as he snatched the blue scrap from Freet's hand, one word being all he could manage until he sucked oxygen through the mask into his single functioning lung.

He didn't want to show Freet any more weakness than was necessary, but at that moment, he couldn't help it. To keep himself from collapsing, Garrett braced his buttocks against the wall and locked his knees in place.

"Translator," Freet told him.

Garrett shook his head. His fingernails on his right hand, the one with the undamaged blood supply, had a blue tinge to them.

"Lose translator?"

Garrett glared at him. He hadn't lost it. He had forgotten it the same as he had the mask. Freet had to know that, just as he had to know the state he'd been in when he shot out of those quarters.

"You know, Chief," he panted, "I'm beginning to wonder if a monster sense of humor doesn't lurk behind those steely eyes of yours."

"Talk less, breathe more." He pointed to the tube they had come out of. "Others no know. Better no say."

"Secrets, secrets," he muttered. He pushed away from the wall. His breathing was still a little heavy, but his nails had turned pink again.

"No translator," Freet reminded.

"That will make talking to you like talking to Boss. Boss would never pull a stunt like that on me though. Better be careful who you pull it on next. If I had a weak heart, you could have done me in."

Freet waited until he stopped talking to say, "Two above Phogatres. They territory. We trespass. Reach challenge level, no reason. Shields no meaning."

"They don't help a hell of a lot then, do they?" he quipped.

"Words have no meaning."

"That's nothing new." Garrett turned and walked down the corridor. "Words don't mean anything to a lot of people," he said bitterly. He stopped to look back at Freet. "But never talk to yourself. That's a sure sign of going nuts. It's okay to talk to something that's alive, deaf and dumb maybe, but it has to be alive and capable of looking at you, so you know it's listening."

"Waste words."

"Gonna miss you, Chief." He started off again. "Who am I going to talk to after you've earned your hunts?"

Garrett rounded a corner and stopped dead. "Those sons-of-bitches," he breathed out.

Row after row of clear cages were stacked one on top of another to reach the fifteen-foot ceiling. Each cage held one animal, cage after cage of single animals kept away from any other living thing.

"No like specimens?" Freet asked.

"They're living, breathing—" He stopped with a deep breath and choked down his anger. His lips twisted sardonically under the mask while his voice grew calm and cold. "The only thing they're good for this way is biology. Nothing can be learned of their behavior by watching them like this."

It was very silent for a few moments before Freet said tonelessly, "You finish. We go now."

Garrett backed off. "Yeah, I've seen all of this I want."

He spun only to have Freet shift to block him. "No go back way come."

"Fine, just get me the hell out of here."

Freet led. Garrett pressed him to go faster despite his shortness of breath. Freet wouldn't be hurried. He didn't increase his pace even when Garrett went ahead of him, eyes to the floor so as not to see anymore of the caged animals. Freet trailed behind and gave directions. After he called Garrett back twice for a missed turn, Garrett slowed down. That was what kept him from running into Midradina.

"You are late," she said. "Was there—?"

"Late?" Garrett twisted to look back at Freet. "Did we have an appointment?"

"I was asking a question."

"Oh, excuse me, your highness. Ask your question by all means." He crossed his arms and leaned back against the nearest wall.

"What has happened?" she asked of Freet. Freet stared at her blankly and shook his head when she pointed to his ear. She told Garrett, "Give me your translator."

"Don't have it."

"I have given you both one, neither of you have them?" she asked in exasperation. "How will you communicate?"

"We do all right," Garrett told her sullenly.

"You do not. You did not know I would be here or why."

"I didn't know it was planned either," he retorted. "I thought I was just walking off steam. I didn't realize I was being manipulated again. Looks like I'd catch on."

"Must you make the simplest of things difficult?"

Garrett had a retort ready when the wall he leaned against vibrated violently. He lunged forward, spun to see what had caused it, staggered off balance, and staggered again to stare in open-mouthed shock, unaware his mask had fallen off.

The creature was pure white. She tossed her head angrily, and pawed at the floor with her front hoof. Her mane flew from her agitated dance, and her wings were unfurled.

"Mask, Earthling," Freet said.

Garrett made no move to take it. He was so entranced that he struggled for air without knowing. He blinked, and his gaze flickered when Freet pressed the mask into his hand, but they went right back to the cage as he raised the mask automatically to his face.

"Where…where….?" Garrett stammered.

"Not on your world," she told him.

"Pegasus, magical steed of Bellerophon," he breathed in awe with a deep breath before and after. "Maybe the gods were real."

"I did not know your world had such creatures."

"Neither did I."

There was a brief pause before she said, "Your mask is nearly depleted, Earthling. Have you another?"

Garrett shook his head, but the tone of her voice got through to him. "I haven't flipped," he told her with a self-conscious grin. "In my world this creature was a myth, an ancient legend. Only this one's a she, Peggy I guess, instead of Pegasus."

Peggy held his attention like a magnet. While he stared at the magnificent winged horse, Midradina looked at the yantz with her. It sped off, its body a blur as it disappeared down the corridor.

"Would you, if given the choice, choose this beast over your own?" she asked in a curious tone.

"That would be a tough one," Garrett mused in preoccupation. What he'd give to have the golden bridle of that legend in his hand.

"Perhaps a comparison is needed."

Garrett twisted to face her, wincing with the familiar pain in his back that had been absent until then. He twisted further to look where she pointed. "Are you saying Boss is here?" Midradina moved away from Peggy down the row of cages. Garrett didn't follow her. "I don't want to see him."

"We thought—"

"Not likely," he returned curtly. "He doesn't belong in a cage, lady. He'd been better off if you'd let him die where he was."

There was a slight flicker of her brows and then a slight nod. "It is the creatures in the cages that have brought your anger."

"You got it."

"And what would you do to remedy the tragedy; release them?"

"Yes."

"Now it is you who does not think," she told him with a lift of her chin. "How would they live after years of captivity?"

"They probably wouldn't last a day," Garrett told her hatefully, "but they'd be done with cages and unnatural lives that have turned them into zombies. Even I could think of something better than that."

"That is doubtful," she said crisply. "You may do with your creature as you wish, keep it to accompany you on hunts or set it free on the first suitable planet." She stretched her hand out to the front of the cage. "Set the door or say no. I have other things to do."

Garrett thought open. "Looks like I jumped the gun—hey, wait a minute."

She moved away quickly, and Garrett rushed to overtake her. Freet moved to stop him. Garrett reached out to catch her arm just as Freet reached him. The collision jarred Garrett just enough to drive his hand into her side with a clunk before Freet's arms locked around Garrett and dragged him back.

"No," she shouted.

Garrett's head snapped around to find himself eye to eye with a yantz. Where before there had been tiny three-fingered hands, there were three-bladed claws instead. He didn't move and neither did Freet. He didn't think either of them took a breath until the yantz retreated.

"Never do that again," Midradina told him sharply.

Garrett quickly agreed while his mind took off in several directions. What had clunked hard against his knuckles when his hand shoved into her? How did those tiny, soft little hands turn into such wicked looking blades? Had Freet moved to save him from the yantz, or did Freet think he had saved her from Garrett's attack? All his questions were put on hold when the yantz approached them again. The claws that had only a few moments before been frightening enough to make anyone leery had disappeared. Instead it held out—with three-fingered hands—a fresh mask and an audio translator. Garrett took both gingerly.

He handed the translator to Freet and exchanged masks. "I only meant to say thank you, not attack you," he told her.

"I did not believe you were attacking, only the yantz," she said stiffly. "It should have been explained to you."

It had been, in Freet's pithy manner. Garrett just hadn't believed it.

###

Inside with the door shut, Garrett was relieved to discover the cage was sound proof. No sound came in from the outside; no noises would escape to violate the privacy of his reunion with Boss. Midradina and Freet had moved out of sight to have their own conversation. She would give more instructions to Freet, Garrett was sure, on how to deal with him, but he didn't care. He was too relieved and astonished at the horse's good condition. He wasn't sure how long he'd been there since his watch had disappeared with his mangled shirt, but he was sure it hadn't been long enough for the gashes the wire had torn through Boss's hide to heal to ridges of thin scars. There were enough of them to turn Garrett's stomach, but the horse's coat had a healthy sheen to it. There was no gauntness in his strong body, and Boss was full of energy, making the reunion in the cramped space a trial. Boss pushed at him with his head and bounced Garrett off the walls with his enthusiastic greeting.

By the time Boss calmed down, Garrett had as well. The lump in his throat had subsided, and his voice was steady. He could pay attention to the other items in the cage while he stroked Boss's neck. Whoever had cared for the horse had left the blood-stained and wire-ripped gear. Boss had played with it, no doubt out of boredom, and scattered the canteen, bridle, saddle, and blanket. He had even worked the bedroll from the ties behind the cantle, but the saddlebags, rifle scabbard, and rifle were still in place.

Garret gathered the gear to set outside the door, although it wasn't easy. He could grip with his right hand, but without the muscle structure in his right chest and back he couldn't lift much weight. He had to drag the saddle on the floor and could do no more with his left hand than pat or stroke Boss. Something that should have only taken minutes seemed to take hours. He had to stop for breath, stop to move Boss out of his way, and stop to rest several times before all of the gear was in the corridor. Finally he sat down, exhausted from what should have been a very small effort, eased his back from the return of an old, familiar ache, and looked Boss over again.

The horse obviously had been well taken care of, although Garrett couldn't see how. There was no source of water, no kind of feed, and no waste. The cage was spotless. He had cleaned enough stalls in his life to know they didn't stay clean long if a horse drank and ate.

"It doesn't make sense," he told Boss with a weary sigh. "There's just too damn much to think about in this place, and I'm not doing a very good job of concentrating. I'm not doing a very good job at anything." Boss nickered softly and plucked at

Garrett's pant leg with his upper lip. "Yeah, I know, but they wasted it, Boss." The wry grin was back. "If any of this is true. For all I know, I'm the one in a cage—with paddy walls, but just in case, I'll hang on until I can get something better than this for you."

He dozed off and woke at some strange noises. Along the back wall a trough opened on the floor with running water. A second trough opened in the wall, big enough for Boss to get his head through. It was full of gray pellets. Boss drank from the trough and played with the water, splashing it on the floor and walls. The walls absorbed the moisture. Scraps from the pellets that he dropped on the floor were also absorbed. When Boss emptied his bladder later, the floor absorbed that as well. Out of curiosity Garrett spit. That was absorbed also. Those Thornns really had themselves a system.

"Going to try that when I get back to my quarters," he commented even though he had no desire to leave Boss and return to his rooms. Freet had other ideas.

###

Freet was a taskmaster. After he carried the saddle and gear to Garrett's room, he began to teach. His method was 'I will speak; you will listen,' and Garrett had a lot to learn. There were three hundred hunters and three hundred lists of do's and don'ts in dealing with them. Garrett did not see how he would ever learn it all. If he made even the most subtle of mistakes in dealing with one of the hunters, it could be seen as a challenge.

During the first few days there were no visits to the common room or casual walks through the halls to alleviate Garrett's battle with claustrophobia. The only breaks in the monotony—usually when Freet could see Garrett was about to explode—were trips to the pen room. Even then Garrett was not allowed to wear the spare denim shirt he had dug out of his saddlebags. The shields had to remain visible, and they visited the pens by a shorter route than they had taken the first time, through the intermediate area, well away from the Phogatres territory. Those trips acted as tranquilizers for Garrett. They eased the tension of confinement. They were also the only time Freet left him alone.

Boss was delighted every time Garrett appeared. He romped, kicked up his heels and danced as much as the confined area allowed. Once he calmed down, Garrett took him out of his stall—a concession in terms to make things easier for Garrett—and walked him, always with a stop to visit Peggy. Boss carried on like a young stud in his prime instead of an over-the-hill gelding. He squealed, snorted, and pawed. Peggy's response was to charge the door. She would never be tamed, Garrett knew, though she might someday be ridden, if a man worked long enough to win her trust. After several days, she stopped charging and rearing when he appeared in front of her cage. She accepted his repeated presence by ignoring him.

When Freet decided it was time to expand their routine, they began taking trips to the common room. Other than some covert glances and whispers from the few there, Garrett was ignored. Garrett complained as they left after one visit. The translator was in his pocket, which didn't matter. Freet never cared much for anything Garrett had to say unless it was parroting back his lessons. Nevertheless, Garrett still talked to him as he spoke to Boss, never expecting an answer.

"I don't know what the big deal is," he said as they rounded a corner to see Gunian approaching. According to the rules Freet had taught him, the appropriate way to deal with Gunian was to stare him down, which Garrett did.

"You are looking well, Earthling, but still you hide behind the shields," Gunian said in greeting.

"I got me this terrible affliction," Garrett told him seriously.

"What is that?" he asked mockingly.

"Impatience, just like you. I'm waiting for our meeting behind the barn."

With narrowed eyes Gunian said, "I do not know barn, but we will have our meeting."

"You bet." He grinned and waited quite deliberately until Gunian walked by to call him back, which was considered an insult. "Just one thing, are you going to be a man about it, or do you feel the need for a weapon?"

"You call me a coward?" the Gunian asked in a dangerous tone.

"Nope," Garrett answered lightly, "just asking."

"I will meet you, Earthling, in any way you wish."

"Bare knuckles then, no holds barred, always found that the best way to judge the mettle of a man."

"Only my body," he agreed.

Freet didn't say a word until they reached Garrett's quarters. Once there, he demanded the translator with an abrupt, almost angry motion. "What Gunian say?" he asked.

"Not much," Garrett answered indifferently.

"With you, few words much meaning. Many words little. What he say?"

Garrett lounged on the bench. "Don't let it worry you. What we said pertains to the time after you've earned your hunts."

"Think weak mind," Freet returned coolly. "No court battle with Gunian."

"Don't run away from one either."

"Way to avoid."

Garrett shrugged and picked up his cigarettes. He rationed them for two reasons. He'd stuck three packs in his saddlebags with enough matches for what would have been three days of fence riding before returning to the main ranch. He was down to the last five of the last pack. The other reason was with only one lung, smoking wasn't easy. The first one he'd lit up had caused a coughing fit that nearly choked him to death. It'd been severe enough that even in his oxygen enriched quarters he'd needed a mask to regain his breath. But like any devoted addict he had persevered and forced his lung to accept the smoke again, not looking forward to the time when he would light the last one.

"I don't suppose..." he inhaled deeply and let the smoke drift from his lips. "...I can get anymore of these around here."

"Many wish."

"Come on, Chief, you'd never even seen one of these before."

"Show where, tell what say."

"Show me first," Garrett countered. He didn't believe Freet for one minute.

"Tell first is bargain."

Garrett studied him thoughtfully. "If you're on the level, that's cold-blooded blackmail. What difference does it make to you what we said? Once you've earned your hunts, you could care less what happens to me."

"You insult?"

"Just a little friendly challenge."

"No mistake the Gunian," Freet told him bluntly. "No challenge friendly. He kill."

"He'll try."

"Dead you want; be simpler ways."

"You reckon?" Garrett asked with a twisted smile. The revolver he'd considered sticking in his mouth no more than a few minutes before the whole crazy thing started was still in his saddlebags. The reason wasn't as strong now. His back ached a little off and on, but nothing like it had before; and his legs hadn't gone out from under him once, but then he hadn't been moving around much to strain his back. "If I start quaking in my boots over facing him, I'm sure I can think of something simpler."

"Think fool."

"You think I don't know anything about being the new kid on the block. Wrong, Chief. If I back away from the first challenge, I'll be branded a coward. Gunian's one of the top dogs around here. If I meet him and win, fewer of them will challenge me. If I lose, there's no sweat over anything."

"Always hear many words to know meaning. Speak what think, no so many words, be easier."

Garrett just grinned at him.

"Can avoid."

"Not my style." He held the cigarette up in a reminder of their bargain.

"Bring."

Garrett paid close attention to the route. He still felt like he was in some horrible nightmare or totally insane, but just in case he wanted to make sure he could find his way back.

The room they ended up in had a machine that didn't look like much, just like a conveyer belt that traveled through a gray box. However, as Garrett watched it, he realized it was nothing like the airport scanners it resembled. The cigarette put on one side came out in duplicate on the other.

Garrett sent through the twins and the quads and so on until he couldn't hold anymore. Then he wanted to see it work on something else. As a working cowboy he carried little in his pockets out of habit. Anything in the front pockets always managed to pinch or poke while riding and anything in the back usually rubbed a sore spot. He did, however, have the audio translator and matches. He handed Freet the twin translator as it came out and motioned for him to put it to his ear.

"Does it work?"

"All same," Freet told him tonelessly, but with a hint of impatience.

"This is great. We can make spares and not have to get replacements every time we lose one."

He didn't say every time you lose one, which Freet had managed to do four times. Having duplicates would save trips to the intermediary area for replacements.

"Need no much longer." Freet said indifferently. "Better make what need, clothes, boots."

"You're a real kill joy sometimes, Chief." Garrett shoved the original translator back in his pocket and bent to pull off one well-worn boot. Holding it in his hand, he asked, "Suppose it's a waste of time? Gunian will probably kill me before I can finish wearing them out."

"What he say?"

"Told you." He was sorry he'd brought it up with a bad joke. He dropped the boot on the conveyer belt and pulled off the second. "Too bad this thing can't new them up. They're comfortable though, well broke in."

Freet caught the boot as he dropped it. "Show, now tell."

"You can be down right pesky at times." Garrett reached for the boot. Freet moved it out of reach. "Stubborn too."

"Have bargain."

"I held up my end of it."

"Think I think," he stated astutely.

"Still don't see why you care," Garrett grumbled, but relayed the incident with Gunian in detail since he wasn't getting anywhere with Freet's obstinacy.

Freet's hand flipped when Garrett finished. There was a flicker as his knife disappeared into Garrett's boot.

"We agreed, body only," Garrett repeated and watched the boots disappear.

At the other end Freet handed him the boots as they came out, one minus a knife. "No witness, bargain no good."

Garrett asked seriously, "Are you so sure it could only end in death?"

"Regret before battle, Gunian sense."

"Yeah, guess so." Garrett leaned down to pull on one pair of boots and then straightened to leave.

"One thing," Freet said to delay him and pointed to the knife Garrett held in his hand. "Weapon forbid in quarters, only for hunt."

"More secrets, seems to be the way of life around here."

"Less know, better. Same me, Earthling. Someday may be enemy."

"I'll keep that in mind."

###

Freet wasn't there to lecture him. He wasn't asleep on the bench, or crouched in the corner. Garrett had known the day was coming when Freet would no longer be watch dogging him and had thought he was ready for it. Once it did come, however, he realized he wasn't. Freet was, at least, a distraction. Nothing in the two rooms Garrett paced restlessly in his stocking feet offered much to occupy his mind. More than once his steps took him to the corner where the spare pair of boots stood with the knife still inside. Finally he took it out.

Double-edged and razor-sharp it was a perfectly balanced throwing knife. The feel of it in his hand took him back to his school days when he and all the other cocky upstarts had spent hours playing mumbly-peg to prove how brave and skilled they were. It had been switch blades then, smuggled up from Mexico, cheap construction with snapped blades more often than not when they were thrown. Freet's blade wouldn't snap. Garrett was sure of that before he flicked his wrist and watched the knife fly. Straight and deadly, the knife sank in the soft wool-lined underside of the saddle.

The knife would kill, but could he? Could he kill again for even less reason than he had before? The thought made him chuckle. What the hell was he worried about? He was so out of condition, he'd never win any hand-to-hand combat. His only hope of survival was to out-bluff any possible rivals. If he looked tough and talked tough maybe he could hold off any actual fights until his back gave out. Then to hell with all of them, but to look tough he had to get into shape. That called for working out. For that he needed more space.

He was sure the wall between the main room and bedroom could be moved. He'd seen it move once, but no matter how much he pushed, he couldn't budge it. Finally in frustration he sent a thought for it to move and was amazed when it obeyed him. Once he recovered from the shock, it took him no more than half an hour to have the three wall sections framing the outer door in a six by six foot box. What had been the bedroom door opened into the resulting one large room. The bed went in one of the alcoves created by the new structure, and the table and stools in the other. Afterwards he rested, still frustrated by his weakness. The work hadn't taken much physical exertion, but it had left him exhausted.

After two hours of sleep he started out slowly. He walked through movements of the martial arts the army had taught him to test how much he remembered, how much he could do, and how well he could do it. As far as memory was concerned, he was quickly satisfied that he remembered the moves. The other two aspects were discouraging. His left arm was weak. His right arm was slow to respond because of his chest, and even at a slow pace he was quickly out of wind.

While he took deep breaths through the mask, Garrett slipped off his Levi's, tossed them on the bed, and put on loose pajama bottoms to concentrate on his legs. Though he still got winded quickly, he did much better on the leg exercises. He was stiff, but some stretching exercises would help. The results might be enough to impress those guys as long as they had never seen any karate and the stress didn't finish his back off. He was on the floor with one leg folded back and one straight for stretching when someone knocked. The mask was tucked out of sight when he opened both doors from where he was.

Freet stalked inside. He was as close to exhibiting emotion as Garrett had ever seen. "Open door, no see who," he berated coldly. "Tell weapon forbid, leave in sight."

Garrett straightened, winced slightly from twisting his back, and leaned back on his elbow. "To begin with, you washed out Injun, I don't see through walls." He tipped his head towards the saddle. "No one bothered taking the rifle or the pistol, so I doubt they're going to get excited—"

"Translator."

"In my pants." He bent down over his legs as far as he could go. It wasn't nearly far enough. He was way too stiff and lacked flexibility.

"Translator," Freet repeated.

Garrett pointed to the bed. Damned if he was going to get up to fetch it. "There's no reason you can't carry one yourself." He took a deep breath and pulled down further as he exhaled. "And don't tell me you don't have any pockets. You can carry a knife; you can find some way to carry—"

"Find."

"Find it yourself."

Freet squatted beside him and pulled his head up by his hair. Garrett reacted with instinct he had thought he was going to have to re-hone. His right arm swung up to knock Freet's arm away, and the left shot out with the heel of his hand to catch Freet on the point of the chin. Both blows lacked strength, but they were accurate and totally unexpected by Freet. He landed hard on his butt.

"That," Garrett wagged a finger in Freet's face, "is a touch you need permission for."

"Translator," Freet said again with a cold stare.

Since Freet showed no signs of retaliating, Garrett relaxed and grumbled, "I'm going to tie a string around that son-of-a-bitch and hang it from your neck."

Before Freet could answer there was a knock on the door. Garrett couldn't hear any sound from the hall, and from the way Freet glared at him he knew he didn't dare just open the doors without possible violent consequences. He didn't want to get up either. He had twisted his back when he hit Freet, and made it ache, along with his legs, which would show when he moved and walked, something he sure as hell didn't want Freet to see.

From outside, Midradina called to identify herself. Freet sprang to his feet and dove for the knife. Garrett decided to stay where he was, pulled his legs up and crossed them. As soon as Freet was squatted back in a corner, the knife out of sight, he opened the doors.

She eyed Garrett closely. "You are well?"

Garrett gazed at her blankly. "Yeah," he answered in concern. He hadn't felt anything when he hit Freet, but maybe the yantz had. "Is Bud okay?"

"The yayantz are comfortable, but they are confused. You have no pain?"

"No," he lied. He ached like hell, but none of it had anything to do with the molded areas. "Does Bud?"

"Not specifically." She hesitated briefly. "Your flesh is damp. You have been exerting yourself?" she asked while her eyes took in the new arrangement and the litter of his gear.

"Haven't figured out what to do with all that yet," he told her of the clutter. Let her think what she wanted about his exertion. "Shove it under the bed I guess."

"You may have whatever furnishings you wish. The Freet will show you where to obtain them. He has, I see, shown you the duplicator."

"Yeah," Garrett said with a grin. He had a knife thanks to it.

She turned to Freet. "The yantz have— " Freet showed her empty hands. She turned back to Garrett. "You have the translator?"

"Nope, I gave it to him," he lied. He pointed to Freet as he said it, and Freet contradicted him by saying, "You have."

"You both are irresponsibly careless," she told them in irritation, but turned back to Freet. "Will he— "

"Hey," Garrett exclaimed, "are you talking to him in his own language?"

"Yes, and it is most difficult. Do not interrupt."

Garrett reached for the translator behind his ear. With one nail he pried at it and yelped in surprise at the sharp pain caused by pulling it loose.

"Now what have you done?" she demanded.

"I wanted to hear his language," he retorted. "Mysty said the thing was temporary."

"Temporary, but not unattached. Now you have caused yourself injury."

"No shit," he answered, looking at the blood on his fingertips.

With her brows furrowed she answered with, "Yes, shit."

Garrett grinned.

"What do you now find amusing?"

"If you have to explain it, it isn't funny." Garrett doubted she had ever used that word before in her life or knew what it meant.

"I doubt with an explanation, it would be humorous." she said haughtily.

"That's what I said."

"Then why—" She held up her hand to silence any answer he might give and told Freet, "Take Mord, then go hunt."

"A hunt?" Garrett asked excitedly.

"Wear shields," Freet said.

"Is third planet, no difficult. Need no weapons."

Freet nodded in acceptance. Garrett had a hard time not whooping, his first hunt, getting off the gray ship, his first strange planet. He clenched his hands to contain his excitement, and the shield popped off his arm.

"Look at that," he exclaimed.

"Perhaps that is what the yantz felt," she commented. "How does it feel?"

"Weak." He scratched at the chest pad with his right hand while he twisted and flexed the left arm.

"That will take longer," she told him, "It is of more delicate tissues."

"How long before it comes off?"

"A few weeks," she answered and turned back to Freet. "No lose translator. Important speak."

"He understands."

"May have questions," she pointed out.

"All answer in time."

###

Mord scolded Garrett for his foolishness, but Mysty was delighted to see him. He was too delighted to remember to speak in English, and Garrett couldn't understand anything he said once Mord removed the one translator to repair the damage. He could hear English through the ear that still had a translator attached behind it, but all he heard through the other ear was a discernable garble. The effect of the two different sounds was to make both indistinguishable.

"How do you stand that?" Garrett asked of Freet.

Freet stared back at him, but Mysty asked in English, "Stand what, Garrett?"

"Okay I understood that. With just one of these things, I can't understand anything anybody says. I asked Freet how he stands it when he uses the plug."

Mord answered, but he was on the wrong side of Garrett so all that Garrett heard was a high whine.

Mysty translated. "Hears Freet with one ear only. Deaf is he in other, but among the others known this is not."

Another secret Garrett thought. How many more he was going to be given before he forgot who was supposed to know what? Mord demanded his attention with a tug on his ear.

"He said—" Mysty began.

"I got that message," Garrett grumbled.

"Restricted to his language only vocal is," Mysty went on. "For all language audio plug is and efficient more, when lost not. How many to replace have you?"

Garrett shrugged and got his ear tugged again. He sat still. "He loses those too. I don't think he likes them any better than the vocal."

"A religious fear or superstition seems he has. Refused he various types for him Mord has devised. Briefly use will he, but to carry refuses."

"So much for tying one around his neck," Garrett muttered.

"Still would lose it he, sure am I," Mysty said with a chuckle. "How fair you with him?"

"Strictly business." Garrett caught Mord's hand. "Let me see it," he said of the thing Mord meant to put back in his ear.

Mord was in an impatient mood. He barely let Garrett get a glimpse of the pea-sized, paper-thin wafer before he pushed it into Garrett's ear. He scolded, still in his oscillating whine that in an instant turned into English, as he worked to attach the wafer to the wire through the outer ear to the external unit.

"It would be better," Mord whined, "to place the translator permanently."

"You aren't burying anything in my head," Garrett told him sharply, with a reason that was no longer vague to him. A deep suspicion was growing and clarifying in his mind as to a dual purpose for those translators.

"It is only beneath the skin," Mord argued.

"No." Garrett jumped off the table. "Come on, Chief."

"For a time can stay you not?" Mysty asked.

"We've got things to do."

"Anxious are you for your first hunt. Understand I, but return can you not to visit?"

"I don't think that's a good idea," Garrett told him coolly. "The others are already down on me for favors. It's better if I'm just one of the boys."

"But—"

"Come on," he told Freet and walked out. In the hall he started to ramble. "You know how things sit in the back of your head. You don't even know they're there, but they talk to you, telling you things you don't understand."

"No translator," Freet told him in disinterest.

"Yeah, I know, doesn't matter. See I just figured out why I don't want that damned thing in my head. And I've got me a mean idea it's the same reason you don't want anything to do with them, suspicion not superstition. Like how did she know where the Karoz was to catch him?"

He paused for breath. "With it—Hi there, Gunian, how's things going?" The last Garrett called out as he, without a break in stride, continued walking. He held up his left arm. "Shouldn't be long now. Just as soon as these others fall off, we'll have our little meeting."

"I look forward to it," Gunian returned with a slight bow. "But I would first ask a question."

"Sure."

"As he has no translator and cannot understand your words, why do you speak to him?"

"He never interrupts," Garrett answered glibly.

With a half-shake of his head and a wicked smile Gunian said, "It does not seem sporting to kill a fool."

"You don't think so? Well, I'll tell you what, I'll take that into consideration. Depending on how you prove yourself, I may let you off."

Startled for an instant, Gunian laughed. "I think I begin to like you, Earthling. If you are as brave in battle as you are with words, it would indeed be a shame to kill you."

Garrett smiled, but he didn't trust Gunian's sudden change of humor. "I sure would think so. That's why I won't let you."

"It is time for refreshment. Join me. We will see if there, perhaps, is an alternative."

"What refreshments?"

Freet spoke. "Talk long. Much do."

Not sure what he would be getting into, Freet's interference came at an opportune time. Garrett told Gunian, "Sorry, maybe next time."

Gunian eyed Freet and asked, "You do everything he tells you?"

"Got to bide my time..." Garrett said with a shrug, "...until them yayas let go of me." He hooked his thumb toward Freet to follow. Let the Gunian chew on that for a while.

Freet took him straight back to his quarters and nearly tore the room apart to find the translator. The bedroll Garrett had on the bed, preferring it to the bare mattress even with the controlled temperature, flew into the air a piece at a time after Freet shook them in his search for the earplug. Garrett didn't help. He knew where it was, in the pocket of the Levis he wore. He also knew why Freet wanted it. Freet finally realized where it was and backed Garrett up against the wall as he demanded it.

"What say?" he asked curtly as soon as he had the translator.

"It's none of your business," Garrett told him. "And don't try blackmailing me with showing me things again. There isn't anything you can show me I won't find on my own sooner or later."

Freet tossed the translator at him. "Find hunt."

"Don't think I won't." He shoved the translator back in his pocket and stormed out the door. Two left turns and a right took him to the common room. He walked straight to where Gunian sat. "Invite still open?"

Gunian's eyes darted behind Garrett and back. "For you, not the Freet."

Garrett didn't even know Freet had followed "Since I'm stuck with him, I guess that means no."

He half-turned to walk away when a movement caught his eye. He threw his left arm up to block the arm and knife that came at him. From there Garrett gripped the thumb around the knife with his right and twisted.

The man's head was narrow at the top with small eyes and nose, and enlarged at the bottom with a huge mouth. The last offered a convenient target for Garrett's fury. He'd never seen the pear-faced man before, which made the attack even more maddening.

"Want me, sucker?" he asked as the man quailed at the pain from the twisted thumb. "Come on!" Despite his weakness a jab with his left hand split the man's lip "Come on!" Blood trickled from the man's nose from a second jab.

Terrified, pear-face let go of the knife and screamed, "The Freet. Was not for you. The Freet, it was for the Freet."

Garrett shoved him away, confused, not sure if he believed him, but still furious. He warned coldly, "Better make damned sure when you go after someone, it's not someone close to me."

The man nodded vigorously and dropped to a bench cradling his hand. Not one of the others had moved, for or against Garrett. Freet hadn't moved, for or against him either. But they all watched him.

"That goes for all of you," Garrett snapped. He walked to the door and turned to face them. "And don't think I'm going to learn three hundred different sets of quirks. You can learn mine. I look at a man when I talk to him, I look at anyone walking towards me, front or back, and I speak when I damned well want to. Any of you want to take offense at what I do and how, we'll settle it when these come off."

He knew Freet followed before he reached the second turn. It wasn't because he heard Freet. He was high on adrenalin, his sixth sense sharpened. He felt him.

"Turn left," Freet ordered from several feet behind.

Garrett turned without asking where they were going. He had the translator with no intentions of giving it to Freet to be cross-examined again, no matter how many walls Freet backed him into.

"Hunt be short."

"I'm not going on any hunt with you, even if I felt like it." Garrett didn't feel like it. His back and legs hurt, but he changed his mind about the translator. He had a few things to say.

Freet walked towards the back wall of the new room they entered. Garrett followed holding out the translator. In one step he went from bare, gray walls to a pink world. There was no longer any sense in telling Freet he wouldn't go on the hunt. He shoved the translator back into his pocket, more than a little amazed over the transition to an alien world, though he refused to show it.

He might have enjoyed his first visit to a strange planet, if he hadn't been so mad. He just couldn't appreciate the uniqueness of a world colored in the spectrum of pinks, ranging from almost red to a pale shade with just a slight tinge of color. He poked absently at a pretty, little pink flower that tried to eat his finger and swore when another, with yellowish, pink colored petals and a purple stem, left welts on his arm.

Freet stopped in a field of pink grass. "See enough? Go back now?"

"If you're staying on my account, don't bother," Garrett returned in the same sharp tone. "I've had all the looking through rose colored glasses I wanted a long time ago."

Freet stared at him until Garrett nodded, then walked off. Leaving had become Freet's second favorite method to let Garrett know he didn't want to listen to his rambling. Not much caring at the moment, Garrett followed. They walked back into the ship with the same suddenness and lack of warning. One step they were surrounded by pink, the next by gray. Garrett didn't even ask how it was done. Freet took them back to Garrett's quarters, and Garrett went straight to bed, not even bothering to take off his boots. He didn't go to sleep, however. The pain that kept him awake gave him the opportunity to overhear Freet and Midradina in the hall.

"He sleeps," Freet stated flatly.

"At this time of day? Has the short hunt tired him so badly?"

"No have night day. Sleep short time all time."

"That must make it difficult for you. Do you feel he will be able to—?"

"Feel same as say before," Freet cut her off abruptly.

"The answer is the same," she countered. "Can you teach him enough in only four hunts for it to be safe for him to go alone?"

"Safer hunt than here."

She moved to a different subject. "You are making ready for the next hunt?"

"Go soon wake."

"Do you not hurry too much? It is not a good place in the cycle."

"Better be done soon."

There was a slight pause before she said, "I am grateful—"

"No be," Freet told her coldly. "Make bargain, favor for favor, no more."

"You have shown him many of the things you have discovered with your wanderings. Will he be as discreet in not disclosing them to the others?"

"Will see."

There were no polite farewells. The conversation just ended, leaving Garrett in a depression. Hell, he didn't feel like tromping around in a bad place in a cycle anyway, whatever that was. Freet could just go alone. Freet, however, wouldn't co-operate. He came through both doors a few hours later and shook Garrett when he didn't answer his knock on the door. When Garrett didn't respond, Freet shook him harder.

"Damn it, Chief," Garrett grumbled, "let me alone."

"Time ready hunt."

"Not now, I'm tired."

"You weakling?"

"That's me. All talk, no show, stupid Earthling," Garrett hissed and rolled with his back to Freet. "Go on your damned hunt, and leave me alone."

"Hunt for two. You go. There do what want. Lie down, be weak."

"Or," he reared up to snatch the translator from Freet's hand. Freet was faster. He kept it from Garrett, but he didn't return it to his ear. "Or punch your lights out," Garrett continued, knowing Freet didn't understand. "I should have let that pear-faced bastard have you. Then you wouldn't be able to badger me to keep your damned bargains for whatever your twisted sense of honor is."

All Garrett's outburst accomplished was to satisfy Freet that he was awake. As soon as Garrett stopped talking, Freet gave orders. Garrett was to choose what he needed for an overnight stay and duplicate it. Garrett clenched his teeth to keep from wincing at the pain in his back, rolled his bedding, and picked up his saddlebags. "Okay," he said without interest.

Freet added the jacket Garrett had tossed to the side when he first unpacked, his change of clothes, canteen, cigarettes, matches, and the shirt he had kept Garrett from wearing on the ship. "Now maybe," he said before he led the way to the duplication room.

Before they reached it, Garrett reconsidered taking what he carried in the saddlebags. When he rode away from his pickup and horse trailer, he'd gone out for three days of work. There wasn't any need for the tools he'd carried, and no reason to add the burden of the excess weight. He doubted he'd ever have any use for them on that gray stick-everything-together ship either, but running the saddlebags through just the way they were was easier than sorting through it first.

Freet duplicated one thing, the translator. He held both out for Garrett to take, which Garrett did with a smile. "I bet if I shoved them up your ass, you'd know where they were," he told him and dropped them in the saddlebags.

Once back in his room, left alone while Freet went for his things, Garrett did more than discard the tools and translators from the bags. He also re-discovered a few things. The first was food. The memory of the taste and smell of coffee made his mouth water. The dehydrated, bland meals he'd carried for the convenience of their light-weight and compact size suddenly seemed like a feast compared to the odorless, tasteless, liquid substance. He repacked those packets along with his battered coffee pot, utensils, and pans and looked forward to building a small fire to enjoy them. He put a canteen full of water in next. The pistol, belt and holster were the first things that went in on the other side, with his spare clothes and jacket packed in tightly over them. A short length of rope from the coil on his saddle made a sling for the bedroll. A small first aid kit, flashlight, and Freet's knife finished his packing, except for the medication.

He considered that for a long time before he shook out two tablets. If the pain increased to the point he needed numbing, he wanted them where he could get to them without Freet seeing. He put on his shirt, dropped them into the pocket and shoved the worn cigarette pack down on top.

Freet returned with a blousing shirt belted at the waist added to his costume and carrying a small sack, a very small sack.

"So?" Garrett retorted. "You know where you're going. I don't."

"Translator."

Garrett used hand signals to tell Freet to forget it. Freet stepped in front of him, much to Garrett's short-tempered annoyance. "It'll be interesting to see if my back holds up as long as my patience with you," he growled.

"Translator."

Garrett nodded and smiled and said, "Sure, on the bed though, not in my pocket." Freet held out his hand, which really irritated Garrett. "You don't need it now."

"Translator."

Garrett rolled his eyes and made a pretense of searching for it in his pockets before he went to the bed where he knew it was. "This better be important," he warned, tossing the translator at Freet.

Freet caught it deftly and put it to his ear. "Have masks?"

Garrett shook his head and waited for a question Freet needed a translator for. None came. Freet added a stack of masks to his small sack and tucked the translator under his belt.

"You son-of-a-bitch, what are you up too?" Garrett muttered. He grabbed up his saddlebags and bedroll and followed Freet. "You never carry that thing. You know it wires you."

"No talk hall."

"Asshole," Garrett growled and lapsed into silence.

###

"Where is your mask?" Midradina asked when they entered a room Garrett had never seen before.

Garrett panted and pointed at Freet. Talking made regaining his wind harder. His lung had expanded enough to allow him to move normally in the halls without enriched air, but the additional stress of the weight he carried and the pace Freet had set had taxed his lung's capacity again.

"His mask," she told Freet. He stared at her. She asked Garrett, "Translator?"

He pointed at Freet again. Freet, after Midradina motioned to her ear, showed her empty hands, stirring Garrett's curiosity. For him to antagonize Freet was one thing. Freet antagonizing Midradina was something else.

She turned on Garrett. "The Freet is not responsible for your every need. To struggle for breath until your color has altered is irresponsible."

"Bullshit, lady," Garrett exploded. "I can—"

He had to either stop for air or faint. Freet held a mask out to him. He snatched it, glaring, no longer appreciating Freet's game.

To further irritate Garrett, Midradina told him, "You will be responsible for having with you what is necessary for your well being. I will not give you another translator. Now you will learn as everyone before you has, by observation, without someone to conveniently answer your questions."

"Listen, you—"

"I will not." She put her hand to a door within a wall of doors. "A locker has been prepared for you. Your weapon is within. Think open, Earthling, or do without."

Garrett thought open, walked over to it, and nearly laughed.

"No much weapon," Freet observed as she disappeared.

"It's not," he snapped.

It was his six-inch hunting knife and scabbard, old and worn. Garrett used it for everything from cleaning his fingernails to skinning a steer, although he had never used it for killing.

He was struck with a sense of ridiculousness. They had taken what was more a tool than weapon from him and left him his rifle and pistol. Each of those was a hundred times more deadly than the knife, and he had used them to kill, which was one reason he had held on to his job. Whether it was a deer for camp meat, a rogue lion after the stock, or a pack of coyotes, Garrett never missed with that rifle. He did nearly as well with the pistol, but here they didn't even recognize them as weapons?

"Other weapon here." Freet said and led him to a side room.

The collection was ludicrous. There were weapons ranging from caveman clubs to crude fifteenth and sixteenth century equivalents of swords and lances. The most advanced thing was a crossbow Garrett wouldn't trust to send an arrow straighter than two feet.

"You guys actually hunt with this stuff?" he asked incredulously.

"No," Freet answered, making Garrett's head whip around. "These no want in hunt."

Garrett eyed the hand to Freet's ear. "I can see why." What he didn't understand was Freet's sudden, constant use of the translator.

"No like, make own. Show where when return."

"So I'm stuck with only a knife for a hunt?" he asked, even though he had no intentions of hunting and did have his pistol.

"Two think, if wise."

Garrett hadn't duplicated the knife and shot him a go to hell look before he picked up a rapier to examine. "I could always be Zorro." He slid the thin blade out of the scabbard. With a few experimental slashes through the air, he discovered the blade was well balanced and handled easily.

"Know weapon?"

"Did some fencing in college," he answered in preoccupation. Although he'd like to test it with a lunge, he knew better. His back already hurt like hell.

"No good to hunt."

"Depends on what you hunt." He returned it to the scabbard and set it down, hesitated, and picked it up again as he followed Freet. "The romantic in me," he said when Freet looked at him. He changed his words when Freet's hand went to his ear. "Never can tell; it might come in handy."

"No sound same."

"As close as you're going to get."

"As think. Say much, no mean hear."

That explained the increased use of the translator. "Oui?" Garrett asked, using some of the little French he knew.

"No translate."

"Just goes to show I can still say what I don't mean for you to hear."

###

A locker near Garrett's popped open. Freet pulled out a pack and dropped in his small sack. The pack sat on the floor while he put two knives sheathed in leather through his belt, handles crossed over his belly. A scabbard, long and narrow, hung from the belt he looped around his waist and tied down on his thigh. Short arrows filled it. The crossbow he took out made the one Garrett had been offered really look crude. Freet carried it in front on a sling over his shoulders. He put the pack on last and adjusted the shoulder straps.

Garrett had the feeling he had been had again. "How long…?" He waited for Freet to raise his hand to his ear, "How long a night is it?"

"Ten your hour, day twenty-three."

"I don't have enough then," he snapped, not for thirty-three hour days.

"Me do. Better no carry in hands." He talked as he walked. "Need hand for mask."

The brief warning was all Garrett got before he stepped from the safe, gray room in to a howling sand storm. A hurricane force gale drove sand to rip at exposed flesh and tore the mask from his face. He failed in his attempt to catch the mask because of the foil in his hand, losing the foil in the attempt. Just to stay on his feet was a struggle, especially when Freet pushed him. Garrett's first impulse was to slug him and let go of some of his frustration and animosity. Common sense prevailed. He couldn't see far enough to hit anyone. He buried his face in the bedroll, stepped in the direction Freet pushed and found the foil by tripping over it. Freet tripped over him.

"Hold on," Freet shouted in his ear and guided Garrett's empty hand to a strap on his pack. Garrett held on. He could kill Freet later for the unexpected walk into hell. At that moment he couldn't breathe or see, and twice he lost his hold, forcing him to grope frantically until he found it again. Each time was because the sand shifted from under his feet as Freet led them crosswind and downhill. The third time, determined not to lose his hold, he dragged Freet down with him. An avalanche started, with them riding the sliding sand. The ride took them out of the wind, didn't stop for twenty feet, and ended with a jolt. Garrett clamped his jaw tight to hold back a cry of agony as more sand slid down, burying him where he sat.

Freet jerked Garrett clear of the sand by his shirtfront and set him down on top. He turned to slip his pack off. Garrett spit sand out of his mouth and blew it out of his nose, holding his breath so he didn't inhale it. When Freet turned back with a mask Garrett hit him with an old fashion jab and caught the mask as Freet fell. Freet landed as he had the first time Garrett hit him, on his ass. Garrett put the mask over his face, took a breath and removed it to spit again. He really wanted to hit Freet at least once more, but knew better than to try to get up. His legs weren't numb, but the pain from landing in the ravine was just as crippling. They would not, he knew from experience, hold his weight. Since he couldn't hit Freet, the only other thing he wanted to do was lie down and roll in agony. He had to settle for a glare over his mask.

Freet glared back. He sat cross-legged to clear the sand from his eyes, nose, and mouth. After he shook his head to free his ear of grit, he took out the translator. "Have reason strike me" he asked in a dangerous calm.

"Good old G.P."

"No translate."

"Shove it, Chief. I'm not explaining anything to you."

"Have reason no strike back?"

"You want to hit me?" Garrett challenged. "Go ahead. Get rid of some of your hostilities. It'll be mentally healthy for you."

"No healthy you."

Garrett wished Freet would hit him. One good punch to the jaw would do as much as the tablets in his pocket. "Don't start worrying about my health now," he taunted. "Just drop me down another hole to see if it kills me."

"You drop us," Freet told him. "No reason you strike me."

"Take a hike. I don't need you to hold my hand. I can find my way back all by myself."

"Why strike me?" Freet asked again.

"Get out of here," Garrett shouted at him. "I'm sick and tired of looking at you."

Sand fell from every fold of Freet's clothing as he stood. "Scout. Maybe not crazy when come back. Make sense."

"Don't count on it," Garrett said grimly. He expected to be good and high just as soon as he could dig the pain pills out of the sand in his pocket.

###

Garrett had one boot off to shake out the sand before he spotted the spider. In a floating, happy mood from the morphine, he didn't see it as a threat. He didn't like spiders on him though, especially ones as big as saucers. Nor was he too high on morphine to forget that the spider might be poisonous, but he made no move to get away from it. He knocked it away with the top of his boot. The spider flipped, landed several feet away, and reared back on its hind legs.

"Uh," he grunted. "A feisty little shit, aren't you?"

He leaned further to flip it again. The spider jumped and landed on the boot. Garrett shook it off. It reared again. Garrett leaned further, threatening his balance, and the spider changed into a rock. One instant it was a spider, the next it was a rock the size of his head. Now that was curious, and Garrett wanted to investigate. Freet stopped him. He pushed the boot out of Garrett's hand with his knife and jerked him straight up in one swift motion.

"It touch you?" he demanded.

"Did you see that?" Garrett twisted to look and point.

Freet jerked him around. "It touch you?" he asked again.

"No, man, I don't like spiders, but—"

He wanted to tell Freet about the spider that turned into a rock, but Freet wouldn't let him. Garrett twisted to point; Freet jerked him back by to his shirt.

"Have venom on you? Have place feel numb?"

"All over," Garrett told him with a lop-sided grin. He stared at the sand that coated Freet's face and added, "Boy, you look like you've been dragged through a knothole backwards."

Freet let go on his shirt and squatted as Garrett slid down. He pulled up each hand to examine it and turned Garrett's head from side to side.

"Did you see—" Garrett pointed again.

"Answer." He held Garrett's head between his hands. "Burn by now. Have burning?"

"Wouldn't know if I did. That's...," He pointed a finger in Freet's face for emphasis. "...what it's supposed to do."

"Crazy Earthling," he muttered. "Better take no chance."

He hauled Garrett up and started him walking, not an easy chore. With his co-ordination inhibited by the drug, the dull pain in his back and legs discouraging the desire to walk, and only one boot on putting him off balance Garrett staggered and continually tried to sit down. In his drugged state he didn't get angry, he just didn't co-operate. Freet had to drag, push, and shove to keep him going to the spring where he dumped Garrett. Garrett didn't get mad over that either. The water was cool and washed away the grit. He didn't know Freet was gone and didn't care. He stripped down to the yantz shields and didn't think of Freet seeing the mass of scars on his legs and back below his waist where the body armor hadn't protected him. The water felt too good. He rolled in it to lie on his back and found Freet next to him, still on dry ground.

"Out now," Freet ordered.

"Come on in. Feels good."

"Dark come," Freet told him. "Creatures come to water."

Garrett leaned back on his elbows and told him as seriously as he was capable, "You could use a bath. You're filthy."

"Out now. Cold soon."

"Don't want to."

"Come now," Freet said firmly.

Garrett rolled from his back to his stomach. Freet threw his hands in the air and went after him. He stood Garrett on his feet, held him up with one hand at a shoulder and pressed his wet clothes to his chest with the other. Garrett took them automatically and stared behind Freet.

The spring ran away from them, down a sandy, barren bed that dropped enough to have hidden the explosion of green until he stood. Beyond that was a jungle too thick to walk through, filling the ravine between the sand slopes. That wasn't where Freet walked him even though it was where Garrett tried to go. Freet took them back to the gear and supplies with no more cooperation from Garrett than before. Garrett stayed on his feet while Freet shook out his bedroll and within minutes of being laid down, Garrett was asleep.

###

He woke with a jerk and shoved himself up before the cold hit him. He huddled quickly back under the protection of his covers. The air was freezing, and it was pitch-black in the direction he faced. Careful to keep the covers up close around his neck he rolled towards a flicker of light. Freet sat on the other side of a small fire with a sheet wrapped around him and, suspiciously, with his hand to his ear.

"Most ever sleep," Freet commented.

"How long have I been out?"

"Night end soon."

Not soon enough, Garrett thought. He had made an ass out of himself. Pain be damned, that was the last time he'd take any morphine where anyone could see him.

"Think hit head," Freet told him. "Make crazy. Do silly things."

"Yeah, well I'm fine now," Garrett retorted and hoped Freet went right on believing his idiotic behavior was due to a hit on the head.

"You remember?"

"Enough to stay away from spiders."

"Spit venom. Eat flesh away. Come with daylight."

"I got the message. You don't need to harp on it."

"Why strike me?"

"Just scratch it off to crazy."

###

Garrett dressed quickly, but with caution, and kept his back away from Freet in the hope Freet hadn't seen his scars the day before. He used the foil to pick up each article of clothing from his briefs to his socks to check for spiders before shaking them free of as much of the sand as possible. There were no spiders, but when he went for his boot, he saw why Freet had dropped a rock on it. A fourth of the top of his boot was gone. He didn't need Freet's warning to not touch it and told Freet so. They were the first words they had exchanged all morning.

"Wear these." Freet held out a spare pair of moccasins with one hand, the other hand to his ear.

Garrett refused to take them. "I'll get by without anything more from you."

"No in sand with octum. Octum spit, legs, feet."

He jerked the moccasins from Freet's hand. "Damned sure wouldn't want it said you didn't pay your debts."

"No owe you."

"You damned sure don't, so quit acting like it. I don't need or want a babysitter." He tucked the moccasins under his arm, picked up the saddlebags in one hand and the foil in the other. "If I get killed for my own stupidity, it's no skin off your nose or theirs, but if there was a way to do it, I would stick around forever just to spite the whole damned lot of you."

"No understand," Freet said quietly.

"Tough shit," he retorted and walked away.

"Where go?"

"To be alone," he called back. "And you'd better stay the hell away from me."

"Be back eight your hours."

"I'll be back when I feel like it."

He felt like returning after what he estimated to be one hour. There wasn't much to see. Below the wind level he walked the length of the pocket of jungle on one side of the sand slopes, crossed the ravine beyond it and walked back on the other side. Just short of reaching their camp he perched on the soft sand and spent another hour on his gear, first to check for spiders and then to clean the sand out of everything, including the pistol. He kept a constant watch. Just because he had moved out of Freet's view, didn't mean Freet hadn't moved to where he could watch him.

The foil made a suitable substitute cleaning rod with patches cut from his shirt to clean the barrel and cylinders. When done, he made the foil serviceable as a weapon. It was of no convenient use to him if he had to carry it in his hand, and its previous owner had been a much smaller man. There was no way to lengthen the belt to fit him. He had to alter his belt to accept the straps attached to the scabbard instead. He carved while he chewed on jerky and dried fruit with frequent checks of the surrounding area for spiders and Freet.

Maybe his anger at Freet was unfair. He hadn't overheard Freet say anything more, in spirit anyway, than Freet hadn't already said. Freet didn't want him as a friend, had told Garrett it was better to consider him an enemy. He'd made no secret of the fact he helped Garrett for reasons that had nothing to do with generosity or kindness. The only thing new Garrett had heard was that Freet wasn't receiving four extra hunts for his services. He had agreed to take Garrett on four to repay a debt, four he was so anxious to finish, he took one in a bad place in the cycle.

The last Garrett could do something about. This was the last hunt they would go on together, even if it meant being killed on the next one by going alone. He didn't want any friends anyway. He had spent the last twelve years of his life making sure he didn't have any, and the reason hadn't changed. He just hoped when the time did come, it wouldn't be on the dismal space ship.

After three more hours of morbid, angry thoughts, Garrett had had all he wanted of the second planet. Freet waited in the same spot.

"Hunger?" he asked, his hand going to his ear and his eyes on the foil hanging at Garrett's side.

"No. If you're ready to go, I've seen enough of this place."

"No much interest."

Garrett gave no answering comment, not even on the fact that he had seen nothing to warrant the possible need of Freet's bow. He went to his bedroll, shook it out as carefully as he had his clothes before he re-rolled it. When he finished, he picked it all up, took up the mask, and started for the ridge. Midradina had said to observe and listen. All they'd done when they returned from the pink planet was retrace the way they had come. Easy.

When he reached the top the wind wasn't as severe as it had been the day before, making Freet less of a jerk for walking him into that hell without warning. That didn't mean Garrett felt more like talking to him, and it didn't keep him from being furious with him when they got back.

On the first trip they had left for the pink world and returned to the same room. Garrett hadn't thought that leaving from a different room the second time would be of any importance. It was. The first room had not had access to weapons. If one left the ship to hunt, one had to go through decontamination on return, which was a nice way of saying, strip naked so you can't smuggle a weapon into quarters. If he came into the weapons or locker area for any reason, he had to leave through decontamination with fresh pajamas provided on the other side.

"Body naked, hands empty," Freet explained in his succinct manner.

Because he hadn't listened closely enough before they left he was going to lose accessibility to his only whole shirt and Freet's knife, and he for damned sure wasn't going to ask for another one. Freet had told him to make duplicates of everything. He could have explained why, but then Garrett felt he should have anticipated for himself that there was a reason. He hadn't listened closely enough, and not for the first time.

Because Freet put the translator into his locker and stripped, Garrett talked out what was bothering him. "My head isn't working right, Chief. I've never been a genius, but I've never been this slow either."

"No translator."

"Yeah, I know just like I know two and two make four, but my head isn't putting it together. I got two over here and two over there," he waved his arms as he talked, "but it doesn't go the next step until four walks up and hits me, and then I think, yeah, I should have known that."

"Go now, others wait," Freet told him.

"It sounds like a fool proof plan." Garrett's thoughts took off in another direction. He had two guns, Freet had a knife, and the Dapho, the pear-faced man, had a knife. Who knew what other weapons were hidden under all those hides and furs. His hunting knife had been taken off his belt, but the Karoz had a litch. Whoever was responsible hadn't recognized it or his guns as weapons.

The scholars knew what a musket was; Vizron had asked him about them. That was close enough to a rifle to have been recognized. They could implant a tiny device in their heads capable of translating at least three hundred languages and, if his suspicions were correct, transmit a tracking beam, yet they didn't recognize a gun. That didn't make sense.

"Earthling," Freet called out.

Garrett nodded and hurried, too preoccupied with his thoughts to remember to return the moccasins as he had intended. Something was wrong, really wrong, with the way things were done there. Mysty knew what century he came from and had spoken of technology. The scholars didn't. Mord did, at least somewhat, but Midradina, as well as the scholars, had thought him a primitive savage. Then there was Freet. Where did he stand in all of it? He dressed and behaved primitively while knowing how to operate think tubes no one else knew existed and refusing to wear a translator.

Garrett was still wondering about Freet when they reached his quarters. He went for a translator and asked, "How long have you been here, Chief?"

"Time little measure."

"And little meaning?" he asked soberly.

"No end."

"Yeah, well, I'm tired, Chief."

Not entirely a lie, but Garrett had no intentions of sleeping. As soon as Freet was gone he went to the intermediate section. There was no reason to tell Freet what he was going to do. Freet would find out soon enough, to his pleasure, Garrett was sure. The problem was he couldn't find Midradina. Mord sent him to Mysty. Mysty didn't know where she was either, but he was thrilled to see Garrett.

"Garrett, come in, please, do," he cried happily and dragged him in. "So good to see you it is. Well looking you are, tired though perhaps. Resting well you are? Oh, the air, I adjust it will."

"You don't have to do that," Garrett protested as he was pushed down in a chair high enough that his feet barely touched the floor.

"Easy it is and fear do not, no harm to me it does. A mask wear will I if difficult becomes. So happy to see you am I. Well it goes? Good teacher is Freet? Stoic, yes, but leave you will he to learn what safe is to learn alone and dangerous point out. A good man, but silent, so closed within. Drawn him out have you? Speaks with you does he?"

"No," Garrett inserted into Mysty's non-stop questions.

"No? Oh, sad that is." Mysty dropped down into another massive chair. "Hoped I had friends you would become. Why recommend him did I. In two, qualities common sense I."

Garrett scoffed at that. "We aren't anything alike."

"Yes, Garrett, are you. Outwardly not, but here." He touched his chest. "And here, think I." One long finger touched his temple. "But discovered this not you have?"

Garrett shrugged. "I came to find Midradina." He looked around the room. Mysty's quarters were pretty much the same as his. There wasn't even a higher ceiling to accommodate Mysty's excessive height. There was a larger table and two stools on one side and the two large chairs in the other. Everything was the same drab gray, making Garrett curious as to what might be in the bedchamber, if maybe more of the real Mysty was there than in the reception room. Despite his curiosity, he got straight to the point.

"I'm tired of Freet dogging me all the time. I want her to release him from whatever promise she got from him."

"Believe I not how that it is, Garrett."

"He feels like he owes her something. Taking care of me was his way of paying her back. Freet's done more than enough to pay off any debts and having him around isn't making it any easier for me with the other men. They resent the yantz treatment and the special accommodations. I can't do anything about the treatment, but I sink or swim from here on out with them. It's my responsibility, no one else's, and that's how I want it."

With a deep sigh Mysty leaned back to study Garrett. He said thoughtfully, "I think difficult for you it is to accept a person special are you, deserving treatment special."

Garrett retorted. "There hasn't been a damned thing done for me, and it's not that I'm not grateful—hell, I'm alive—but it's all been done for the yantz. I feel like a parasite."

"Live off the yantz you not do."

"I've never had to depend on someone or something to keep me going."

"Or had on you something depend?" he asked.

"Not long enough to count."

"Perhaps think failed then have you?"

Garrett jerked up straight. The conversation had definitely gotten away from him and too personal. "Just tell me how to find her."

Mysty shrugged causally. "A message there is no way her to send. Comes she, goes she. If comes here she, tell her will I wish you with her to speak. No more do I can."

"The scholars sent her a message," Garrett reminded him curtly.

"Not they did. Cause that of delay in knowing need were you in. Not know did she what happened to disturb yantz until the head scholar went she to learn how faired you. Unfortunate not meet him you did. Very interesting is he and like not those you meet did."

"He must have been too busy to be bothered," Garrett said tartly.

"Chosen was Vizron for the reason same as Esten."

"You don't have any form of communication in this place?" Garrett cut him off with.

"Midradina only the sections between and with the Thornns through yantz. Very much it is for one only, think you not?"

"Really makes me appreciate the time she's squeezed out for me," he said with a terse smile as he stood and headed for the door. "I bet she damns the day she brought me aboard for evidence against the Karoz."

"Do not mistake, Garrett," Mysty told him with sharpness in his voice. "No trials here there are. Midradina it is who accuses, judges, and punishes." His voice became mechanical. "That first thing, despite what has happened since, was done for your sake alone."

Garrett didn't turn to face him. Mysty's words took him back to the thing that tormented him about everything. All of the yantz's work had been for nothing. She could have saved him from an agonizing death without involving the yantz. The Karoz would have only taken a few months of life from him. She, with the yantz, had given it back, but the amount of time hadn't changed. In a place where time had no measure, he was still counting days and weeks to reach those same few months, even more so. There was no way he could survive there with half a body.

"Let me out," he said quietly.

Mysty saw the stiffness in his body and the muscles jerking along his jaw line. He opened the door, but he called out, "Return to visit, Garrett, please."

V

Being alone was still hard on Garrett. He didn't completely understand why. He had lived alone pretty much all his adult life, deliberately. He supposed the difference was he had always known that when and if he took a notion for company, there were places he could go where he could find a congenial welcome and interesting conversation with people who didn't want to kill him. He was also bored and constantly fought claustrophobia. The only solution he could think of was to keep busy. He visited Boss and Peggy, worked on his gear, rearranged and straightened his quarters—cleaning wasn't necessary since there was no such thing as dust—and worked out until he couldn't anymore. Without a watch to keep track of time he figured that took half a day. After a glass of substance, with nothing more to do, he started the whole routine over. By the time he thought it was evening, he had expanded his routine by checking out his saddle and bridle for needed repairs and taking them, huffing and puffing, to the duplicating room. He then made two trips, one to take a set back to his quarters and the second to his locker.

A sleep attempt after that failed and set him off to prowling. He stayed clear of the Phogatres territory and ended up back in the locker room. From there he went to the workroom with the foil and scabbard. The tools and available materials were just as antiquated as the weapons, requiring some improvising. Instead of getting frustrated, Garrett just accepted the additional work and inconvenience of the trips in and out for what he needed as giving him something to do.

He went back to his quarters, took the reins off the bridle to take to the duplicating room. He dropped off one set at his quarters and took the other set to his locker and the workroom. It took some engineering, but with his hunting knife for slicing and Freet's knife for punching, he put together a belt to hold the scabbard on his left thigh at the proper length for drawing the rapier. Every time he picked up Freet's knife, he regretted not having listened more closely about duplicating everything he wanted to take to the planet. If he were ever challenged with one of those in his hand or better yet, one in each hand, they would be less willing to chance being slashed to ribbons.

The others had weapons that were recognized as such. There had to be a way to take them through decontamination. "Where there's a will, there's a way," he murmured. He ran Freet's exact words through his head again, which wasn't difficult as brief as Freet's vocabulary was.

"Naked body and empty hands?"

He walked from the locker room with the knife in his hand and stood at the door to the decontamination center. It was really no more than a long hall with another door at the end. There was a chute at the entrance to dump the clothes if he didn't want to keep them and a niche at the other end with fresh pajamas. Somewhere in there was a sensor of some kind, had to be. If you had clothes on before you reached the niche, the door wouldn't open.

"It can't be that easy," he said aloud, but he gave it a try. He stripped off the pajamas bottoms and kicked the knife down the hall on the floor. When he got to the other end there were fresh pajamas. The door opened. He wrapped the knife in the shirt he wasn't allowed to wear and carried it back to his quarters, puzzled with disbelief over how easy it had been.

He discussed the situation with Boss during his next visit. "Do you suppose they figured all their specimens are just so stupid all they had to do was tell them they couldn't take a weapon out and make-shift some half-ass system to fool them into believing it? Too arrogant? That's what it looks like. They think we're all stupid, not that I haven't been. My head just hasn't been working right, Boss. Maybe all this goop I've got in me is doing something to short-circuit my thinking."

Boss nickered in response and shoved at him with his head for an ear scratching. "Well, hell, maybe they aren't that much smarter. All that 'think it done' stuff they do could mean their brains are just different than ours, but if that was so then how do they set the things to work for us? Or do they? No one set the duplicating machine, but it worked for me."

Boss lost interest when the feed and water slots opened. Garrett sat down in the corner of the pen, his back against the wall. He still wondered if some of the things would work for anyone, while some were set to work for specific people when he drifted off to sleep. It wasn't restful.

He jerked awake, not remembering his dreams, but woke drenched in sweat and with an overwhelming sense of the walls closing in. Panting, he left the pen and its closeness, and dug a mask out of his pocket. By the time he was steady again, he stood in front of Peggy's pen and smiled slowly. To his disappointment he couldn't open the door with thought. That didn't stop him. The doors to the pens were swinging doors, not sliding like those of his quarters. After a little experimenting on Boss's cage he was back at Peggy's pen springing the catch with his knife.

Peggy charged immediately. He back-pedaled, slammed the door, tripping in his haste. On the floor, he looked up at her and smiled despite the pain he had set off in his back. "No letting you out," he told her while she reared and pawed the air, "but you'll get used to me in time."

###

The day didn't start well, if it was another day. Garrett had no sense of time, a fact driven home to him when he rounded a corner at not too fast a pace because of the pain in his back. "Good morning," he said cheerfully to the group of five.

"It is evening," Gunian replied. He looked over Garrett's attire, Levi's, pajama shirt left open to compromise with the yantz, and his boots. He smiled and laughed softly. "It would seem you have your days and nights in reverse. An easy thing to do when there is no sun or moon."

"Or...," sneered a companion, a green-tinged man with oversized ears, "...the Freet has taught him to sleep the day and walk the nights for safety."

Garrett countered with, "Or you've got your days and nights reversed. How long has it been since you lived with a sun or moon?"

Gunian raised his hand to stop the angry mutterings. "Another possibility is that your days and nights are different from those set for us, and you have not adjusted to the change. Until the days and nights were set, it was difficult for us to sleep. You have found this so?"

"Nope," Garrett lied with a poker face.

"You are fortunate."

One of the other men grumbled, "In more ways than one."

"They are jealous. You understand?" Gunian asked pleasantly.

Garrett still grinned and told him, "They can set their green-eyed monsters to rest. It won't last much longer."

"It seems some things have already changed. Your friend is not with you."

Gunian looked behind him. Garrett didn't. He wasn't too sure he wasn't going to get jumped. "If you mean Freet, he wasn't doing it out of friendship."

"He stood behind you. His knife was drawn when the Dapho attacked."

Garrett hoped his surprise didn't show. He hadn't seen Freet move at all and certainly hadn't seen a knife. "Or to protect himself," he suggested blandly. "He was the one the Dapho was after."

"More a possibility," Gunian said with a wicked smile. "He has never stood with any other."

"You know him better than I do."

With a slight nod, Gunian asked, "Do you go to the common room for orders of the hunt?"

"He does not need to," the big-eared man said belligerently, "She goes to him."

"Go," Gunian ordered. "We will be late." To Garrett he said, "Walk with us."

"Sure," he said brightly and stepped back. "Age before beauty."

Four walked by him while Garrett stood with his back to the wall. Gunian faced him. "You say I am older while you are more handsome?"

"I don't know how long you've been here, but I figure I've got some catching up to do."

"Time does not pass here. We do not age." He looked at the lines etched in Garrett's face and the gray in his hair. "As you have."

"Touché. You still go first."

"That did not all translate."

"Too bad."

Gunian smiled slowly. "I would not attack you while you wear those shields. I do not wish to lose my head."

"I don't trust you any further than I could throw you, and right now that wouldn't be very far."

"You look stronger. Your strength returns?"

"You'll find out."

Gunian chuckled and started off. No one paid any attention when he walked into the common room. They all turned to look when Garrett appeared. There wasn't anywhere near three hundred, but there were enough of them, and none of them looked friendly. Garrett walked around the outside wall as much as possible and sat down with his back to it, legs stretched down the bench, a position that eased his back as much as it gave him the appearance of nonchalance. Midradina was in the center, surrounded by them. He couldn't see her, but he could hear her calling out names, or rather where they were from. Hunters didn't rate names.

Blue faces, red faces, pink and purple, they were nearly all distorted in Garrett's eyes somehow. They all turned for a furtive look at him and then looked away until the yantz approached. Then they pushed and shoved at each other to clear a path from Midradina to him even though the yantz wasn't threatening. It moved slowly to stop a few feet from Garrett's face, its bulbous eyes level with his. The way he sat, it hovered over his legs with four of its legs folded up under its body. It wasn't Bud, Garrett knew instinctively, and something tugged at the back of his mind to be remembered while he kept a casual attitude. He and Midradina were the only two who didn't seem interested in the creature or what it did. She continued to speak without interruption or hesitation as Garrett watched down the opening left by the yantz.

The yantz extended one front hand and tugged at the lapel of Garrett's shirt. Garrett could guess what it wanted and was annoyed at being the center of attention. "Go away," he whispered.

The yantz didn't leave. It tugged at his shirt again, obviously wanting him to remove it. Garrett raised his arm to block a third tug, making the beings in the room gasp. Ignoring the yantz didn't work, maybe doing what it wanted would make it leave him alone. He took his shirt off in an indifferent manner with his attention on Midradina, giving only occasional glances to the yantz. It floated from one side of him to the other, and its tiny front hands rubbed over the chest shield.

Garrett's ability to feign casualness exploded when the yantz picked up his left hand with its front two hands and unfolded its back four legs to snap another shield over his arm.

"What the hell?" he roared and shot up to his feet. "What is that for?"

Midradina acknowledged what was going on for the first time. "The arm is sensitive."

"It is not!"

"Not to you, but it is to them."

"Because it's weak! It won't get any stronger with this damned thing on."

"It is because," she told him coolly, "they wish no further damage from battle such as the one you had with the Dapho, the one you did not report."

"Just how the hell was I suppose to report it?"

"The same way you leave messages," she shot back coolly. "Combat here is forbidden, of that you are aware. Do not pretend the innocent with me on that issue. Just as with the others, to ignore a law will bring you punishment. Do not think the shields give you special privilege, and do not again show neglect in the care of the yantz. You will not wear a shirt even if it is open, so all will be reminded clearly that you are not to be attacked until the shields are removed, or it is the yantz punishment they will receive. Now, if you have finished your disruptive behavior, you need not stay, as you are denied one hunt for not reporting the attack."

Garrett's fists clenched and unclenched. His jaw flexed from the pressure of his clamped teeth, but he moved quietly. He snatched up his shirt and walked out of the room. He was down to a slow simmer when he reached Mysty's quarters.

"Oh, Garrett, so happy you to see I am. Well it went?"

"What went well?" he demanded.

"Dina was—"

"It was all a set-up?" he exclaimed.

"Set-up I do not know." He took Garrett by the arm and led him to a chair. "Explain while rest you. Weary look you."

He was and showed it. He leaned forward with his elbows on his knees and held his head in his hands. "You told her what I said, and she staged that scene."

"Was distress it not to you for them to believe receive special advantage have you?"

Garrett grinned and leaned back to slough in the chair. "Yeah, sorry for being so dumb and getting upset about being cut down like that in public."

"Without humor you smile, Garrett." He sat down in the chair opposite him. "Know I quite stern can be she. Very angry was she to discover the Freet had not of the attack informed her, but not would he. A betrayal would have been it. A great disturbance it did among the yantz cause."

"So why didn't they report it?"

"Report the disturbance they did, but recognize did not the cause until learned of the battle they. Your exertion felt before had they and recognize did not the difference or such is what I believe. Of the yantz, so little know we and think I also things there are to Dina they tell do not."

"She's the only one they talk to?"

"Yes," Mysty said slowly.

"You've told me that before?"

"Yes, though very weak you were."

Garrett gave a derisive scoff. Weak in the head, but he did recall what he'd been trying to remember in common room. Midradina had told Mord that her bayantz could not touch him, and the yayantz could not leave their sanctuary. So where had that one come from? "What's the difference between a bayantz and a yayantz?" he asked.

"A yayantz to a bayantz progresses when a transformation completed has it. Only bond with one and can bond with others not though many know this not."

More secrets, but he didn't dwell on it, instead asking, "And become guards afterwards?"

"Yes." He took a breath and said quickly, "Others we believe capable may be with the yantz telepathy, yourself as such."

Garrett scoffed again, forgetting where his thoughts were going. "I'm not and don't try to get me to learn. There's too much to learn now."

"Quickly you do learn, Garrett, and no time limits are there. Age you will only when on a planet you are, days few at a time. Years yours will be expanded to centuries."

Not as a cripple he thought and stood. "Kind of tired, Mysty, I'm going to see if I can get some rest."

Mysty's lips went out of sync. "What is it that troubles you so, Garrett?"

His smile was sardonic again. "Besides the obvious?" he quipped.

"There are many ways to assist the obvious to be better. Freet has shown you the learning and create rooms?"

"Nope, must be some of those things he figures I can learn by myself."

"The learning room provides information." Mysty rose and lifted Garrett's shirt, twisted and winkled from the wringing he had given it while walking off his anger. "The create room will provide for other needs. It would be my pleasure to give directions to locate them and instructions to their operation. For one with as active a mind as yours, all would be possible. One need only picture what they wish for in their mind, for it to be theirs. Visuals are provided for those who cannot."

"Sounds interesting," he said without enthusiasm. He felt like Mysty was humoring him. As dull as his mind was, he would be using those visuals.

"Both would make it easier for you."

"I'll find them eventually," Garrett said with an indifferent shrug.

"Did the Karoz take you from family, Garrett?" Mysty asked suddenly.

"No, I'm just a worn out old saddle bum, no ties and no strings."

"Saddle bum I do not know, but worn and old, no. I see the results of your exertions. Your body grows stronger each day, as does respect for you among the hunters and their fear."

"Who told Midradina about the fight?" He wanted at least that settled in his mind.

"Do not be angry, but it was I. I would not have done so, had not the information been useful in the set-up."

Garrett was too tired to be angry or grateful. "How did you know?" was all he asked.

Mysty hesitated before saying in a rush, "I have dreams. It does not make you fear me?"

Garrett considered the worried look in Mysty's eyes and shook his head. "We gave up burning witches at the stake a long time ago. We call them psychics now." He didn't believe in them or Mysty. He figured Mysty was protecting whoever had told him.

"It is something with which you are familiar," he said in relief.

"I've read about it," he answered drolly.

"I believe you are one."

Startled at first, Garrett laughed. "Sure, Mysty, and if I had wings I could fly."

Confused, Mysty said, "Yes, but—"

"I am no psychic," Garrett said flatly.

"The abilities may lie dormant within—"

Garrett cut him off coldly. "There is nothing dormant in me I don't know about."

"What is it that—?"

"See you around." He went to the door and ended the conversation.

Mysty didn't try to hold him any longer, although he requested that Garrett return. Garrett made no promises. Aside from the distrust Garrett had of Mysty, he didn't want friends. He hadn't let anyone close enough to him for them to mourn his leaving for over twelve years. Nothing in that regard had changed.

###

The old routine wasn't enough. There wasn't enough in the repetition of working out or visiting Boss and Peggy to keep his mind occupied, even if he did continue to make slight progress with Peggy. Garrett had to have something else to distract him from the same thoughts over and over and the feeling of suffocation the ship gave him. He prowled around until he found the create room, easy to recognize from what little Mysty had told him.

One shelf over a long table on one wall held dozens of thick books, each about the size of notebook paper with page after page of clear sheets adhering to a blank white sheet. On the clear sheets were black and white sketches of costumes ranging from caveman furs to creations a Star Trek designer would have loved. They had to be the visuals Mysty had mentioned, but there was no system to the drawings. Futuristic, primitive, and what could be historical Earth were all mixed in together. Some were crude, other ridiculous, and still others appeared to be practical or comfortable. He chose several and set about learning how to operate the machine.

The machine was a three-foot square closet built in the middle of the room. Nowhere, inside or out, could he find a knob to push or pull, a switch to flip, or even a plate to press. Inside the only break in the smooth gray walls was a rough spot the approximate size of the visuals. He stuck a sheet there. It adhered, but nothing seemed to happen. Since everything there worked by thought, he thought "Create." Still nothing happened. There was no buzzing, clicking or hums, but when he stepped out, a bright pink jump suit with matching boots and gloves lay on the table.

Garrett cleared the table with a sweep of his arm and a chuckle. Pink was not his color and even if it was, the suit wouldn't have fit him unless he was five foot tall. In seconds he had another complete costume. Though reminiscent of a Russian peasant dress, a high necked, full shirt with blossoming pants tucked into boots, Garrett doubted any peasant, Russian or otherwise, would wear one made in a bright red vinyl looking substance.

Three costumes later he still hadn't found anything in a tolerable design of an acceptable color or fabric to suit him, let alone the right size, but it was interesting and amusing. With hundreds of pages to a book, he'd found a new source of entertainment. Three costumes later he had learned how to transfer his size and the color he wanted into those visuals. Six or so later he had a pretty fair stack of different styles of shirts, pants and boots to a color and size in materials more like what he was used to, but he was bored and tired. He disposed of the costumes down the waste chute and went in search of the learning room, knowing he wasn't yet tired enough to sleep. He found something else.

###

At first he thought the Phogatres were playing some kind of kick ball, which made a nice change from them trying to kill someone. He walked by the intersection without a direct look at them until the fur ball skidded in his direction. He meant to side step away from it. Instead he nearly jumped out of his skin when the fur ball exploded and encased his foot and ankle.

"What the hell?" he exclaimed. He shook his foot furiously until he realized it was Glemm clinging to him, trembling violently.

"Give back," the lead Phogatres commanded.

Glemm crawled up his leg. "I don't think..." Garrett flinched and grabbed for the tiny hand that grabbed at his crotch. "Watch where...." The hand had already gone to his waistband as others gripped his arm, back waist, and shoulder. Glemm's arms wrapped around Garrett's neck in a strangle hold.

"Give back," the Phogatres commanded with the menace in his intentions obvious.

Angry over what they had been doing and embarrassed by the thing wrapped around his neck, Garrett smiled dangerously. He pulled at the arms so he could breathe. "I don't think he wants to play anymore."

Two Phogatres moved closer as a unit. The third didn't, saying, "He is the one. See the shields." All three turned away, but not before giving him a look that promised nothing pleasant.

"Assholes," Garrett muttered. He walked as fast as he could. "They're all assholes. I'd like to give the whole lot of them a hot foot."

He pulled one of Glemm's arms loose so he could get more air, but the creature had six of them, and the poor thing was frozen in terror. No sooner did Garrett pull one arm loose and start to work on another, than the first one was wrapped tightly around him again. Garrett was staggering by the time he went down the ramp to the infirmary. He dropped to his knees as he reached the door. Fortunately for him, Mysty and Mord were there. Mysty pried the Glemm loose. Mord picked Garrett up and rushed across the room, setting him on the counter. He nearly jerked the drawer out in his haste, and he had no difficulty getting Garrett to accept the mask.

The single lung had again met with a condition it couldn't cope with. Garrett had not had to use a mask under normal conditions, in normal air for some time. Recovery after being strangled was another story. Even with the mask, it was difficult, especially when he tried to keep Mord from chastising Glemm and because of Glemm, Mysty.

"You see," Mord shrieked, "what that stupid creature has done. Now not only is it a nuisance, it is dangerous."

Glemm didn't look dangerous, rolled in a quivering ball in the crook of Mysty's arm, and Garrett knew it hadn't meant to hurt him. "I—" he gasped out.

"Be still," Mord ordered and turned back to Mysty. "Have I not told you—?"

"It did not attack him, I am sure," Mysty cried in anguish.

Garrett tried again. "No, it—"

"Be still and breathe," Mord ordered.

"Garrett," Mysty cried, "I am so sorry. I do not understand what made it do such a thing."

"Fear," Garrett managed to say.

Horrified, Mysty exclaimed, "You attacked it?"

"Phogatres kicking..." Garrett held up a finger to request a minute.

They gave him several minutes for his breathing to level off and his color to return. They were also silent while he relayed what had happened, though Mysty's hold of Glemm became more protective.

"Better check him for broken bones," Garrett said as he finished. "They were kicking him pretty hard."

"It does not have bones," Mysty told him with an unsteady voice. "I am so grateful to you."

Mord rudely cut him off, "It is not a he."

"Like the yantz?" Garrett asked.

"No," Mysty answered. "Both, but I wish to thank you for—"

Midradina came in, in what Garrett supposed was a run though the movement of her legs and feet could not be seen under her gown. She saw him and stopped so abruptly her skirt swung forward and back in a sweep of the floor. "You do not look ill," she said in obvious puzzlement.

"I'm not."

She looked at Mord and Mysty, who offered no explanation, and back to Garrett. "Why are you here, if you are not ill?"

"Came to visit," he told her blatantly. He knew if she found out what had happened Glemm and Mysty would be in trouble. "Mord's going to give me a tour of the medical facilities."

She asked of Mord, "What is there he has not already seen?"

"Little." Mord went along with the lie. "It will be a short tour and a long visit."

His comment gave rise to something Garrett hadn't considered before. He had accepted the condition of his back and the prognosis as irreversible. A possibility that it may no longer be true occurred to him. After Midradina left, he told Mord he actually was interested in seeing his facilities. The comment made Mord chuckle.

"It is as Dina said; there is no more to see than you have already aside from ointments and a few instruments."

"Be grateful," Mysty told him, "the yantz gave your arm support for healing. His way is to smear the limb with gray mud, both uncomfortable and cumbersome."

Garrett hid his disappointment. "Sounds like an old fashioned plaster cast, heavy and itchy as hell."

"I have heard this complaint. There is a better way?"

Garrett described the lighter weight methods and watched Glemm slowly recover from its fright. He would rather talk about Glemm as it cautiously unwrapped itself than answer Mord's questions. The questions made it all too obvious Mord did not possess skills superior to Earth's, especially when Mysty asked about the types of treatments for spinal injuries, making Garrett uncomfortable.

"I don't know much about that," Garrett lied and abruptly changed subjects. He pointed at Glemm. It sat on Mysty's folded arm with two legs dangling, two holding to Mysty's arm, and two around Mysty's neck. "What was he—it doing up there?"

"I do not know," Mysty said with a sigh, "but I am so grateful to you for rescuing it, Garrett. The Phogatres are particularly vicious towards it, and unfortunately they can see it in camouflage. I pray it has not caused you a lasting injury. It is much stronger than it appears and than it realizes, I'm sure, in its fear. I do not know of anytime it has ever deliberately caused pain."

Garrett joked. "Just so it doesn't have claws hidden away in those little hands."

With a weak smile Mysty said, "I have heard of your exposure to the claws of Dina's bayantz. Had it not been for your yayantz, there would not have been any hesitation to give her time to assure it you meant her no harm."

Although he didn't understand what one had to do with the other, he nodded and walked to the door. "Why won't they treat the hunters?"

"Their wounds are the result of their violent way of life, a life they choose."

"I hadn't chosen it yet?" Was that why he had been granted the treatment?

Mord corrected him. "That is why Dina was allowed to call them to you."

"Or they came of their own accord," Mysty said. "She had requested before and been denied. As I have said, there is much of the yantz we do not know and the Thornn."

Garrett was reminded of where he had been headed before he had encountered the Phogatres. He asked directions to the learning room and received them, along with complete instructions on how to use it. Both were simple to follow, especially the latter. He did nothing more than sit down on a bench and wait for the room to talk to him. The room responded to his thoughts, fast-forwarding to pass over something that did not interest him or rewinding to replay something he didn't quite catch the first time.

The information was disappointing. There were a few facts, such as substance could be ordered in a solid form as well as liquid, and he could think any flavor he wanted into the otherwise tasteless food supplement. He also heard instructions on how to self-create in the create room, but no facts on the Thornns or the yantz. The room provided less information about the ship than he already knew, except for how to know while in his quarters when he was supposed to go to the common room for instructions for a hunt, when it was his turn to leave, and how he could know who stood outside his room. Freet had failed to tell him the purpose of the prism over the door or the significance of the color changes. Freet, he decided, either had a hidden sense of humor or was vindictive.

All that 'think too much and too little' business with the doors had been a bunch of malarkey. No matter how ignorant Freet was—and Garrett didn't believe for a moment he was at all ignorant—he couldn't have misunderstood the simplicity of the instructions. Had Garrett been unable to think the door open, Midradina would have set the door and room to his voice command. Having some flavor in substance and to be able to chew on something instead of always drinking it would have made all those past meals more pleasant too. He was sure the old saying 'still waters run deep' applied as a vast understatement to the phlegmatic Freet.

###

Garrett's second trip to the create room was with a completely different agenda. His head still worked at a sporadic level, and he hadn't taken a vague thought any further the first time when he had noticed the costumes were not just bare shirt, pants, and shoes. They were complete with underclothes and miscellaneous objects of decoration. The visuals seemed as though they were a picture of some kind taken of those clothes that eliminated the man inside, but included everything inorganic right down to a thin gold chain and medallion from one of them.

Things had happened so fast when he'd been attacked, Garrett didn't remember more than a general idea of the Karoz's covering. He certainly hadn't taken any hide-by-hide account. It turned out none was needed. There were only ten fur costumes, which contradicted his theory of the visuals being the clothing the specimens wore when they came onboard. The number of fur visuals was far short of the number of those men he'd seen wearing furs, and he hadn't found any visual of the clothes Freet wore. Also, unless there were many more scholars than hunters, there were more volumes of costumes than there were men, meaning the visuals had to have come from somewhere other than what the specimens wore. To him that meant he probably wouldn't find the litch Mysty said the Karoz had when he was taken.

About to give up on what he considered a wild-haired notion, Garrett decided as long as he was there, he would create the four closest visuals to what he remembered of the Karoz's clothes. He knew when he found the right one. The stench gagged him immediately and worse, set off a reaction he had never anticipated. He started to shake and fought the urge to vomit while he stabbed at the fur with his knife to get it down the disposal chute without touching it. The smell sickened him, but it was more than the smell. With the last piece gone, he staggered to the door and fell to his knees, wanting to curl into a ball and cry.

Once the air cleared, he could breathe and the dizziness had passed, he sat up and held his trembling hands in front of him. He had read somewhere that smell was the strongest of memory triggers. The Karoz stench had damned sure triggered something. He didn't remember being terrified when it had happened. He didn't consciously remember anything more than his concern for Boss. But then he hadn't believed what was happening either. He hadn't accepted the Karoz or events as being real. So why was he shaking? Had he finally accepted what was happening to him as truth? Was a man insane when he started believing the figments of his imagination? Or was all of this really happening?

With his knees drawn up to lean his elbows on, Garrett held his head. He was tired, so much so that what he saw on the floor didn't excite him or make him feel smug in proving his theory. He picked the litch up and turned it in his hand. It was the size and shape of a TV's remote control. He wondered abstractly what channel he would get if he pointed it at a wall and pressed one of the buttons on the side. Cartoons? Reruns of Star Trek? A hole in the wall? Was he in a Thornn research vessel, thousands of light years away from Earth or was he in a hospital, really holding a remote control in his hand? And did it even matter anymore? Real or fantasy, would anything he did or thought he was doing matter?

He grunted over that last question. It would damn sure matter if it was real and any of the hunters got a hold of that litch. He took it and the visual sheet with him to be sure none did.

VI

Garrett rolled out of bed, stood straddle-legged to keep his balance, and tried to orient himself. Something had awakened him. He didn't know what, and he was in such a drug induced stupor, he just stared at Midradina when she sailed through the inner door.

"How could you have done such a senseless and cruel thing?" she demanded furiously.

"Huh?"

"This is unforgivable. You will be punished." The more he stared dumbly at her, the more furious she got. "Now those that are not killed by the others will starve. How could you be so cruel?"

"I don't know what you're talking about," he mumbled and wished he hadn't taken those pain pills.

"Do you deny you know how to open the cages?"

"You're mad because I opened Peggy's cage?" he asked in confusion.

"All of them!" she shouted.

He started to understand what she was saying. "I never—"

"Who else? Only you have spoken of such a thing. Free them you said, but how could you so stupidly have freed them here on the ship?"

"I didn't."

"No one—"

"I don't care what anyone else did," he shouted at her. "I didn't open those cages. You're going to have to find someone else stupid and cruel. I said you could find something better for them, not turn them out to starve or kill each other."

"You—" She spun to face the yantz behind her. After a few seconds she turned back, stiff-faced, and spoke with a forced quietness. "They do not believe you released the creatures."

"Bully for them." Garrett dropped on the edge of the bed. "Maybe you should have asked them before you came busting in here with your accusations."

She took a deep breath and said, "They recommend I ask you for suggestions on how to remedy the situation."

"Catch them and put them back," he answered hatefully.

"There are hundreds!"

"You've got hundreds of hunters. Put them to work."

"Were they to know the creatures exist, they would slaughter them."

"Hell," he dragged a boot from under the bed, "it was probably going to be a boring day anyway."

"You would help?" she asked in surprise.

"I'll help the animals," he told her coolly as he pulled the last boot on and picked up his shirt. He wasn't going bare from the waist up to capture animals. "You'd better round up anyone you think you can trust. Some nets would help."

"Very well, we will meet in the main corridor."

After she left, he muttered, "And thank you too."

He was still sluggish when he reached the pen area. The poor substitute of coffee flavored substance did little to clear away his drug holdover. A cigarette hadn't helped either. He thought he would just have to work it off, but then he looked into the pen room and received an instant adrenaline rush. Inside was pure bedlam, filled with ear shattering screeches and squalls. The floor thronged with animals that ran, jumped, and fought one another. The air was filled as well with birds of every size, shape, and color, flying in fear and confusion.

Garrett was more than a little nervous about going into that mass of moving creatures he'd never seen before. Some were similar to some he knew—as much as the octum had looked similar to a tarantula—and for all he knew just as deceptive, but Boss and Peggy were back there. He worried more about them and was relieved to discover the freed animals were afraid of him. They ran and skittered out of his way.

Boss and Peggy were still secure in their pens, safe from any harm they might do to themselves or in panic with their hoofs to the freed, smaller animals. Reassured, he took his time going back, and closed cages that still held animals that were too terrified to leave the only thing they knew.

"It's not quite as bad as it looks," he called out to four others as they arrived, Mysty, Mord, Freet, and a stranger. He shut three more doors on his way. "There's only four rows opened, all smaller cages. We shouldn't have to wrestle down anything bigger than we are." He spoke to them as a group, not acknowledging Freet in anyway special. "Some are still in their cages, and others will probably go back when they get hungry."

"What of those that do not?" Mysty asked.

Garrett shrugged and looked directly at the stranger. He was no hunter. There were no furtive glances from him, but instead a direct, open appraisal that Garrett returned. He wasn't much over five and a half feet tall, and his marble-white coloring and white pajamas made him look like a statue. He had no body coloring except for a slight blue tint to his irises with slightly darker pupils. Not even the inside of his mouth, tongue, or lips had color. He would have made a beautiful statue, well formed, well proportioned, and with a handsome face. As a man he left Garrett cold. Not even his smile helped, especially since it was condescending.

"Garrett," Mysty said, "this is Radshab, a Vasian."

There had been a little flicker of annoyance in Radshab's eyes at the order of the introduction, but his smile stayed in place. "Strange is it not," he asked, "how races are so similar and yet so different?"

"Yes, it is," Garrett answered. In his own world, he was called a white man. There would have been some real adjustments made if there had been any like Radshab.

"Our forms," Radshab went on, "are most similar although in my world your size would be considered grotesque. Are you large for an Earthling?"

"About average," Garrett lied. He didn't care for being called grotesque no matter how veiled.

"We must meet sometime, Earthling, and compare our worlds."

Garrett gave a non-committal nod, knowing that would never happen. He turned to Freet. Freet may not want anything to do with him, but he preferred Freet's company over the arrogant Vasian. Freet surprised him by already having his hand to his ear. "Any ideas?" Garrett asked him.

"Catch with hands."

"That's about as far as I got. Be some easier if we could herd them into a smaller area."

Freet nodded. "Big cages other end. Chase there."

Garrett pulled his gloves on. "Anything in there poisonous or carnivorous?"

"No, but frightened." Freet pulled a pair of gloves from his belt. "All bite and scratch."

"Don't you think," Radshab asked, "you should wait for Midradina?"

Garrett really didn't like him then. Beneath his smile, it was obvious that Radshab considered himself far superior both as a Vasian—whatever the hell that was—and a scholar. He was the kind who used subtle and constant reminders. A hunter was not, his last question implied, intelligent enough for any independent action without someone superior—Midradina in that case—to guide them.

"Okay," Garrett said. He sat down on the floor, his back to the wall.

Without comment, Freet squatted beside him. They were a stoic pair when Midradina arrived in a manner that did not placate Garrett's mood. Behind her was a man instead of a yantz, no more of him visible than his dark, elfin head. Black hair, skin the color of well-weathered leather, and brilliant downcast black eyes peeped out from a five and a half foot mound of mesh wrapped around him. Not even his hands were visible. Midradina, with empty hands, introduced him only as the Fray. All the scholars had been introduced by name, but the Fray was just another species of a primitive hunter not worthy of the personalization of a name.

"You have assessed the problem?" she asked Garrett and Freet. "And have formulated a plan?"

"Not us, lady," Garrett answered as he watched the mesh reform in a neat pile on the floor and a man emerge. "We're just the peons around here."

Beneath the nets was a little man who reminded Garrett of a spider monkey. He was dressed in brown cloth the color of his skin. His body was short while his arms and legs were long. The hands were the most interesting thing about him. He had four fingers, all of the same length, and two thumbs per hand, one on each side. He was also painfully shy.

"What is a peon?" Midradina asked.

"Someone who waits for their betters...," He looked directly at her, "...to give them instructions before they make a move."

"That is ridiculous," she retorted in exasperation. "If your only objective was to wait for instruction, why did you request nets?"

"I didn't request. I suggested," Garrett answered blandly, irritating her all the more. "I heard tell how smart men, scholars like, used nets to capture, not kill critters. Figured y'all would know what to do with them."

She asked stiffly, "For what reason are you acting the fool?"

"Just remembering my place."

"It is my doing, I fear," Radshab said smoothly. "They had formulated a plan, but abandoned it when I suggested they wait for you. I am afraid the Earthling took offense when none was meant." He turned to Garrett and ignored Freet. "I was referring to the nets I knew she was bringing."

He hadn't been referring to any nets. Even his off-handed apology, which was only for Midradina's sake, was offensive in its insinuation that they didn't have the ability to understand the simplest of words.

Garrett shrugged in answer. "Don't make me no never mind. I never hunted with nets." He turned to Freet. "You?"

Freet shook his head and pointed to the Fray. "Him do all time."

Everyone looked at the little brown man. His head shook as Midradina asked what should be done.

"Garrett and Freet," Mysty said quickly, "had discussed first closing in the creatures still in their cages and containing the others in smaller areas to make their capture easier."

With a look of gratitude, Midradina asked the Fray, "You have nets large enough to do this?"

The little man twisted and leaned for a better look into the large room. His eyes were quick and bright, but they dropped to the floor when he turned back and nodded.

Garrett rose to his feet. "I'll give you a hand."

The Fray shrank back, Freet lunged up, and Mysty jumped forward to stop him. Mord settled for shouting. Only Midradina and Radshab did not react. Freet was the fastest and stopped a confused Garrett.

"You must not touch him," Midradina told him. "He would cause you pain."

Garrett looked around Freet to ask the Fray, "Why?"

"I do not mean to," the Fray answered miserably.

"His body is different than yours," Radshab said patronizingly.

"I can see that," Garrett snapped. "My problem is ignorance, not blindness."

"The difference is not visible," Mysty said.

"It is," Radshab told him, as if he explained something to a small child, "a primitive defense system he cannot control."

Garrett mentally ground his teeth. "Like Esten?"

Midradina answered. "It is not heat, but very uncomfortable."

"Or deadly," Radshab had to add. "It intensifies if he becomes frightened or excited."

"So I don't touch him. I got the message." He turned back to the Fray. "I'd still like to give you some help, and I'll be careful not to touch you."

"Better I do alone," he murmured softly.

"Okay, just tell us what we do."

Startled Fray exclaimed, "Me?"

"You're the one with the nets," Garrett pointed out.

"I—I hang nets and go."

"You aren't going to stay and help?"

"Better," Freet commented, "five men than four."

Garrett fought not to smile over the well-aimed shot at Radshab. And Radshab didn't like it. A sharp edge came into his tone. "He cannot touch the animals."

"No need," Garrett assured him. "He'll throw the nets; we'll take them out."

Midradina told the Fray, "They need your help."

"Some object to my presence," he said softly.

"Not here," Garrett told him cheerfully. "Anyone object?"

No one did, not openly. Mord and Mysty voiced their desire for him to stay. Radshab simply said he had no objections. With a little more coaxing the Fray went to work. While the others moved down the rows to close the cages that were still occupied, he used open cages for a ladder to string the nets at the ends of the first row, closing the top and bottom doors on the nets to serve as anchors. In a very few minutes a portion of the animals were confined in a smaller space. His skill became even more apparent once he began tossing the net.

With his long arms and legs, the Fray leaned his short body out to whip a six-foot circle of net towards his prey. With his double thumbed hands, he had enough control to throw the net in any direction. The first flip of the net sailed out to pluck a bright colored parrot from the air and dropped on two furry creatures that ran together, each slightly different from the other, yet each resembling a squirrel.

Garrett praised the Fray's skill and worked his hands under the net to capture a chattering, furiously squirming squirrel creature in each hand. Their needle sharp teeth penetrated the leather of his gloves, and to get rid of them as soon as possible he tossed both into the nearest cage and slammed the door shut.

"You cannot do that," Midradina cried.

Garrett rubbed his stinging hands on his thighs and asked in bewilderment, "Do what?"

"Only one per cage, there must be no breeding."

Garrett raised one eyebrow at her and looked at the squirrels carefully. "They're both males."

"It makes no difference."

"It does where I come from," he said blandly.

She colored slightly and snapped, "It is the law. Only one creature per cage."

With an indifferent shrug, Garrett moved off. "Then move them."

She followed. "I have no gloves."

"They don't do much good." He pulled one off to show her the bites and smeared blood. "Just catch them as close to their head as you can. That way they can't twist to bite you."

"Bird too," Freet said, with one hand to his ear and the other showing a tear in his gloves. "Be more careful."

"You got it." Garrett nodded to the Fray. "Ready when you are."

They were ready, but the Fray could not throw. Midradina still stood in the center with Radshab near her and Mysty and Mord a few feet away.

"You folks want to kinda move to the back and shoo the critters this way so our partner here can drop a net over them?" Garrett asked.

Radshab whispered something to Midradina. She shook her head and said, "Let it be," to him and asked Garrett, "Will those two injure one another?"

Since they had been running together he doubted it and asked, "What are they doing now?"

"Eating," she said in perplexity.

"Food would be about the only thing they would fight over. If they're sharing without a fuss, I don't reckon they'll fight any."

Radshab started to say more. Midradina waved him into silence. "We will be of some use," she told him, "and shoo the critters."

From that point things moved rapidly. At Garrett's suggestion the Fray concentrated on the ground animals and left the birds for the last while keeping them contained within the nets from aisle to aisle. Mysty and Mord with their great height herded the flyers.

Garrett soon began to enjoy himself. They all danced, ducked, or flinched to avoid the various animals that squealed, screeched, ran, or flew. Mysty did the most intricate dance when a monkey sought refuge under his robe. Mord achieved the fastest twenty-yard dash when, while on his way to help Mysty, the same monkey broke from beneath Mysty's robe in a screeching run to find a safer place. Radshab achieved the lowest duck by going face down on the floor to avoid a large bird that resembled a raven and made the quickest return to his feet when he found himself face to face with a large land tortoise.

Midradina exhibited the most control. She was terrified of the animals no matter how small, yet she never ran from or slapped at any creatures when any came near her while she herded them toward the nets. That was why Garrett took the rabbit to her during a lull while the nets were being reset.

It was a small cottontail, not much bigger than his hand, and once it quieted down, it seemed to like the inside of his shirt. "This little guy," Garrett took it out, "was so scared he couldn't move. He's still trembling."

He held it out to her, one hand under and one hand over, and stroked it with his thumb. She made no effort to touch it just as she had made no attempts to take an animal from the nets. Nor did she move back, but she was tensed, ready to do so.

"He's more afraid of you, than you are him. You could calm him down, talk soft to him, and scratch his ear. His fur is one of the softest things you'll ever feel."

"And," Radshab said, "hides claws and teeth."

"A lot like the yantz," Garrett returned tightly. "They only use them when they're frightened or threatened."

"One does not fondle a yantz."

"More's the pity," Garrett replied in irritation and walked away, putting the rabbit back in his shirt.

Garrett started around the corner of an intersection to herd more animals towards the net and performed a quick u-turn. With one foot still in the air poised to step forward, he pivoted to go back the way he'd come.

"We're going to need a bigger net," he told Midradina as he walked by her.

"Why?" she asked. "What is it?"

"Damned if I know." He turned back to watch the corner. "Or want to find out."

Midradina moved enough to peer around the corner. "It is a trohog," she said.

"That," he said with a jab of his finger, "is the ugliest thing I've ever seen."

"No doubt we are just as ugly to it. Most likely we look like worms."

"That's fine as long as it doesn't eat worms," Garrett replied.

Mysty and Mord chuckled behind him. Garrett glanced at them and then at the Fray, who was busy with his nets, his shoulders shaking. Freet, his hand to his ear, wore a particularly blank expression.

"It is a foliage eater." She looked from one to the other of them. "This was one of your humorous remarks?"

"Not for me," Garrett answered in complete seriousness.

While he stayed as far as possible from the corner, Garrett moved along the wall behind Midradina and Radshab. He leaned out for another look. He didn't like what he saw any better once he knew what the thing was called. At eight foot long and three foot high the trohog looked like a headless slug of giant proportions, covered with foot long spikes and colored a sickening shade of purple. The only thing needed to make it totally repulsive was a coating of slime.

"Does it have a head or a tail?" Garrett asked.

"You can see it does not," Radshab told him.

Garrett had had just about had all he could take of Radshab. He asked, "Since you know so much, how about telling me if it's coming or going?"

"It moves," Midradina answered, "in either direction."

"And just how," Garrett still spoke to Radshab, "do we get it to go the way we want it to?"

"To where?" Freet put in.

"Better to leave alone," the Fray answered to surprise everyone.

"I'll go along with that," Garrett agreed.

"You are afraid of it?" Radshab asked.

"Radshab," Mysty gasped.

"That was rude," Midradina reprimanded coolly.

"It was not meant to be," Radshab said smoothly. "I was only curious as to what would frighten an Earthling."

Garrett still smiled. "Don't go judging Earthlings by me. That Karoz kinda took pot luck, but then he probably wasn't looking for the pick of the litter."

"Your words translate, the meaning does not."

"I keep hearing that. You scholar boys must have screwed up somewhere when it comes to translating. It just goes to show—"

"Earthling," Midradina began sharply, "you will—"

"Not insult your precious—?"

Garrett didn't finish that particular taunt. The trohog rose up soundlessly to tower over them. Garrett stiff-armed Radshab away as he jumped at Midradina in a twist, pushing her backwards into Mord. Garrett's momentum carried him forward, head and shoulder first into the cages, nearly knocking him out.

The trohog flopped to the floor where they had been standing, its quills quivering. Its middle immediately began to pull up, and the front end lifted two foot up off the floor, moving to flop again in their direction. Garrett knew there was no way he could move fast enough to avoid being hit. He was bracing himself for impact when the Fray jumped over his legs. With one touch of the Fray's hand, the monster threw itself backward and curled into a ball of shimming spikes.

"Thank you," Garrett said with sincerity. The twist to his back and the slam into the cages had numbed the lower half of his body. He rolled over, pushed with his hands to sit and swung back on his arms to lean against the cages. He hoped it looked casual rather than necessary because it was all he could do. The movement only carried his legs so far. They were crossed and crooked, but he would not, under any circumstances, lean down to straighten them. He also hoped everyone's attention was on Radshab, not on his lifeless legs.

Radshab rushed towards Midradina. Mord stepped in front of him. Mysty turned her away, holding her in his arms. Garrett knew why they were so determined that no one get close to her. Once before he'd inadvertently touched her, and his knuckles had clunked. He'd felt whatever it was that time with both hands. Midradina's upper body was encased in something hard and unyielding.

"It is not safe for you here," Radshab cried. "Allow me to escort you back."

"No," she said, her voice unsteady.

"It would be a disaster if you were injured or killed."

"The Thornns would simply choose another Midra."

"It is my wish to assist you," Radshab insisted, not easily rebuffed. "It is too much for but one."

"I shall relay your opinion of my abilities to the Thornn."

"That was not my meaning!" he exclaimed in horror.

"I do not wish to discuss it." She turned to Garrett. "Will you accept my gratitude, Garrett Maniam?"

He gave her a genuine smile. "That's easy, you're welcome,"

That seemed to perplex her as she turned to the Fray. "And you, Advavotory, my gratitude to you as well."

"It was my honor," he murmured in embarrassment.

"Both," Radshab said, "have quick instinct and reflexes."

"Asshole," Garrett muttered.

Radshab's phony act slipped to show his contempt. "You spoke, Earthling?"

"The name...," Garrett told him coolly, with a smile of the sardonic variety, "...is Mister Maniam. I'm who, not a what. Remember that the next time you address me."

As an interruption, Freet asked, "Trohog dead?"

"No!" Advavotory cried. "It sleeps for a short time."

"Why attack?"

"Searching for food, not caring what is in its way."

"From your world?"

"Yes."

"What do we do with it now?" Midradina asked.

"Barbecue it," Garrett grumbled.

"What?"

He looked up and shrugged. "Put food in its cage, and hope it can find its way back without running over anyone or thing."

Freet grunted and pointed to several brown spots on the floor. "He bleeds."

"It is nothing," Advavotory claimed immediately.

"Go with Mord," Midradina ordered. "We have all spent long hours without rest or substance and can do little more until the trohog has returned to its cage."

"Don't forget the way back," Garrett called out to the Fray with a twitch as the rabbit ducked back inside his shirt.

"Mystaleah, you will escort Radshab back to the scholar's entrance so he may rest. I will open it from here."

"I'll stay here to close that thing back in," Garrett offered to give a reason for just sitting there.

Midradina turned to Freet. "You will bring substance?"

Freet studied Garrett intensely, making Garrett uncomfortable. If anyone was to notice his twisted legs or anything odd about the way he sat, it would be Freet. Garrett was just about to say something caustic when Freet nodded and walked away.

As soon as they were alone, she asked, "You have pain?"

"Nothing I can't..." he began cuttingly. His first thought was that he hadn't done as good a job of covering up the numbness in his legs as he had hoped, then he remembered the yantz. "My chest doesn't hurt."

"It is more discomfort they sense; intense when you fell, but now they are uncertain."

"That's the drawback to these shields. I don't feel anything. I must have strained a muscle or something," he prevaricated and worried over just how much the yantz did feel.

"That must be it," she said, but she looked confused. "Perhaps it is the creature disturbing the shield."

Garrett shook his head and took the rabbit out. "He isn't touching it. Cute little guy, isn't he?"

"It has the look of innocence while bearing teeth to bite and claws to scratch."

"Everything does in one way or another," he told her. "What makes the difference is if it's done out of meanness or only for protection."

"And Radshab?" she said, perceptively seeing the point he made.

Garrett shrugged. "You don't care what my opinion of him is."

"He is, we believe, insincere and untrustworthy. Mystaleah was curious, if you too would feel this way."

"My opinion doesn't matter."

"You do not like him, did not immediately, if Mystaleah is correct," she went on.

"So?"

"But you do like the Fray. It angered you when he was treated as one less worthy."

"If you're getting at something..." He looked back down at the rabbit, "...I'd just as soon you said it than beat around the bush."

"I am merely making an observation."

"Passing the time in idle conversation doesn't seem to be your thing." Nor did he appreciate it. The feeling in the lower half of his body was coming back in the form of pain.

"I do not believe I have ever engaged in idle conversation. There is too little time," she stated matter-of-factly. "What is meant by cute?"

"Adorable," he answered, the closest word he could think of as a simple translation, but he didn't believe her real objective in talking to him had anything to do with the rabbit. "I won't say anything about whatever that is that you wear under your gown." Whatever it was that was hard and unyielding when his hands slammed into her.

"It is better you do not," she commented in preoccupation. "Why is a wild creature so comfortable in your hands?"

He was puzzled by her casualness on the subject after the way Mord and Mysty had kept Radshab away from her, but he let it drop and answered her question. "I just let him know I mean him no harm."

"Could I do such a thing?"

"Not if you're scared of it." When she looked at him in confusion, he explained, "Your fear would make you tense and nervous. He would feel that and that would in turn make him nervous. Even then he probably wouldn't bite unless you held him down. He'll bite at anything that keeps him from getting away from what frightens him."

"It is too bad the same cannot be said for the hunters," she commented.

"Most men," he said in a terse correction, "are the same under normal circumstances."

"These are not what you would classify as normal circumstances."

"They could be more normal."

"Perhaps you will be a Midra..." Her voice grew cool. "...and tell the Thornn how that might be accomplished."

"I've no desire to be a Midra," Garrett told her, "and meant no slight to you, but maybe if you took more time for idle conversation, you'd be able to see what hunters need to feel more like men than animals and what the scholars need to feel less like gods than men."

"Perhaps that is why."

Garrett would have asked for clarification only the trohog was too much of a distraction. It flipped itself out flat and immediately drew itself up in the middle. Garrett held his breath. There was no way he was going to have enough control yet over his legs to get out of the way if it moved in his direction. Midradina didn't move either. When the end that rose told him it was going the other way, he let his breath out slowly, not realizing until then that he held the rabbit protectively against his stomach under both of his hands or that Midradina watched him with a puzzled look on her face.

Before they could resume their conversation, Freet returned with substance crackers, and Midradina left. They ate, something Garrett did slowly to gain time to recover before returning to work. The pain had eased to tolerable by the time Mysty and the Fray came back.

As they began again, Mysty reported that Radshab had insisted on staying in the infirmary rather than going to his quarters for rest. He would return with Mord as soon as Mord was finished with a patient they had found waiting.

"I predict it will take a long time," Mysty told them with a twinkle in his eyes, "perhaps longer than it will take us to finish."

Mysty brought more than that information, though he hadn't meant to. He brought Glemm. The creature was so shy, elusive in its camouflage coloring that Garrett and Freet both tripped over it before they realized it was there. Once called to by Mysty, it reverted to its natural black color, and startled the Fray by suddenly appearing near him.

Glemm's closeness and its curiosity over what Fray was doing gave them all a scare. Glemm darted in just as Fray swung the net and touched Fray. Glemm shot up in the air, all six legs straight out and quivering. It seemed to hang there for a second and then fell, straight down to the floor to lay stiff and still.

Advavotory thought he had killed it and cried out his regrets to Mysty. Mysty also thought it was dead and ran the length of the aisle with his robe held high. Just as he knelt down to reach for it, Glemm sprang up to the tips of the fingers of each of his tiny hands. Mysty recoiled and fell on his bottom with a resounding thud. Glemm then darted off stiff-legged to where the net had landed to investigate a chattering blue creature under it. Glemm's legs folded, and it bobbed up and down to tease the trapped animal while Mysty held his head in both hands.

"Don't act like it hurt it none," Garrett commented, all he could get out before he had to turn away to hide his amusement.

He didn't think Mysty or Fray would appreciate him laughing. He developed an imaginary itch under his nose and got busy retrieving the latest catch, being careful not to look at Mysty. He had to control his laughter several times during the time it took to recapture the ground animals.

With six legs, a small body, and six tiny hands, Glemm could and did get into everything. Whether down on its belly or up on its fingertips, it moved with incredible speed in any direction, even able to duck free of Advavotory's net as an irate small cat-like thing chased it. It tripped them, closed doors on their hands, or closed the doors before the animal could be tossed in, all while Mysty scolded or threatened it uselessly until he could stand it no longer.

"Advavotory can you not catch it in a net?" Mysty pleaded.

"Hell, Mysty, let him be." Garrett slid down the cage fronts and sat on the floor. "He's having more fun than any of us. Watching him you'd think he let them out just for the fun—what?"

The last was when Mysty paled and gasped. "By the heavens." He colored in embarrassment and shook his head. "It cannot open doors."

Confused, Garrett asked, "You think he would do something like that?"

"It has an impish nature. One is never too sure what direction it will take." He hesitated and repeated, "It cannot open doors."

Freet squatted across the aisle from Garrett with his hand to his ear and suggested, "Maybe someone teach."

"Glemm," Mysty asked sternly, "did someone teach you how to open doors?"

Glemm bobbed up and down once, and Mysty sighed in relief, astonishing Garrett. "He answered you?" he exclaimed.

"But of course, one bob is no, two is yes."

"I'll be damned," Garret said and added quickly, "Just in case, you better explain to it, this kind of thing is only fun once."

"It does not lie."

"Glad to hear that," he said, but he wondered about the trip and fall he'd had when he opened Peggy's cage the first time. He shook his head as Mysty had done. Even if Glemm had watched him, it didn't have a knife. He changed the subject with a weary sigh. "I don't know about the rest of you, but I've about had it for a spell."

"Thank the heavens," Mysty sat down right where he was. "I began to fear you would not stop before it was all done."

Freet grunted, his only response to the decision to rest.

Garrett waved at Advavotory. "Pull up a piece of floor and join us. We're going to rest for a spell."

The little brown man hesitated for a moment before he moved closer. "Mister Maniam." He pronounced each syllable carefully.

"Whoa a minute," Garrett told him with a light laugh, "That long version is for folks I don't care for much. Folks I like, I appreciate them calling me Garrett."

Advavotory squatted, which put his knees above his head, and smiled shyly. "I am Vo."

"Well, Vo, it's been a pleasure working with you. We'd never have gotten much done without you."

"I am honored at your words. It has been a pleasure for me also, but I must leave soon."

"Is it your hand?" Garrett asked quickly.

Mysty explained. "He must rest. His body grows weak without sleep."

"You should have said something sooner," Garrett told him.

"I am not yet weak," Vo answered indifferently, "but my strength will not last as long as it will take to net all the birds."

"Yeah," Garrett looked up at the incessant movement over their heads. "Mysty are there any two species alike?"

"I do not believe so."

"I don't think there are any females either. There's not much chance they would cross breed if there were. Are there any big cages empty?"

Freet answered with, "No breed. No female. Be big cages back."

"The Thornns won't like it, Garrett," Mysty warned.

"I'm too tired to give a damn. All I promised to do was help get them into cages so they wouldn't starve."

###

Garrett took morphine to sleep and flopped on the bed with his socks and pants still on. Midradina with her yantz at her shoulder woke him, just as abruptly as she had the day before.

"You cannot fail to realize some of these hunters are so primitive they can smell it. They will find a way to take it from you and probably eat it."

Garrett's response was the same groggy, "I don't know what you're talking about," while he sat on the edge of the bed rubbing his eyes.

"That cute creature," she answered tightly, "You must return it."

"I don't have it."

"I looked in the cages. It is not there."

"Then you didn't look in the right one." Anger woke him rapidly. "I left him with Boss." He had done so with his shirt wadded up in the corner to make a nest for it to burrow in.

"That monster will kill it."

"He will not," he retorted. "Boss doesn't have a mean bone in his body. Damn it to hell, will you give me some credit." He jabbed a finger at her. "You don't even know a rabbit from a horse. How the hell do you know how they'll get along?"

Garrett was starting to vent his frustrations when someone knocked on the door, and Freet called out.

"At least someone knocks," Garrett told her pettishly and headed for the bathroom. "He probably wants to see you."

"Why do you dislike him?" she asked as he walked away.

"I don't," he shouted back as he disappeared inside the bathroom, wishing he could slam the door instead of thinking it closed.

He didn't dislike Freet, which was one of his biggest frustrations. He liked him, and he missed his company. To keep a strictly business attitude around him was hard to do, especially when they worked so well together. He had to constantly remind himself that Freet didn't care in the least what he thought about anything. He didn't want to hear anything Garrett had to say unless it pertained to what they were doing, and he certainly didn't want to just visit. Considering the circumstances, that was the way it should be.

There was a problem with the birds. With so many to a cage, the birds were too crowded to rest on the floor without squabbling. Midradina's solution, of course, was to capture the birds and put them in individual cages.

"No do me alone," Freet told her.

Garrett stepped out. "You are as far as I'm concerned." He leaned back against the doorframe with his arms crossed. "I'm not getting bit or scratched anymore because the Thornns don't know their ass from a hole in the ground."

"They will injure themselves," Midradina cried. "Surely you do not wish this."

He told her curtly, "All you have to do is make them some perches. If you knew anything about birds, you'd know that."

"They will not suffer out of my ignorance," she stated haughtily.

"They have for years," Garrett said. She jerked her head around, making him regret his remark. It wasn't her fault that she didn't know how to properly take care of the animals. He pushed up from the wall. "All they need are perches, something resembling a tree to sit on." He opened both doors, hurrying them on their way.

"You will not help?" she asked.

"He doesn't need my help, and I've got plans."

What he said was a lie. He didn't have plans and felt like a heel, but it was the way Freet wanted it, and it was the way he wanted it too. Freet sure didn't argue when Garrett refused. Garrett wandered the halls before he ended up at the infirmary in search of something to ease the swelling and soreness in his hands from all the bites and scratches. Mysty and Vo were there. Mord was removing the stitches from Vo's hand, careful to avoid touching Vo with anything other than the instruments.

"Wow, you do heal fast." Garrett leaned, one hand on the table to look closer and jumped with a yowl, shaking and rubbing his arm furiously.

Vo jumped up and cried, "I am sorry, I am sorry," over and over again.

Garrett's jump and yowl were more from surprise than pain. He had been shocked—literally. Poor Vo was the cause with the charge his body gave off transferring through the metal table.

"Boy," Garrett exclaimed, "you carry one hell of a jolt. Now I know why..." His voice broke with a grin. "...Glemm jumped..." The grin became a suppressed chuckle. "...like that."

He struggled not to laugh. The more he thought of how Glemm had shot into the air, and how Mysty had looked when he ran to him and landed on his butt, the funnier it got.

"He is not angry?" Vo whispered in amazement.

Mysty told Garrett with a grin, "Glemm did not jump as far as you, but it jumped higher."

Garrett's control broke, and he laughed uproariously. Mysty joined in, and Mord chuckled while Vo smiled uncertainly. The laughter was contagious as they recounted their various jumps, dashes, and Garrett's u-turn. The stoic, taciturn Freet walked into the jovial scene. He stood without comment while each brought their laughter under control before he spoke directly to Garrett.

"No fast enough one. Birds hurt other. Hunt come soon."

To Garrett that was a curt reminder that Freet had already lost one hunt because of him. "Okay," he retorted and then asked Vo, "Want to give us a hand?"

Mysty translated with, "I believe he asks if you will assist." He asked Garrett, "What to do?"

"Make perches for the birds."

"Also assist will I."

Garrett asked Freet, "What progress have you made?'

Freet shrugged. "Can only carry few poles one time."

"Let's go get a couple of handfuls then."

The supply section, new to Garrett, was full of poles of varying lengths and platforms from table to bed sizes. While they searched through them Garrett flinched from touching one of the poles at the same time Vo touched the opposite end.

Garrett joked. "We need to create a pair of rubber gloves for him."

"Wish you why to do this?" Mysty asked.

"So he doesn't shock us anymore."

Vo exclaimed, "This is possible?"

The idea seemed simple to Garrett, but because it seemed so astounding to the others, except for Freet who didn't have his hand to his ear to listen, he said uncertainly, "It's just electricity, isn't it?"

"I do not know electricity or rubber," Mysty answered in his own language, "but if so simple a thing will help Vo, let us try."

That puzzled Garrett. If it was just an electrical shock, similar to a stingray, why hadn't it been recognized in this highly advanced place before? It puzzled him even more when the three of them, watched by Freet, created a pair of double-thumbed rubber gloves for Vo from the machine. To create something from nothing more than Vo's hands on a plate for measurements and Garrett's mental image of what the gloves should be made of had to be far more complex than the concept of a bio-electric field, even if Vo's was so intense. Yet the gloves worked.

Mysty volunteered to test them. He gave Vo's finger a tentative tap, a quick touch, and then gripped Vo's hand tightly. Tears moistened Vo's eyes as he attempted to thank Garrett.

"Sure," Garrett said gruffly.

"Garrett," Mysty explained emotionally, "Vo has never been able to touch any living creature here, man or beast, until now. For him this is a miracle. To be able to touch without hurting, it is a new life for him."

"Glad I was able to help," he mumbled.

"Anything—ever—anything I can do for you," Vo swore.

Garrett grinned. "Help us get those perches made."

"That is not enough."

"It is for me. Let's get them done so Freet…"

He looked at Freet as he said it and caught a thoughtful, studying look from Freet. It was gone quickly when Freet saw him look his way. His eyes dropped briefly, and when he looked back up his hand was to his ear. The new look wasn't as cold as some Garrett had gotten from him, but it was just as closed and remote.

"…can have his hunt," Garrett finished.

"You hunt too," Freet reminded him.

He clapped his hands with an enthusiasm he didn't really feel. "Let's hurry it up then."

VII

It was his first solo hunt. He'd never admit it, but Garrett was feeling more than a little nervous. Between Octums, screaming sand storms, and flowers that tried to eat his fingers, he knew the precaution of sending someone with him was warranted. He just couldn't accept Freet's terms, anymore than he could accept being dependent on someone.

To Garrett's surprise, Boss waited in the portal room when he went in. He didn't waste any time. He pulled what he needed from his locker to go with the sack of replenishing supplies he already carried. He put the bridle on Boss first. Then he tied all he could to the saddle and dragged it by the horn with his right hand. He led Boss with his left hand. The shock of going from the gray walls to a sun bright, green field with a gentle breeze blowing was almost too much for the Boss. He jerked away from Garrett's weak hold of the reins, and Garrett let him go, more than a little shocked as well.

It was beautiful. There was grass—green grass—up to his knees. A gorgeous blue sky with white fluffy clouds was overhead and trees, green trees, circled the meadow of the high mountain valley. He could easily believe he was back on Earth, not the high desert of scrub oak and juniper, but the higher mountains of the

Rockies. Lush grass covered the meadow and towering, majestic conifers and aspen surrounded it. Everything was like Earth, at least as long as he didn't look too closely. Compared to what he'd seen before it was close enough for him or rather would be for Boss, if it was as good as it looked.

Boss decided it was okay. He trotted back to Garrett. Everything was strange, but his ears, nose, and eyes told him there was nothing threatening. He greeted Garrett with a nicker to be sure his return was accepted and his leaving in such a manner forgiven.

"Okay, but stand still now. We aren't taking anything at face value. I've done too damned much of that already," Garrett said with an uncertain half-shake of his head over whether he believed any of it at all.

Garrett removed the bedroll, saddlebags, and sack from behind the saddle to lessen the weight. He wasn't sure even then if he would be able to heave the saddle up high enough. After a struggle that left him panting, he hefted it onto Boss's back. Once the saddle was cinched down, re-tying the remainder on—after a pause to rest—was easy. The next obstacle was mounting the horse with all the gear behind the seat. Were there anyone around to see, he would have been forced by pride to use a standard mount despite having to twist his back to get his leg high enough. Alone, he led Boss until he found a rock to stand on, slid onto the saddle sideways, and lifted his leg over the horn.

An absent pat on Boss's neck signaled he was ready as he settled his feet into the stirrups and took up the reins. He'd spotted a ridge above the treetops, and wanted to see more before he had to return. If he liked and trusted what he saw, if it felt right, he may not return to that invisible portal, back to the cold, gray ship. He'd stay if he decided to, despite the Thornns' precautions against one of their specimens breaking free of their control.

He started off in the opposite direction from where he wanted to go and worked free the section of the translators from behind his ears. As careful as he was he still tore his ears enough to cause a little bleeding, but nothing like when he had grabbed and pulled. He left the section inside his ear alone for two reasons. He didn't know how or if it was connected to his eardrum in some way and the possibility of some yet to be discovered factor could make the planet too dangerous for him to stay. If that turned out to be true, he would have to replace the translators behind his ears. He left them where he could easily find them before turning Boss for the ridge. If they were transmitters, something he didn't even know for certain, it would look as if he were stationary.

A game trail led the way through the increasingly dense forest taking him in a wandering direction to his ultimate goal. He estimated he'd gone half the distance before night fell, but long before he stopped to make camp, Garrett knew he was being followed. He couldn't see anyone, had heard nothing, but Garrett knew he was being watched. He set up camp carefully. His fire was small, only large enough to heat water for his dehydrated food and coffee. A bed of pine needles and his bedroll were just far enough away to be in shadow, but he wasn't under the blankets after the fire died down. He slept back further in the trees with his revolver tucked into his waistband, depending on Boss for a warning if anyone came near. No one did, but Garrett's belief that someone was out there didn't lessen, someone very good at tracking and staying out of sight.

Garrett knew he was too ignorant. He didn't know how long a cycle ran from planet to planet, how long between visits back to the same planet ran, or how long a cycle was on each. He didn't even know for certain that he would ever be back to the same planet. He had assumed, and he was beginning to hate that word, he would be back sometime. Freet had been well acquainted with both of the other planets from what had to be experience from previous visits, but for all Garrett knew it could be years between visits to each planet. He didn't have years. If they did have a tie on him, and he was being followed, he couldn't stay, but if the planet proved to be as good as it seemed, Boss could.

He had seen nothing threatening. All the wildlife or signs of any were like the rest of the planet, similar to Earth's. Even the insects were similar to those of Earth, just as the trail he was on the next morning. When the slope became too steep for straight up travel, the trail zigzagged, giving him the opportunity to check behind them. Not once could he spot someone. When they reached a section of loose rock that was too dangerous for a horse with a rider, he dismounted. He turned his head to appear to be looking at Boss and swept the area behind him. He still couldn't spot anyone.

"Maybe I'm just paranoid," he mumbled. "But there's never been a time when I had this feeling, I wasn't right, Boss. Saved my bacon more than once. Could be an animal. Just never known an animal to stick for so long. They'll watch until you're out of sight, then go on about their business. Some, once in a while, will tag along out of curiosity, but not this long, not any I've ever known. That may be the problem. It may be something I've never seen or even imagined before."

He remounted and told Boss, "Could be the smart thing to do is go back to where we came from." Boss snorted. "Yeah, you're right, not my strong point. Besides I still want to see what's over that ridge."

Boss snorted again. He was tired. The climb was steep after weeks of no more than short walks around the pen area, and he was out of condition. He didn't lift his feet quite as high as he should, and he raised his head to look and smell the air instead of watching where he stepped. The rock wasn't much, but it slipped from under Boss's left foreleg. He whip-lashed Garrett when he lunged to keep his footing.

Garrett caught the saddle horn with both hands, clinched his teeth, and ground out, "Keep going," as he began to slide out of the saddle.

Boss obeyed. He hopped the last few feet to a level and clear spot. Garrett slid off the saddle with the first hop and was dragged by his hold to the last. When Boss stopped with an alarmed snort, threw his head, and danced over something he saw, Garrett let go and reached for the gun in his waistband as he fell. Even though the pain was agonizing, taking his breath and most of his strength, Garrett managed to roll belly down to face whatever had spooked Boss. It was nothing a bullet could be used against. Boss had nearly walked off into nothingness.

The ridge they had worked so hard to reach appeared to be the edge of that world. They were on a level, bare spot no more than fifteen feet wide with the thinning forest edging the one side they came in from. The other side just ended, literally and abruptly. Straight down as far out as he could see and to either side there was nothing. That side of the mountain was a sheer, smooth drop into a haze. An unpleasant odor of rotten eggs wafted up to him when he leaned out far enough that the breeze from behind didn't carry it away.

Garrett pushed back with his arms, scooted far enough for the air current to carry the smell clear and grimaced as his legs caught on the rough surface. Boss had already moved away, but the same breeze brought a new scent to him. His head lifted, and his ears twitched to point to the trees down the ridge from them. He blew and nickered softly when Freet appeared.

Garrett swore under his breath. He slipped the pistol under his belly and propped one fist on the ground, the second on top of the first, and his chin on his fists, pretending a lazy, nonchalant attitude. The pistol was close enough if he needed it. Freet had warned him not to trust anyone. Garrett wasn't going to, especially someone who could follow a man the way Freet did.

Garrett did not look around or give a greeting. Neither did Freet. Freet walked silently to the edge and leaned out to look over the abrupt drop. Still looking down he asked, "You jump, Earthling, I have your Boss?"

Startled at first with a flash of anger, Garrett reverted to his own particular brand of humor and laughed instead. "I guarantee you, Chief, I ain't jumping anywhere." Nor would he walk until the pain let up.

Freet backed off from the edge and squatted a few feet from Garrett. His arms lay over his knees with his hands clasped together, and his blank, show-nothing gaze was steady on Garrett's face. "No say no, no say yes, must no think to jump."

Garrett shook his head and thought of the gun against his gut. He had never considered jumping as a way out.

"Many do such thing, jump high place, hang self. Many do first move quarters. More after. No can live alone Thornn world. Not same you. You friends, worlds yet see, have curious."

"I'm not in any hurry to do myself in." He was puzzled and suspicious of the way Freet talked. It was the most Garrett had ever heard Freet say at one time that hadn't been lecturing. The change made Garrett uncomfortable. It was almost as if Freet was attempting to be friendly, which was ridiculous. He didn't have a translator for any real conversation.

After a short pause, Freet said, "Bad place. Sides fall."

"So leave." He flipped his fingers at him. "I didn't invite you, and I don't want you to stay."

Freet waited again until Garrett finished. "No safe."

"What do you care?" Garrett asked, before he shook his head. "You can't even understand me. If you want to talk to me use a translator." He tapped at his ear.

Freet shook his head. He said, "No expect."

"Bull shit! You've been dogging my trail for two days."

Freet rose and looked back towards the edge. "No safe," he repeated with more urgency.

"Then get the hell out," Garrett shouted, angry and frustrated. He couldn't move unless he crawled, and he wasn't going to crawl in front of Freet.

Freet jumped him. Garrett threw himself to his back, one arm going out to hold Freet off, the other going for the pistol. He was slow with fatigue and pain, and Freet moved faster than anyone he had ever seen. One hand closed over Garrett's on the pistol butt, and one jerked him up by the front of his shirt and flipped him. Freet wrenched the pistol free, and his other arm wrapped around Garrett's neck. Garrett saw the knife as he twisted to go after Freet with his hands, but he never knew where it touched him. In the time it took for one beat of his heart, he was unable to move. He didn't even feel the scratch that did it to him. Just as when the Karoz attacked him, Garrett was fully aware of what was happening and was totally unable to do anything to stop it.

Freet rolled him to his back and picked up the gun. Garrett thought Freet was going to shoot him, but Freet shoved the gun into his belt and hoisted Garrett up to his shoulders. Garrett thought then that Freet was going to pitch him over the edge of the cliff, but to his surprise, Freet ran downhill with Boss trotting after them. Garrett knew Boss followed because he could hear him. He also heard an ear-shattering roar behind them that spooked Boss, making him jump ahead of Freet and Garrett.

Just as Freet had warned the sides of the cliff fell away, or so Garrett assumed from what he heard. He couldn't see anything more than Freet's back and legs and a very small portion of the ground. He could hear Freet panting when he finally laid him down.

Freet leaned over him. "Too stubborn, Earthling. Be anger. Remember, strike twice no can strike back. Strike again, wait no shields." He sat back on his heels, out of Garrett's range of vision. "Midradina say four hunt. Be three. Be me go or be yantz, no Boss. Sleep now." He stuck a pill in Garrett's mouth. "Make hunter drug go."

Garrett wanted to bite Freet's finger. He couldn't anymore than he could spit out the bitterness in his mouth or stop Freet from straightening his arms and legs. He was totally helpless with his anger quickly replaced by fear. As Freet removed his boots, Garrett wanted to scream at him even though he knew it was irrational. He knew the real cause of his building panic was not the temporary paralysis Freet had caused, but the fear of the rapidly coming time when he would be permanently paralyzed. His chest heaved, and he knew he was having what the doctor described as an anxiety attack, which was to Garrett the essence of his own weakness. His fear was out of control, and Freet's efforts to help made things worse because he couldn't tell Freet to leave him alone. He had to control it. He didn't need a mask. He wasn't suffocating. He was hyperventilating even though he only had one lung.

Concentrate on something else, he mentally screamed. What? What was going to happen when the drug wore off if he still couldn't get up because of the pain in his back and legs? What if they were dead and the feeling was never coming back this time? Freet had the gun. He had to have that gun. He couldn't be a hopeless cripple.

Hopeless cripple was what she'd called him when she'd stood beside his hospital bed. She couldn't devote her life to taking care of a hopeless cripple. He shouldn't expect his child to have a crippled, useless father, sign the adoption papers, relinquish your rights, give the baby she carried a good life, don't drag it down with your...

"Hear me," Freet shook Garrett by the shoulders. "Breathe when say breathe."

He drew Garrett's wild thoughts to him. Garrett wanted to tell him to give him the gun. He had to have the gun. "Sleep," Freet told him.

Freet pressed his fingertips to Garrett's eyes to close them and poked a pill in his mouth. Sleep came quickly, but in Garrett's frame of mind, sleep only brought disturbing dreams. The first was the same one he'd had in some variety for eleven years of his blonde-haired, blue-eyed daughter. Through those years his imagination had shifted the image of the toddler in the only picture he had ever had of her. In the first ones she had been too young for words. She had sobbed and held out her hands to him. The sobs had become words as he imagined her growing. She called him Daddy while she held her hands out to him, told him she needed him, and she loved him. He told her not to, don't need me, don't love me, I can't give you anything; I'll soon be a hopeless cripple.

The familiar dreams changed to a jumble of past and present. Midradina reached out to him and tears spilled from her eyes. He ran from her through a jungle with the mortar shells exploding closer and closer to him. He ran faster and faster until he broke free of the jungle to run in sand that dragged his feet down, and he careened into a carved, wooden cigar store Indian with tears running down its cheeks. The collision knocked it over, and it fell and fell, finally landing on a gray floor and shattering. The pieces flew in thousands of different directions, showered down, changed into animals that swirled, glistening until they settled, and formed into the eyes of a yantz. The yantz said to him, see yourself as others see you, they need you. Garrett fought the dream.

He didn't tell the yantz no or tell it that no one needed him as he had told Carolyn over and over through the years. He just fought to stop the dream. He didn't like the direction it took off in.

The yantz eyes scattered into thousands of mirrors, first with his image and then with those of others he had known in the past or knew in the present. All reached out to him. He shook his head. He had nothing to give them. He turned his back to them to face black emptiness and stepped towards it. Something caught him and drew him back. He couldn't see what, but it was gentle in its strength and warm. They need you, it told him. He said no. They need you, it repeated, and Garrett laughed. They don't, he told it, I wouldn't bring them anything but grief, and let go—I don't like this dream.

Whatever held him released its hold as he fought his way out of sleep with a movement so violent it took him to his knees with the gun in his hand. The first thing he saw was Freet, squatting ten feet away on the other side of a small fire.

"Enjoy the show?" Garrett asked hatefully.

He knew he moved around during dreams and sometimes spoke. He felt exposed and vulnerable under Freet's cool eyes, especially after Freet had witnessed his anxiety attack, and from the way Freet had talked to him, he had known the symptoms for what they were.

Anxious to get away, Garrett dropped down on his rump. The gun went into his waistband before he automatically knocked each boot on the ground to dislodge anything that may have crawled in and shook them before he pulled them on. Freet didn't have his hand to his ear, and Garrett used the opportunity to vent some of his anger.

"At least you don't ask me about it," he ranted. "I don't have to tell you it's none of your business why I squirm around in my sleep. Hell, you wouldn't understand anyway. No more than you understand why I couldn't come down off that ridge. Just a stupid, stubborn, Earthling trick. Well keep thinking that way. You start feeling any different, and I'll..." He went to his feet, "...beat the hell out of you to make you hate me if I have to. I won't be responsible for putting anyone through that kind of grief."

He started for Boss, who was still fully saddled and bridled several feet away. While Boss nickered a greeting, Garrett looked around to check the sun. He had slept the remainder of one day and the night away. It was the next morning.

"The god damned least you can do..." he raved, "...when you knock a man out is unsaddle his horse."

He unknotted the main cinch and unbuckled the second. He leaned down to unsnap the breastplate as Boss nickered in greeting again. Garrett spun in time to see Freet jump back. Garrett looked from one to the other. Boss didn't usually give strangers that kind of a greeting, yet he had done the same thing on the ridge. He behaved as if he were familiar with Freet, which didn't make much sense if Freet were afraid of him.

"Carry." Freet indicated the saddle and blandly ignored Garrett's questioning look.

"No, you won't. You—where's the translator?"

Freet gazed at him blankly until Garrett pointed at the side on his head. Only then did Freet slip a finger under his belt and hold his hand to his ear.

Garrett used the time to calm down and organize his furious thoughts. "I didn't think of you not being able to hit back when I hit you," he told him coldly. "You have my word it won't happen again. You also have my word, if you ever do that to me again, I will do more than just hit you as soon as I can."

"Stop hunter drug." Freet held out his hand with two small brown pills in his palm.

"Something you just didn't think to tell me about before?" he asked caustically. He knew then why he'd been unable to move during the Karoz attack. Their weapons were treated with a drug.

"One each seven day."

Garrett snatched the pills and turned his back on him. Freet's reasoning was something he couldn't understand. Let him learn what was safe on his own, Mysty had said, and teach what was dangerous. Maybe paralyzing him to show him how easily it could be done had been a lesson, but Garrett didn't like his methods. To be told about the drug and the antidote would have been a lot less humiliating.

Garrett slid the saddle off onto his back and held it by the horn with his right hand over his shoulder. With it already up he thought he could manage. The left was strong enough to slip the bridle off. He knew Boss would follow. He hadn't expected Freet.

He fell into step beside Garrett. "Why carry, no Boss?"

Garrett didn't explain the possibilities of saddle sores from wearing the saddle for a prolonged period of time. He said, "Go away and leave me alone."

"Must be portal."

"Fine, just don't go the same way I do to get there."

He increased his pace, walked away from Freet, and fought the desire to look back. What he'd heard Freet tell Midradina was contradictory to the way Freet was behaving. The contradiction disturbed Garrett, especially after that dream.

VIII

Midradina waited for them when they stepped through the portal, minus a yantz floating behind her shoulder. Garrett held Boss' reins short to keep him from dancing nervously and asked, "Why is it I don't think I'm going to be happy to see you?"

"You will not," she stated. "The animals are free again."

Garrett gave the reins a rough snap. "Hold still," he ordered sharply and asked her, "When?"

"Sometime yesterday." She stared at Boss. "It is quiet simply because you tell it to be so?"

"Yes," He put a comforting hand on Boss's neck. He didn't often speak to Boss in that tone and wouldn't have if it hadn't been for her. He felt especially bad when he felt how Boss trembled. His harsh command had been obeyed, but Boss was frightened. "Where can I put him?"

"In its pen, but the pen must remain in the passage until the room is cleared of the creatures."

"You moved his pen up here, not just him?"

Midradina nodded and indicated the wall behind Freet. It slid open to expose the large pen, door closed, and Garrett's shirt still wadded up in the corner for the little rabbit. The pen floor was level with their floor, its walls flush with the walls of the opening.

The floor of the passage, visible through the pen floor, was sloped away while the ceiling was about level and even with the cage.

"Convenient," Garrett commented.

"Way Thornn take captive," Freet said coldly. "Walk through portal to cage."

"The Thornns realized that mistake long ago," she answered just as coldly.

"Do little make better."

"Is Vo around?" Garrett asked to interrupt them.

"He has gone for his nets," Midradina told him.

"With all the practice they've had, they won't have much trouble."

"They?" she questioned.

"No help?" Freet asked tonelessly.

Garrett felt like a jerk but still told him, "You can manage."

"You are not well?" Midradina asked him.

"I feel fine," Garrett retorted. "I'm just plum worn out from having so much fun, and I'm tired of chasing animals to put back in cages, I don't think they belong in."

None of what he said was a lie, though those weren't the reasons he wasn't going to help. Freet, as well as some of the things Freet had said, bothered Garrett, his comment about having friends for one. Garrett didn't see those he had met on the ship as friends. They were just people he'd enjoyed spending time with and liked. But if he felt that way about them, maybe they felt the same in reverse. That was a foundation stronger ties could easily grow from, ties that would cause grief, if he allowed it to happen. The way to prevent strong bonds from forming—on his side as well as others—was to keep away from them, the way he had with Mysty. He hadn't thought it necessary with Freet, but after the way he had acted on that hunt, Garrett wasn't so sure any longer. He was sure he needed to avoid Vo with his over-zealous gratitude mixed in with possible friendship.

"Did you have an injury on the planet?" she asked, bringing his head up with a jerk. "The yantz—"

"I'll tell you, lady, I have just about had it up to here..." His hand slashed across his forehead, "...with the yantz. I feel like I've got a gremlin in my pocket reporting every move I make. If they're not there, he is." He pointed at Freet, "I'm sick of it." Even if the pill Freet stuck in his mouth had kept his back from hurting after the wrenching Boss's near fall had given it.

"Has anger," Freet supplied blandly. "No leave falling mountain. Feel ground move, use hunter drug to take."

"Was such an extreme necessary?" she asked calmly.

Freet's expression suggested it was because Garrett lacked good sense.

"Get in line," Garrett told him furiously. "You're after Gunian."

"You win," Freet returned without a change of expression.

Midradina asked Garrett, "What is the meaning of your statement?"

"Private," he retorted and bent over to unsnap the breastplate from the cinch.

"Since it appears you have no regard for your own life, I remind you, you cannot die until the yantz transformation is complete."

"If I'm dead, no one has to worry about it hurting," Garrett said indifferently and pulled the saddle off to his back.

"If you die, the yantz will die. You have been told this."

"No," Garrett answered explosively. "No one told me that."

"I told you, you cannot damage yourself until the bond is finished."

"Damage is not the same as dead." His anger built. Then he grinned with a half-shake of his head. He was being ridiculous over her not caring if he died as long as the yantz didn't, when he planned on killing himself in the near future, and didn't want anyone to care.

"Do you wish for death?" she asked in puzzlement.

"Nope." He took the saddle to the locker. Death was just preferable to the alternative. "Let's just hope nothing happens to change my mind before the yantz is safe."

"I did not mean to imply I would rejoice in your death," she told him.

Garrett chuckled over that. "I'd think you'd be glad to be rid of me."

"I would not be gladdened by your death."

Or saddened, he thought. She didn't seem to be capable of either. He asked, "Will these things be off before the next hunt?"

"I do not believe so."

"Then I'll do everyone a favor and stay here until they are. Once they are, you won't have any reason to keep a watchdog on me."

She may not have understood the exact terms he used, but she understood his meaning. Her eyes darted in Freet's direction. "As you wish."

"I wish," he said fervently. "Now if you will excuse me?" He tipped his head towards the decontamination door. "A little privacy would be appreciated."

###

Garrett took Boss into his pen and stayed, taking longer than necessary to brush Boss down, to wait until both Midradina and Freet left. Because of his delay he was caught inside the cage when the wall shut and knocked the door closed. He got a ride down to the pen level where he'd had no intentions of going. The journey ended at the bottom of the ramp, but until someone, meaning Midradina, moved it further, he couldn't open the door far enough to squeeze out because of the ramp rising up in front and the closeness of the wall. There would have been nowhere to go even if he could. The ramp was a chute. With the pen still inside on that end the only way to go was up, and the door to the locker room was closed. Since the pen wouldn't go back into place until the pen room was cleared, he was in for a long wait.

He sat down, picked up the wadded shirt and talked to the rabbit when it poked its head out cautiously. Boss leaned his neck over Garrett's legs to greet his little roommate. They touched noses, Boss blew, and the rabbit popped back inside, squirmed around, and popped its head back out again making Garrett smile. He started to relax and put other things out of his mind when Boss jumped sideways, slamming into the side of the cage.

The combination of a slick floor and a panicked horse didn't put Garrett in a very good position. He scrambled up to his feet and started nearly as bad as Boss. There was an open space where a solid wall had been a moment before, and Midradina stood on the other side of the cage wall. Boss snorted his displeasure. Garrett glared his. The cage moved back until there was room for him to squeeze through the door sideways on the opposite side from where she stood. Peggy caught his attention as he stepped out.

Peggy was one cage down. She always caught his attention, but this time it was out of concern for her. With the soundproof cages, she couldn't hear the noise from the animals that were running loose. He could, and he didn't like what he heard. She didn't like what she saw and reared and pawed at the floor. A quick look confirmed what he feared, and he hurried back.

"You must return up the ramp," Midradina told him.

"Have Vo and Freet gotten down here yet?" he asked in an urgent whisper.

"No, Vo—"

"I haven't got time to go back up there and go through decontamination." He shut the pen door and moved to the side she was on. As he slipped through the small opening between the pen edge and the wall, he gave orders. "Move the pen back up to keep this blocked and show me a way around so I can intercept Freet and Vo."

"You said you—"

"Damn it, don't argue with me. I've got to keep them from going in there."

"I do not—" She shrugged her shoulder as if a hand had touched her and gave him a belligerent look, but the cage slid forward. Resentfully she said, "I will show you."

They moved parallel to the chute, and she opened another section of wall into a long hall, parallel to the cages. Garrett left at a run. He took the first opening he found, hoped Midradina had opened it for him, and ran into an intersecting hall. Vo came towards him, bundled in his nets.

"Have you seen Freet?" Garrett panted.

"No, I—"

Garrett didn't wait for more. He didn't know where he was in the halls and left a confused Vo at a run. He overtook Freet before he could open the door. Too winded to talk, he threw himself against the door in front of him.

Freet turned as Vo and Midradina reached them, hand going to his ear. "What?"

"I do not know," she answered stiffly.

Vo shook his head. "Trohog maybe," he suggested.

"How him know?"

"He could see into the main area from where he was." She raised her hand and half-turned. A blur materialized into a winged, big-eyed yantz. She took the blue masks it held, and the yantz disappeared. "I do not know what he saw," she continued as if there had been no interruption and held one of the masks out to Garrett.

Garrett took it gratefully and held up one finger as he sucked enriched air deep into his lung. All three watched him until his color returned and he could talk again. "Whole different ballgame," he said still taking deep breaths between words. "This one is a peck of trouble."

"It is a different, more difficult situation?" Midradina asked for clarification.

He nodded. "Can this door be opened just a couple of inches?"

He scrambled to his feet at the unexpected swiftness of the door moving against his back. He twisted, ready to run until he saw it stop at the couple of inches he requested and settled down on one knee. Freet moved closer, stood behind him to watch through the opening a few moments, and then squatted next to

Garrett with his back to the door. Freet tipped his head to Vo. Vo took his place, still loaded down with nets, and looked inside for even less time than Freet before he moved to the other side of Garrett and started shedding his nets.

"They are what you call monkeys," Midradina said, confused by their attitudes.

"Apes," Garrett corrected. "Those are simians. They're as big as we are, approximately four times stronger than a man of equal size, and they have canine teeth to back them up."

"They would attack?"

"Yes, ma'am," he told her solemnly, "and win."

"You have nets."

"Not strong enough," Vo answered. "They will tear through."

"Then what must be done?"

Freet answered with, "Ask Thornns."

Garrett was a little annoyed with Freet for saying it, even if he was right. It was a Thornn problem, not theirs.

After a short pause, she told them, "They say I allowed the situation to happen, I must find a solution."

"Those sons-of-a-bitches." Garrett exclaimed. "Who the hell do they think you are, Wonder Woman?"

"It is my responsibility," she answered stoically.

"Bullshit! You didn't cage them up. They did."

"That is irrelevant now."

"The hell if it is. Let them clean up their own messes."

Midradina shouted back at him. "They will not. It is my responsibility."

"Did you ask for it?"

She opened her mouth to answer, got a look of amazement on her face, and snapped her jaw shut. With visible effort she told him coolly, "You do not understand. You do not attempt to. You only make things difficult."

"Maybe it's time someone did."

Mysty's arrival interrupted the argument. He saw her flushed face, Garrett's set expression, Vo's expression of astonishment, and Freet's blank one. "Is something wrong?"

"You could say that,' Garrett answered tartly and hooked a thumb at the slit.

"Oh, dear," Mysty said as he looked inside.

"Yeah," Garrett drawled. "You got any ideas on how to recapture those brutes?"

"One cage for all," Freet suggested.

"They'd kill each other," Garrett said. "The damned things have already split into groups, two that I've seen, and they're territorial. You go shoving them in together, they'll fight."

"That cannot be allowed," Midradina stated, drawing a look of irritation from Garrett.

"Why don't you just call Radshab for a solution?" he asked sarcastically.

"Make cage for group," Freet said before she could answer.

"I cannot form cages in the pen room." She spoke directly to Freet, attempting to ignore Garrett. "Nor is there space for more large cages."

"Would be if you moved the smaller, empty ones out," Garrett snapped.

"Could you do that?" Mysty asked.

"Yes," Dina answered, "but I must be able to see which cages are empty and which are not."

"Not to move them," Garrett said thoughtfully as he turned back to watch through the slit.

"You have an idea?" Mysty asked hopefully.

"Maybe." He squatted down to study the situation and put his anger with the Thornns aside. "The first thing we have to do is separate the groups." He half-shook his head and rubbed the back of his neck. "Hell, we can't tell from here how many there are."

"Forty-three," Freet supplied.

"Great," Garrett grumbled. "This group's got eight. If they broke up into groups of about the same size, then we've got about five groups to deal with." He twisted to look at Midradina. "Are there more than two places where we can get a look in there?"

"As many as you wish, but of what use will that be?"

"To locate the groups," he growled and fought for patience. "You can shut them away from one another by shifting the cages."

"How will they eat in such a way?"

"Would you like to take this one step at a time?" he snapped, since he didn't have an answer.

###

The pen room was surrounded by a hall like the one Garrett had run down to stop Freet and Vo from walking into the pen area without warning. The walls that surrounded it were sections Midradina could manipulate for peep holes. Each group was located and isolated by swinging out a section of cages to close off the aisle they were in. The ruptured feeding and water tubes answered the question of how to feed them. Food and water poured onto the floor in abundance. Once Garrett convinced her not to turn the flow off, the apes barely squabbled among themselves as they gathered up pellets or drank.

The apes who had not been accepted into a group were free to roam the area at large. A single stack was moved to provide food and water for them. The corridor to Boss and Peggy's cages was closed off, and Boss was moved back in place. Only the smaller animals in displaced cages were left without food or water, a fact Midradina pointed out when they reached the main corridor again.

"We'll think of a permanent solution," Garrett said wearily, "before they get too hungry. Freet's idea sounded pretty good."

Freet grunted. "Speak fast. No wish chase portal room."

"No," Garrett agreed. "They'd probably chase us." He slid down to lean back against the wall. "We'll have to think of some other way to make them move." He looked at Midradina. "Can you teach any of us to move those cages?"

"Why do you ask?" she asked evasively.

"Just thought it would make things go faster," he said with an irritated shrug. Let her keep her control if she wanted it.

Mysty exclaimed, "You do not intend to continue?"

"Isn't finished," Garrett remarked simply.

Mysty turned to Midradina. "They must rest. They have just returned from a hunt and are already weary. Fatigue will make their reactions slow and their minds dull."

"I do not argue," she answered in puzzlement.

"He will." He pointed at Garrett. "Without you it would serve him no purpose." He took her by the arm and led her off. "We will meet back here in ten hours."

"Now what was that about?" Garrett asked of no one in particular.

Vo answered, "For me."

"You don't run out of steam any sooner than the rest of us."

"Her maybe," Freet suggested. "Hard think much long time."

Vo murmured in agreement as he dropped to sit on the pile of nets he left behind to traipse the halls with them. "Must concentrate; focus thoughts on just one thing."

"You do?" Freet asked softly.

"Try," he answered shyly. "I think if I can open my door, I should be able to open others. Things—others here do not hear my thoughts."

"No translators," Garrett joked absently. He was tired. "You should try pictures."

"You do?" Vo asked excitedly.

"Me?" he asked with a start and then laughed. "I'm not telepathic."

"Try?" Freet asked.

"No," Garrett answered lightly, "and I think that's something you would know without trying."

Vo shook his head. "Children do not know unless taught. You teach Earthling children?"

"We aren't telepathic," he told him, his smile a little forced. "Are your people?"

"We learn as children. I had forgotten our first lessons were with pictures. How do you know this if—?"

"I was joking," he cut him off with sharply. "I don't know anything about it."

Freet leaned forward, elbows on his knees to hold the communicator to his ear. "Teach us, Vo?"

"Have you got a burning desire to talk to the yantz?" Garrett asked him lightly.

Freet twisted his head to look at him. That cold, deadly look was back in his eyes as he answered. "Maybe can open door no can now, find where Thornn hide, kill."

"You find Thornn, you will kill?" Vo asked. Freet nodded in answer. Vo nodded in agreement. "I have never wanted to kill until the Thornn. It is not right take me from my mate and children. Did you have a mate? Children?"

Freet nodded to answer the first question and said, "One female, one male not born."

"Two sons and two daughters for me." Vo turned to Garrett, "You?"

"No." Garrett got to his feet and walked away.

Whispering, Vo asked Freet, "Did I make him angry?"

Garrett heard, clenched his jaw, but didn't stop. He doubted if Freet's feelings were dented, but he knew how sensitive Vo was before he heard the worried whisper. It was better to hurt Vo's feelings a little now than to stick around letting the camaraderie grow. A friendship between Freet and Vo was better. They had a lot in common. They should have been friends long ago, probably would have been just as others would have been, if the Thornns hadn't compounded their cruelties by setting up an atmosphere of fear and distrust to convince them every one of the others was a cold-blooded killer. Unfortunately some were. The problem was in knowing who were the monsters the Thornns painted them all to be.

Picturing Vo as a loving parent and mate was easy. Not Freet. To learn he had had a wife, one child and another on the way and realize the depth of Freet's hatred for the Thornns because of being taken from them was too intimate a glimpse of the man behind that carved face. And Vo? Garrett would have never thought Vo ever hated any living being—man or beast—but he did, strongly enough for the gentle, little man to wish he could kill.

With the subject of family fresh in his mind, he searched through the debris from his saddlebags until he found his wallet. He held it in his hands and hesitated to open it. Inside was the only photo he had of his daughter, the only one he ever would have. Garrett looked at it and waged the same mental argument he always did, logic over emotion. Logic always won; she was better off without him. He had never looked for her to tell her the truth, but his emotional side had never given up the thought of someday tracking her down. Whether he was crazy or the fantasy was real, now there was not even the slim possibility of someday.

###

Despite how tired he was Garrett couldn't sleep. He could have taken morphine, but he didn't need it for pain—which still surprised him—and he didn't like the way the drug made him feel or behave. He drank a glass of substance instead, showered, and changed into fresh clothes. He stuck the worn pack of cigarettes into the pocket of an open pajama shirt.

All he planned on doing when he left his quarters was to peek through slits in the walls and check on Boss and Peggy. As soon as he peered through the main door, however, things started off in a direction he had never intended. The red maroon hair was wrong for Earth, but it looked like a chimpanzee. It looked forlorn both in the fact that it was alone and in the way it sat, arms folded tightly around its body while it rocked back and forth. It didn't run from a man either. When Garrett squatted and talked softly to it through the slit in the door, it talked back in a low whimper.

"Are you hurt, buddy?" Garrett asked. He successfully tested to see if he could control the door as Midradina had with a few inches instead of the wide open he had always used. The chimp still didn't run away. "Sick maybe?"

It curled its lips up, tipped its head back and shook it. It had no canine teeth. Garrett opened the door a little wider.

"Were you someone's pet? Huh? Is that why you don't have your fighting teeth?"

Though he didn't believe the animal was threatening, he knew that didn't mean it couldn't be dangerous even without those fangs. His attention was riveted on the animal to the exclusion of everything else, not that Freet wasn't good at not being heard on those moccasin covered feet of his.

"What..." He paused when Garrett spun, shot half up, and dropped back again. "...do now?"

"Damn you," Garrett exclaimed with his heart in his throat. "Don't sneak up on me like that. What are you doing here anyway?"

"No sleep."

"So? What do you think you'll accomplish down here?"

Freet shrugged and asked blandly, "What you do?"

"Checking on Boss," he grumbled. Freet was pretty good at sarcasm, brief vocabulary or not.

"No Boss you talk," Freet pointed out and rose up on his toes to look through the door.

"He was someone's pet," Garrett explained belligerently. He turned back to the door and softened his voice. "It's okay. We're not going to hurt you."

The chimp had risen to its feet and the knuckles of its hands, ready to run during their exchange. He looked from Garrett, over Garrett's head to Freet, and back to Garrett before settling uneasily down on his hunches.

"Make new pet, need bigger cage Boss," Freet told him.

"Wouldn't work. Chimps aren't something Boss is familiar with. Talk to him, maybe he'll understand you."

"No my world."

"Vo's maybe?"

"How Vo have such pet?"

"Good point. He's as big as Vo. Wonder where he came from."

"Wonder," Freet said tonelessly and tensed when the chimp scooted forward, "what think you do with."

"I don't know," Garrett admitted, but still held his hand out to coax the chimp closer. "Too bad we can't return him to his owner."

Freet watched the animal closely. "No think good do."

"Leave if you're worried."

Freet was worried. As the chimp edged closer, his hand closed on Garrett's shoulder. He didn't pull Garrett back, but he was ready to if anything went wrong. It was a protective gesture that Garrett found both annoying and touching. He tried to shrug the hand off.

"It's more frightened than you are," Garrett told Freet in irritation.

"No think so," Freet returned dryly.

Freet's grip tightened, and he pulled Garrett back as the chimp rose to its feet again. The animal's head swiveled to look behind it and then back towards them as it moved forward. Something back there frightened it more than they did, and its rapid movement towards them set Freet into motion. With one hand still gripping Garrett's shoulder, the other came around Garrett's chest and dragged him back.

Garrett fought to get free of Freet's hold. The chimp moved over his feet and slipped along the wall, huddling in the furthest corner. It watched them and the door anxiously, poised for further flight. That, of course, aroused Garrett's curiosity. He wrestled out of Freet's hold and slapped at Freet's hands as Freet attempted to catch him when he saw which way Garrett was headed. A shove sent Freet back far enough for Garrett to get through the door. At first glance, there wasn't anything he could see or hear to account for the chimp's behavior, so he moved in further to investigate. He had gone as far as the first cross aisle, Freet at his heels, when all hell broke loose.

Garrett had just noticed that some of the smaller animals were free again when a thunderous crash vibrated off the walls. Before the sound faded the air was filled with frantic screams from the apes. He needed no more urging to turn and run. He and Freet were barely halfway to the safety of the door before the second crash. The wall of cages separating them from the nearest group of apes fell to the floor. Looking over his shoulder, Garrett saw the reason for the panic, and he knew they couldn't outrun the apes swarming over the cages. He dove for Freet and took both of them down as the first of the apes reached them. Once they hit the floor there was nothing they could do except hold their arms over their heads until the stampede of seven frantic apes ran over them.

The apes were afraid, a fact Garrett had trouble conveying to Freet. When the apes were gone, Garrett staggered up and pulled Freet towards the door. Freet, since that was the way the apes had gone, tried to go in the opposite direction. They both pulled at each other until Freet turned to look where Garrett pointed. The Trohog was slithering towards them over the scattered cages. Freet ran into Garrett before Garrett could move. They both ran outside of the pen room and stared down a long empty hall with the door shut behind them, bending over to catch their breath.

"Hurt?" Freet asked.

"Hell," Garrett panted, "I don't know. Adrenaline's too high." He leaned back against the wall to take a few deep breaths before he continued. "It's not every day I get run over by a herd of screaming gorillas being chased by a six foot slug with swords all over its back." At his own words, Garrett laughed. "It sounds like somewhere along the line, I started believing all this stuff."

"Lose translator."

"Yeah, I know." He brushed absently at something tickling his neck and stared curiously at the blood on his fingertips.

Freet blocked Garrett's attempt to locate the source of the blood. "No touch," he warned. "Wire may puncture ear. Go Mord."

"Ha, ha." Garrett pointed down the long hall where the apes had disappeared. "I'd rather try out running the trohog than that pack of rascals again."

He pointed to the door behind them, pantomimed going around and up. He thought it would be easier to work their way around the trohog and go up the gravity tube.

Freet disagreed. "Maybe trohog knock down more cages."

"So what do you suggest, just sit here between a rock and a hard place?"

They both stiffened. From somewhere out of sight they heard the apes scream. The apes were coming closer, and they had no place to run. One quick look through a crack in the door told them that. The trohog was only a few feet away on the other side.

"Yantz," Freet stated and pointed to the air behind the apes as they came into view.

"Open the wall!" Garrett shouted. Midradina had to be with the yantz, and he opened the door behind them a few more inches.

"Crazy!" Freet exclaimed. He jerked Garrett nearly off his feet to get away from it. "Close!"

"Its scent might keep the apes back," Garrett explained, not even thinking of Freet not having a translator or that Freet was too flustered to remember he could close it himself. "And it can't get out." He shouted down the hall again, "Open the wall."

The apes grew nearer, and the trohog, despite its size did come through the door, oozing out like a horror movie blob with its spears folding like a fan to pass through. The apes stopped their advance, but Freet and Garrett were pressed against the wall to avoid the sharp spikes.

"Open the damned wall," Garrett screamed.

The apes, afraid to go either way ran in circles, into each other, and into the walls. Because of their screams, Midradina couldn't hear what Garrett was shouting. She finally saw him throw his arms wide and point to the wall, but he shrunk back against the wall when the trohog hunched up and flipped itself forward. Garrett shouted at her again, and the apes compacted their frantic milling. They were afraid of the yantz and the human, but they were more afraid of the trohog. They began to move in her direction. If they broke and ran, even with the yantz slashing at them, they would run over her.

Garrett was just beginning to think that the only way to make her understand was to run the gauntlet of trohog and apes, when the wall next to the apes opened. Garrett sank to his knees in relief. Freet dropped beside him and released his hold of Garrett's arm that Garrett hadn't even felt until then. Freet muttered as the trohog, for who knew what reason, followed the apes through the new opening.

Midradina glided up silently in front of them. "You attempted to move the cages," she accused.

Garrett, still wound tight, shouted. "We did not! That damned trohog knocked them down. I didn't turn it loose either, but someone did. It was in its cage when we left here. Where's Mysty?"

"He searches for the Glemm."

Garrett shot to his feet and grumbled, "He better find it before I do."

She turned as he stormed by her. "You are bleeding. Go to Mord."

"I will," he shouted back, not adding that he would do so when he got damned good and ready.

###

To further irritate Garrett, he had to go to Mord in his search for Mysty. He didn't get any further for some time. Mord was too big to argue with or get around. His ear got repaired. The tear was so severe the translator had to be removed temporaily. Mord also noticed the small tears from when Garrett had removed and replaced the back sections before. Garrett told him they itched, earning a lecture in gibberish he couldn't understand until Mord taped a thick pad over the injured ear to block the jumble of sound. By then Mord was pressuring him to have the implants. With his nerves still raw, Garrett stormed out. Damned if he didn't just walk into another mess. Glemm was leading the maroon-colored chimp down the hall in the hunter's quarters.

"Glemm," he called out in a hoarse whisper and hurried to overtake them.

He didn't know how the two of them had gotten in there, but he knew he had to get them out. He might get mad at Midradina for saying it, but there were men there primitive enough to smell an animal and savage enough to kill it for the fun.

"Glemm, you little shit," he whispered hoarsely, "Get him out of here." The only move Glemm made was to take the chimp further, making Garrett grit his teeth. He forced softness into his tone and held his hand out to the chimp. "Come on, big guy, we've got to get you out of here before someone sees you."

The chimp didn't resist or pull away when Garrett took one of its hands. It just wouldn't follow him. Since anything said in the hall could be clearly heard in the rooms, Garrett was afraid to speak to it anymore. He squatted and was able to coax it closer, but still couldn't get it to follow him. Garrett considered just picking it up and running in the hope that he could make it to his quarters before anyone could hear if it screamed. Before he could do so, the door to the nearest quarters opened.

From where Garrett squatted the man looked to be about twenty feet tall. He had to lean down to look through the door and had the eyes of a mad man. A chest-length beard, matted hair that hung below his shoulders, and the tattered rags he wore all combined to complete his image of insanity.

Garrett's hand dropped to the knife strapped to his calf. "I don't want any trouble with—" he began.

"Shama?" the man whispered with his wild stare on the chimp.

The chimp looked, screamed, and leaped into the huge man's arms.

Garrett rose to his feet and flinched from a stab of sharp pain in his back and knee. He didn't stop to think about it. "Get him inside before someone sees him!"

The tall man did so with tears glistening in his eyes, leaving a dumbfounded Garrett alone in the hall. Glemm had disappeared before Gunian and half a dozen others ran around the corner a moment later.

"It was you?" Gunian asked.

"Huh?" Garrett asked in genuine bewilderment. He had just told Freet he'd like to find the chimp's owner. It was spooky the way he had.

"He is an idiot," someone retorted.

Gunian held up a hand for silence and restated his question. "Was it you who screamed?"

While he asked, his eyes darted over the bandage covering Garrett's ear, giving Garrett an idea. As long as his hair had grown, Gunian couldn't see the translator behind his other ear. "I can't understand you. Damn sure wish I could. There was a scream or something a few seconds ago that put my hair on end. Sure would like to know what it was. Is this damned place haunted?"

The question set the group to mumbling while Gunian asked, "Why can you not understand?"

Garrett grinned. "Sure was silly of me to ask a question when I can't understand the answer. Had me some trouble with the translators. I'll just have to wait until Mord can rig me up something new. Wish to hell there was someone who spoke English. I'd like to know what that sound was. Man, it sounded like it came right out of the walls. Weird, it was just plain weird."

From the pack of men someone asked, "What does he say?"

Several answered that they didn't know, Gunian among them. In disgust, Gunian led the group away with some uncomplimentary comments about Garrett's intelligence. They all laughed, and Garrett smiled. He preferred having them think him an idiot rather than knowing he had just lied through his teeth. There certainly was an advantage to having people believe you couldn't understand what they said. It gave him a perfect excuse not to answer their questions. He was feeling pretty pleased with himself when he pivoted, winced violently, and fell into the wall.

The pain wasn't of an intensity he hadn't experienced in the past, but it was sudden and without warning other than the slight twinge he'd had a few minutes before. The twinge had intensified, shooting down through his legs with an additional throbbing in his left knee. The back and leg pain was usually a constant ache that gradually built up to a crippling degree unless he did something to aggravate it. It had never hit him so suddenly before. The pain in his knee was even more puzzling. It was swollen. Damned strange he hadn't noticed it before. He hadn't been aware of any kind of an injury. It had to have happened when the apes had trampled over him and Freet, but why hadn't he felt it then? And why hadn't he felt the pain in his back that was rapidly growing to a crippling degree? For that matter, why was he just now feeling the aches and pain all over his body?

He didn't have time to figure it out then. He had to get out of sight before he dropped. Unexpectedly, the chimp's owner offered a way to accomplish that. He stood at his door and motioned Garrett into his quarters. Garrett wasn't sure he wanted to accept. The man was at least as tall as Mord, and the idea of being locked in a room with a creature that appeared to be as mad as the proverbial Hatter was not appealing. Garrett was relieved when the offer was withdrawn. The man jerked back inside, and the door slid shut. The man had looked terrified as he disappeared. Garrett didn't blame him. He would have had some problem himself over seeing Freet coming at him with a knife in his hand.

"Asshole," he grumbled on principle as Freet walked up to him. "He was just trying to be friendly, and you scared the hell out of him."

The knife had already disappeared back under a fold of cloth at Freet's thigh. As usual he waited until Garrett finished before he said one word, "Cannibal."

Horror was Garrett's first reaction. Suspicion and a narrowing of his eyes followed. "Bullshit," he retorted as he walked off.

Within five feet, he knew he couldn't make the distance to his quarters without the building pain becoming too obvious to Freet who followed beside him. Altering his course, he headed to the much closer common room. He could sit there to relieve the pressure until the pain let up enough for him to walk normally.

"No know hunter, no go in," Freet lectured.

"Yeah, yeah."

"In first many do. Many disappear."

"Damn it, Chief, go away."

Everyone in the common room heard the last as he stepped in. Gunian sat at a table with four others and looked from Garrett to Freet. "Now neither understands," he said to his companions, "and still they talk."

Garrett grinned at him and ambled to the closest table to hide how difficult it was to take a normal step without dragging his feet. He gave them a cheery wave and sat sideways on the bench, his legs down its length and crossed at the ankles, to listen, paying no attention to where Freet went. Since they believed he couldn't understand what they said, he was about to hear an ear full.

"Little that creature does makes sense," said the antagonist, elephant ears from before. "He is a fool."

"But a fighter," added another.

"A poor one."

"Why do you say poor?" Gunian asked.

"His blows were weak, and what test of skill is the Dapho? Against one who would fight back, he will be a coward."

Gunian snorted. "If that is what you believe, Mata, you are the fool."

"I do not believe the fight," the forth of the group said. "We all know the Dapho for a coward. For what reason would he attack the Freet? If he were to attack anyone, it would not be one so dangerous, and the Earthling's blows were weak without doing serious damage, nor were they to kill. For reward the Dapho would do whatever Midradina asked. What is a bruise for a special hunt?"

Garrett gave the man a closer, covert look. Like Gunian, he wore plain pajamas. His features were thick and coarse. Heavy brows dominated his features, nearly hiding his eyes. He was a no neck variety with a head that seemed to sit directly on his massive shoulders, and he turned his shoulders instead of his head to look from side to side.

"Interesting theory, Zalano," Gunian remarked.

"And supports mine," Mata claimed. "He is a coward. We all saw his arm is healed, yet the yantz replaced the shield to protect him."

"For what reason?" Gunian asked.

"To spy on us."

Gunian scoffed. "There are enough informers among us they do not need one so obvious."

Zalano turned to Mata. "There is an easy test. If the shields are false, the yantz would not know if he were struck."

"Do you make this test?" Gunian asked Zalano maliciously.

"Not with the Freet here."

"He is not an informer."

Garrett leaned down suddenly to hide any change in his expression at the sudden end of his pain. Of all the times for his back to give out, this was not the best, not when Zalano was trying to goad Mata into an attack on him, and most certainly not when the Phogatres walked in during a discussion of the possible fraudulent nature of the shields. If he walked out then, trouble could be averted. Couldn't happen. He couldn't get up, let alone walk. Nor could he shift to a better defensive position without exposing his paralysis. Even attempting to get to his knife on the down side of his right calf would expose his inability to move his legs.

Zalano said clearly in a raised voice, "The shields are fake, used only to deceive us and protect him while he spies on us."

The effect on the Phogatres was immediate. One headed straight for Garrett. "Take our kill," he growled and reached out with both hands to close on Garrett's neck.

With no way to avoid it, Garrett jerked the nearest table leg out from under the top, braced his back against the wall, and rammed the pole end into the man's solar plexus. As he dropped to his knees and gasped for air, Garrett bounced the table leg off the top of his head. The man's eyes rolled back, and he dropped face first to the floor, his head even with Garrett's knees.

"If you two," Garrett pointed to each of the remaining Phogatres with the pole, "don't drag him out of here, I'm going to get up and really start whipping ass, whether the yantz like it or not."

Shocked, neither of them moved until Freet walked up behind them. With a glass in each hand, he didn't threaten them, but the sight of him startled them. As he crossed to the opposite side of the table from Garrett—with no more than a glance in their direction—they each rushed to grab one of their companion's feet. Freet set a glass in front of Garrett and sat down opposite him as the Phogatres dragged the unconscious man out.

"Thanks for the help," Garrett told him tersely as he returned the leg to under the table.

"Refreshment," Freet answered.

"Asshole."

"Only one."

Being suddenly dry-mouthed, Garrett picked up the glass and drank in gulps, two before he choked, coughed, and gasped for air. With his eyes watering, he gasped a second time and caught enough air to get out in a squeak, "That's booze."

"Too strong, Earthling, add water," Freet told him blandly.

He reached for the glass, and Garrett knocked his hand away. "You think I can't drink? I'll show you, you son-of-a-bitch. It's a damned sight different when you know what's coming. I've drank enough of the worst rotgut in the world to know how to handle this stuff."

With a deep breath, he exhaled half, held the air in his lung, drained the glass, and then blew out quickly. He managed not to gasp as the fiery liquid went down or shudder when it hit his stomach. The empty glass hit the table sharply next to Freet's full one.

"It ain't bad, but I know some moon-shiners that could teach you boys how to make some really good stuff."

"No more," Freet told him. "Only one."

"Naw," Garrett drawled. "I've had a lot stronger. White lightning is what we call it back home. This stuff would be okay for polishing silver, but—"

Gunian couldn't stand it any longer. "Do either of you understand what the other says?" he asked.

"Sorry," Garrett told him. "I can't understand a word you're saying. Don't suppose any of you speak English? Just nod your head or shake it. I can understand that in any language."

Gunian did shake his head, as he left. The other four followed. There were whispers and backward glances, but nothing was said loud enough for Garrett to catch. He watched them out of sight and turned back to find Freet studying him in the same thoughtful manner Garrett had seen when he had made the gloves for Vo, only Freet didn't alter or hide it as he had then. He pushed the second glass to him. "Water take burn."

"No refreshment for you, Chief? Are you a purist, nothing to affect your thinking or reflexes? I bet you've never wanted to be so drunk you were numb, so numb you couldn't think or feel. Well, I do." He picked the glass up and saluted Freet with it. "Too bad this won't do it."

The refreshment had burnt like fire and spread warmth through his body, but it had no kick. There was no buzz, and it didn't dull the pain eating its way back into his body as the paralysis let up. With a flinch he reached for his knee.

"Apes hurt?"

Since that would give him an excuse for limping, Garrett nodded. Freet made no further comment on that. "Refreshment slow. Soon be stagger."

"If that's your way of saying drunk, that's okay with me."

"Help sleep."

"That's okay too." He laid his head back against the wall and closed his eyes. He could go to sleep right there. He guessed the refreshment was having an effect after all. He hadn't felt so relaxed in too many years to count.

"Trouble come," Freet whispered, spoiling the moment.

Actually it wasn't Freet who spoiled it. A furious Gunian, his four equally furious companions, Midradina, and her yantz did. "What has happened?" she demanded without preamble.

Garrett knew he couldn't answer without Gunian knowing he had lied about the translators and overheard everything they had said. He also knew she would be angry if he didn't answer so he propped his chin in his hand and grinned at her.

"Have refreshment," Freet told her. "Staggers."

"Yes," Mata exclaimed, "and the Freet brought two. How can he have two when none other can?"

"He cannot," she said, dismissing his question. She held out her hand for the glass Garrett still held.

Garrett looked at her hand, his glass, and back to her, and then asked querulously, "What do you want my water for? Something wrong with me drinking water now?"

He slammed the glass down on the table and started up. He forgot his legs weren't ready to cooperate. To hide the lack of co-ordination and strength, he let his hand slip off the bench and rolled off to the floor.

"With whom did he battle?" she demanded, a look of disgust on her face as he grinned up at her. "And do not think I will tolerate a conspiracy of silence or denial, or all will be punished."

"The Phogatres," Gunian told her, "but do not be concerned. Your Earthling was not injured."

"Why did they attack?"

Gunian hesitated, and Zalano answered with, "It was said the Earthling had taken a kill."

Zalano was clever. Garrett would give him that. Devious as hell, clever, and Midradina believed it. She turned back to Garrett as he floundered his way back on the bench. The grin he gave her was just as lopsided as before as he leaned an elbow on the table edge, deliberately slipped, and nearly went to the floor again.

After a roll of her eyes, she turned back to the group of men. "Are any of you ignorant enough to ignore the shields?"

"No," Gunian answered for all.

"Do not mistake either that there will again be this long a delay in response. The yantz will no longer wait for me, but will come immediately if there is a disturbance. There will be no one to distinguish for them who is guilty and who is not. The responsibility is for you to prevent attacks. Do you understand me?"

"It is clear," Gunian snarled. "We all are to be his guards or suffer the same consequences as the attacker. Why do you not forbid him to leave his quarters, if you so fear he will be damaged?"

"It would be as easy," she returned coldly, "to restrict all of you to quarters for insolence and disobedience."

Zalano stepped forward. "We will not disobey, Midradina, and the Gunian is always insolent. It is his nature."

She didn't respond to his fawning manner. "It is not within the yantz's nature to be tolerant. Twice now their welfare and comfort has been disregarded while you watched an attack upon their shields."

"Including the Freet," Gunian pointed out hatefully. "What has he done to earn your favor? Become—?"

"Beware," she cut him off. "My tolerance is also at an end. I will not again explain the Freet's presence."

The yantz, either signaled by her or sensing the tension, moved closer. It hovered over her shoulder instead of behind her.

Gunian held his ground. "The Freet as a reminder seems inadequate, and the Earthling does not want him."

"Adjustments will be made."

As a departing line it infuriated Garrett. Adjustments, as if he were a piece of machinery that needed a screw tightened. He seethed and drank more water. He wasn't drunk enough. He could still think and feel. "Can you get me some more of that stuff?" he asked Freet. He tapped the empty glass. "More?"

Freet gave him the carved 'even if I could understand I wouldn't answer' look.

"Yeah," Garrett muttered and twisted to face the others. The look he got from them wasn't friendly. Midradina had made him into a complete outcast as efficiently as if she had hung a leper sign on him, more so since they couldn't read. "Hey, Gunny, old boy, where can I get more of this stuff?"

"Let us go," Zalano said.

"No," Gunian answered and walked to Garrett. He pointed to the empty glass, to a far wall, and motioned for Garrett to follow him.

"I gotta go with you to get it?"

Gunian nodded and motioned again for Garrett to follow.

"What scheme is in your mind?" Zalano asked,

"No scheme," Gunian answered.

"I know you. You do not do for others without reason."

To the astonishment of the others, Gunian offered Garrett help walking. He held his arm out to him and tipped his head to it. Garrett, in a vindictive impulse, lunged up and threw his arm around Gunian's shoulders. The Gunian hadn't been the one to set the Phogatres off, but just as Midradina said, he did nothing to stop it, and using a man's drunken state for schemes against him didn't set right either. Garrett decided to do some getting even. Despite his lack of motor coordination, he didn't have any trouble thinking clearly. At least he didn't think he did. His arm around Gunian's neck had the result he wanted. Gunian went rigid, so much so that it felt as if he moved he might break. Now, Garrett thought, play your buddy-buddy games.

"You're not..." Garrett slurred out, "...such a bad old boy after all, Gunian."

Gunian relaxed with a supreme effort. He didn't go so far as to hold Garrett's arm in place. He just walked, dragging Garrett with him by the arm hooked around his neck. Once there, he raised Garrett's hand and placed it palm flat against the wall. A niche opened with a dull, gray glass in it. Still without pulling away, he went so far as to catch Garrett by the waistband to keep him from going over backwards when Garrett tipped his head back to drain the glass.

"Whoa," Garrett exclaimed. He missed the nearest table by several inches when he set down the glass, something he didn't do deliberately. "This old boy better get his ass home before he ends up face down in the gutter."

As drunk as he was and getting drunker, Garrett knew discretion was definitely the better part of valor. If his tongue got as sloppy as his body, he'd give away his deaf act. He spun around. Two staggered steps were needed to stop, and the effort for balance put him in a stumble off in the direction opposite to the one in which he wanted to go. Gunian caught him.

Garrett leaned on him, gave Freet a come-on wave, and told Gunian, "Gotta have my watchdog, ya know. She don't want me going nowhere without my watchdog."

His watchdog apparently had no intentions of helping. Freet made no move toward him, and it seemed Gunian had decided whatever he wanted was important enough to endure being touched. He pulled Garrett's arm over his shoulders and started him in an unsteady, wavering line towards the nearest exit. Zalano stepped up to the other side and took Garrett's other arm over his shoulders. The other three followed, and Freet followed them.

"You are a clever one, Gunian. What better way to learn his secrets than to see his quarters?" Zalano whispered.

"Believe what you wish," Gunian answered indifferently.

Whatever Gunian had in mind didn't matter. He was never going to get inside, and they would be disappointed in what they saw in the small foyer. Garrett chuckled with the thought of disappointing them.

Zalano grunted in disgust. "Never have I seen one stagger so badly."

"Never have you seen one drink two refreshments," Gunian reminded.

"He staggered from the first. None have been so weak as to stagger so from only one. Why do you think the Freet gave him his?"

"Ask the Freet."

Zalano lapsed into silence, and Garrett analyzed. Zalano had talked the most earlier and held the others' attention. He was by far the largest, which suggested that he was the strongest, but he didn't seem to impress Gunian. The others listened to him unless Gunian spoke. Zalano seemed intelligent, but it was Gunian the others seem to follow. Well, hell they had had years to observe each other. They must know something about Gunian he didn't, and Zalano had been wrong about him being a spy. As to the fight being a fake, he didn't think so, not after Midradina's reaction, but that could have been part of a ploy.

"Never have I seen one talk so much and say so little," Zalano said, interrupting Garrett's train of thought.

Gunian grunted as he pulled Garrett to a stop in front of the door to his quarters. He stepped in front of him and held him by the arms to steady him while he motioned with his head for Garrett to open the door. Garrett obliged with a grin, but he only opened the outer door. Zalano and the others rushed in, not seeing Gunian's look of disgust over their actions. Garrett did see it, however, and knew Gunian wasn't going to go in unless he did.

"Hurry," Zalano ordered, "before the Freet interferes. We may never have another chance to search his belongings."

Gunian shifted positions to move to beside Garrett. "You better come out," he said, as he moved Garrett towards the door.

Four was better than none. Garrett shut the door. He let his legs fold up under him and closed his eyes. He nearly gave his fake pass-out away when Gunian caught him and eased him to the floor.

"Crazy Earthling," he muttered before his voice hardened back into a snarl to talk to Freet as Garrett went to sleep. "You were stupid enough to give him your refreshment; you can spend the night with him in the hall."

###

The instant Garrett groaned awake, he knew he had a hangover, which was the only thing he knew. With an attempt to lift his head he immediately decided it belonged on the floor, being held with both hands. With concentration, achieved only with supreme effort, he remembered he was on a Thornn research vessel, which accounted for all the gray he saw. Okay, but why was he lying on the floor in the hall, and how had he gotten a hangover? And why did he hurt more the longer he laid there? He felt like he'd been run over by a truck. No, his memory corrected, it had been apes.

Still holding his head with both hands, he rolled carefully and managed to sit up. He reached for his knee with another groan and memory slipped into place bit by bit. He remembered the wild man, Glemm, and the maroon chimp, the encounter with Gunian, his knee and back suddenly hurting, and then, oh, yeah, going to the common room. There was something about the Phogatres, he wasn't sure what, and Freet had given him something called refreshment. After that things got real hazy. He didn't know how he'd gotten where he was or how long he'd been there. He wasn't even sure of where he was until the door he sat in front of opened at his command. Relief turned to astonishment when four men rushed out, shouting obscenities at him.

"If you can't take a joke," he groaned, "piss on you."

He managed to hang on to his head, get his elbows and the knee that didn't hurt under him. His head throbbed so much that his vision blurred. When Freet spoke, he jerked, lost his balance, and fell holding his head again with both hands.

"Damn…" What started as a yell subsided quickly to a groaned whisper, "…don't sneak up on me."

"Time go."

With another groan, Garrett released his head with one hand, groping blindly for the doorway. He used everything he had to crawl inside, grateful that the door closed automatically. He thought he was alone and jerked again when Freet spoke.

"Tell Midradina have stagger sickness."

"Tell her whatever you want," he whispered miserably. "Just let me die in peace."

"No die," Freet told him dispassionately. "Only think."

Even though Freet half-dragged him with his arm over his shoulders, it was a contest to see if Garrett would reach the bed before he passed out. Once on his bed the intense throbbing in his head gradually eased to a horrible ache, and he could see if he only opened one eye at a time.

"I don't want anything," he told Freet in response to a touch on his arm and a bleary-eyed look at the glass in Freet's hand.

"Help head."

Anything would have been appreciated, but not by starting that pounding off again if he had to move to get it. He closed the one eye and told Freet, "Later."

"Others wait."

"They better not be waiting on me."

"Me go. First you drink."

Garrett knew him well enough to know Freet wouldn't move an inch until he did what he wanted. Correction, Freet did move. He lifted Garrett's head and held the glass for him. Even that movement started the throbbing off, and Garrett passed out, but not before he choked down three swallows. It helped. When he woke again, there was only a dull, heavy feeling in his head. He felt drugged. Hell, he probably was. He didn't know what Freet had given him. He sat up slowly to discover that Freet had split his pant leg open from the hem to the thigh and wrapped a blue cloth around his knee.

"No more refreshment for you, Garrett old boy," he promised himself fervently and narrowed his eyes to make them focus on a slight movement. Once he was sure he saw what he saw, he groaned again. Glemm stared back at him from across the room. "I hope you aren't up to anything. I don't think I could handle it."

He didn't think he could handle much of anything. Just to stand was a real chore and walking to the bathroom a challenge with the stiff knee and his definite lack of coordination. Splashing water on his face didn't help clear away the dullness. Neither did soaking his head in the filled basin. Neither did Glemm.

Any other time its antics would have amused Garrett; not when it took intense concentration to keep his own movements in control. Glemm continually distracted him. Just as when it was in the pen room, Glemm was into everything. It was everywhere. It hung off the side of the sink while Garrett soaked his head and slipped up between Garrett and the mirror to look closely at the toothbrush and paste Garrett used in the hopes of taking the 'something died in my mouth' taste away. Every time Garrett moved, it jumped or dodged to avoid being touched, making Garrett jerk or hesitate, and destroying the concentration he needed to keep from staggering or falling down. After he nearly got a toothbrush in his eye, Garrett snapped at it to get out of the way. It disappeared instead, which distracted Garrett to the point he needed to hold onto the basin with both hands to look for it. He called its name, and it became visible again, chinning itself on the basin to look at him over the edge.

"I'm taking you back to Mysty before you drive me crazy." Garrett took a step towards the door, and Glemm dropped to the floor. It darted in front of him, nearly tripped him, and ran on its front and back legs with the center pair tucked against its body. In the center of the room it sat, back legs folded and front extended. It looked more like a dog than a mutated spider while it watched Garrett change his pants and put on his boots.

The walk helped work off the drugged feeling, and Garrett's coordination improved, but not his mood. He had to go all the way to the pen room to find Mysty, making his mood even more belligerent when all he wanted to do was lay down. He couldn't even get interested when he saw they had decided to recapture the apes with little danger to themselves by drugging them. He sat down on a fallen cage to rest and watch, easing the dull pain in his back, legs, and swollen knee.

Apes of all sizes and colors sprawled around the vast cleared area. Several big cages lined the back wall. Vo, Freet, Mysty, and Mord dragged the sleeping creatures to the big cages while Midradina arranged the smaller cages into neat rows.

As soon as Glemm reached Mysty and crawled up his robes to curl around his neck the others knew Garrett was there. His reception was mixed. Mord and Mysty both had amusement in their eyes. Freet was as indifferent as ever, and Vo was sympathetic. Midradina was righteously angry.

"I have no sympathy for the results of such foolishness," she told him.

"God forbid you should waste such a precious commodity," he returned rudely.

No doubt to prevent an argument between the two of them, Mysty said quickly, "I am surprised to see you moving about after the amount of refreshment you consumed."

"I wouldn't be if I wasn't afraid of what it would do." He pointed to Glemm. "The idea of it loose in my quarters with its 'impish nature' didn't appeal to me."

"It was in your quarters?" Mysty asked, somewhere between amazement and disbelief.

"I damned sure didn't go looking for it."

"It sounds as if..." Mord mused, "...the after-affects of the refreshment have left you in a querulous mood."

"That stuff does have a built in deterrent to over-indulging," Garrett admitted.

Midradina told him, "Which is why consumption is limited to one serving."

"Yeah, well, no one told me, and it wasn't on those information tapes. I've just been doing some of that learning on my own." He had also learned another lesson about listening to Freet though he didn't say it. Freet had told him "only one" several times, although he hadn't said why.

"It is most odd," Mysty interrupted him, "that Glemm was in your quarters."

"The least said about that creature the better," Midradina snapped. "Had it not been for it being where it did not belong, the Phogatres would never have attacked the Earthling."

"Huh?" Garrett grunted.

Freet entered the conversation. "Too bad no remember. Good battle."

She turned on Freet. "What is good about any battle?"

"Him win."

With only a vague memory of fighting a battle, Garrett stood up with every intention of leaving.

"What is wrong with your leg?" Midradina asked sharply. "Is it a result of your staggering about while intoxicated or your battle?"

"Apes," Freet answered.

"Another circumstance Glemm is responsible for," she told Mysty, turned back to Garrett and added, "because you can not learn discretion."

"What did I do?" he asked in bewilderment.

"Since you are responsible, you will assist, after-effects of intoxication or not."

"Responsible for what?" he asked of her receding back. He turned to the others. "What did I do?"

Mord motioned at Freet and Vo to join him in the chore of dragging the apes to the cages, disassociating them from the situation. Mysty, with Glemm still wrapped around his neck, was left to explain.

A simple enough statement began. Mysty had questioned Glemm more and discovered it could open cages. It had learned when Garrett had opened Peggy's and improvised to open the others. Garrett had already suspected that, but Mysty had more to say. Glemm was a simple, yet complex creature. It willingly allowed no one other than Mysty to touch it and would not deliberately touch anyone else except in extreme circumstances such as when the Phogatres attacked it, which did not mean it did not take an interest in others. It was capable of sympathy and compassion, and it seemed to have taken an interest in Garrett, primarily one of curiosity Mysty suspected.

"Well, damn it, how am I supposed to know it's around to 'maybe' see me do something it isn't supposed to see?" Garrett exclaimed.

"I have instructed it to show itself to you. If it will not endanger itself to do so, it will."

"Great." Garrett pushed up from his cage seat.

Mysty held out a hand to delay him. "I will make every effort to convince it to make itself known to you when in your company.

I do not believe it will use the gravity tube again after its experience with the Phogatres, but—"

"It can operate the gravity tube?" Garrett asked incredulously.

"No," Mysty said with a pained expression, "it climbs it, but the door—"

"Has the same kind of latch," Garrett finished for him. That was how Glemm had taken the chimp into the hunter section too, something he wasn't going to tell anyone.

Mysty nodded. "But it is restricted by the corridor doors."

"We'll just hope no one accidentally teaches it to think—"

"Garrett!" Mysty exclaimed in alarm. "Do not even say such a thing where it may hear."

"Say?" He looked at Glemm and jerked up straight. "You mean that thing understands me?" Mord and Mysty spoke English, but he had never considered Glemm understood it. He could kick himself. It had understood him well enough in his quarters when he said he was going to take it to Mysty.

"But of course," Mysty said in amazement. "How else would it know you could devise something better for the animals?"

"I didn't say that."

"You said—"

"I said," Garrett shouted in agitation, "that something could be done, not that I could do it."

"Your exact words were—"

"That wasn't what I meant."

"Glemm takes everything it hears literally. You said—"

"Next time," Freet said from behind them, "no say want apes move. Say want control."

Garrett groaned and sank back down. That was why Glemm had released the trohog the second time, and the giant slug had made the apes move. That was also why Glemm had taken the chimp into the hunter section, to return it to its owner. "I hope I haven't said anything else hair-brained that it's going to do." He waved his hand at the shambles. "I'm sorry."

Mysty answered. "Don't be sorry. A change was needed. You and Glemm caused it."

"There's easier ways to do it," Garrett retorted.

"No," Mysty said. "I believe the Thornns had to be forced into allowing a change by a desperate situation. This is ending well. The Thornns have released their rigid control of the area. Perhaps it is a beginning."

###

Garrett learned several lessons that day. Exertion cleared away his hangover. More importantly, he discovered why he hadn't had any pain from the bruising he had taken from the apes and why he'd had the reprieve from the pain in his back after Boss's stumble. The tablet Freet had stuck in his mouth to counter the hunter's drug didn't just make the hunter's drug go away. It also protected the victims from the extreme pain the drug caused as it wore off. Because of Freet's overbearing—in Garrett's opinion—behavior in using the hunter's drug to get him off the ridge, he had inadvertently saved Garrett from a lot of pain.

The hunter's drug was to ensure a merciful kill. All their weapons were to be treated with it to cause immediate paralysis to prevent any pain and suffering before a second, finishing strike could be made if one was necessary. The antidote had been developed when it was discovered the hunters used the drug on each other. One pill every seven days prevented the drug from working. One taken after exposure not only countered the drug but also the painful after-affects of the drug wearing off. None of that information nor a description of the consequences of imbibing too much refreshment had been included on the information tapes simply because they had never been updated. Garrett's lack of knowledge earned Freet a piercing look from both Mord and Mysty.

Mysty told him sternly, "Those are things you should be teaching him."

"Teach many," Freet said indifferently. "Teach many more."

Garrett didn't remind him that his services were not wanted. He had every intention of standing fast on his decision not to go on another hunt until those shields came off. But the damned things stuck like glue.

With his knee injury as an excuse for limping, wincing, and taking Mord's pain pills, even though they never worked as well as the hunter's antidote had that first few days, he helped to settle the apes into their new homes. They devised artificial trees, swings, sleeping lofts, and miscellaneous oddities to catch the ape's attention, giving them something to investigate or just plain play with.

He also convinced Mord that the translator wires irritated his skin, and he refused to have the implants. He ended up with plugs similar to the one Freet used that fit inside each ear like a hearing aide and were easily removed. Between trips to the infirmary he spent time in the create room. Even after the satisfaction of his success in self-creation and the interesting things he found in other visuals, the tension was building to an explosive level. He couldn't stay still, his agitation grew, he fell into a depression, and his back ached without relief despite Mord's pain pills. It didn't help when the prism over his door turned green signaling his time to depart. He was pacing when Freet walked in, without knocking, with his hand to his ear.

"Get out of here."

"Time go." Freet stood like a statue as he spoke with only his eyes moving to follow Garrett and take in the changes in his clothing. Freet's eyes flickered over the side opening, knee high moccasins, the close fitting pants tucked into them, the tailored shirt, and waist length vest, all in black.

Not caring what Freet thought of the clothes, Garrett retorted, "I told you, I'm not going until these shields come off."

"Hunt for two. No do me favor no go. Do favor do."

"Who says I want to do you any favors? Who says I'd even bother to spit on you if you were on fire?"

Freet ignored the question. "You no go, I no go."

"Tough."

Freet's eyes followed Garrett pace the room twice, before he said, "Good hunt. No stay together."

"You won't follow me?" Garrett demanded.

Freet hesitated, but finally answered, "No."

"I mean it, Freet, if you follow me; I'll come back whether it fouls you up or not."

IX

Garrett made sure Freet didn't follow him, at least not easily. He mounted Boss and rode off at a lope. Freet might follow, but he'd have to run to make up the distance. His speed didn't keep him from looking at his surroundings. With green meadows and blue sky, it was a beautiful place, but then the planet before had been beautiful, and it had turned out to be a crashing disappointment. Prepared for another one, Garrett rode from meadow to meadow and followed faint game trails, too faint. There were few signs of wildlife and few glimpses of anything. It was not encouraging. When he spotted a structure tucked away amongst the trees on a hillside he went to investigate, putting his uneasiness over the lack of wildlife temporarily aside.

He expected something he had never seen before. Instead he was puzzled by how familiar it looked. Columns surrounded the outside of the structure, supporting the excessively high open breezeways and rooms built around courtyards. It reminded him of pictures he had seen of Greek and Roman ruins. In that aspect it was disappointing. In others it was fascinating. The structure obviously had been there for a long time. The floors were covered with a layer of dirt and leaves that had blown in through the open arches and windows, and the walls and columns had vines trailing up them, but the walls and floors showed no sign of weathering. There was no deterioration of the marble-like substance used for construction. The courtyards were overgrown with wild plant life, but the pool in the center of the first and largest had a giant urn in the center over-flowing into a fountain of crystal clear water, and the pond had no algae on the sides or dirt on the bottom. There wasn't even a dead leaf floating on the surface despite the leaves littering the stone walkways around the pond. Smaller ponds and what appeared to be a bathing pool inside were the same.

With no litter in the empty rooms to show an occupant had ever been there, the building gave off a feeling of waiting, leaving him with a sad, lonely feeling as well as a sense of intrusion. He didn't prolong his stay. The place made him uncomfortable, and he still had a ridge to climb to see if this really was a whole planet or one rotting away as the other Earth-type planet had been.

The level of pain in his back worried him. The medication he had taken since his return from the last planet had kept it from being so intense that it crippled him, but it was constant. The doctors had told him that intensity and duration were warning signs of the time when there would be no recovery from the paralysis.

"In a way," he told Boss, "I wish it would just get over with. No more waiting, wondering if this will be it." Boss nickered in reply. "I know. It's Mord's pills. They make me morbid and irritable, but I've got to think about it. I don't want to take a chance on you getting trapped in that damned cage. If this place is as good as it looks, I'm leaving you here. You'll be lonely, but no lonelier than in that cage and this is a damned sight nicer place to be lonely in. I should have quit procrastinating months ago. You'd be loose where you belong, not..." He gave a short and bitter laugh at the sound of his own words. "Hell, if I'd given up when I should have, neither of us would be in this mess."

Garrett started the climb to the highest ridge to see if the world continued in beauty or dropped away into a smelly abyss. He discovered the ridge rose to a bluff, too steep and rocky for Boss to climb. To ride around it would make him late in getting back to the portal, but he couldn't be sure it was safe to leave Boss until he saw the other side. One choice remained as far as he was concerned, climb the rim-rock face on foot.

Giant bug or not, he owed the yantz. He had agreed to the treatment, even if he hadn't understood what it entailed or believed any of it. They had saved his life and held up their end of the bargain. The least he could do was to honor his and protect Bud. Where he pulled the trigger didn't really matter, on that gray tomb or on some strange planet, as long as he didn't do it before those shields came off. The yantz had said the healing would take a month. Even as messed up as his sense of time had been, that couldn't be much longer.

He stripped Boss down and turned him out to graze. What he didn't take with him, he stored under a tree. What he did take pretty much fit in the pockets of his chaps and shirt; cigarettes, some substance wafers, and pills, his and Mord's. The canteen and binoculars hung across his shoulders. He carried the rifle in his hand and strapped the holster on for his pistol.

Even in his depression, Garrett could appreciate the beauty of the view spread out on both sides of the ridge. On one side more ridges and valleys climbed into majestic mountains reaching high into the blue sky with clouds building on the horizon, promising rain. On the other, the ridges diminished gradually, flattening out to green plains as far as the binoculars would let him see. The only thing bothering him was the scarcity of wildlife. He did see some herd animals too far off to distinguish, but in a place where wildlife's greatest enemy was absent, he expected to see an abundance of it. There had been intelligent beings living here. Perhaps what had taken them had taken the wildlife population as well.

For his peace of mind, he rationalized that whatever was responsible for the absence of wildlife, it was no longer a danger, or the Thornns would not allow the hunters to go there. He convinced himself of this so thoroughly he didn't return the way he'd come. There was nothing back there he didn't already have duplicates of, and there was no reason to tell Boss good-bye.

Between Mord's drugs, leaving Boss behind, and what Garrett knew he had for a future, his mood was dangerous. Freet recognized it immediately. He looked at what little Garrett carried and looked for Boss, but he didn't speak a word. He stood back for Garrett to go through the portal first and followed Garrett, walking into his back when Garrett stopped suddenly.

"What do you want now?" Garrett demanded with enough fury that the yantz with Midradina flew forward.

"You will go to the infirmary," she told him steadily, though she watched him closely.

"For what?"

"Mord will examine you."

"No, he won't." He walked by her to his locker to throw in the rifle, pistol, binoculars, and canteen.

"The yantz desire—"

"I don't care what the yantz desire," he told her hatefully. "Those little dictators have had all they're going to of me."

"Dictators?" she exclaimed with her voice rising. "How can you say such a thing after they have saved your life?"

"Just because they saved it doesn't give them the right to live it. It's my life, my body. There's damned little else you leave a man on this floating tomb, and they're not going to take it over piece by piece."

"You will do as ordered, or you will not hunt."

Garrett shifted into cold fury. "If you try that I'll cause so much trouble you'll damn the day you tried."

"You threaten me?"

"Yes," he answered coldly though he had no idea what he would or could do.

"You..." She made an impatient gesture as if shrugging a hand off her shoulder. "...are..."

She was distracted, but not by a physical touch. She looked at the yantz. During her silent conversation with it, Garrett stripped off his chaps, boots, and socks. It took that long for her to speak to him again.

"They are confused..." she informed him stiffly, "...over your obvious anger."

"Tough."

"What they request is for your benefit," she said through clinched teeth.

"In whose opinion?"

In exasperation she exclaimed, "You do not even know why the yantz are concerned."

"No, and you didn't bother telling me. You just ordered."

"I have the authority to order."

"Not as far as I'm concerned."

"Nothing was done against your wishes. You accepted treatment."

"I didn't know what treatment meant." he yelled at her and slammed the locker door. "You didn't bother telling me it would tie me to them like some kind of leech, draining everything I feel from me."

"They do not," she shouted back.

"They know everything I feel. At least the others have some kind of privacy."

"They—"

"Damn it!" he shouted at her. "Leave me alone!"

He had to get away from her before he did something stupid like shake her until her teeth rattled. He started towards the decontamination chamber, remembered the knife still strapped to his calf, and veered off to the weapons room.

As the door closed Garrett heard her ask Freet, "Do you know the cause of his irrational behavior?"

"Mord drug maybe," Freet offered.

"They feel it is more than his leg or the drug. The transformation is not progressing as rapidly as it should, as if something drains his strength."

"Why say to me?"

"Would you speak to him?"

"No listen. Better do as say, leave lone."

She did, to Garrett's surprise. He half-expected her to be at his quarters when he got there and fully-expected her to show up when enough time had passed for it to be obvious he was not going to the infirmary. After two hours, or so he estimated, he decided he had won, got drunk on his own pain pills to celebrate, and stayed that way for two days. He gave that up because of the dreams.

He supposed digging out the picture of a smiling toddler had started them off in such quantity again, coupled with knowing there would never be any chance of him ever seeing his daughter. Or maybe the morphine in such constant doses had opened doors in his mind he was able to keep closed when he was in control. With the hope that it was the morphine, he switched back to taking Mord's drug. After a few more days, he was able to stop taking either. The pain finally began to ease off to the dull ache he was accustomed to. The dreams, however, didn't stop or decrease in frequency.

The last was what drove him out of his quarters. The create room was only another closed-in room. The only place with any space to it was the pen room. He headed for it only to be intercepted by Mysty in the intermediary area.

Mysty's face immediately creased in concern. "Please, Garrett, tell me what it is that troubles you."

"There isn't anything to talk about."

"The yantz only wish to help you."

Garrett shrugged. "They can help best by letting me live what there is of my life on my own."

He didn't hear her coming. He didn't know she was behind him or how long she had listened until she spoke. "They only wish your well being," she told him.

"Which means Bud's," he said without bitterness. "I'm sorry for him. If I'd had any idea what..." He waved his hand at the gray walls that surrounded him, "...it was going to mean, I wouldn't have said yes."

"It is the closeness perhaps you are unaccustomed to," Mysty suggested.

"I don't call it closeness," he retorted and walked off.

###

Peggy, though fascinating to watch, still would have nothing to do with him. She had stopped charging when he opened the door as long as he stayed back and didn't attempt to venture inside.

"Too bad I can't turn you loose with Boss," he told her. "You'd be company for him. Then again, maybe you wouldn't." He thought about that for a moment before saying, "But you'd be free. How would you like to feel the ground under your feet again and eat real grass? And fly, if your wings haven't atrophied?" He muttered with a shake of his head, "I've got to pull out of this. I've got to think of something to entertain myself. Everything is too damned depressing around here."

He closed the cage and returned to the create room. At one time the visuals had entertained him. He hoped something would spark some kind of interest. He wasn't having much luck even before Midradina popped in through what he thought was a solid wall.

"Are there any real walls in this place?" he asked curtly, annoyed over being startled.

"All are walls, but most are not stationary," she answered, her delicate brow furrowed in puzzlement.

"Next time knock or something."

"I do not wish to quarrel with you. I wish to ask you a question," she told him wearily. Garrett looked at the yantz over her shoulder. "It is for me, not for them."

"How did you know where to find me?"

"I asked them."

She braced for him to explode, but he didn't. It only confirmed what he thought. The yantz knew where he was every minute. He sat on the table edge with his ankles and arms crossed. "What do you want?" Maybe a quick answer would get her to leave.

"Why is the closeness of the yantz of such repugnance to you?"

"I don't consider it closeness. It's like there's something other than me in my body, telling them everything I feel. I can't even stub my toe without them telling you, and you running me down to find out why I hurt."

"I have not been coming."

He derived little satisfaction from verification that he was right about that too, telling her, "No, but you know."

"It is not that they know everything you feel. They can only feel actual pain in the bonded area."

"I'll try not to fall."

"But not for your own sake. This is what confuses us. There is indifference in you for your own welfare. You are more cautious for the safety of even the small creatures than for yourself."

"Was your question just an excuse to deliver a lecture?" he asked tartly.

"No, and I would not have, had you given a comprehensive answer. Why is privacy so important to you?"

"Because it's me, damn it. You can take everything away from a man or make it worthless with create machines and duplicators, but you can't take that. It's mine, where all that makes me who and what I am dwells. It's my body, my mind, and my soul. They..." He jabbed a finger at the yantz, broke off, and dropped his arm. "Body snatchers," he quipped sardonically. "Too many movies, maybe."

"I do not know movies."

"Doesn't matter."

"Perhaps, but the other thing you said, do you mean their intent is to take your body?"

"No, not actually," he said.

"I do not understand, nor, I think, do you. You speak of being invaded when the yantz only sense as you would touch or taste. It is stronger with you because of the bonding."

"Do they know what I think?"

"No, they only sense physical effects. If you would—"

"But it knows what you're saying?"

"It cannot hear sound. It only hears what is said to it in thought."

She went on about his cooperation hastening the transformation. Garrett only half-listened. As soon as she finished he asked, "Doesn't it hear through you?"

"It hears only what I say to it in thought," she repeated.

"Telepathically, in words?"

"Yes, why, do you wish to speak to it?"

"No," he exclaimed with a jerk. "And don't start on that they want me for a Midra stuff."

She turned to the yantz for a moment. "They do not," she said as she turned back.

"Good because I don't want them in my head."

Midradina shook her head slightly. "This is hopeless," she said and disappeared back through the wall.

Garrett agreed. She hadn't understood anything he said, and she certainly hadn't convinced him to accept bonding as no more than closeness. She had, however, killed any interest he'd had in searching through visuals. He returned to his quarters and received a distraction, but not one he wanted. He caught movement out of the corner of his eye as he stepped inside. Glemm came into view as it dragged to the corner of the foyer.

"What are you up to now?" Garrett asked in suspicion. The big, black eyes stared at him unblinkingly. "Come on, you're going back to Mysty right now."

Glemm did not move except to draw up into a ball. Each of its six legs wrapped tight to rock back and forth.

"Are you sick or something?" Glemm unwrapped one leg to sluggishly bob twice in the affirmative. "Did you have another run in with the Phogatres?" One weak bob no barely pushed its body up before the leg wrapped tight again. "Shit," he grumbled. "I could spend all night playing question and answer games with you and still not know what's wrong. Stay here. I'll go get Mysty."

It was Mysty's pet; he could figure out what was wrong. Only he couldn't find Mysty. He wasn't in his quarters, and he wasn't in the infirmary. Midradina was there, annoyed and totally lacking in sympathy when she discovered what Garrett wanted. That, in turn, annoyed him.

"I know it's a pain in the ass," he retorted, "but there's something wrong with it. Just tell me where I can find Mysty."

"I do not know where he is."

"You've got a better idea of where to look than I do. Point me in the right direction."

Mord volunteered to help find Mysty and suggested she go with Garrett to judge if the situation warranted a trip by Mysty into the hunter's quarters. The insinuation was both that Garrett was excited over nothing and that Mysty shouldn't be exposed to the nasty hunters. Both further irked Garrett. He left without waiting for her. He was ready to boot Glemm out, tired of the lot of them, until he opened his door and saw Glemm convulsing on the floor. He knelt beside it, but even in that condition, Glemm pushed away from him. It was pretty hard to help something when you couldn't touch it.

"Mord is looking for Mysty," he told it. "He'll be here soon, and he'll know what to do." Silently he added, "I hope," as another bout of what had to be severe pain gripped Glemm, leaving it limp and exhausted. Sure the silly creature was dying; Garrett lost his temper with Midradina when she arrived. Glemm went into another fit of convulsions, but she announced it was not serious.

"How can you be so damned cold?" he shouted at her. "It's in agony. It could be..."

"It is producing," she stated flatly,

"...dying and ....huh?"

"The yantz say it is producing."

"It's having a baby?"

"Perhaps."

Garrett rolled his eyes, closed them, and rubbed at his face. "Unless reproducing means something else to you, it's having a baby," he said tersely.

"Producing is more accurate. They say it is uncertain what a Glemm will produce until it has arrived."

"How," he asked through narrowed eyes, "can it produce something besides itself?"

"They do not know, but—oh, no! Take it. Take it quickly."

The only thing she could mean was the rock between Glemm's front two feet. Garrett leaned down, not understanding why a rock would upset her, and yowled in unexpected pain, dropping the rock instantly.

"It is hot?" She moved to see around him as Glemm snatched the rock.

Fighting against the urge to dance, blow on or shake his hand, Garrett retorted, "No, it just don't take me long to look at a rock."

"It is a Creeg stone creature,"

She was still trying to see around Garrett when someone knocked. Garrett, expecting Mysty, opened the door without looking.

Midradina cried, "No!" and Glemm darted out of the door on its front and back legs while it held the rock with the center two.

Freet stood in the open doorway, his head tipped to watch Glemm scurry by. He stepped aside quickly when Midradina and the yantz followed in a rush.

Garrett couldn't ignore his hand any longer. Instead of the pain decreasing, it had increased. He shook it. The pain intensified. He blew on it, which did not help at all, and asked Freet, "What the hell is a stone creature?"

Freet didn't answer. No surprise. He walked by Garrett. Garrett blew a while longer, gave it up, and headed inside to see if a dousing in water would help. Freet stepped in front of him with a glass of substance.

"I'm not hungry," Garrett growled. He had some real pain and rapidly rising blisters.

Freet caught his wrist, twisted his hand up, and poured the substance on it. The immediate cooling stopped Garrett's first instinct to shove Freet away. Instead he opened and closed his hand to spread the liquid relief while Freet poured more until Garrett's hand was coated.

"It would have been handy to know it does that when I had all those bites on my hands," he grumbled.

Freet didn't have his hand to his ear, and Garrett was in the mood to fight. He motioned to his ear, but forgot about it when they heard yelling.

###

The common room was in bedlam. Rocks went off like firecrackers, multiplying in numbers with each pop. One turned into dozens. Twenty or so hunters slipped on rocks, failed to outrun them, and jumped on tabletops to avoid being hit. Even then they weren't safe from the flying missiles. They dodged and flailed. Through it all, Glemm high-stepped, not only to dodge flying rocks but also to avoid the hands of the furious hunters.

"Stop it," Midradina shouted. "Follow it," she corrected as Glemm shot by them. "See that it has no more."

"What are we supposed to do if it does?" Garrett asked.

"Throw substance on it. Do not let it multiply."

"Sure," he muttered. He turned and stopped dead. A mass of men bore down on them, drawn by the commotion. "I wouldn't go in there," he called out with a jerk of his thumb over his shoulder. "There's some kind of rock things loose." He saw the rocks coming closer and moved faster. "They burn like hell too."

A traffic jam developed. The crowd continued towards the common room out of curiosity. The ones in front saw the horde of rocks coming toward them and turned, colliding with those still pressing forward from behind. Garrett, with a sudden feeling of dread, shoved. He didn't realize he was holding his breath until they broke free of the main bunch and moved quickly away from the latecomers to a relatively empty corridor. He started to breathe easier, not knowing why he had felt so threatened. When he saw the scratch on the back of Freet's hand he thought they were lucky to have gotten through with no worse injuries than that and then puzzled over why he thought it.

"Be smart go Mysty," Freet suggested.

Garrett attributed his worry to some form of claustrophobia, shook it off, and muttered, "Yeah, but I don't think it's particularly smart." He also knew where it might go instead.

As fast as he could walk without breaking into a run, he opened the door to his quarters long before he reached it. Glemm was inside when he and Freet got there. It appeared as soon as Garrett said its name.

"Have you got anymore of those things?" he asked.

Glemm, on five legs and shaking on rear one, bobbed once.

"Got burnt, didn't you, you little shit?"

Glemm answered yes and backed away from them as Garrett and Freet entered. Garrett opened the inner door and went straight to the substance dispenser. Freet squatted just inside the inner door to watch.

"Hold your foot—hand—whatever up," Garrett ordered. Glemm held up a front leg. "The one that's burnt."

Glemm flopped on its back to hold all six legs straight up in the air. Garrett looked from its feet to the glass and back to Glemm. "It would be easier if you just took a bath in it."

He poured the substance out on the floor. Glemm rolled back to its feet, stepped into the puddle and slid, stiff-legged down into the pool of substance to its belly. "That," Garrett told it while it wallowed in the liquid before the floor could absorb it, "was a dumb thing to do. If you wanted to get even with the hunters for something you should have picked a way that didn't hurt you. That's the craziest, damned way I've ever heard of to give a hot fo—fo..."

Garrett stuttered to a stop, remembering the crack he made about wanting to give them all a hot foot the time he rescued Glemm. Glemm bounced up and down twice.

"You didn't!" Garrett exclaimed.

"What hot fo—fo?" Freet asked.

"It's a gag, a joke—damn, Glemm, you didn't do that because of what you heard me say." Glemm stared at him. Garrett asked weakly, "Did you?"

Glemm bobbed a yes and hopped from one leg to the other. It ran across the room and jumped from the floor to a chair to the table where it flailed four arms while standing upright on two.

"Good imitation," Freet said dryly.

"It is not!"

Freet grunted. "Tell Midradina safe," he said and walked out.

"Stop that," Garrett shouted at Glemm.

Glemm immediately disappeared making Garrett feel guilty. It wasn't Glemm's fault. It didn't know any better than to do something it had heard him say. Garrett told Glemm so. It still took several minutes to coax it into appearing under the table.

"I'm sorry I yelled at you," he told it seriously, "but you've got to quit doing this kind of stuff. I know you did it because of something you heard me say, but you didn't understand what I meant. Because of that you caused a lot of trouble. Those guys..."

A flash of the memory of those guys—the big, bad, and vicious hunters—hooting and scrambling to get away from those rocks suddenly struck Garrett as funny. A smile twitched at the corner of his mouth. He fought against it.

"...got painful burns."

He knew from experience how painful those burns were and how quickly the pain subsided with a dowsing of substance. He still struggled to stay serious.

"And you got burnt."

That brought the image of Glemm hot-footing it through the rocks and Glemm again, flopped on its back, its legs flag-poled in the air for treatment. Garrett had to pull his lip between his teeth. The memory of Glemm's antics afterwards was too much, and he burst out laughing. Glemm responded by going back to mimicking the hunters making Garrett laugh even harder.

"Okay," he gasped and fought for control, "But please don't do anything like that again. You'll get us scalped." Glemm stiffened and bobbed once. "Oh, not literally." Garrett took a deep breath and did sober. "Now I'm serious, Glemm, don't do things because of something you hear me say. It gets us both into trouble," he said, but started to chuckle again. "You sure did have them jumping though."

The good humor was quickly put away when Freet returned. Freet's stoic attitude had a way of doing that. He stepped inside and squatted with his hand to his ear, telling Garrett tonelessly, "Say keep here until safe."

"Is she mad?"

"Mean anger, yes."

"What will she do to punish Glemm?"

"No know."

"What'll I get this time, lose another hunt?"

"She no know…" Freet's voice caught. He shifted slightly and finished, "…you cause."

"She will. I wouldn't let Glemm take all the blame." He watched Freet shift again. "Is something wrong?"

With a shake of his head, Freet stood. He turned for the door only to stop, hunched slightly with a grunt. Concerned, Garrett touched him on the shoulder. Freet twisted away, putting his back to the wall.

"Sorry," Garrett retorted angrily. "I forgot to ask permission."

He backed off, but Freet's hand shot out to grip him by the arm. Garrett caught him by the shoulders. Freet hadn't twisted to keep Garrett from touching him. He had put his back to the wall to keep from falling.

"Beware," Freet gasped. "Fear you. Try kill."

"I'll get you to Mord."

"No good." The pain eased a little, and he straightened slightly, panting, but not gasping. "Mord no physician. Waste time. Take quarters. Die there."

What had been a scratch on his hand no more than an hour before was swollen, red, and oozing. Red streaks radiated out from it, up Freet's arm. "You aren't going to die from a scratch," Garrett told him. "It's infected, but—"

"Poi..." Freet collapsed before he could finish. His body hunched as he fell and his legs drew up. He clawed at his belt. "Red—you..."

He didn't finish. The small leather pouch he had pulled from under his belt fell to the floor as Garrett heaved his limp form to his shoulders.

X

Garrett's chest was heaving when he eased Freet off his shoulders to the table. Though Garrett normally would have had little difficulty carrying Freet, his lack of lungpower had him gasping by the time he reached the infirmary.

"What has happened?" Mysty cried and rushed to help Garrett straighten Freet.

"Looks like poison," Mord supplied holding Freet's hand up.

"Do something," Garrett gasped out.

Mord laid Freet's hand down. "There is nothing I can do," he told him, "Except ease his pain."

The doom materialized over Freet, and Garrett, nerves stretched to the limit, shouted, "What do you mean there is nothing you can do?"

"The hunter's poison antidote did not protect him; therefore I have nothing to treat him."

Garrett forced down a building sense of panic. He wouldn't, couldn't accept that there was no help for Freet. "Where's Midradina?"

Mysty showed him with a tip of his head as she drifted into the room. "I am so sorry, Garrett," he began.

Garrett cut him off and told her, his voice cold and hard, "Get the yantz to treat him."

"They can treat only open wounds," she answered dispassionately.

Garrett pointed to Freet's swollen, blackened hand. "He's got a wound."

"That is too insignificant for a yantz treatment."

He stared at her for moment in disbelief and then exploded. "You want a wound?" he demanded in fury.

Before any of them had any idea of what he was going to do or could stop him, Garrett pulled the knife Freet had given him from his calf. In one swipe, he gave Freet a wound in a slash from his collarbone to his navel.

Midradina was horrified at his action. Mysty was stunned. Mord simply picked him up, set him out the door, and held him out with a hand to Garrett's chest to explain tersely, "To treat any wound would not treat the poison."

"Then give him some of their precious essence!" Garrett shouted as the door shut in his face. He pounded on it and kicked. "Damn it! Open the door! Give him some essence!"

He stood there a moment longer, hands clinched in fists and breathing heavily. They weren't going to let him back in, and there was nothing that could or would be done. Freet was going to die, and some son-of-a-bitch was going to pay for it.

Garrett spun away with no clear plan in mind, other than committing mayhem. He had no plan even as he entered the common room. He walked across the floor littered with dead stone creatures and sat across the table from Gunian.

"Stone creature burn?" Gunian asked of Garrett's blistered hand.

Garrett went into his idiot character with a grin. He wanted information, and Gunian could give it to him. "Yeah," he answered. "For such little things, they pack quite a wallop."

"Acid," Gunian stated. "It is not the first time a hunter was taken with curiosity and unwisely brought one back from a hunt. Fortunately they have a short life and breeding span."

Gunian thought Garrett was responsible for the stone creatures. He let him. He looked around at the mess and picked up one near him. "What'd you do with the bodies?"

"Midradina made the hunter responsible dispose of them," he said without a smile.

Garrett was sure the thought of seeing him pick up thousands of rocks amused Gunian. He tossed the rock in the air. "It would make a good baseball," he commented and pitched it across the room. It sailed by a small group of hunters and surprised him as much as them with his accuracy by hitting the disposal bin.

"What are baseballs?" Gunian asked.

"A game, sport, where I come from."

"Throwing stone creatures?" he asked in scorn.

The tone cut at Garrett's already volatile temper. It took supreme effort not to do more than ask sarcastically, "How accurately can you throw, huh? Well enough to bet your refreshment against mine that I can't throw better than you?"

"Bet?"

"Wager."

"Ah," Gunian drew out. With a wicked smile, he shook his head. "I know my abilities well enough not to gamble so limited a commodity."

"It's the only thing limited around here. I suppose you know where to get anything you want."

"Except additional allotments of refreshment."

Garrett leaned forward and asked softly, "How about poison?"

Gunian blinked. He stared at Garrett for an instant and then his features hardened. "You disappoint me, Earthling. I did not think you would use such a..." He paused to give the impression he left a word out, "...way. Who do you wish it for?"

"What do you care, as long as it isn't you?"

"That is so," he agreed, "but you will be punished."

Garrett smiled at that. "What's one or more hunts? Are you going to tell me?"

"I will take you."

Garrett didn't ask why Gunian would go to the trouble of being a guide. He did stop Gunian from learning anything more of what he was going to do. He blocked Gunian's way into the quarters of what Gunian called a chemist and told him it was private business.

The chemist was a small man with skin the color of tallow. He could more accurately be described as a witch doctor. The room was lined with narrow shelves stacked high with bundles of dried plants.

"I want some poison," Garrett said without preamble. "I want it to hit fast, cause lots of pain, and kill slow enough for him to know he's dying."

"Oh, yes," the man chirped. "I have just the thing, very good, new, and very good. But the cost is high. What have you to offer?"

"Before we decide on any price, I want to know more about what I'd be getting. Is the stuff easy to give?"

"Oh, yes." He picked up a small gray vial with a cork in the top of it. "Just a little on a glass or in a small scratch."

"And the antidote?"

"Antidote? Oh, no, I—"

Garrett cut him off curtly. "I want the antidote."

Startled by his sudden change in tone, the man said, "There is none."

Garrett growled and sprang. He snatched the vial from the chemist's hand and bent the man backwards over the table. With his arm pressed down on the man's throat he repeated, "I want that antidote."

His eyes were wide with fright as he told him, "There isn't one."

"No one makes a poison without an antidote. You'll give it to me or else."

He intended to use the man's own poison against him. He couldn't get the cork out with one hand. He grabbed up an empty vial from the table instead. The sight of a vial without a cork was enough. The man squirmed in panic and screamed. He sobbed, and blubbered incoherently as the vial neared his mouth, but his eyes lit in hope at a knock at the door. Midradina's voice sounded. The man sobbed anew as Garrett jerked him up and pinned him against his chest with an arm around his neck.

"Stay out of this," Garrett told her in a growl when she and two yantz entered.

"Release him," she ordered.

"He's mad," the little man sobbed, "attacking me in my own quarters."

Garrett gave the man's head a twist. "You'll tell me or die along with Freet."

"There is none," he sobbed. "The formula just came to me. I haven't created an antidote. I swear."

Garrett saw a blur from the corner of his eye as he wrestled the man to get the vial to his mouth. A yantz materialized in front of him. The vial was knocked from his hand and sent sailing across the room.

"Release him," Midradina repeated.

The yantz did not have its claws out, but had nevertheless struck him. Garrett stared at it and told her, "I'm not through."

"I will question him."

He told her hatefully, "Your methods aren't very effective."

"Yours are cruel and savage."

Garrett smiled coldly. "They get results." He tightened his arm around the man's neck. "Who did you give that poison to?"

"The Dapho," the chemist choked out, "only the Dapho."

He picked up the real vial. "Is this all you've got?"

The chemist's eyes flickered when he realized he'd been threatened with a harmless vial, but it didn't lessen his fear. His head bobbed.

"You better not make any more of it. Understand?"

His head bobbed again, and he dropped to his knees when Garrett released him. Garrett stepped over him and through the door she had left open, going face to face with Gunian.

"You told me an untruth," Gunian said in accusation.

"I didn't tell you anything." Garrett looked at the men crowding the hall. "Get out of my way. I'm not in the mood to walk through or around you."

"Return to your quarters," Midradina ordered from behind him. "And you, Earthling, go to the infirmary."

Garrett didn't argue. He knew she would see to it he didn't get near the Dapho, and he already planned to take the poison to Mord for analysis, but Gunian still stood in front of him.

"He is your friend," Gunian said, still with accusation in his voice.

"No, but I owe him."

###

"What the hell kind of a doctor are you?" Garrett demanded in frustration.

"It would take a chemist to analyze that," Mord answered. "I regret, Earthling, there is nothing I can do."

"This is a research vessel. It's got to have a chemist."

"The Thornn will not interfere with anything the hunters do to one another. I will take that to..."

Mord reached for the vial, and Garrett spun away in agitation. He caught a blur of movement from the corner of his eye from a yantz as it moved to stay behind him. It had stayed with him all the way from the chemist's quarters even though Midradina had stayed behind. A new guard, Garrett was sure, and he was furious about it. He flung the vial into the disposal chute and walked to the dome-covered table.

"Take that thing off."

"Garrett," Mysty exclaimed, "it eases his pain."

"And prolongs his agony. Take it off. He wanted to die in his own quarters. I can do that much for him unless the Thornns object to that too."

"They would not, but..."

"Remove it." Midradina gliding in. "And then you may both leave us."

Confused and worried by her order, they exchanged glances, but did not argue. Mord dissolved the dome before they left, but watched Midradina until the door closed.

"Of what is to occur," she told Garrett, "you will speak of to no one." As she spoke a section of wall opened to expose a long narrow hall.

"The yantz?" Garrett asked in confusion. "They're going to help?"

"They will treat him. They do not know if it will be of benefit. You must carry him to the treatment room. You can manage the weight?"

Garrett glanced at the monitor board. He would manage it if it took every ounce of strength he had. If he read those lights right, it might already be too late, but it was a chance. He heaved Freet to his shoulder and started off at the fastest pace he could manage. "They'll have to hurry. They can't wait for bonding to give him essence."

She kept pace with him. "Essence cannot be produced without bonding."

"Why?"

"Only a bonding yantz can produce essence and only during transformation."

"There's one already in transformation with me."

"Its essence is only for you. It would be either ineffective or harmful for any other."

He could see the room ahead and increased his pace despite his own struggle for air. Two yantz waited. The light came on so quickly when Garrett put Freet down he felt a flash of numbness as he straightened and moved back out of the way. One yantz used an unsheathed claw to cut away Mord's bandage from Freet's chest and sliced the sutures. What happened next turned Garrett's stomach. The yantz began to lap up the blood oozing from the wound with a long, thin tongue, replacing it with green molding.

"Do not interfere," Midradina warned quickly.

"It's like," Garrett choked out, "a vampire."

"This is what you requested."

Garrett backed away. Each time the tongue flicked out, his stomach twisted. "It's not...I didn't..."

"You can not stop it now. You have gotten what you demanded. Now you find it repugnant? Have I not warned you many times to not interfere in what you do not understand?"

"I understand what I'm told," he shouted at her.

As he shouted Midradina's yantz moved forward. The yantz behind Garrett moved as well until each was in front of their counterpart, facing each other.

"You must stop this," she cried. "They will destroy each other."

"Hasn't one gotten its priorities mixed up?" he asked nastily.

"The bayantz has but one priority, one purpose."

Garrett blinked a couple of times and stepped back with a lot of little facts sliding into place. They were like pieces of a jigsaw puzzle suddenly forming a picture. A yayantz could only touch the one they were bonded with. Four had worked together to dress him and two of those had given him essence while two stayed with Bud. A yayantz became a bayantz after bonding ended. A bayantz was a guardian, a protector. The second yantz had not accompanied Midradina to the hunter's quarters to protect her. It had slapped what they all believed was the poison from his hand, not to stop him from poisoning the chemist, but to protect him. And it didn't protect him just to protect Bud, not if it would attack another yantz. It had to be one of the ones who had bonded to his arm, freed to become his guardian when the shield fell off

"You better make them understand," he told her unsteadily, "I might get mad as hell at you, but I would never hurt you."

She didn't look like she believed it. She hesitated before she turned to the yantz. Garrett went back to Freet. The wound was nearly closed with a thin green line instead of the open cut. It still sickened him to watch, and it might well be for nothing. The poison darkened Freet's hand completely and worked its way up his wrist.

Another bit fit into the picture and Garrett groaned. "If he dies the yantz..."

"Will die as well," she finished for him when his voice trailed off.

"I didn't think of that. Will you tell them I'm sorry? I didn't think of that."

Her brow furrowed slightly. "Would it have made a difference?"

He looked at the yantz hovering over Freet's chest. "It would to Freet," he said evasively. If he had to knowingly choose the possible death of a yantz over the chance of saving Freet's life, he didn't know what he would do.

"Your assistance is required," she told him.

"Doing what?"

"Lifting the Freet," she said as a strip of black guard went over Freet's chest, and the light went out. "You must hold him for the administration of the essence."

"It's only been a few minutes."

"The transformation time for so slight a wound will be short. The essences must be administered quickly."

"He's unconscious," he pointed out as the yantz flew off. "How can he swallow it?"

"He need not." She glanced at the yantz behind her and added, "You must hurry."

Garrett didn't argue anymore. He slipped an arm under Freet's shoulders and lifted him just as the yantz returned with a cone-shaped cup. It painstakingly dipped one hand into the cup and moved the liquid to Freet's mouth, drops at a time. In half an hour the guard on Freet's chest popped off.

"The transformation is complete," she told him. "The yantz is safe now."

"That's something," Garrett remarked feeling something between gratitude and resentment. It reflected his confused feelings about the yantz.

"You will speak of this to no one."

"Not even Freet?"

"No."

That presented Garrett with a dilemma. Part of him argued Freet had the right to know. Another part countered that if Freet had any idea what it entailed, he wouldn't have wanted anything to do with it and would really hate Garrett for what he'd done. There was another part that pointed out that it may save Freet's life, and if it didn't none of it mattered.

###

Freet's quarters were as ambiguous as the man. With the exception of a change of clothes neatly folded on the bench and a pile of the so-called lost translators on the table Garrett could just as easily have walked into an unoccupied room. Freet had not even rearranged the walls. The only individual touch was a wall of cabinets in the bedroom, the contents of which Garrett did not investigate. Whatever Freet had stored in them was none of his business.

He could just as easily have walked to his own quarters, executing a left turn instead of a right. Freet's quarters were just across the hall from his, a fact that both surprised and annoyed Garrett. He should have already figured that out. It made sense to place his quarters as close to Freet's as possible since Freet was his appointed guard. It also explained how Freet had kept such close tabs on when he came and went.

To be the only source of Freet's care was not a responsibility Garrett cared for and, again, was something he hadn't anticipated when he had demanded the yantz treatment. He worried every minute that what he did for Freet was wrong or was not enough. He ended up feeling like a Peeping Tom while he bathed the burning skin of Freet's face with cool water. If he'd had any idea why Freet wore his hair long or held it in place with a band, he wouldn't have disturbed it. Instead he removed the headband and exposed the reason for Freet's partial deafness. More than half of his left ear was gone, with scar tissue covering the external opening. Only a third of the top remained, just enough to form a lump under his hair to give the impression there was a whole ear. Garrett put the band back with a pretty good idea of how Freet had learned about the octum venom.

More than once, more than a hundred times, he considered carrying Freet back to Mord. Each time he had to discard the idea for the same reason, Freet's healed chest. The irony tormented him. Freet had the yantz treatment, still needed more than the sponging Garrett could give him, but couldn't be taken to Mord because of the yantz treatment. No, it wasn't the actual treatment; it was the silence forced on him by Midradina and the yantz. A vicious circle with him caught in the middle. No, it was a vicious circle he had created, with Freet caught in the middle.

"Maybe I should have minded my own business," he told the unconscious Freet.

While his mind wrestled with the problem, another arose. The second was one he was accustomed to, which didn't make it any easier to deal with. His back, no doubt from the strain of carrying Freet, threatened to cripple him as the pain radiated down into his legs. Taking his own medication when he had the responsibility for Freet's care wasn't an option. Mord's drug left him depressed with a flash point temper, neither of which he needed under the circumstances. He tried a different method. He reconstructed the bench to the side of Freet's bed. All he had to do was reach out to sponge Freet's face in an effort to cool the fever. The arrangement relieved his back, but it did nothing for Freet.

Midradina gave Garrett control of Freet's quarters as she had given Freet control of his. Garrett could leave and come back anytime he pleased, but he was afraid to leave for even the few minutes it took to get the oxygen masks from his own quarters.

The rest of the day and the first night Garrett saw no difference in Freet's condition. Not until the next day did he start to hope. The swelling in Freet's arm and hand began to lessen; though so slightly to start he wasn't sure it wasn't his imagination. By afternoon it had accelerated to such a degree he could almost watch the blackness and swelling as it receded. Freet, however, still labored for breath even through the masks, and his fever was still high.

Fatigue became a factor for Garrett. He would jerk awake, riddled with guilt, to sponge Freet down and leave a cool compress on his forehead only to doze off again until the time Freet woke him in convulsions. Garrett was determined then to take him to Mord and damn the consequences, but Freet's contorting body threw him off balance. Doubting that he could even get to Mord, he used the only other method he knew of to cool a fever. He took Freet to the shower.

He was as wet as Freet when Freet finally stopped jerking. Water sloshed in his boots on the walk back to the bed, and water dripped from his hair as he leaned over Freet. He reached for the sheet, pulled it up to Freet's chin, and froze when he saw that Freet's eyes were open. Freet's empty gaze gave Garrett a chill. What if Freet's brain had been burned up by the fever? What would happen then?

"Don't look at me like that," Garrett exclaimed and shook Freet roughly.

"No feel well," Freet mumbled with his eyes still vague and out of focus.

"You shouldn't, you—"

"Why wet?" He raised his right arm weakly and with extreme effort focused his gaze. "Think die."

In exhaustion and relief, Garrett sank down to sit on the side of the bed.

"Why wet?" Freet repeated.

"I don't know why you ask questions," Garrett said wearily, "when you can't understand the answer." He gave a short laugh followed with a heavy sigh and talked even though he had just said Freet couldn't understand. Or because he knew Freet couldn't. "You scared the shit out of me, Chief. I didn't think you were going to make it. You're too good a man to be taken out like that."

###

A week passed, not that Garrett had any real way to do more than estimate the passage of time. He stayed alone to get back on balance and do a lot of thinking. Nothing about his future had altered because of the bizarre new life he lived. He had been living for the moment for a long time, and the reason hadn't changed. He'd just forgotten it while he tried to make sense of the things that were really not his problems. He'd lost touch. Living for the moment meant looking around corners, as many as he could in the time he had left. It also meant not getting overly excited about anything, such as being denied the next hunt because of his attack on the chemist or when Midradina arrived at his quarters, yantz hovering protectively over her, to demand his knife and chew him out.

"If this is about slashing Freet," he began in argument.

"Weapons are forbidden in quarters," she told him coolly. "Be grateful you are not denied another hunt for what you caused with the refreshments as well."

"What do I have to do with refreshments?"

"You taught them a foolish game which has resulted in excessive drunkenness and brawls. Never before had they discovered a way to—"

"They played baseball?" he asked incredulously with a chuckle and shake of his head. He handed the knife over without further argument and took private pleasure in seeing the distrust in Midradina's eyes.

"I would have thought with more serious matters on your mind, you would not have taken time for something so frivolous," she told him stiffly.

"Did they get rid of all the rocks?" he asked in curiosity.

"That was your objective to avoid the responsibility of cleaning the debris."

"Damned clever of me," he told her sarcastically. All he had wanted was for Gunian to tell him where they got their poison, although he didn't tell her that. He asked, "In all the time they've been here, none of them thought of gambling to get more?"

She hesitated and then didn't answer his question. "You will be notified when you are again eligible for a hunt."

Garrett shrugged that away. He'd just have to wait a few more days to see around any new corners. Detaching himself from his concern over Freet wasn't quite as easy. He figured Freet for the kind of man who wouldn't appreciate being nursed—being dependent on someone. Before Freet woke a second time Garrett had rearranged his quarters. Once Freet woke, he got him to the bench long enough to place the bed between the bathroom and the substance dispenser on the long wall he had formed. While he worked there had been an uncomfortable silence. Freet didn't speak even though his eyes followed every move Garrett made, and he looked away whenever Garrett glanced towards him. Garrett only spoke once, after he got Freet back to the bed and after he handed him a translator.

"We're even," he told him and walked out.

It had been damned hard not to walk back across the hall every few minutes to convince himself he had done enough to provide Freet's unassisted recuperation. He had only gone back once, with an excuse. When the door opened Freet stood at the other end of the large room Garrett had constructed. He looked a little pale, but steady. Assured the man had the constitution of a bull elephant, Garrett tossed the leather pouch that Freet had dropped the day of the attack. Freet didn't say a word, and Garrett counted on the discomfort to keep Freet away. His next hunt would be totally alone, no Boss and no Freet, or so he believed.

XI

Loose gravel trickled through Garrett's fingers. It felt real just as the knife-sharp pain that had shot through his back and down his legs when he'd slipped on the creek bank. All too real was the sudden cessation of pain that pitched him face down on the rocky ground without any feeling in his legs. He'd experienced that enough times.

All of it had to be real, even the Earth-type planet rotting away at the edges. Who the hell would let or make themselves go insane to avoid facing reality and not imagine away the reality they wanted to escape? If he imagined giant bugs that could cure imagined wounds, he could just as easily imagine them healing his back. Why not escape completely? Or was death the only complete escape? Was the final irreversible act of putting a gun to his head what he really avoided?

Garrett shoved the saddlebags off his shoulder and pulled the revolver from his holster. Propped up on his elbows, he held it with both hands. Was that what he was afraid of the most? Had the whole complex mess been imagined for nothing more than to create someone, something that depended on his being alive, without any emotional attachment, as an excuse not to take that final step?

"Looks like I could have done better than a bug," he grumbled glumly.

He thought again of the daughter he would never see and sighed. He'd had twelve years to do something about seeing her. Instead he had spent those years making sure there were no bonds in his life, no personal or emotional ties, and no relationships that had any special meaning. The decision had been his, something he had consciously worked at, and it was a little late to regret it because no one gave a shit if he lived or died. Nor was there any reason to put off getting it over with, unless he wasn't in fantasyland and the life of a bug, five of them, if he had counted correctly, depended on his staying alive. No, four. At least one of the bugs had graduated to bayantz.

Deep in gloomy, confused thoughts, Garrett didn't hear Freet's approach. He jerked when Freet entered his field of vision, but no more than Freet. His sudden movement caused Freet to stop so abruptly his feet went out from under him. He continued down the short slope of the creek bank on his rump, heels, and hands, hitting the bottom with a jolt and a grunt.

"No follow," he said quickly while his eyes flickered over Garrett. They came to rest on the pistol in Garrett's hand.

"Relax," Garrett told him with an indifferent look back down the creek bed, "it isn't for you."

"Who is it for, Garrett?" Freet asked softly, making Garrett's head snap back around.

"You understand me?" he asked in astonishment.

"Not all." He slipped the pack from his back and leaned forward with his elbows on his knees. "You use words differently than I have learned and use words I do not know. I doubt my wisdom in revealing this to you while you have that weapon in your hands, but attempt to understand and not be angry. My intention was not to deceive you anymore than any other, and I did attempt to dissuade you from speaking more than you meant for me to hear."

Garrett had to agree to last statement. Freet had at first attempted to keep him from talking by not having a translator.

When he realized Garrett was going to talk anyway, he sought to shut him up by having one.

Freet continued, "I will not divulge what you have said to me believing I did not understand nor of what I have observed." His eyes flickered down Garrett's length and back to his eyes. "You are in pain?"

"No," Garrett answered in a daze. He had suspected Freet understood more than he let on, but never that Freet understood and spoke English perfectly. "Why? Why pretend?"

"A combination of reasons," Freet said. "I had hoped that by introducing you to Mord's medication, it would not be necessary to involve you further in my deceptions. His medication, like your own is not efficient, and its side-effects cause me concern. As with everything Thornn, there is a double edge. Refreshment gives euphoria and pain after, pain relief causes depression, agitation, and mental confusion."

He shifted for more comfort before he continued. "It is your own medication you have taken," he observed. "Its effects are more pleasant, but just as dangerous and ineffective in relieving your pain. Do you remember clearly what transpires while under its influence?"

"Enough," Garrett answered emptily. He hadn't taken anything, but didn't correct Freet.

Freet had expected him to be angry and looked at him closely. "You have decided again that none of this is true?" Garrett shrugged in answer. "I have watched your many moods. Sometimes you believe and are angry, wishing to make better the things you see. Others times you believe it is not happening and treat all as a jest."

"Insanity, Chief, I believe I have gone stark-raving mad."

Freet nodded slowly. "When you first arrived I did not believe you would survive the hunter's section. Like the owner of the foil before you, you thought yourself no more than a character, acting out some part in a fantasy dream. He was killed quickly during his first battle. In your first battle I saw that you are one who disassociates from emotion when threatened. You are calm and deliberate with instinct taking over. I thought then you could survive, but to do so you would be like this poisoned sea planet with the bad eating away the good, becoming like the rest of us with only hate and self-interest. This was not something I wished to see. I thought it best to stay away."

Freet shifted slightly to continue though not from physical discomfort. "It was too late for that even when I told Midradina what I wished. I said it out of anger with myself for what I considered a weakness. For the first time since being taken from my world I felt something other than hatred. Since then I have felt shame. You made me remember what it was to be a man, not an animal. I had not once thought or cared that I may be able to help the others or the creatures in the cages. I have seen, Garrett, not our poison taking the good from you, but your good reaching out to others."

Garrett commented with a dour, "I'm not crazy, Chief, you are."

"Your greatest fault is you have no concept of your effect on others. To help is natural for you, an instinct you are not conscious of. Just as with Vo when he felt pride and enjoyment. You provided it from the first time you spoke to him as a man to devising those gloves. Even Midradina has been affected."

"Sure," Garrett answered with a wry grin. "She cherishes every minute of time she's around me."

"You make her furious, and you confuse her," Freet stated. "For one who has never felt emotion it is a beginning."

"Give the credit to Glemm then. It did it, not me."

"Because—"

"No," Garrett cut him off. "I don't know what you and Mysty are up to, but I'm not going for it. I'm not some damned messiah, and I won't be. You, the yantz, and all the rest of them can go to hell and leave me alone."

"Or you will beat me," Freet asked calmly, "to make me hate you? It would serve little purpose when I know why you do it."

"Just what the hell do you think you know?" He couldn't remember all the things he had said while he ran off at the mouth. Freet couldn't know all of it.

"How long?" Freet asked with his eyes shifting straight to Garrett's back.

"Maybe right now," Garrett snapped.

What Garrett meant was that maybe now was the time he wouldn't regain feeling. Freet obviously thought Garrett meant he would turn the gun on himself that instant. He lunged up and grabbed the barrel. He jerked to take it from Garrett's hands, flinched when it discharged, and jerked again, freeing it from Garrett's grasp. As he stepped back, Garrett caught Freet's ankles and pulled. Freet went over backwards, landing with a force that knocked the air out of his lungs, and he discovered that even while partially paralyzed, Garrett could move and was a formidable enemy.

Garrett came up on his hands and lunged forward with his arms. Freet was still trying to catch his breath when a second lunge dropped Garrett over his chest to hold him down while he took back the gun. Garrett shoved away, tossed the gun to his right hand and pushed up on his left elbow ready to use the gun on Freet if he went after it. Then he saw the blood.

Freet held one hand up in a stop motion. His other hand held his side. "Possibilities," he gasped. "Discuss possibilities first."

"There aren't any," Garrett shouted at him.

Freet mimicked the gesture Garrett used when he needed time to catch his breath. Freet held up one finger. Garrett couldn't tell if Freet needed to recover from having the air knocked out of his lungs or if he couldn't breathe because of a bullet in his chest. He returned the gun to the holster. Using his hands while balanced on both elbows wasn't easy. It would have been impossible if Freet had fought him. Freet didn't. He leaned back on his hands to let Garrett remove the belt from his waist and push his shirt up.

"That," Freet gasped, "is painful."

"It ought to be, you stupid son-of-a-bitch," Garrett ranted. He used the edge of the shirt to wipe away some of the blood and calmed down when he saw it wasn't serious. "It's only a graze. You're damned lucky."

"It burns and it cuts. How does it do this?"

Garrett dabbed at the four-inch gash across Freet's ribs. "It throws a piece of hot lead. It's not deep." He pressed the shirt over the wound. "Have you got something in your pack to use for a bandage?"

Hunched over, Freet answered by rolling to reach his pack. He snagged a strap and dragged it toward him. As the initial shook wore off, the more it hurt. He was gasping again as he pulled the shirt off over his head.

"Neat," Garrett said sarcastically of the twin knives strapped to Freet's forearms, handles down.

Freet choose not to answer. He handed Garrett a small white jar from the pack. Garrett pulled his eyes away from the nearest knife and shifted around to be able to reach the wound. The knife was smaller than the one Freet had given him, but he was sure it was just as deadly. Freet hadn't been wearing them when he had slashed his chest, but he wondered how often Freet had sat or stood near him, arms crossed with his hands in easy reach of those weapons.

"Need to stop the bleeding first," Garrett said.

Freet leaned back on his hands and told him, "That will."

"What about cleaning it?"

"Antiseptic and analgesic."

That seemed an awful lot for one paste, but Garrett shrugged. "You're the doctor."

"This is a physician?"

"Yeah."

"Yes." Freet flinched and caught his breath as Garrett dabbed the paste on. He let it out in a hiss before he said in a pant, "I am a doctor or was in my world. That is why I did not wish you to use your weapon on yourself before we can discuss it."

"Don't go offering me any miracle cure to prove I am crazy."

"I am sorry. I can not...offer a cure." Freet paused to take several deep breaths. "I was not a surgeon. For removal of such a tumor—"

"Would you shut up?"

"I do—"

"Chief, shut up." He put on a couple more dabs before he said softly, "It isn't a tumor. It's glass cutting into my spine. I appreciate your concern, but there isn't anything you can do, so drop it."

Garrett was impressed with the cream. Blood was smeared over Freet's side, but the wound was closed. There was no fresh flow, a translucent layer covered the wound, and Freet's pain eased.

"You're lucky it didn't bust a couple of ribs." He replaced the lid and held the jar out to Freet. "How long will it take to heal?"

Freet returned the jar to his pack. "Four or five days."

"You treated Boss," Garrett stated. Mord didn't have any such paste, Freet frequented the pen area, and that explained Boss's attitude toward Freet, something else he should have put together sooner. "He must have kicked the hell out of you before you got all those cuts covered."

"Many times," Freet agreed, "and bit."

"He wouldn't have," Garrett said in the wounded animal's defense, "if he hadn't been hurting, and you hadn't been a stranger. He wouldn't now."

"I was not serious when I asked for him. I did not realize you were in such pain until I turned."

"Kinda wish you had been," Garrett said of the first and ignoring the last. "I'm uneasy about leaving him, even there."

"Then I will learn not to be fearful of him." He took out the small pouch Garrett had returned to him the last time he saw him. "Watching you with him, I see he is a gentle creature who responds to affection." While he talked he shook pills of assorted colors into his palm. He chose a red one and held it out to Garrett. "It is not a cure, but it will help. With it you will feel no pain. No pain, Garrett, a fact you must remember. This does not have the mood altering effects such as yours or Mord's. Its danger is you can be injured, as with your knee, and be unaware of it. Its duration is fifty of your hours, no matter the amount of pain, and it ends very quickly."

It had ended quickly, nearly dropping him in the hall. Mord's drug wasn't what Freet had stuck in his mouth after paralyzing him, something else he should have realized. "You're a devious man, Chief,"

"Outwitting you has challenged my cunning. I prefer we combine our efforts."

"To do what?"

"Whatever we wish," he said in a dismissive manner and changed subjects. "Why do you call me Chief?"

"Because you look like an Indian," Garrett answered in preoccupation. He ought to be hateful, be doing something to push Freet away. He could see the wooden Indian again from his dream, the one he had shattered. "Damn it, I wish you weren't doing this."

"I know, but if you think to save me grief, it is too late. You have already touched my spirit and heart as a brother. Now we will be brothers, something I thought to never experience again, and I will have memories of something other than hatred."

"I'll admit..." Garrett broke off, not quite willing to admit what it would mean to him. He was still reluctant to encourage Freet. To let him in was contrary to a policy he'd held to obsessively for twelve years. He warned instead, "When the time comes, it won't change anything. I won't—can't live as a cripple."

"As I could not, I understand this, but not that way." He looked at the gun on Garrett's hip and held out another pill, a bright yellow one. "One will give you sleep, more restful and natural without after-effects. Three will give you a peaceful ending. What is an Indian?"

Garrett took the pill slowly. He knew of at least one time when he'd had one of those too, to end a panic attack, but didn't comment. Instead he told Freet of the Plains Indians the first sight of him had brought to mind. He told him as much as he could remember of their culture, their pride, and their prowess, their horsemanship, skill as warriors, hunters, how they lived off the land, and that their leaders were called chiefs.

"It is interesting," Freet told him, "with the translator it is my name. It startled me to hear it after so long a time."

"You did a damned good job of hiding it. What is it in your language?"

"Long and tedious; from you I prefer Chief."

"Were you a chief, a leader?"

"Yes, curious, is it not?"

"Curious you chose that costume to wear. I've got a pretty good idea it wasn't what you arrived in."

"It was not. My clothing was too telling by design and fabric that I came from an advanced culture. It is an advantage to be without the others knowing."

"As dense as I've been it's a good thing Gunian didn't stick around," Garrett grumbled.

"It was predicted he would not. Midradina is fortunate to have Mystaleah as sage and counsel. Do not mistake Mystaleah is in league with the Thornn. His hatred for them is as strong as his love for her. He is and has been her guardian for many years. While others would try violence to destroy the Thornn control, he attempts to accomplish change through her, but until now the Thornn influence has been unshakable."

"Don't start that again," he warned.

Freet shrugged. "It is easy to deceive Midradina, but not Mystaleah, and he can be trusted. He will not inform her of transgressions against the Thornn rule as long as it does not endanger her." Without a pause for breath, he asked, "Why was the tumor—glass not removed?"

With a sigh, Garrett asked, "Do you know what tenacious is?"

"Yes, and I am. I will not stop asking questions until they are answered."

"Yeah, well my elbows are getting sore," Garrett complained.

###

He'd put Freet off, but just as Freet had warned, he did not stop asking questions until Garrett answered. Getting mad at him didn't do any good either. Garrett had rolled and moved his legs with his hands. Freet wisely watched without offering assistance while Garrett put into practice what they had taught him after telling him he would never walk again. He pushed up on his arms and swung his body backwards to lean back against the bank, the same method he had used to get in and out of his bed or wheelchair. If it had been left up to the doctors, he would have spent the rest of his life that way. It had taken him three years to walk without braces, crutches, or a cane and not a minute of it, then or any time after, had been without some degree of pain.

"They can't see it," he finally told Freet. "They figured to dig for it would do more damage than leaving it alone."

"Why can they not see?"

"Glass—do you know what it is?" Freet nodded. "Well, it doesn't show up on x-rays. Do you know what they are?"

"When last were you examined?" he asked instead of answering.

"A couple of months ago, why?"

"Were they able to determine if this glass was embedded in the vertebra or simply resting against it?"

"They figure it's wedged between a vertebra and disk, sawing its way through," he said impatiently.

Freet nodded thoughtfully. "I could feel a lump approximately the size of the end of my finger. That is why I assumed it was a tumor."

"You felt?" Garrett asked tersely.

"The body has—"

"Wait a minute. You examined me without my knowledge or permission?"

"I could not request it without disclosing I am a physician," he stated blandly.

"Right, now that makes sense. So when did you do this—without me knowing?"

"On the wind planet while you slept." He anticipated Garrett's next question. "I ensured you would not wake. I could see in your eyes and the way you held yourself you were in pain, but not the cause. I could not assist you without that knowledge. Do not argue with me now over so minor an issue, diverting our attention—"

"I don't consider it a minor issue," Garrett snapped.

Freet continued doggedly. "You body has encapsulated the glass."

"So what?"

"Now it can be seen."

"And I ask again, so what? What the hell difference does that make?"

He studied Garrett quietly for a moment before saying, "None now."

Garrett drew his eyebrows down and studied Freet. "Meaning it will?" he asked suspiciously and shifted slightly as feeling began to return.

"It is possible it delays your prognosis. I hesitate to say this and give false hope, but you are aware of the healing properties of substance. It is possible it has caused encasement of the glass to prevent further damage as well as repairing the existing injury."

"It hasn't gotten any better, Chief."

"The glass has been encased. That is causing pressure as would a tumor."

"But?"

"I do not know with any certainty, Garrett. I speculate. There is previous damage and weakness to the spine, and I do not know if the substance can repair it. But there is a possibility. This is why I have not warned you against using it."

"Why? What's it do?"

"Steals mental clarity and potency. Have you noticed the last?"

With a wry grin, Garrett told him, "If you want to know if I'm impotent, just ask."

"Had you been before, you would not know if still you are. Substance while having great healing properties suppresses the desire as well as the ability, a wise ingredient in a society of only men. Were you before?"

"That's not really any of your business," Garrett told him without rancor, but he wasn't going tell him he had been since he'd been hurt.

"You said to just ask."

"I didn't say I'd answer," he quipped and turned serious again. "That's why I haven't been able to think right?"

"That and the drugs you have been taking. I think now you take only my drugs."

"And the substance?"

"Better for now that you continue using it."

A wry grin twisted Garrett's mouth. "So I sacrifice 'mental clarity' on the chance it will heal my back?"

"For now," Freet answered with a nod, "I know of no alternative."

###

The paralysis let up without pain through the medication provided by Freet. As they ate, things Freet had said shifted back and forth until Garrett's head jerked up. He damned himself for not having thought of it the instant Freet uttered his first word. "Where did you learn English?"

Freet sat his plate aside. "I learned English with the translators while listening to Mord, Mystaleah, and Midradina speak."

"She has never spoken English to me."

"Always in your presence she uses Mystaleah's language."

Facts slid around in his head until Garrett asked, "Why would she hide being from Earth from me?"

"It is from the others more so than you, I think. Already there are many charges of favoritism. For them to know she brought you from her planet—"

"No one knows she's from Earth?"

"No one knows where she is from. Some believe she was a child, taken from the pens by the yantz and cared for until maturity. Some, of course, believe she is Thornn. Others believe she was a specimen chosen by the Thornn, trained to use the yantz, to be their Midra. It was the Midra who began the transfer from cages to quarters."

"Cage?" Garrett jerked up straight. "You were in cages like those animals?"

"Whoever walked into the portal walked into a cage with the door closing behind them."

Freet's voice took on a chilly coldness, understandable considering what he described. Once caged, sleep was induced. He woke, stripped naked, in a new, smaller cage. The cages were moved to the pen room just as Boss's had been moved, to be stacked two high, sides, back, and floor opaque. The only other captives visible were those straight across with occasional glances at those above or to the sides of them. Once when he slept the cage was moved, the back wall of the quarters opened, and then the door to his cage. Everything he had had with him when taken was there. Another time he woke with the translators in his ears, and Midradina appeared for the first time to instruct him on the room's operations and question him as to which section he would be in. Sometime later she reappeared to give him further instructions on finding the learning room and gave him control of his outer door. Once that had been done, permanent translators implanted in the other prisoners, and the hunts established, nothing had changed until Garrett arrived.

"I have discovered many things, Garrett," Freet ended with, "but never the hiding place of the Thornn."

Garrett cleared his throat to find his voice. "What do they look like?"

"No one knows. None have ever seen them."

"Then how do you even know they exist? How do you know that whole damned ship is nothing more than a computer?"

"My concept of that machine may be faulty, but does not a computer need someone to create a change, such as moving specimens to quarters and separating the sections?"

"Yeah, but maybe the Thornns are machines, capable of thought, but not emotions. That would explain their cold-blooded treatment of their specimens." He spat out the last word. "It'd serve them right if some of their specimens had wiped them out and taken over."

"Difficult to do without communication. The cages were all sound proof."

"Unless you're telepathic," Garrett said lightly, with a twist to reach his canteen. He turned back to find Freet gazing at him in deep thought. "Now what?"

Freet asked quietly, "Have you ever attempted telepathy?"

"Vo already asked that," Garrett answered in sudden irritation. "No, and I don't care to. When I get an idea, I want to know it's mine, not one put there by someone else."

"That would not be telepathy. Telepathy is no more than a form of communication."

"If you want to play around with that kind of stuff, do it with Vo."

"That stuff?" Freet queried.

"I'm not into E.S.P.," Garrett retorted. Nor did he want to talk about it. He pushed up, going for his saddlebags.

Freet followed, asking, "E.S.P.?"

"Extra sensory perception, witches, and spirits."

"Superstition?"

"No, not really, it's..." He stopped to look at Freet in perplexity. "Maybe it is," he admitted. "But scientists were doing a lot of research on E.S.P., telepathy, clairvoyance, that kind of stuff."

"You have no belief in these things?"

"No."

Freet nodded and changed the subject. "You have been on many very strong drugs, and you have suffered a great shock, physically and mentally. You have coped admirably with each.

Over and over you have amazed me with the things you see that those of us here have failed to see. Now without the drugs or pain to drain and confuse you, you will see even more."

A memory flashed in Garrett's mind of a soft, warm voice telling him they needed him. He shook his head against it. No one could depend on him. He wasn't going to be around that long. He hadn't let anyone depend on him since his wife had walked away with his daughter in her belly, and he was never going to again. With those dark thoughts in his mind, he grew pensive and withdrew from Freet. Freet had given him more than enough to think about and even if Freet hadn't said so, Garrett knew there was more. He wasn't ready to hear it. He didn't want anymore yet, but when they walked back through the portal, Midradina was waiting for them.

"Now what are you going to tell me," he asked in resignation, "that I'm not going to want to hear?"

"The yantz 'request' you allow Mord to examine you." She went on quickly before he could explode. "The transformation is not progressing as expected. They fear a physical problem they are unaware of inhibits the process."

"I'll think about it," he told her well aware of the concession she was giving by making 'a request' instead of issuing an order. He appreciated it, but he still didn't want to see Mord, especially with the yantz suspecting a physical problem.

"You are the most exasperating being I have ever encountered," she told him angrily and spun to leave.

The motion of her dress reminded Garrett of the metal vest she wore. "Armor?" he asked after telling Freet about it.

"They say she has no legs. What will—?"

"What?"

"What will you think of?" Freet finished with the tenaciousness Garrett accused him of.

"Don't think you're going to say something like that and just drop it. What do you mean she has no legs?"

Freet shrugged and went to his locker. "It is something I have heard the others say. What—"

"Why?"

"Because they have never seen her legs possibly. What—"

"None had ever seen the yantz claws either," he retorted, "but they all knew about them."

Freet shrugged. "Perhaps they say this because none have seen her legs because of the gown she wears. You will think over what?"

"If you want to eavesdrop," Garrett snapped, "wear a translator."

He went to his locker and grimaced when Freet told him, "I have been forced to do so on the ship since you are so stubborn."

Garrett raised an eyebrow over that. Something else he hadn't noticed. That was why Freet had stopped badgering him to tell him what others said during various encounters. Just to put an end to the questions while they stripped he told him, "They want Mord to examine me."

"It would come to nothing. He would not discover what you wish to keep private."

"You did easy enough," he grumbled. "How soon did you know?"

"I suspected soon after you began moving about and exerting yourself enough to aggravate the injury, but I doubt any others have. Even the sharp-eyed Gunian did not realize you did not stand to meet the Phogatres because you could not."

Garrett slammed his locker door shut. "You've thrown a hell of a lot at me, Chief, awful fast."

Freet agreed. "I should have broken my silence sooner. There is much you have seen with its significance lost on you because of the drugs, though I am puzzled by your repulsion to telepathy."

"I'm not repulsed by it."

"Feel fear?"

"Asshole," Garrett retorted and headed for the decontamination door.

"That," Freet followed along behind him, "is one of the words I do not know, also shit."

They dropped their knives to the floor and kicked them to the other end. "Shit is a big pile of smelly, worthless manure. That's what the idea of me being telepathic is equivalent to."

"Is not manure used to fertilize plants?"

"Meaning what?" Garrett demanded while he strapped the knife to his calf.

Freet strapped his knife to his thigh. "I do not believe the idea is shit."

Garrett jerked on a pair of pajama bottoms "That's it." He stormed to the door, tying them around his waist as he walked. "You are the most pig-headed, most stubborn..." The door slid open and Midradina stood on the other side. "What do you want now?"

Midradina blinked in perplexity. "You still argue with the Freet?"

"I never stop arguing with him."

"Then why do you stay together?"

"Because..." The significance of the question hit him. She had not ordered Freet to stay with him, and the hunts hadn't been programmed for two. "...I like to argue," he finished lamely.

It sounded ridiculous even to him.

"How can there be an argument when he does not understand?" she asked.

He told her in a surge of humor, "I always win."

Behind him and with his hand to his ear, Freet said, "No always win."

She left with a look for Freet that indicated she was as exasperated with him as she was Garrett. Garrett watched her leave and wondered about the legs nobody could see. He turned to find an altogether different expression on Freet's face as he watched until she was out of sight.

XII

With Freet's assurance that Mord's examination would find nothing, Garrett went to the infirmary. As Freet had suggested whatever Mord's skills had been on his own world, he lacked the knowledge to do more than a perfunctory exam. He took Garrett's vital signs and asked Garrett questions. Garrett admitted to difficulty in sleeping, rapid and erratic mood shifts, and depression. He also admitted to a noticeable inability to concentrate. Most of those problems had either been caused by or aggravated by the drugs he'd been taking, which he did not point out.

He did say defensively, "What do you expect? I never know if I'm coming, or going, or what's going to happen next."

Mysty nodded in understanding and answered in his poetic version of English with, "My world as yours not as advanced. Technology our greatest a simple hoist. Tallow for candles our light only, no..." He switched to his own language, his mouth going out of sync with his words, "...controlled power or vehicles for the ground or air. You have an advantage over most others here. The possibilities of all this has at least been envisioned in your world."

"In fiction," Garrett clarified. "That damned portal is no looking glass, this is not Wonderland, and I'm no Alice." He shook his head. "Wrong analogy, this is Star Trek and Star Wars, Heinlein and Jules Vern, every science fiction thing I've ever seen. If I told anyone on Earth about this, they would think I'm crazy."

Glances were exchanged quickly and covertly. Mord asked, "This is what you fear?"

Garrett answered with a shrug.

"Perhaps you prefer to think yourself insane with a hope of a cure than this which is endless?"

"Mord!" Mysty exclaimed.

Midradina moved to in front of Garrett. "You are not insane. I have seen madness. It is not in you."

The yantz behind her took his attention. "What do they want from me?"

"Only your well being, they do not ask nor do they expect anything in return. They wish for you to understand, they comprehend emotional stress can create a physical effect."

"And?" Garrett prompted.

"That is all."

Garrett had the feeling it wasn't, that there should have been a 'but we know there is more' to finish it.

"There is perhaps..." Mysty asked hesitantly, "...some other problem?"

"Don't go wishing anymore on me than the obvious," Garrett joked and hopped off the table. "I've got all I can handle right now." He stopped as he reached the door and turned back. "Should there be? Is there something else I don't know about?"

"No," Mord said too quickly while Mysty looked evasively to the floor.

Garrett turned to Midradina. "What are you worried about?"

"Your welfare," she answered immediately.

"In what way?"

"Every way."

It might have been a touching answer if it hadn't been given coldly, drawing a tart remark from him. "Your concern is overwhelming."

She responded in kind. "It is not mine. It is theirs."

"Touché," he told her with a mock salute as he went out.

The instant he stepped into the halls a depression settled over him. It was all that damn gray.

It should be something cheerful, he thought, *like a bright yellow daisy.*

Garrett started violently. In the blink of an eye, as far as he could see, the walls, ceiling, and floor of the hall were a bright yellow, the exact shade of yellow he had pictured. Stunned to a degree of stupor, he didn't move. He couldn't move. He'd done that. He'd thought it, and it happened.

"You do?" Freet asked from behind him, making Garrett start again.

"Damn it, don't sneak up on me!" he exclaimed furiously.

With one eyebrow raised, Freet told him, "Better me than enemy." He dropped his eyebrow and pointed to the wall. "You do?"

"I think so," he said uncertainly.

"Why?"

"I didn't mean to. I was just thinking they should be yellow, and they were."

"Think too hard."

Garrett laughed. "If you mean it's too much yellow, you're right. How about some blue?"

Nothing happened, drawing a dry, "Think too little," from Freet.

It was Garrett's turn to raise an eyebrow. "This isn't anything new to you. You've done it."

"In quarters," Freet admitted, "no hall."

"Just another of those things I can learn for myself?" Garrett queried tightly.

"Learn much more soon than me," Freet said and dropped his voice. "Talk more private."

By the time they reached Garrett's quarters the ceilings were blue and the floors were brown to go along with the yellow walls. In his quarters, Garrett experimented, first with simple designs to wall size murals of outdoor scenes. It was so simple. All he had to do was mentally visualize the scene while he thought at the same time of the area he wanted to cover. He hadn't tired of the new game when all his walls were transformed. He applied it next to the common room, visualizing the room one wall at a time with a scene reaching to the ceiling of blue with white, fluffy clouds.

"Nothing change," Freet told him.

"Not here," Garrett told him with a grin. "Let's go see what results it had."

"I do not know what you have done," Freet advised, "but it will be better, I am sure, if you do not admit to it."

"Why?"

"Not all can do this, and I have heard none speak of the ability."

The more primitive the man, the more frightened he was of the sudden change Garrett had made to the walls, floor, and ceiling. One member of a hide and fur species was on his hands and knees on a table, the table and benches being the only things still in the cold gray he was accustomed to. Another sat in a trance, mumbling about the end of the world, a prediction totally out of place as far as Garrett could reason, since it wasn't a planet to begin with. Still another jiggled a leather pouch, chanting to ward off evil spirits.

Garrett was aware of all of that as he stepped in and waved to the group gathered in the center. "Nice," he called out. "Who's the artist?"

Someone muttered something he couldn't hear as Zalano said, "What does he know? He has not seen it for endless years."

With an innocent demeanor, Garrett asked, "Is something wrong?"

No one answered. Comments about his intelligence started, and then there was something to capture his attention. With one talking over the other it was hard to hear for, but there were bits he picked out; soon be mad, not such a gift, the Sicasee, and laughter drowning out the rest.

"Do not listen," Freet whispered.

Garrett had already heard enough. His amusement was gone. He shot out of there, headed back to his quarters, and caught one more little bit to make him furious, Midradina's pet.

###

Freet answered stoically. "Four have been treated by the yantz before you."

"And?" Garrett demanded while he paced from one side of his quarters to the other.

"One showed no sign of change, another swore he was being spoken to by God and was killed for his efforts to convert others, the Sicasee went mad, screaming of voices, and took his own life. The first was Midradina."

"Before or after she became a Midra?"

"Before."

Garrett grunted. That explained why there was so much talk about him becoming a Midra. "You let me believe there were no others."

"I said nothing, but had there not been others, how would we know what the yantz can do?"

"The same way you know about their claws," he growled.

"Someone saw them attack and told the story."

"Who? Why?"

"The story is a man was attacking a child, that the struggle brought them through the portal. The movement of the cage was automatic, carrying them to the pen room where several saw the yantz go to them." He waited while Garrett sat down. "They killed the man. It is believed the child was Dina."

Garrett groaned. "Oh, Christ, no wonder she hates me."

"Many more saw the yantz carry her from the pen room, me among them. As a physician, I believed her already dead so severely was she beaten. It was not until after we were moved to quarters I knew she had survived. Others who had seen her knew she had been saved and help was asked for. After the fourth, we were told the yantz would no longer treat hunters. None were, none, Garrett, until you."

He didn't ask why Freet hadn't told him all that before when they had talked about Midradina. He'd known there was more and that Freet was giving it to him slowly. He asked, "How old was she?"

"It would be difficult to say, but I believe from the size she is now and the size then, perhaps early puberty. I do not know the age for this in your world."

As sickened as he was by what he heard, Garrett attempted to get an idea of time. Midradina appeared to be in her early twenties. If she had been brought there before changing from child to woman, figuring thirteen or so as an age for that-—near Carolyn's age, which gave him a chill—at least ten to fifteen years had passed.

Freet went on. "A hunting cycle has never included an inhabited planet. Someone or something altered the controls to send the Karoz to your planet for some purpose. Dina and her yantz went in pursuit. I can understand why they would remove you and your Boss from the planet, and I would understand a merciful death, but not why the yantz treated you. Either she or the yantz guardian must have called to them."

Garrett was again struck by the similarity to bees. "Where the hell is the queen?" he asked absently.

"I do not understand the question."

"The yantz, where is the queen?"

Freet obviously still did not understand, but he said, "There are three. Perhaps the third is the one of which you speak."

"There are nine at least," Garrett corrected, still preoccupied.

"Three," Freet insisted.

"Nine, damn it," he snapped and lunged up off the bench to rummage through the odds and ends he had carried back from the create room. "I might be crazy, but I can still count. Four had worked on me, five counting Bud, at least one for Dina, and the other three." Ten, though he didn't tell of the last.

"There has always been only three."

"I've seen five at once." He went on to explain what Mysty had told him about yayantz and bayantz. "That means there has to be at least nine."

Freet said. "They must have been more than we have ever seen or they are reproducing."

"Stop worrying about their sex life and worry about this."

"What is that?"

"I can't believe I know something you don't." He shook it for emphasis. "This, old buddy, is a litch, and with it no one on this ship is safe, including the yantz. With this the Karoz punched a hole as big as my fist through my chest and took my arm off."

"If this is as you say, then I must tell you more than I have intended so quickly. Things are happening, strange things."

Garrett grunted. "I think I get the dubious credit for that."

"These things started before you came."

Garrett sat down. "Like someone sending the Karoz to Earth?" he asked while he remembered the soft voice telling him they needed him. It wasn't as easy then to push it away.

###

It was a dream. Garrett knew he was asleep when the soft knock came. He told them to come in. They came in single file, arms tucked into the loose sleeves of their floor length robes. The cloth was something soft and glistening like velvet in dark shades of blue and green. Heavy chains of gold hung about their necks with large medallions of interesting patterns, similar to Aztec sun calendars. An odd combination, he thought. Medieval robes, artifacts of an ancient race, and the Phogatres. There was no doubt in his mind they were the Phogatres. Dressed differently, different attitudes, but it was their faces. The first introduced himself as Lamphin, the second as Wastrol, and the last as Famala.

Lamphin explained he was their speaker while Wastrol and Famala were the listeners. He spoke more strongly while they heard more clearly, but Garrett had neither heard them as one nor spoken that they could hear. It was taking a combined effort to make him hear, and to create a mental image, a complicated process as they must all concentrate on the same message in unison. They asked if he understood.

Garrett answered yes and asked what they were doing there, what did they want, and why had they tried to kill Glemm?

Their images wavered for a moment before they steadied and answered. "A new voice had come to us, one we have since recognized as false. We were deceived as it spoke to us in our own language, clearly that we all may hear. It had told us the Ancient's pet was a spy, reporting what we do to the Thornn to betray us, just as it told us you are evil and must be destroyed. Your protection of the Glemm made this seem so. Your mercy in not killing Famala did not. We have counseled with the old voices, those that have never deceived. Unlike our old voices, the new does not speak with us, only to us to never answer a question. We come now to tell you, we will use deception as caution. We speak to you so you may know we are not enemies, though we will pretend to be."

Garrett accepted what they said without question. "Do you speak with Vo?"

They wavered again, came back into clear focus and answered, "We hear many without understanding. If the Vo you speak of were to learn your language, then we might understand him."

Even in his sleep, Garrett started. "Why my language?" he asked.

The answer was simple. "It is the language of our old voices." They wavered again and came back with, "We must go now; we grow weary. First we must warn you, just as with your quarters, allow no entry in thought without identification. Also though we now recognize the deception, and we do not believe we will be misled again, as a precaution you must not trust us without first asking the yantz."

Garrett grinned. "How do I ask them?"

Their images wavered again. Only Lamphin's image stayed clear to tell him they would search for a solution. Then all three faded away to allow Garrett to drift into a deep sleep, undisturbed by further dreams.

When he woke, Garrett wasn't sure it had been a dream. It certainly wasn't like any he had ever had before. Similar to the ones he had of Carolyn, but not quite the same. He was still in bed thinking about it when Freet came in.

"You are ill?"

Garrett shook his head. "Who was the fourth, the one who showed no change after bonding?"

"One of the Phogatres."

The answer both excited and disturbed Garrett. Had his subconscious been talking to him in his dream? Had to be. It was just organizing subconscious thoughts. The yantz had bonded with four. Two had gone crazy, claiming to be hearing voices; two had not. Dina didn't. Because she was telepathic before the bonding and knew what she was hearing? If the voices the other two had heard were the yantz attempting to speak to them, then maybe there had been no change in the Phogatres because they were already used to hearing voices.

"You are not going mad," Freet said to interrupt Garrett's thoughts.

"I don't hear voices, but I was wondering if maybe some of the others are."

"The yantz attempting to make others hear?"

"Someone else who's telepathic that no one knows about." The new voice, Garrett thought, who had talked to the Phogatres.

"I do not understand."

"Neither do I," he admitted. "But I think I'll poke around a little bit, see if it goes anywhere."

###

Garrett needed Midradina to access the only place he could think of to start his investigation. She, understandably, resisted letting him anywhere near the Dapho or chemist despite his promise of no violence.

"Okay," he finally said in frustration, "ask the yantz."

"Why would they—?"

"Ask them," he insisted without being sure why he thought it would help.

Midradina gave him an 'it is useless' look that quickly altered to surprise and puzzlement and then, if Garrett was any judge, resentment. She was stiff when she agreed to take him. Unfortunately it was a pretty much a useless trip. The chemist insisted that the formula had just come to him in a flash of inspiration, a term he instantly regretted when he saw the look on Garrett's face, but Garrett kept his promise. He controlled his fury with the stupid little man.

The Dapho wasn't in his quarters, and Garrett left Midradina to walk back to his quarters alone. Deep in thought he didn't pay too much attention to what was going on around him until a blow struck him in the back. He put a hand to the wall to keep his balance and looked down to see the end of a crossbow bolt sticking out of the left side of his chest.

Garrett's first reaction was a detached wonder. It didn't hurt. He hadn't had one of Freet's pills in nearly five days. The ache in his back had been constant, but not of a degree to warrant using medication, so he should feel the arrow.

He wasn't given time to dwell on it. The Dapho came at him with a knife. Garrett threw up his left arm, knocked the blade aimed at his chest to the side, and struck with his right to the throat. The Dapho staggered back, gasping for air, and the Karoz took his place, swinging his club at Garrett's head. Garrett's left arm blocked the blow, but the force drove him into the wall, and then he hurt. He noted and wondered why the Karoz didn't stink at the same time he knew he was going to die. He coughed and blood filled his mouth and weakness swept over him. He dropped, sitting on his feet, and leaned a shoulder against the wall for support. He knew a second blow was coming and couldn't move fast enough to throw himself completely out of the way. The club slammed into his back, and he heard the Karoz grunt from his effort.

Then the Karoz screamed. The club and his arm fell to the floor. The scream cut off abruptly. His head hit the floor and rolled to Garrett's knees. The Dapho tried to run. The yantz was a blur as the Dapho's head flew, landing beside the Karoz's, both staring sightlessly.

Garrett couldn't take his eyes off those heads. Even as he choked on his own blood, he couldn't take his eyes off the heads, not until he heard Freet shout at Midradina.

"Tell move away. Drown in own blood. Must have help now."

The yantz hovered above Garrett's head. The claws dripped with blood, and it jerked from side to side to keep anyone from coming near, ready to kill again if any dared.

"Make understand," Freet continued to shout. "Must help or die."

In a daze Garrett thought the yantz was frenzied because he was in pain. If he could stop the pain, the yantz would stop hurting. The least he could do for it before it died when he died was to stop the pain. The pills were in his pocket where he would always be able to get to them. He tried to straighten, to drag his right arm up. His feeble effort was blocked by the wall. He was still struggling to push up when Freet pulled him up against his chest.

Freet shouted at Midradina, "Need help to carry."

"Gunian," she ordered immediately. He stood with the dozens of others staring in disbelief and shock, "you will assist."

"Tell Bud…" Garrett gargled, "…sorry."

XIII

A tube ran through each of his nostrils; he was in his own quarters; Freet sat beside him, and his legs were dead. All of those things registered as Garrett's eyes opened. He looked accusingly at Freet.

Freet ignored the look. "One tube is oxygen to increase the supply to the right lung; the other is suction to remove fluid from your left."

Garrett rolled his head to face the wall.

"It may be shock, Garrett. The blow may not have done the damage you believe."

"Go away," he told him quietly.

"I must stay." He took a deep breath. "Not my arrow."

Garrett didn't answer. There wasn't any reason to. There was no reason for anything except waiting for a chance. He waited for two days while he suffered silently through the necessary administrations from Freet to keep him living. On the third day Freet went outside to speak with Midradina. As soon as the door closed, Garrett rolled from the bed, gagging and choking as the tubes pulled from his throat. He heard Freet and Midradina whispering to prevent him from understanding the words as he laboriously dragged his half-dead body to his saddlebags and the three little pills he had tucked away there.

In the hall, Midradina told Freet, "They sense something is wrong."

"Transformation no go as expected?" Freet asked tersely.

"Is there a problem they are unaware of?" she asked just as curtly.

"Is thing they no know?" he countered.

"Why are you so hostile when you see what they have done for a hunter?"

"A man," Freet corrected. "He no hunter as say before."

"He is capable of killing."

"All are, even yantz."

"You..." She broke off to clinch her hands and teeth for a moment. "They wish to know is there anything they may do?"

"Is depression. Must have interest to live."

"He..." She hesitated again and said, "They sense something now."

Garrett levered himself up one last time and fell forward, his arm stretched. He had no pain. Either the yantz or Freet had seen to that. He did have weakness. He struggled for breath, but in just a few more minutes he would have the quick, painless, and neat death Freet's pills promised him.

Freet's hand gripped his wrist. He rolled Garrett to his back, and stuck only one pill in his mouth.

###

The same feeling of nothingness was within him. What Freet did had no more interest to Garrett than why he was on the floor of the portal room with a gray cylinder up against his stomach. A tube ran from what had to be an oxygen tank through his nose to his lung to keep him alive. He would have to wait until a chance came again.

Freet, loaded with a backpack and crossbow, knelt beside Garrett, tying a rope loop on the cylinder top. He hooked the loop over his shoulder and pulled Garrett up. He took care to move the tube over his shoulder before he heaved Garrett up to avoid pulling it free and having all his care go for nothing. With Garrett on his shoulders, he started for the portal just as the wall from the pen room ramp opened. With an exclamation that did not translate, he bolted and ran, a difficult thing to do with the weight he carried.

It was not difficult for Peggy.

Without time to even question what Peggy was doing free of her cage and in the portal room, Freet hit the irregular surface of a green meadow and ran several feet before he tripped and fell to one knee. He was urged back to his feet by the winged horse coming out behind them. Like Boss's first trip from the ship to a planet, the instantaneous change startled the equine. She reared on her hind legs, front hooves pawing the air, and her wings unfurled. Freet dropped his pack, weapon, and, unnoticed in his haste, the rope loop for the cylinder. The oxygen stayed when he heaved Garrett up again just as Peggy dropped to paw at the ground, sending clumps of grass and dirt flying. The magnificent head tossed and she snorted, blowing huge bursts of air from her lungs.

Each slow step Freet took pulled the tube tighter until it went from uncomfortable to gagging, and Garrett began to choke. Peggy's head swung to locate the sound, and Freet froze. When Peggy turned to face them, head lowered, and one front hoof pawing, Freet held his breath. Confused by the onslaught on all of her senses, Peggy looked away. Freet pulled the tube, eased the tension, but also moved the cylinder and drew Peggy's attention again. He froze in a test of patience and endurance. Garrett was not a lightweight man. Peggy lifted her head to smell them and snorted. Freet could not know how familiar Garrett's scent was to her and how strange was his. He only knew he could not outrun her if she charged, and his experience with Boss's feet and teeth told him it would be painful.

The only shelter of any kind was a fallen tree. When he reached it, he eased Garrett off his shoulder and rolled him face up against the flimsy protection. He finished just as Peggy charged and tromped over his pack and the cylinder coming straight at them. Freet ran. She followed, but only as far as five feet from the log where she stopped, pawed the ground, and squealed.

Freet ran to the side, waved his arms, and shouted to draw her away from Garrett. She charged towards him a few feet before she stopped with a spray of dirt from each hoof, and a new stand off began. Freet waved his arms furiously and shouted. She charged in a short run only to stop, and Freet gained very little ground. She was still too close to Garrett, and Garrett hadn't moved. When Freet saw the smashed valve of the cylinder, he feared Garrett was unconscious. That fear forced him into a dash for his pack, which took him closer to her than he had gone before. She retaliated with a closer charge.

Garrett rolled from his side to his back.

"No move," Freet shouted. He held the pack with one hand and dug into it with the other.

Garrett rolled his head towards the sound, his eyes instantly being drawn to Peggy. He blinked rapidly with a bewildered expression on his face as Peggy charged again.

The battle between the equine and the man altered. Instead of Freet trying to draw Peggy away, she kept Freet away from Garrett. "No move," he shouted at Garrett again as Garrett rolled clumsily to his stomach, pulled the tube from his nose, and rose up on his elbows to watch.

Freet dashed to the right. Peggy rose up on her hind legs and spun to charge. He darted to the left; she spun and lunged to block him again. Garrett grinned slowly.

"Is not humor," Freet exclaimed incredulously.

"Is from where I'm watching." When he twisted to look back at his lifeless legs the smile faded, but he said, "Just walk towards her."

"She will trample me."

Garrett looked back at Peggy where she tossed her head and pawed the ground. "She'll move..." He broke to take a deep breath. "...away as long as... she's able."

"Hope you right. You need mask."

A dazed expression was the only answer Freet got. Garrett watched him inch his way forward for a few feet, then Garrett dropped his head on his arms and closed his eyes.

###

The sound of birds, the smell of coffee, and a bright blue sky above were not a bad combination of things to wake to, if he knew where he was. Garrett blinked to orient himself and had a difficult time doing it. The only thing he was sure of was the absence of feeling below his waist and a mask over his face. When Freet appeared beside him holding out the battered tin cup from his saddlebags, he knew how he had gotten to where he was and thought he recognized where, only not even that was quite right. The dwelling he had found on his other visit to that planet had been covered with trailing vines and dirt. This one was spotlessly clean.

"Taste," Freet told him. "No know prepare right."

Garrett took the cup and held it while he assessed his condition, something he had only been vaguely aware of before. The pads on his chest were backwards, visible from beneath the blanket that covered him from the middle of the chest downwards. The left side of his chest was covered with a black patch, the right was free. He was lying on a bench of some kind, his head and shoulders elevated on cushions with a mask over his face. "I must have gone through the looking glass again."

"Come through portal," Freet told him.

"No beam me up, Chiefy?" he asked with a crooked grin. Freet's expression was too sober and worried. "TV." That explanation did nothing to clear away Freet's concern. "Programs of fiction, actors, performers, science fiction."

Freet squatted beside him. "You think again you are insane?"

"Naw," he drawled sardonically as the memories slid in quickly, "everyone else is."

"Garrett, you..."

Garrett waved his right hand weakly to stop him. "What was wrong with me? Why did I act like that?"

Freet let out a pent-up breath. "Shock, maybe."

"I've been in shock before. It wasn't like that. This was..." He hesitated while he remembered how it had been, how he had felt until he started coming out of it. "Like part of me was asleep or something?"

"Awake now," Freet said in relief. He leaned elbows on his knees. "You have been given many strange medications. We have no way of knowing how they react together."

"Have you given me Mord's drug?"

"No, only mine for the pain."

"There won't be any more pain, Chief," Garrett stated matter-of-factly.

"Will be with no medication." He pointed to the right side of Garrett's chest. "It has not finished bonding, delicate. Must stay calm. Had to open so you can breathe until this one heals now."

"How long?"

Freet knew exactly why Garrett asked. "A week the yantz estimate for so small a wound. Maybe two for first. You can tolerate so short a time?"

"All I've got to do is lay around. You have to do all the work."

Freet nodded without comment. He stated in a rush, "Not my arrow."

"Didn't think it was," Garrett told him with only a slight twinge of guilt while he removed the mask for a sip of coffee. Freet was the first person he had thought of when he looked down to see that bolt sticking out of his chest, and the flash of thought that Freet had been the one to do it, had ripped at his insides nearly as badly as the arrow.

Freet cupped his hand under the cup and raised Garrett's head with the other. Garrett took one small sip, grimaced over the barely warm, watery coffee, but only said, "A little weak."

"Do better next time," Freet promised and replaced the mask. "Think did believe why no talk me."

Garrett felt another twinge of guilt. He had thought it possible over and over. Each time he discarded it or believed it didn't matter. Whatever had held him in that state of apathy was gone. "It wasn't the Karoz or the Dapho either." He suppressed a shudder of how both of those men had looked the last time he saw them.

"No see who?"

"No, but he's a mean son-of-a-bitch. Killing me wasn't enough. He wanted me to believe you'd been the one to do it."

He didn't need to elaborate. Freet understood. He switched to English to say. "I think they wanted Midradina to think so too."

"Did she?"

"At beginning, she hesitated to move the yantz away so I could help you."

"I don't suppose you asked her if they knew who it was."

"They say not."

"Whose quarters are in that corridor?"

"You have thought of these things while you have lain so quietly?"

"Not that I was aware of." He looked beyond Freet to the slender columns holding up the roofs of the covered walkways around them. How he had felt worried him. A lot of times in the past he'd thought about giving up, but never had, not until then and never so single-mindedly bent on killing himself.

"It was the Karoz on one side," Freet told him. "All others in corridor are empty. The Dapho must have been with the Karoz, though none have ever been before because of his stench."

"He didn't stink. I can remember that. He didn't smell like he did the first time."

"Strange, but the bow was found his quarters. If a third was there as well, it would have been easy to slip into the hall when all eyes were on the yantz."

Garrett grunted. He preferred not to comment on what the yantz had done. "I found a place something like this one."

"This one is lower, the opposite way from where you went." He pointed through one of the open breezeways to ask, "Why equine follow?"

"Lonely." Garrett watched Peggy graze peacefully. "Whatever possessed you to turn her loose?"

"Me no do!" Freet exclaimed in his own language. "Think you!"

"Hell, Chief, I wasn't in any condition to do anything, let alone something like that and I can't...move..." Garrett's words slowed to a stop.

"What?"

Garrett started to rise up on his elbows. He gave the idea up and settled for just lifting his head. "Glemm?" he questioned apprehensively. A black glob bobbed up next to the bench on the opposite side of Freet. Freet startled to his feet, and Garrett dropped his head back down with a groan.

"Him do?" Freet asked incredulously. Glemm bobbed up and down in a yes, and Garrett groaned again. "How?"

"It doesn't matter how," Garrett moaned. "I'm going to get blamed for it whether I'm the one who accidentally taught it how to open those doors or not."

"Maybe all do when speak with Vo on learning with pictures," Freet suggested and frowned when Glemm bobbed up and down in a yes.

At the end of his words a yantz materialized. Glemm disappeared, and Freet turned into a cigar store Indian. Garrett was prepared to face Midradina and the second yantz when they arrived, only it wasn't Garrett she was furious with.

"I would expect something like this from him." Her hand flipped violently in Garrett's direction while she talked to Freet. "Not such irresponsibility from you as well. You will return immediately."

"No," Garrett exclaimed in real dread.

"Yantz say?" Freet asked coolly.

"You have exceeded acceptable tolerances of the liberties allowed you."

"Yantz say?" he repeated in the same tone while Garrett withdrew to watch.

"I say," she told him haughtily. "I gave you an order."

"Only Midra," he answered rudely. "No speak for self. Speak for yantz, Thornn."

"I have the authority."

"When they say. Ask them we go back."

"You ask them," she retorted childishly.

Freet was unimpressed. He squatted. "See me; see no go. They want, they force."

The yantz didn't move. With those eyes of theirs it was difficult to tell if they were even observing what was going on. Even when she spun to face the one behind her, neither yantz showed any change. She did. Her fury did a rapid alteration to slack-mouthed shock and back to fury. She left fast enough to ruffle her stiff gown in the breeze she created. Her yantz accompanied her, leaving Freet stoned-faced and Garrett with a twitch at the corner of his mouth.

"You planned that," he accused. Freet dipped his chin. "Why? What are you up to?"

"Later," Freet answered as the remaining yantz drifted closer to them.

"It can't hear you."

Freet grunted and watched the yantz stop a foot from Garrett. It extended one hand towards him and just hung in the air puzzling both Freet and Garrett.

Freet suggested, "Want see shield, maybe."

"They never bothered asking permission before," he said, but he had the same feeling and pushed the blanket down further. The yantz moved closer to rub its hand over the shield. "I wish there was a way to talk to them." Freet grunted again while he rolled Garrett carefully to his side so the yantz could reach the back shield. "You do that well."

"Roll patients many times."

"With a yantz?"

Freet shrugged and maintained a stoic attitude until he had returned Garrett to his back. His mouth dropped open when the yantz hovered over Garrett and extended its arm out to touch Garrett lightly on the cheek. That astonished him enough. Then Garrett touched the tiny hand. The yantz turned its hand to close its fingers around Garrett's finger.

"That was Bud," Garrett explained as the creature disappeared.

"You have named them?" he exclaimed.

"Only Bud," he said, his brow drawn down in puzzlement.

"Why only one?"

"He was the one that stayed with me. The other four came and went." He didn't say aloud that only one had touched Freet or fed Freet essence. Despite the outcome, the process still made his stomach heave. He could still see the yantz tongue flicker in and out of the wound. The thought of four or five of them doing the same to him caused him to shudder involuntarily.

"What is it, Garrett?" Freet asked in concern.

With a weak smile, Garrett told him, "It's just that every time I think of bonding, I think of vampires or ghouls."

"What are those?" Freet asked.

Before Garrett could answer, Midradina reappeared, even more furious than she had been before. "Not only have you irresponsibly left the ship, you have compounded the carelessness." She turned directly to Garrett. "The equine must be returned to the ship."

"I didn't turn her loose."

She clenched her fists and hissed, "Do not again attempt to place the blame on the Glemm. It is, and has been, with Mystaleah. I made certain before returning."

"I didn't do it," he repeated as stoic as Freet. He would not tell her Glemm had just been with them and expose Mysty's protective lie.

"Him sick," Freet pointed out.

"Then you did it," she accused.

Freet gave her that face carved of wood look. He knew as well as Garrett that Glemm had to have returned to the ship with her the first time. "No can move cage," he told her tonelessly.

"Neither can the Glemm," she shot back.

"Or me," Garrett retorted.

"You..." She shook her shoulder as if someone had put a restraining hand on her. "...will..." In exasperation she twisted to face the yantz. She obviously did not like what it said anymore than she had the time before. She waved her hand and pointed furiously at the men. She didn't like the outcome and left without another word.

"Tell yantz," Freet called after her, "need more masks."

"Throwing a little salt in an open wound?" Garrett asked in a whisper while she glided out of sight.

"No know meaning."

"Don't give me that no know crap either, speak English."

"Better no do with ears to hear."

"If you mean Glemm, it's—"

He was going to say Glemm had gone back with Midradina when she had returned the first time and somehow gotten to Mysty before she did. He would have been wrong. The instant its name was said, it appeared. It sat on Garrett's ankles, a rather grim reminder of his condition since he had been totally unaware of it.

"How be here and there?" Freet asked.

"It moves fast. The only other explanation would be there are two of them—oh, no." The last accompanied a double bob from Glemm. "There are two of you?"

Glemm answered no, making Freet say, "Maybe no can count."

The glemm showed it could by bobbing twice just as a second glemm appeared at Freet's feet. Its sudden appearance and close proximity made Freet jump back several feet. His exclamation didn't translate, but it did shock the glemm at his feet back into camouflage.

Garrett couldn't resist teasing, "Ah, you scared it."

"No so funny," Freet retorted.

The glemm reappeared, again at his feet, and Freet again did a long jump. Garrett still teased, "Careful, it will get you."

"No so funny when strangle."

"That was only because…" Garrett's mind ran ahead of his words. He looked back at the glemm comfortably nestled in the space between his ankles. Mysty's Glemm would not touch or be touched by anyone else unless it was an absolute emergency. Yet the one on his legs was obviously comfortable with him just as the other one was attempting to touch Freet. Garrett didn't like the direction his thoughts were going, but had to ask. "Are you Glemm?" To answer, the glemm squirmed to be more comfortable. "Now wait a minute..."

"Careful," Freet mimicked, "it will get you."

"I'm not the one who is being followed," Garrett pointed out tersely.

"No want pet!" Freet exclaimed and backed away as the one attached to him moved closer.

"Neither do I, I don't plan on being around long enough to enjoy one."

"Think have anyway," Freet grumbled while still being stubbornly pursued.

###

With persistent questioning they learned they both had a glemm, whether they wanted it or not. Glemm had reproduced two of itself, one specifically for Freet and one for Garrett. "Others?" Garrett asked, again with dread.

The glemm bobbed and bobbed and bobbed until Freet cried, "Six more—with nine of these creatures there will be bedlam."

Garrett stared thoughtfully at the glemm nestled on his legs. "Each one for someone in particular?" The glemm bobbed twice, and Garrett shook his head. "They're like familiars."

Freet gave up trying to escape and endured the one on his feet. "These are something from your world?"

"Usually cats, fiction, witches—they created them or bound them to them using something of themselves." Garrett ran his hands through his hair. "Hell, I'm so tired I can't remember how that went."

"You do need rest, but first I would ask this familiar is something repulsive?"

"No, not really, it's just—just…"

He drifted off, and Freet asked, "And the others that you mentioned, vampires and ghouls, they are repulsive?"

Garrett felt silly and defensive and said, "They're fiction."

"And Peggy?"

"Yes, what are you getting at?"

"A prejudice, perhaps, from what was written about creatures similar to these."

Garrett laughed, a short and shallow one to accommodate his lack of lungpower. "Why not, Chief? If the gods were real, why not demons and spirits?"

"That is how you feel about the yantz, they are demons and spirits?"

Demons of hell and evil? No, that wasn't how he felt. He shook his head. "How do you feel about them?"

"I do not know. I am confused. Before it was always hate. Now I am not so certain they are loyal to the Thornns. I feel they wish to help us."

###

Wanted or not the glemms made themselves right at home and proved to be a source of distraction, amusement, and aid to Garrett. They were smaller than Mysty's Glemm and obviously younger. Their antics were typical of those of any child. They snooped into everything, chased, pounced on one another, rolled in wrestling matches, and dropped wherever they were when they were exhausted to curl up to sleep together.

After watching it crawl into Freet's pack to investigate its contents, Garrett named his Mischief. Mischief fetched and carried for Garrett. His pride was saved in that he didn't have to ask Freet for the simplest of things, and Freet did not have to make so many trips for those trivial items. Mischief proved to be so efficient that Freet felt secure in leaving Garrett alone for a short time. Peggy's ambling had taken her out of sight. He wanted to check on her. He also, though he didn't mention it to Garrett, wanted to find Boss; if Boss was close enough to locate in the short time he was going to allow himself to be gone. He felt certain that having Boss around would help keep Garrett's morale up.

Garrett told him to quit hovering like a mother hen. Freet had already left a fresh mask, water, and one pain pill on a small table beside him. Everything was in easy reach, and he was going to take a nap as soon as he felt the first twinge of one pill wearing off and took the other. Naps were easy for Garrett. That told him more about his condition than anything. He was weaker than the first time. Even if he had the use of his legs, he could not have gotten up, a fact that would have distressed him had he planned on spending more than a week or two as a cripple. He could stand that long for the yantz's sake.

He was so weak he fell asleep before he took a pill. A dream began immediately. Lamphin was there. Garrett saw Lamphin clearly, he heard Lamphin, but the man he looked at did not move his mouth to speak.

"To reach you is easier now that we have connected once," Lamphin explained. "Only I need come, and I have done so to wish you well and a speedy recovery from us all." His dignified demeanor broke when little black hands pulled up his robe. He actually smiled.

"Oh, you've got one too," Garrett told him with a chuckle.

Lamphin held the glemm in his arms. "We are confused. When first it appeared we thought to return it only to discover there are three which show no desire to leave us."

"A present from Mysty's Glemm."

"What are we to do with them?"

"Damned if..." His breath caught in a twinge of pain he ignored and went on. "...I know. Just..."

"What is it, Garrett?" Lamphin asked in sudden concern.

A scream answered him. Garrett heard the scream without knowing it came from his throat. All he knew was pain everywhere, all encompassing. His body convulsed with it in wild spasms, each muscle and limb with a mind of its own. The violent contractions threw him off of the bench and knocked over the small table. The items laid out so carefully for his use scattered. A black hand snatched up the single pill and tucked it into Garrett's mouth.

The pain stopped as suddenly as it had begun, but Garrett couldn't draw in a breath. Mischief tried to help. It pushed a mask over Garrett's face. Garrett couldn't draw air in. He was on the edge of consciousness when Freet jerked him up, wrapped his arms around him and drove his fists into Garrett's diaphragm. Something filled Garrett's mouth, but his first attempt at a breath choked him. Still choking, he passed out.

He regained consciousness slowly, and Garrett knew time had passed. He didn't know how much. Freet still held him, arms around his chest, but the two of them were on the floor. His legs were stretched out in front of him, and his head rested on Freet's shoulder. When his vision cleared, the first thing he saw was Mischief, pressed up against him, arms wrapped around Garrett's.

"Rest quietly," Freet warned, his voice strained.

There were yantz. They hovered and showed their distress in erratic jumps. Their state didn't ease when Garrett whispered weakly, "Chief?"

"Must rest."

"What happened?"

"Be silent. I tell."

Garrett tipped his head in agreement. The yantz calmed down, but Freet was still so upset he couldn't remember English, and Mischief was about to cut the circulation off in his arm it held so tight.

"Lung rupture. Bonding no finish, break loose, block airway." He shifted slightly and drew Garrett up a little more. "Move shield back to right side. Now be careful no rupture other lung."

"Promise," Garrett whispered sincerely. He didn't want to go through that again. "Better leave a pill in my hand." He took a deep breath and continued. "Or give one to Mischief to carry."

"No leave alone again."

Garrett half-smiled and half-shook his head. That was an argument that would have to wait until he felt stronger. "Feels like I've had essence," he said sleepily.

"Yes, sleep soon."

A nod agreed, and the crisis, the yantz decided, was over. All but one left. Garrett raised his free hand though with his strength he only managed a few inches. The yantz glided forward and dropped to take Garrett's hand up in two of its.

"Sorry, Bud," he murmured as he drifted off.

The yantz lowered Garrett's hand gently to his lap and disappeared. Freet stared after it with a very thoughtful look on his face.

###

"That was a neat piece of understatement, Chief," Garrett complained pettishly.

Freet leaned back in a new piece of furniture, a chair of gray pipe frame with a sling seat of cloth. "You had been told when in bonding without light or shield the pain is excruciating."

"It was from my toenails to my hair."

"You exaggerate."

"Felt like it," he grumbled. "Why did I hurt where there isn't bonding?"

"Say feel like."

Garrett's eyes narrowed. "Anytime you switch back to your own language, I get the feeling you're trying to hide something."

"What to hide?"

"My legs hurt," he answered in preoccupation. "They didn't hurt like that when…"

Freet spoke quickly when Garrett broke off to stare at him, "No say, fear give false hope."

"They couldn't have bonded it," Garrett exclaimed. "It's closed."

"Open, take tumor." He raised a hand to stop Garrett's retort and switched back to English. "It had become a tumor, encased in a cartilage-like substance, but they did not know if bonding it would be successful. They have never done such a thing before."

Garrett's thoughts reeled. He grabbed a hold of one. "I felt it go when that club hit me."

"The damage is being repaired," Freet stated emphatically. "Before you had no feeling in your legs. Now you have pain."

"They're still paralyzed," he argued in confusion.

"The bonding is not complete." Freet leaned forward. "While you absorb this information, there is something else I feel you should know; Midradina does not know of the injury to your back."

"She knows everything they know," he stated in distraction while he still attempted to absorb the information Freet had just given him. The yantz had bonded his back.

"She knows what they tell her. They have not told her. They have deliberately kept it from her."

"Why?"

Freet shrugged. "I communicated with them through her before. Not in words since. Mord was useless. He said nothing could be done while you drown in your own blood. I pushed him aside..."

"I bet that was a neat trick."

"Figuratively speaking," he answered to dismiss what it would have taken to move Mord. "The yantz, your yantz, did not interfere as I inserted an airway, but there was too much blood. When I told her the other lung must be opened they reported, through her, the transformation was not complete. I had hoped they had been delaying the removal of the shields for your protection, but it was not complete. Still it had to be done until the hemorrhaging could be stopped. Even then they did not know if your right lung would function sufficiently. The only way to find out was to put you under their light and remove the shield. It was with great relief when you drew your first unobstructed breath, yet I knew there was much to be done. I expected much argument. Midradina expected them to refuse. She was horrified at what I proposed. She could not believe when they accepted I would open your chest to tie off the bleeders." He grinned suddenly. The change it made in the stern-faced man was amazing. "They told her to leave. She was galderka."

"That didn't translate."

"It is slang. To say she was upset is sufficient. Our little Midra is learning many new emotions."

"And that tickles the hell out of you."

"If this means it gives me pleasure, you are correct. For too long she has not known she is human or what it means. You have taught her much in a very short time."

Garrett smiled slightly over that. "All I've done is irritate the hell out of her."

"Yes, something she has never felt before. She has always accepted what the hunters have done; the killing, the violence, and brutality as something to be expected and unchangeable. You have done the unexpected, many times over. You have disturbed her perception of hunters and humans." He lost his smile. "You have disturbed our perceptions of one another and mine of the yantz."

"I haven't done anything, Chief, except cause trouble."

"Good trouble. You have come among us with fresh eyes, seeing what we have seen for unnumbered years, yet seeing them not as we see them. You do not blindly accept things are as we've been told or that it is how they must remain."

"The Karoz is the one you ought to thank then. He's the one responsible for me being here."

"I have a theory on that I will discuss later. For now I do not wish to tire you over much, and we wander from the subject of your treatment. We have always been told and always believed the yantz to be incapable of independent thought, reason, or emotion. Now I know it cannot be true. I have watched you with them and them with you. They can be touched, with affection, and they touch in ways other than bonding or killing. And after telling Midradina to leave, they did not allow me to open your chest. They bonded. The bonding stopped the hemorrhaging."

"Quickest little tongues in town," he quipped while he suppressed a shudder.

"I thought it a specialized appendage for the purpose, not a tongue." Freet said with a shrug. "It does not matter. What matters is what they did. After they had made certain earlier I understood without the light you would be in pain on your right side without the shield, they began to slowly withdraw the light. They knew I had been giving you something to block your pain and waited for me to do so again. Reason, Garrett, they do think."

Garrett agreed with that. "They had to know there was some reason I stopped disturbing them."

"They also knew something more was wrong," Freet added. "They were waiting for me to show them what must be done."

"No, you were waiting for the opportunity to show them," Garrett retorted in sharp accusation. "That was what you meant when you said not now. You've been planning this all along."

"It was not something I planned," he stated coolly.

"You said you wouldn't interfere."

"If the paralysis was permanent, and you choose death over living that way, I would not interfere even though there is still much for you to teach—"

"I'm not a damned teacher," Garrett said hotly. "Don't you or anyone else depend on me for anything."

Freet's mouth went out of sync with his words. "No depend you."

"No, and you aren't the one flat on your back and helpless."

With a tip of his head, Freet asked, "Want let die, let yantz die?"

"You could have kept me alive without screwing with my back. You didn't have the right to do that without my permission."

After a moment of quiet study, still in his own language he asked, "Think right have yantz treat, no tell?"

"That's what I said," he said with a guiltily start. Freet didn't know he'd been treated by the yantz. That couldn't be what he meant.

Freet half-shook his head. "No mean you. Regret take me yantz, no tell?"

Garrett shifted to the defensive. "That was different," he grumbled. "You weren't in any condition to ask."

Freet shot back. "You no tell after!"

"I had to agree to not telling you, to get them to do it."

"No say—"

"Stop talking that gutted gibberish to me." He clawed at both ears, pulled the translators out, and threw them. "If you want to talk to me, talk so I can understand you."

Freet stood and calmly picked up the two earpieces. He rolled them between his fingers and looked down at them. "I do not speak gutted gibberish. My language is as full and complete as your own. The translator is incomplete, omitting words it does not know. It is unfortunate. I feel more comfortable with my own words, more able to express my thoughts."

"Just drop it."

"In your words I fear I do not convey my thoughts concisely."

Garrett really didn't have any trouble understanding him in either language, with or without the translators, not that he mentioned it. He just always understood what Freet meant even when he tried not to. "Look, I know what you did and why. Your why is all screwed up. I'm not some damned hero or a Messiah going to save you all. I'm just me."

"Just you was who I wished to save for myself, no other." He raised his hand to stop Garrett's retort. "Allow me to speak without interruption that causes me confusion in your language." He sat down and still rolled the translators in his fingers. "My first thoughts were selfish. Mord's abilities as a physician are minuscule. As I worked I did not wish for you to die because I did not wish to lose your company, but I again became a physician. I was the physician with a single purpose to save a life. Not until you were breathing, and I found myself alone with the yantz, did

I realize you would not appreciate the life we gave you, for you it would be a torturous wait for the bonding to be complete so you could end the life we labored to save."

With a sigh, he shifted position. "When before I said not now, it was not the yantz I think of. It was small hope held that the change within your body from the substance would prevent further damage."

"You said that before," Garrett said wearily.

"No think—not think of yantz—"

"Okay."

Freet shot to his feet and jabbed a finger at Garrett. "I no do more than you, same reason."

"Probably," he admitted.

"Why angry?"

Garrett shrugged. He wasn't sure why he was angry, nor did he think he wanted to attempt to explain all the emotions raging in him. Instead he asked, "Why did Midradina tell you?"

"Did not." He sank back down in his chair. "Know I was dying. Know Mord no healer."

"You guessed?" he exclaimed.

"Logical deduction." He leaned forward and placed the translators on the table. "Why they not want any to know?"

"They didn't explain, but I do know they didn't know if it would work." He told him the rest and ended with, "Even Mord and Mysty don't know, Chief. They thought I took you back to your quarters to die."

"How explain I lived?"

"I didn't. It was the first time that poison had been used. Everyone just figured it wasn't as good as the chemist thought it was."

"No surprise. He isn't much good at anything. Stomach ache maybe."

"Then how did he come up with something like that?"

"Not by self, I think."

"He said the formula just came to him. I'm thinking telepathy."

"From what I know of it, it does not function that way."

"The Phogatres said there was a new voice, talking to them in their own language."

Puzzled, Freet asked, "When have you spoken to the Phogatres?"

Garrett grimaced slightly. "I didn't talk to them actually. I dreamed talking to them." He grimaced again and suppressed a yawn. "It just seemed real."

"It is said Mystaleah has dreams to show him of events he was not present for," Freet said with a speculative look Garrett missed.

Garrett nodded and suppressed yet another yawn. "He told me about one of them, but I didn't watch an event. They talked to me. They were talking to me when I had that bad spell."

Freet grunted over Garrett's choice of words to describe near suffocation and excruciating pain. "I think this is something we should discuss more after you have rested." He leaned forward to exchange Garrett's mask. "I will have the yantz bring a new cylinder of oxygen for you."

"I prefer the masks," Garrett told him sleepily.

"Then I will have Mord prepare more."

Garrett nodded and asked, "Why didn't Dina come?"

"She did. She does not move as quickly as the yantz. You were asleep while she was here." He paused slightly before he asked, "You have great feeling for her?"

"I'd like to take shake some sense into her most of the time." His thoughts became jumbled as he drifted with sleep. "I can't look at her without thinking of Carolyn, what she'd look like at that age. I won't ever be able to see her grown now, not ever." His eyes closed. He sighed heavily and whispered as he drifted off, "Probably wouldn't like me any better, father or not."

XIV

"Just lay, wait die?"

Garrett shrugged and rolled his head to face the opposite direction. Somewhere in the back of his mind a thought nagged that he should regret the frustration and worry he caused Freet. Depression drowned it out. The nagging part told him Freet was right. The depression told him not to bother. The returned feeling in his legs no longer gave anger or hope. There was no strength in them to breed too much fatalism.

When Freet jerked him up and threw him over his shoulder, Garrett asked wearily, "What are you doing?"

"Need bath."

Garrett hung there, ready to endure. He was apathetic until Freet put him down by throwing him into the pool. A spark of interest ignited when he lost the mask, and a gasp choked him on a mouthful of water. He drew his first deep breath to give his flailing arms the strength they needed to overcome the lifelessness of his legs so he could pull himself to the side of the pool. As he struggled, his anger ignited, and he went after Freet. As he levered up and flopped the upper half of his body onto the deck, Freet stepped back out of reach making Garrett even more furious.

"You son-of-a-bitch, I'm going to break your neck."

"Have catch first," Freet told him calmly. "Be better exercise, bring strength back to legs."

Garrett screamed at him. "It took three years the last time, damn you! Can't you understand that, three years to walk right again?"

"Then the pain made longer. Now no pain."

Garrett pushed up, saw Midradina and her yantz, and pushed backwards instead, sinking in the water up to his chest. "What do you want now?" he demanded.

Midradina ignored him and moved to stand in front of Freet, saying something in a singing sound Garrett couldn't understand. "I don't have the translators in," he told her tersely. "If you want to know something about me, ask me. I know you speak English."

Her eyes narrowed for a moment before she told him, "You will give me foolish answers that I do not understand."

When Freet raised his hand to his ear Garrett glared at him. He knew damned well Freet didn't have a translator in that hand any more than he had the times he had faked it before to shut him up.

"I'll try to simplify it for you," Garrett told her hatefully.

She clenched her jaw briefly before stating, "You have no use of your lower limbs."

That was obvious as far as Garrett was concerned. He stared belligerently at her and waited for more.

"How," she asked tersely, "did this happen?"

"That Karoz swings a mean club."

She spun to face Freet. "Why was I not told?"

"Ask yantz why no tell."

She spun to do so with hardened features before she turned back to Garrett. "You said before. It happened to you before, yet you walked. How can life be given back to dead limbs?"

Garrett's anger was gone as quickly as it began. Midradina was angry, but more than angry, she was hurt. He suddenly knew where the story that she had no legs had come from; it was a distortion of the fact that she had no use of her legs, and he knew the reason for the metal undershirt she wore. She always looked like she was gliding because she wore some kind of anti-gravity device.

"I'm sure they didn't keep it from you out of cruelty," he told her gently. "Not all spinal injuries—"

"How is it done?" she cut him off with.

"Do you have any feeling in your legs?"

"I have..."

Tears flooded her eyes, and she spun off. Garrett called after her. When she didn't stop, he told Freet, "Go after her. See if you can help."

Freet shook his head dumbly. "No can force treatment."

"You did me," he retorted.

"You no have yantz on shoulder." He stared after her and told Garrett absently, "Kick, make legs stronger." He straightened and with his show-nothing tone of voice and his chiseled face, he asked, "Why no tell?"

His face and tone may not be showing anything, but Garrett knew when Freet was upset because his English wasn't clear. He told him honestly, "I didn't realize it until just now."

Freet's eyes narrowed as he studied Garrett closely, and Garrett knew why. This last bout of depression hadn't been as long as the ones before, but it had been as severe, and there still wasn't any reason for it.

"What makes me give up like that, Chief?"

Freet shrugged.

"Hell of an answer."

Freet grunted and unhooked his belt. "Think perhaps you know as well as me."

"I don't," Garrett retorted. He rotated to put his back to the pool edge and hooked his elbows on the edge to stay up while Freet stripped. "I just know it isn't me."

"Glad you are back."

A splash announced Freet's entrance into the pool. The time it took for him to swim from one end of the pool to the other gave Garrett an opportunity to think. Not only of his behavior, but also of everything that had happened, things he hadn't thought of, examined, or questioned while the depression held him. It was as if part of his brain kept going to sleep or closed off in some way. Anger had opened it this time, excitement at seeing Peggy free the first, both like flipping open the lid to Pandora's Box.

"Someone," he told Freet as he popped up in front of him, "is trying awfully hard to kill me."

With a grunt, Freet brushed his wet hair back from his face. He reached under the water and pulled one of Garrett's legs up. Garrett gave only the resistance he was supposed to. He'd had too much practice at therapy to forget.

"It's more than just the hunters accepting me." Freet grunted again. "There's a conspiracy afoot." Freet only grunted once more. "Are you going to give me some input or just let me flounder around in the dark by myself?"

"You talk; I listen."

"They tried," Garrett retaliated, "to make me think it was you."

"Say this before," he stated indifferently. "Say you did not believe."

"Yeah, well, how many hunters use a crossbow like yours?"

"None I know of." He straightened to ask, "You wake from a stupor to be frivolous?"

"You've noticed it's like waking up, like part of me was asleep. You said a lot of it was medications, but the only medication I'm taking now is yours."

"It does not do this." Freet thought about it for a moment and ended with a shrug. "It seems like a drug, but none you are taking now would do this. I can only think perhaps it is a residue of some variety from the drugs before."

"We had drugs that caused flashbacks." Garrett thought of the stories he had heard of LSD. "It would be Mord's. His is the one that caused depression. As to being frivolous, I've got to balance silly with serious, Chief, be a little crazy to keep from going insane. I had an Irish grandmother. Maybe I got it from her. The Irish always said they had to laugh to keep from crying."

"You wish to cry?"

"No, I want to laugh, and it's damned hard to do when some asshole is instigating morons like the Karoz and Dapho to kill me while they hide and take me down with my friend's weapon. It's not nice, Chief, and I don't like not knowing who or why."

"I do not know who or why."

"Then let's talk it out, see what we come up with."

Freet returned to the exercises. "The Karoz and Dapho, men of low mentality, easily manipulated."

"Add Zalano, he's the one that set the Phogatres..." That reminded him of something. "Where are the glemms?"

"Gone." Freet looked down quickly. "For a full day, they have not shown themselves."

"Probably off exploring."

"I do not think so." He looked up, guilt on his face. "The creatures make me uncomfortable, so close to only one yet in communication with each other. I..."

"Wait a minute, what do you mean in communication?"

"It is the only explanation."

"Of what?"

Freet took a deep breath and blurted out, "The glemm made me return. It pulled at me until I followed. I should be grateful it saved your life, but to know they communicate over distance with it always so close, always watching, I—"

Garrett cut him off with, "What did you do?"

"I shouted at it."

"What," he growled, "did you shout?"

"To go away, I am apologizing. I did not believe it would go or it would take your Mischief as well. Why is it you wish the creature now?"

Thinking of the Phogatres had made him think of the glemms and reminded him that he hadn't seen them lately, but his mind had taken off on a new train of thought as soon as he did think of them, especially after what Freet said. The glemms seemed telepathic; the yantz, Vo, and the Phogatres were. No, he had dreamed the Phogatres were and that they had a glemm each. For the second time he had remembered the strange dream as real.

"Call for it maybe," Freet suggested when Garrett failed to answer.

Garrett called, and Mischief appeared several hundred feet outside the house, loping happily.

"There Nuisance too," Freet remarked, a little too casually for Garrett not to guess he was relieved to see it.

"Good name," he commented with a wry grin. Freet had accepted it enough to give it a name.

Nuisance leaped on Mischief. Mischief rolled, shot straight up in the air and pounced on Nuisance. They rolled through the grass, wrapped together until Nuisance broke free, shot into the air backwards and spun, all three hands on one side rapping Mischief before it hit the ground in a run. The chase was on. Through the grass they ran onto the slick floor of the house, slipping and sliding around a pillar trying to get traction. Mischief, in the lead dove under a bench. Nuisance leaped to land on Mischief. The rough and tumble wrestling match took them to the pool's edge, over and out of sight in the water.

Both men watched the spot where they disappeared, waiting for them to surface until Garrett asked, "Are they drowning?"

Freet watched for a second longer before he pushed through the water. The glemms were on the pool bottom, still clinging to one another. They continued to grasp one another in frozen terror as Freet lifted them from the water and sat them safely on the pool edge.

Garrett exclaimed, "They look like kids."

What appeared to be a round ball with two eyes covered with fur wasn't. The water had packed the fur against the tiny face with a neck and body beneath, a very human looking face and body. They only thing inhuman was all that hair and a spare pair of arms.

Freet questioned. "Human babies?"

"Yes." Garrett pulled himself along the edge to them. "They're scared half to death. Mischief?" He laid his hand gently on one tiny head. "It's okay now. You're safe."

Mischief turned its eyes towards him and began to tremble. The other remained frozen in terror.

"Tell Nuisance it's okay. You're both safe now." Nuisance stayed frozen. "Chief, talk to it."

"I—"

"We'll talk about it later. For now, calm it down."

"Be fine now," Freet told it stiffly with no change at all in the glemms. He inched closer to repeat the words. Still no results. Not until Freet touched the back of his fingers to Nuisance's head did it roll its eyes towards him. "Safe now."

Both glemms released their hold of the other and turned to their humans to reach out with their top two arms. Each man took his creature, Freet with awkward reluctance, and Garrett with one arm since he couldn't let go of the pool edge without sinking. Mischief crawled up to Garrett's shoulder, top arms around his neck. Nuisance clung to Freet's chest.

Garrett told Freet. "You look the way I felt when Mysty's Glemm wrapped itself around my neck."

"Before it strangle?" he asked tightly.

"Nuisance isn't going to strangle you."

"What I do with this?" Freet implored. "Can not have on ship. Others see, think I…I—"

Garrett laughed. "Hell, I don't know. Forget about the ship and just stay here maybe." Both glemms bobbed twice in unison. Garrett looked at Freet's astonished expression and knew his own was the same. "Is that what you want?" Both bobbed twice again. "Would the yantz let us?" Neither answered. Garrett shifted Mischief to look straight in its face. "Mischief, can you talk to the yantz?" Mischief answered no, disappointing him. "Hell, I thought I was on to something."

"If tell truth," Freet pointed out.

"It is." He sat Mischief on the deck. "Get me out of here, Chief. I've got a bunch of questions to ask."

###

Garrett's legs came back. They just came back. One night he could barely move them on his own; the next morning all feeling and most of the strength returned. His legs were back, and he hadn't needed a mask since Freet had thrown him in the pool. A few days of concentrated workouts and he felt ready to tackle the ship again.

The information he had been able to get from the glemms by asking yes or no questions frustrated and confused him. The glemms were telepathic among themselves. They couldn't talk with the yantz, or Vo, or even their humans. The glemms didn't know if the Phogatres were telepathic, but each did have a glemm with no explanation as to why. That left three unaccounted for, along with the mystery of the sudden population explosion.

More information from Freet was very interesting and probably significant. The house they were staying in hadn't been cleaned by Freet. It cleaned itself the same way the ship did. The first time Freet found it, it had seemed as cold and unwelcoming to him as the one Garrett had found. The difference was the circumstances. He had been desperate for shelter to recover from injuries from a bad fall and the bad weather of a winter month. He'd passed out on the floor and woke to warmth and cleanliness. It stayed clean and stayed at a constant temperature even with the open windows and breezeways, and Freet always returned to the same place, something only Freet, as far as he knew, could do. He had found a control panel in the portal room. He had learned how to operate those controls—by his thoughts in English, and since then he had not taken a hunt anywhere else except for those times he had accompanied Garrett. He could set the control board for any of the four planets at anytime a hunt was called despite what hunt was designated for him by Midradina. There were only four sets of controls, no Earth, which led Freet to a theory.

He didn't believe Midradina had followed the Karoz as he had stated before, but that the Karoz had somehow blundered into a trip she was taking or one on which she was accompanying the yantz. Garrett rejected his speculations as to their purpose. No matter how much Freet argued, Garrett saw himself as a result, not a cause. There was no rational reason for the yantz to be in search of him.

Despite disagreeing with Freet's reasoning on the last, Garrett was sure he had learned some valuable facts and was determined to put all of it together to get a whole picture. His intention was to go straight to Mysty and his glemm. His plan went slightly awry when his anxiousness took him out of decontamination without waiting for Freet and into Zalano and gang coming from one direction with Gunian approaching from the other. Zalano was in a nasty mood and snarled what he had to say, which drew an equally nasty amount of accompanying snarls from his companions.

With a smile, Garrett told them, "Just a minute. I don't want to miss any of this." He dug the translators out of his pocket and nodded to Gunian while he carefully turned his back to the wall. Yantz shields or not, he didn't trust them. "Now, what did you say?"

"Coward," Zalano spat out.

"Boy," Garrett said with a grin and shake of his head, "that was clear enough. Figure you've got a reason for saying it?"

"The day will come when you will not have the yantz to hide behind."

"Right and when they don't have a leash on me, we'll see if your guts are as big as your mouth." He turned to Gunian. "You got any objection to being number two on that list?"

"I can wait," he returned blandly.

"What list?" Zalano demanded. "What do you speak of?"

Garrett ignored the question and rambled. "I choose rapiers. Since I don't know the territory that well, I'll forego my right to choose the place. Who will be your seconds?"

"You babble like an idiot," Zalano retorted. "Nothing you say makes sense."

Garrett dropped his jaw in mock astonishment. "You don't...?" He shifted his eyes to Gunian. "You know what I'm talking about, don't you?"

Something flickered in Gunian's eyes. It was too quick for Garrett to identify, but not what Gunian said. It was pure bluff. "Of course," he answered in the same monotone, "but it will be necessary for you to explain it to him."

Garrett knew Gunian didn't know. He also knew, even though Gunian's expression and tone didn't change, Gunian was enjoying the play.

Garrett gave him a nod before he turned back to Zalano and was a little startled to see how quickly the crowd behind Zalano had grown, but he kept his idiot smile in place. "I'm talking about a duel of honor, honor being something you guys seem a little shy of along with any real courage. All I've seen is back-shooting, attack in a pack, no one on one, face to face. That's what I'm challenging you to. As the insulted party, I have choice of weapons and place. I'll let you choose the place. Our seconds, two for you and two for me to make sure there's no cheating, can settle on the details, unless you show a coward streak and refuse."

"I do not refuse." Zalano stiffened proudly and smiled viciously. "Who will be your seconds?"

From behind Zalano two men flew out of place and scrambled out of the way. Two Phogatres took their place.

"No," Gunian exclaimed. He blinked and quickly dropped back into his no show mask. "They have attacked you. I will not forfeit our meeting through treachery. Myself and the Freet, if he will agree."

"Sure," Garrett mumbled in preoccupation. If the glemms were right, and a dream hadn't been a dream, something he was unaware of was going on. The Phogatres told him they would appear to be his enemy. Offering to stand for him, if that was what they intended, didn't make sense. Neither did the growing crowd behind the Phogatres and Zalano. It made Garrett think of what the Phogatres called their false voice and made him wonder if that was why they were there.

On the other side two men stood behind Gunian; Vo, confused and worried to such a degree that his hands were bare, and one man as tall as Mord. This last Garrett recognized only because of his size. His hair and beard were trimmed, his clothes neat and clean and the mad look was gone from his eyes. It was the maroon chimp's owner.

"I don't think they were offering their services," Garrett told Gunian in distraction. He didn't know if it meant they were there on his side either.

"Perhaps I was mistaken," Gunian answered his eyes on the crowd.

"I sure hope to hell they aren't making any mistake or that none of them are as stupid as the Karoz and Dapho." He turned back to Zalano to face him squarely. He knew his back was safe, and his expression was one of dead seriousness. "Did you see the Karoz or Dapho when the yantz got through with them?"

"There are no yantz here," Zalano answered smugly.

"There wasn't when it all started then either." Garrett addressed the crowd. "You guys have been here for years. You've all heard what they can do, but maybe you haven't seen it. I have. This thing…" He tapped the shield on his chest, "…is like having a piece of someone else inside of me. I can't get rid of it, and I can't control it. As long as this is here, they own me, and they will tear you apart because of it. There is no in-between for them. They…"

They—in the body of one—appeared so suddenly Garrett jumped sideways. His reaction, although from tension not from fear, did more to validate his words than anything. Garrett did nothing to change the impression it gave. He backed up against the wall away from the hovering yantz and stayed there while the crowd quickly and quietly dispersed. Garrett, Vo, still minus his gloves, Gunian, and the chimp man were the only ones who remained. Garrett nodded to the chimp man, waved at Vo, and asked Gunian in an insouciance he didn't feel, "Something you wanted to talk to me about?"

"We must speak of arrangements for the duel," Gunian answered with equal aplomb.

"Come by my quarters later."

Gunian left with a nod. He went in one direction, and Freet appeared, coming from the other. The chimp man saw Freet and left at a fast pace, no doubt with the memory of Freet with a knife in his hand. That left Vo, the yantz, and Garrett. Freet looked at them questioningly.

"Something has happened?" Freet asked.

"No," Garrett told him with a laugh to release some of the tension, "but I sure thought something was going to."

"Me as well," Vo said with feeling as he pulled his gloves on.

Freet did not miss the significance of the gloves. "What?"

"Mob hysteria." Garrett pushed away from the wall. The yantz moved to keep the same distance between them. "And why," he asked it, "are you here?"

"Midradina searches for you," Freet supplied, which explained why it had taken him so long to catch up.

"Where's she at?"

Freet tipped his head towards the yantz. "It will lead you."

Garrett laughed. Everyone had assumed it had arrived to protect him, when its only purpose had been to act as a guide. "Good timing," he told it gratefully.

"For what?" Freet asked.

"To play the boogey man."

Freet rolled his eyes in exasperation and turned to Vo. Vo gave an answer without being asked. "Had it not appeared, they would have attacked, I am sure. Had they attacked, he would have been dead."

"We don't know they would have." Garrett tried to pass off the incident. "I appreciate you staying though."

"Small assistance that I was, I was happy to give." He took a deep breath and straightened. "There is a matter I would speak to you of?"

"Sure."

"In private perhaps?"

"Can it wait?" he asked.

"Yes," he said with a nod. "You would come to my quarters?"

"Sure," he agreed, but asked, "Alone?"

Vo told Freet, "You are welcome at any time."

Several minutes later, as they followed the yantz, Garrett started to chuckle. "I think I know what Vo wants to talk about. I wouldn't be at all surprised to discover he has a 'nuisance' to deal with."

"You would not seem the best source of information on…." Freet broke off when a wall opened before them.

"One you haven't been able to open?" Garrett asked.

"Yes," he answered tightly.

"You use English?"

"Yes."

"Maybe you need to know Thornn," Garrett suggested.

"That thought has occurred to me; also there may be security codes."

"That makes sense. No doubt there are restricted areas for higher ranks."

"You have been military?"

"Career army," Garrett answered soberly.

"You were a superior rank?"

"An officer." He smiled grimly.

Marsha had liked being an officer's wife. She liked the prestige and pomp of the social life until the image was tainted by an unpopular war with anyone who served in it bearing the stain. She had raged at him not to go until he had grown weary of explaining that he didn't have a choice. She was certain he could receive some kind of deferment. She even, in an effort to force it, was willing to sacrifice her body to become pregnant, certain that would gain him a deferment. He had wanted children; which she knew and had found excuses to delay until she thought she could use it as a way to save what she thought of as her position in life. What an irony she didn't know she was pregnant until after he had shipped out. He hadn't even known she was until three months later when they shipped him home in pieces.

"I have reminded you of something sad?" Freet said, breaking into his thoughts. "This is where you were injured?"

"It was a nasty war, Chief. What got me was not on a battlefield but in town, a kid on a bicycle with a bomb." What he didn't add was how much worse it could have been if the standard orders weren't that they were to wear body armor whenever they left their barracks.

"This is the first you have spoken of a mate."

"She decided I was too much high maintenance," Garrett said curtly. "Did you have divorce in your world?"

"She terminated your bonding because of your injury?"

"They told us I would never walk again," he said tersely. "She married some lawyer."

"To raise your child?"

"How did—what did I tell you?"

"You spoke of a Carolyn you would never see at Midradina's age as you fell into sleep," Freet told him. "You think she would not like you as father."

"I've got to learn to keep my mouth shut," he grumbled.

"Is wrong I know this?"

"I've never talked about it to anyone."

"Perhaps feel better do."

"I doubt it. I've never seen her. All I've ever seen is a picture her grandmother was kind enough to send me." Garrett gave one of his sardonic grins. "You wouldn't think it to look at me, but she's a beautiful baby. She doesn't look anything like me, fine boned, blond hair, and blue eyes."

"Your eyes are blue."

"Her grandmother said they weren't the same," he stated and lapsed into silence.

Freet filled the silence. "My daughter resembled me, and as you say, you would not think so to look at me, but she was beautiful."

"You'll never see her as a grown woman either, and you never saw your son. It's no wonder you hate them the way you do."

Freet only nodded as another wall opened. His hatred was not something to discuss in front of their Midra.

###

"No," Garrett exclaimed, surprised by Freet's suggestion.

Midradina ignored him and asked Freet, "Why do you suddenly believe a guard is necessary?"

"It isn't," Garrett retorted.

Freet ignored him also. "Be battle yantz no appear," he told her.

"Don't mind me," Garrett grumbled. "I'm just the one you're talking about."

"We do not wish to trespass on your privacy," she told him seriously. "We only wish to protect you."

"And others," Freet put in, "from stupid."

"Suicide," Garrett corrected absently with his gaze on the young woman.

"A compromise," she suggested, uncomfortable under his close scrutiny. "Only when you leave your quarters."

"Okay," he agreed in preoccupation. It fascinated him how in his dream the worn out picture of a little girl had interchanged with the woman he looked at. It was the blond hair and blue eyes, he thought, as he straightened and pushed the thoughts away to concentrate on what they was saying. After getting over the surprise, what Freet said made sense.

"You agree?" she asked in shock.

"I'm not likely to forget what the yantz are capable of, even if it was after the fact."

Midradina bristled. "They prevented the Karoz from killing you. This will prevent any possible further injury to you and death to others."

"That's why I agreed."

"Without an argument?" she asked suspiciously.

"I don't like death and killing."

"No," she murmured thoughtfully, "you do not."

"Not all men are alike," Garrett told her soberly.

"You," she returned without malice, "are unlike any."

"If you didn't assume the bad in them, you might see more good."

Midradina looked down. Thinking he had embarrassed her, Garrett changed subjects and mood. With a grin he asked, "What did you want to see me for?"

With a sigh, she lifted her gown a few inches from the floor. "What," she asked as a pair of black, liquid eyes peered out at them, "am I to do with this?"

"Three," Freet commented dryly.

"Three," she exclaimed. "Why have you done this? Do you not know—?"

"I didn't do it," Garrett denied fervently. "Glemm did and not because of me. I never said, in front of it or otherwise, that all of us needed a glemm."

"Say need pet maybe," Freet suggested.

"I did not," he retorted with a 'whose side are you on' look for Freet. "Maybe you did. You're the doctor. You know the therapeutic value of pet companions more than I do."

Freet grunted and pointed at Midradina's dangling feet. "Why let atrophy, no exercise?"

The gown dropped. "Mord has examined me. There is nothing to be done."

"Mord," Freet retorted, "is not a physician."

Midradina's jaw dropped. Garrett grinned. Freet looked from one to the other of them in puzzlement, not realizing his angry retort had been in English.

"You have taught him your language in so short a time?" she asked in astonishment.

"You taught him English a long time ago," Garrett told her.

They were all silent while the significance of that sank in. Her face went slack from surprise to stiff as she said, "So you know I am from Earth. I understand now that your words of differences had more meaning, but I have no memory of the man who attacked me with which to make a comparison."

"But you know what he did."

"Yes, and in the beginning I believed you to be as savage."

Garrett gave her a half-smile figuring that was as close as he was going to get to an apology. He changed subjects. "Let Chief look at your legs. He is a physician, and he may be able to help."

There was a slight wait while she consulted with the yantz before she lifted her gown to knee height. Her legs and feet were, as Freet had already said, in a state of atrophy with the shrunken muscles barely covering the prominent bone structure.

The glemm scrambled away as Freet knelt for the closer examination. He pushed each foot up until she winced with pain and then straightened each knee until she winced.

"Well?" Garrett asked anxiously as Freet backed a short distance away from her.

"It is criminal," Freet answered tightly, "that therapy was not begun immediately."

"Ignorance more likely."

"Then nothing can be done," she stated.

"Much can be done," Freet corrected sharply. "Much that should have been done long before."

"Easy, Chief," Garrett said quietly.

Freet clamped his jaw and looked at the floor until his anger was under control to tell her, "Others fail you. Now up to you."

Garrett told her, "It's hard work, and you have to stick to it, no matter how frustrated or discouraged you get."

"Tell exercises," Freet ordered as he headed for the wall they had come through.

"Where are you going?"

"Create room. Make brace. Stretch legs straight."

"Wouldn't it be better with her there for measurement?"

"Meet tomorrow," Freet called back as the wall opened, and he walked through it at a fast pace.

"He is still angry?" Midradina asked.

Not sure what was wrong, Garrett told her, "He's just preoccupied thinking of what has to be done."

"He seems angry."

"That's just the way he is." He dismissed it uncomfortably. "While I'm here, I'd like to talk to Mysty."

She led the way. "The glemms, you did not jest with me, there are now four?"

"Nine, if what we got out of ours is accurate."

"Nine?" Midradina looked horrified. "Why has Glemm done this? It has never reproduced itself before. Now there are so many, and I do not know what to do with this one. I tell it to go away, and it always returns."

"They can be a lot of fun and company, and it's cuter than a kitten." She looked at him blankly. "Didn't you ever have a kitten or puppy?" A shrug answered him. "You don't remember anything?"

"No, though sometimes there is a feeling of something—"

Her voice trailed off, and one hand went to her chest, just below her throat. Her fingers moved absently as if searching for something and her eyes took on the unfocused look of someone in a daze even though she continued to move down the hall. It seemed an incredibly long time before she blinked and returned to where she was.

"How old were you?" Garrett asked gently.

She answered with a shrug when she stopped to knock on the door to Mysty's quarters and call out.

"Go away," Mysty shouted from the other side. "I will argue no more."

"I do not..." She bit back her angry shout, took a deep breath, and let it out slowly to speak evenly. "Garrett wishes to speak with you."

"Garrett!" The door opened, and Mysty nearly fell on him. He gripped Garrett by the arms, shaking him. "You look so well, so well, younger, more rested than ever." He pulled Garrett inside and ignored her. "I am so happy you have returned. I was so afraid—no—no we will not speak of unhappy thoughts."

"Or hold grudges," Garrett teased.

Mysty rolled his eyes and threw his hands in the air. "What am I to do? She will not believe me. If it will not stay with me, it will not stay."

"You said..." she retorted, "...it was a good idea for me to have one."

"But it was not my idea."

"Or Garrett's, he claims," she retorted.

"Then it was Glemm's alone."

"It has never done this before. Why now?"

Mysty threw his hands in the air again. "I do not know. How many times must I say, I do not know?"

"It is your pet."

"It has its own mind."

"Excuse me," Garrett said.

She shouted, "A childish irresponsible mind."

Garrett tried again. "Now wait a minute. You—"

Mysty shouted back at her, "With a love of fun, which you would not understand."

Garrett twisted his tongue up against his teeth and whistled as shrilly as he could. He got their attention.

Mysty recovered first. "I am sorry, Garrett. This is why she was not invited in. We have already had this argument. I am not responsible for the new glemm, and it will not stay with me."

There was a definite stubborn streak in Midradina. She crossed her arms and glared. "Glemm is your pet," she repeated.

"It's not a pet," Garrett answered quickly. "It's not an animal." He turned red in the face when both turned to stare at him and continued speaking with a 'what the hell' attitude. They already thought he was nuts. "They're individuals, intelligent, and independent except for their apparent need for a human or humanoid counter part." He turned to Mysty. "You ought to see that. You just said Glemm had a mind of its own. You've known them longer than we have."

"Only one, but many times I have felt this."

"Didn't they come from your world?"

"We do not know where it came from, not even how long it had been here before it showed itself."

"Oh." Garrett considered that for a moment before saying, "It must have come on with one of the ones who died."

"Many did die," Mysty said sadly while Midradina grew very quiet.

"Is Glemm here?" Garrett asked.

"No." Mysty gave Midradina an accusing look. "Not since she shouted at it."

"It probably visits its children," she answered tersely. "It always returns."

"Children? Plural?" Mysty exclaimed. "There is more than one?"

Garrett told him, "If we got the right information from the two that showed up on the planet there are nine now."

"But—but where?"

"We left ours on the planet. She has one, and I suspect Vo does. That leaves four more somewhere." If the dream was more than a dream and Mischief was right that only left one unaccounted for, information Garrett kept to himself.

Mysty could not tell him why Glemm would suddenly choose to reproduce, how it chose who the younglings would go to, or why so many. It wasn't hard to see that both Mysty and Midradina thought Garrett had something to do with it although neither of them said so. Even Garrett couldn't help but feel that he had acted as a catalyst someway. He was, after all, the only thing new to happen to the ship except the vague something Freet had mentioned.

That thought of something vague was scary, and something else Garrett kept to himself. He hated to think that the glemms were some kind of a spy as the Phogatres had believed and were connected with the something that turned low mentality beings into mindless murderers.

XV

Garrett wouldn't have been surprised if he had dreamt of a howling mob of hunters going after him with clubs and knives. Even a dream of one of them attacking him wouldn't have been a surprise under the circumstances. Dreaming of any of the hunters would have made more sense than dreaming of Clyde Peters. Garrett had crossed paths several times with Peters in the past, Peters being one of those people who liked to hurt people and animals. On one occasion Garrett had beat the hell out of him. Peters could well harbor a hatred of him because of it, and he might also harbor a desire to beat him, but Garrett thought it would make a lot more sense for his dreams to pick someone from the ship where the threat currently existed than to pick someone so far away as a symbolic villain.

Peters wasn't a particularly tall man, but he was burly and strong. Their battle had been legendary, starting when Garrett caught him beating a horse senseless. The fight didn't last long, but it was brutal, and Garrett never gave an inch. He knew he couldn't. He knew Peters would take any advantage and, if not kill him; deliberately maim him if he had a chance. He had nearly maimed him as it was. He had been laid up for a week with his back afterwards, but Peters never ruined a horse again as long as he worked on the same ranch as Garrett.

Peters was the kind of man who easily fit the villain image, only Garrett had never run from Peters as he did in the dream nor had he ever felt such terror. He fell, rolling down a brush-covered hill before he was jerked up by Peters, but it wasn't his hand he saw reach out to scratch Peters' cheek. Nor was it his own scream he heard making his blood run cold. Peters was hitting a child, kicking the child over and over as the background changed from desert to gray. A child's voice screamed again and again, sobbing hysterically, "Daddy, daddy, help me," with each cry growing weaker and weaker. Then screams, not the child's, ripped to the core of Garrett's being as Peters' raised arm fell and then his head.

As the dream released him, Garrett shot straight up in bed. He panted and shook violently from head to foot, both arms wrapped tight around his middle. His body trembled, his gut was tied in a knot, and sickness was in his mind. He was cold with the terror he felt, and perspiration covered his body.

A small hand touched Garrett on the cheek. He turned, saw the yantz and screamed at it, "Don't you ever do that to me again! God damn you, not ever again!"

He jumped and ran, not taking time for boots. Barefoot he ran straight to the Phogatres' corridor to pound on the first door, nearly hysterical. "You talk..." he began.

Lamphin, dressed in a long robe, pulled him inside.

"...to the yantz. They're your voices. You talk to them. Tell them not to ever do that again, not ever. And you, don't any of you come at me in my sleep again, not ever. Do you hear me, not ever."

"It is the only time you hear—"

"I don't care!" he shouted. "If you want to talk to me, talk to me! Don't ever go sneaking into my dreams again!"

"You are upset..." Lamphin began.

Garrett jerked his arm free and backed away. His body still trembled, he couldn't breathe without panting, and he still felt Dina's terror.

Lamphin took him firmly by each shoulder and led him to a heavily cushioned chair. "Sit and recover."

Garrett sat with his elbows on his knees to hold his head in his hands. "Does she remember?" When Lamphin didn't answer he raised his head with his hands pressed to his temples. "Ask them, does she remember?"

There was a slight pause before Lamphin told him, "She does not."

He buried his face in his hands in relief. Only then did he think of what he had done or how he was behaving. He took a deep breath, straightened and let it out slowly, and took another deep breath.

Warhol came in with a gray glass in his hand. He held it out to Lamphin who held it out to Garrett. "This will assist in calming."

Garrett wondered how he had ever thought them cruel looking. They had the same black eyes and protruding brows, but all he saw in their faces was concern. He wouldn't have refused what they offered him no matter how bitter it tasted. He drank the liquid and leaned forward elbows on his knees, both hands holding the glass, too embarrassed to look at them.

"They wish for me to tell you," Lamphin told him gently, "they will never attempt to communicate in such a way again."

"Thank God for small favors," Garrett mumbled. With a deep breath he straightened. "I'm sorry I came in here like that. You probably thought I was crazy."

"I could see you were greatly distressed."

"Didn't it distress you?" he asked more sharply than he meant to.

Lamphin looked puzzled. "What the yantz said to you?"

"Didn't you see it?"

"We do not see, only hear, and this we would not hear as it was said to you, not to us."

Garrett wanted to hold his head again. He compromised by leaning back in the soft cushions of the chair. "I don't understand that stuff," he admitted and suddenly felt drowsy.

Lamphin eased the glass from Garrett's lax hold. "Sometime perhaps we may discuss it with you."

Knowing he was going to sleep, a knot of anxiety tightened in Garrett's chest. Even as his eyes closed, he prayed there would be no dreams.

###

The Phogatres' tranquilizer put Garrett to sleep for several hours, mercifully without dreams. When he awoke, Garrett understood why the dream had shaken him so badly. If he had just seen what had happened, he still would have been shaken, but he wouldn't have come apart that way. He had felt what Dina had felt.

"I've been scared in my life..." he told Freet later, "...but never like that, never as a child in so much pain and knowing she was being murdered." He shook himself and took a quick swipe at the sweat that had broken out in his palms. "That's what got to me. If they had just told me what happened, not shown me how it looked from her eyes and projected the emotions, I don't think I would have come apart like that." He shot to his feet to pace. "No damn wonder those two went mad. It doesn't affect the Phogatres like that. For them it's no different than talking to someone in a dark room. No different than the way they've always talked to each other. You can imagine how it would be to someone who's never had someone talk to them inside their head. No damned wonder one thought God was talking and the other went mad with no one to explain what was happening. Mysty told me she speaks to them through a device of some kind. I don't think so. While she was recovering her mind was blank of any memories that would have made them strange or frightening."

"She was without prejudices. No vampires."

Garrett let that last bit go by without comment. He sat down on the side of the bed. "But she hadn't forgotten her language. Lamphin said it took them years to learn the yantz language. It's hers. It's English. The second voice the Phogatres heard, the one telling them Glemm and I are evil, was in their own language. It talked to them, but didn't answer if they asked questions."

"Interesting, but of what significance?"

"Telepathy doesn't go through translators."

Freet waited for Garrett to say more.

Feeling his way, Garrett said, "Vo said he couldn't get anyone to hear him."

"You wish to teach Vo English?"

"That's not a bad idea, but it's not what I'm getting at. What if there's someone or some group who are telepathic, that we don't know about, who have learned enough of several languages, such as the chemist's, the Dapho's and the Karoz's to send them a specific message?"

"Much trouble for three with little influence."

"They did all right as hit men. Zalano seems to be the new one chosen for influence."

"Or the Gunian who is often in his company."

"I think he's too smart for it." After Freet's grunted answer, Garrett asked, "What have you got against him?"

"There is much about him which he hides."

"The same could be said about you."

"He is dangerous."

"So are you," Garrett teased and then sobered. "I'd like specifics if you have any."

"I do not," Freet answered. "I have always known he is dangerous and mistrusted him."

"I'd like to feel him out a little more. Where are his quarters?"

"Better he comes here."

"The yantz will be with me, and I've got an excuse for going. Nothing will happen."

"Yes, an excuse," Freet said curtly. "I think now you know that you will live, you will be more careful. Instead you are more reckless."

"Challenging Zalano wasn't reckless." Garrett started for the door. "I'd whole lot rather face him, one on one, than a mob in the hallway. Are you going with me?"

###

One look at Gunian's sleep-filled face and Garrett apologized. "I guess I do have my days and nights reversed. I'll come back later."

"No, I..."

In a sleep haze Gunian was at a disadvantage. His mind wasn't working as quickly as usual. He looked from Garrett to Freet to the yantz guard and back before he straightened and returned to character. "You are difficult to find, and I am awake now. I will come to your quarters shortly."

"No sense in that. We're already here and..."

There was a movement behind Gunian. Garrett knew what it was immediately. With a grin, he jabbed Freet with an elbow and pointed. "Nine."

Freet's look was one of total disbelief. "Why him?" he exclaimed without thinking.

"It is not by choice," Gunian returned tartly. He motioned both of them in. As soon as the door shut behind them, leaving the yantz in the hall, he asked Garrett, "You will return it to the Ancient?"

"It isn't his. It's yours."

"I do not want it."

Garrett struggled to not laugh while he told him, "That's the same thing Chief said."

"And did as much good," Freet grumbled.

"You have one?" Gunian asked incredulously while tipping his head to see if Freet wore translators.

The look of disbelief on Gunian's face over Freet having a glemm coupled with the stiff 'I will not show' reaction on Freet's was more than Garrett's sense of humor could take. He burst out laughing. "You should...have seen Chief when... when Mischief and...and Nuisance..."

"Garrett," Freet implored tersely.

"...skidded across...the floor...."

"They fell into the pool," Freet told Gunian flatly.

"And sank like rocks. Chief had…"

Gunian turned to Freet. "This was humorous?"

"Was not. They would have drowned."

"No, no, not that." Garrett dropped one hand on Gunian's shoulder and pointed at Freet. "It was the look on his face when he had to pick Nuisance up. It was like it hurt."

Freet snapped, "You did not think it was humorous then."

"That," Garrett pointed at Freet, "is something that's funny later, when you remember things," He grinned again. "Like the look on your face." He turned quickly to Gunian who appeared to be intensely studying something on the floor. "You need to know though, they're terrified of water."

Gunian shook his head. "This will not be an issue. You will take it back to the Ancient."

"Wouldn't do any good. If you want to get rid of it, you'll have to kill it."

That startled both men, but Gunian was the one Garrett watched. He jerked around, his mouth opened to exclaim, but he caught himself and jerked up straight. He coldly studied Garrett for a moment before saying, "That was a test of some variety?"

"Some kind," Garrett admitted and took a seat on the bench. "Only I'm not worried about you killing it. Neither is it, or it wouldn't be here."

Garrett leaned back against the wall, looking over the dreary, gray room. The bench he sat on and a matching one on the opposite wall were the only furnishings in a narrow room that had been formed by moving the interior wall several feet from its original position. Behind that wall was where one might begin to get a picture of the man the Gunian really was. The room they were in was a facade, just as his face and voice, which never showed emotion other than insolence or disgust.

"You're found out, Gunny," Garrett told him. "But we won't tell on you, if you don't tell on us."

"Found out?"

"Discovered." Garrett stretched his right leg out to dig his battered cigarette pack out of his pocket.

"What have you discovered?"

"You're not all hard ass." He looked at the bent condition of the cigarette he finally fished out of the crumpled pack and grumbled, "I'm going to have to create me a hard cover case."

Gunian's interest shifted. "It is easy for you to do?"

"Just thinking what you want is about as easy as you can get," he answered off-handedly while he concentrated on straightening the cigarette without breaking the paper. He looked up as he placed it between his lips to find both men studying him. "What?"

Gunian waited for Freet to answer, easily accepting that Freet's past behavior had been as much a façade as his own. Freet waited for Gunian until Freet finally shook his head. He sat beside Garrett and told Gunian, "He assumes all that comes easy to him is easy for all."

"You have never told him it is not so simple for others?"

"It is—"

"Wait a minute," Garrett interrupted with. "Are you saying you can't create?"

"I am saying," Gunian answered evasively, "there are those who can not."

"Or can not easily," Freet added.

Garrett knew neither of them fit into either of those categories. "Why?" he asked with the feeling it was important.

Gunian moved to sit on the opposite side of him. "The one thing I have heard in common from those who complain of the machine not working was their inability to visualize what it is they wish to create."

"Mind pictures," Garrett murmured.

"I believe it has something to do with the frequency of brain waves."

"In volume or band?" Freet asked.

"Band." Gunian leaned out to speak to Freet "It is quite possible that to create a mental image a unique frequency is used, present in some and not in others. I have observed that intelligence seems to have little bearing on the ability. Some of high intelligence can't while others of low intelligence can."

"Like who?" Garrett asked.

"I can name three who are no longer with us because of their boasting of their ability." He looked at Freet again. "Do you think it wise not to have warned him of this?"

"You are the only one he has discussed it with."

Despite the fact he had opened up to speak with Gunian, there was a veiled threat behind the words. Gunian didn't miss it. "I will—"

"Pictures!" Garrett exclaimed and sat up straight. "Mind pictures! Glemm?"

More accustomed to Garrett's behavior than Gunian, Freet asked. "What is it?"

"A connection," he told Freet and asked Gunian, "Where is it?"

Gunian pointed down at his feet, and the glemm materialized.

"Is that how you pick us," Garrett asked excitedly, "by mind pictures?" It didn't answer. Garrett rephrased the question. "By our ability to have mind pictures?"

"You expect it to answer?" Gunian asked.

"Maybe no speak Earth language," Freet suggested dryly.

"Do you understand me?" Garrett asked. The glemm bobbed twice, but before Garrett could ask more, Gunian exclaimed, "It answered!"

"Only yes or no, but—"

"If it understands the question," Freet stated tonelessly.

"I did not realize it could comprehend language," Gunian said quietly.

"It's a lot like talking to Freet," Garrett retorted.

"Better than talking to you, no jabber back," Freet returned.

"Ha, ha." Garrett knelt in front of the glemm. "Is it something in the frequency of our brains that makes you pick us?" Two big black eyes gazed back at him. The body didn't move. "Is there some reason you pick— chose one person?" It answered yes. "Why?" It didn't answer. It couldn't the way Garrett had asked the question. "I'm going to teach you little buggers how to write," he grumbled.

Garrett started again. After a lot of teeth grinding between questions the closest Garrett got was that Mysty's Glemm picked who the next glemm was produced for. As soon as it was born, it went instinctively to that person, already knowing their language as well as any language any of the other glemms knew and any glemm following would know. As far as mental images, it either could not grasp the concept or refused to answer.

Garrett gave up and turned to Freet. "Now tell me they're not like a familiar."

"I do not know what a familiar is."

"Pinpan," Gunian said in a daze.

"What's that?" Garrett asked.

"A creature of fiction." He jerked his eyes away from the glemm. "It is created with the blood of the buyer by Calandry to do their bidding. Perhaps it was not just legend. Perhaps the ancient gods did exist."

"Same as he said," Freet commented. "Is Calandry evil?"

"No." He shook his head slightly. "Calandry was the ancient God of safe journey. An offering to him insured that Pinpan would accompany the traveler to protect them from evil. When the journey was complete, it returned to Calandry."

"This is a familiar?"

Garrett shook his head. "Not exactly. I like Gunny's Pinpan better."

"A familiar was evil?"

"It doesn't matter if it was," Garrett said with a slight shrug. "They aren't familiars or Pinpans. They're glemms, similar to but not quite like any of those."

They weren't fiction either, unless everything was, a thought Garrett hadn't had for a long time. He'd slipped into accepting all of it and all of them as reality. More, he had accepted their problems and set out to solve them. He couldn't very well ignore them when their problems were trying so hard to kill him.

The thought prompted Garrett to ask, "Why are they trying to kill me?"

"They are afraid of you," Gunian answered simply.

"Why?"

The answer for that wasn't as simple. "There is the obvious," Gunian said thoughtfully. "You have shown yourself to be alert and responsive to attack, cunning, using whatever weapon is available to you and calm, showing no panic or fear." He blinked, and his gaze became more focused. "I believe there is more than the obvious. They fear you in groups, but the groups do not unite."

"They united in the hall," Garrett pointed out.

"They seemed to, almost as if a signal had been given," Gunian agreed. "Yet I can not discover who it is who speaks to them all."

"What do you know about telepathy?"

"I am not personally acquainted with telepathy, but I can not see how it could be. Too many are involved, so many languages."

"Guess they can't all be telepathic," Garrett mused.

"Perhaps they need not be to receive a message, but the message must be understood." Freet said, "It is not probable so many languages could be learned even if more than one—"

"Damn it," Garrett exclaimed and shot to his feet. "I don't care if it's one or twenty. I don't want anyone planting ideas in my head that aren't my own, and no one has explained yet why someone wants me dead. And don't tell me they're afraid of me. Why, do they think I'll methodically murder them all?"

"You would recognize a foreign thought I believe," Gunian stated calmly, "or discard it with logic and reason, but that is not what they fear. They fear you will prevent them from killing the yantz."

There was a stunned silence broken by Freet with one word, "Impossible."

"They no longer believe so," Gunian told them. "Hatred is growing for the yantz and an idea that it is not impossible to defeat them. You have isolated yourself too much. You do not go among them, and you have without a translator until now to understand what they say."

"Son-of-a-bitch," Garrett said softly. "It's the damned translators." He laughed shortly. "We've gotten so involved in mumbo-jumbo we overlooked the simplest way." Both men looked at him blankly. "What easier way to talk to three hundred different men in three hundred different languages than using the translators?"

"None," Gunian answered, "but I have been unable to discover any mention of anyone talking—"

"Not talking, broadcasting. We know they're transmitters, why not receivers as well, maybe on a subliminal level they aren't even conscious of hearing." He pointed to Freet. "You and I aren't affected because we don't wear an implant. You...," He pointed at Gunian, "...if you heard it at all, you'd do just as you said I'd do with telepathy, recognize it isn't your own thought or ignore it through logic. It's the poor bastards like the Karoz and Dapho that are manipulated."

"You know they are transmitters?" Gunian asked. "This is why you do not wear them?"

"They track you with them," Garrett said absently while his thoughts jumped ahead. "If their objective is to destroy the yantz then they want control."

"Of the ship," Freet finished the thought for him.

"That doesn't make sense," Gunian put in. "Only the Thornn can operate it."

"As well as the translators," Freet said with a nod.

Garrett's brow furrowed. "Unless the Thornn aren't in control any more," he said thoughtfully.

"I do not understand," Gunian said.

"Nor I," Freet added, "unless you were correct and one of their specimens took control from them."

"That wasn't what I said," Garrett snapped.

"Perhaps accurate in retrospect. It would seem the Thornn wish to take control from the yantz."

"Someone does." Garrett looked from Freet to the Gunian. "If he's right, should we warn the yantz?" he asked uncertainly.

"Are the yantz any better than the Thornn?" Gunian asked.

The glemm jumped out in front of Garrett to get their attention. It bobbed twice, went up to the tips of its toes and bobbed twice again. It did it three times to convey an urgency all three recognized.

"Must be very bad, the Thornn," Freet murmured.

Glemm bobbed twice again.

"It kinda makes you wonder, if we're locked in or they're locked out," Garrett said with a grimace.

"Ask," Freet urged.

The look Garrett gave him told him he wasn't too sure he wanted to know. He did so with trepidation, and it was warranted. "Did the yantz take the control from the Thornn?" he asked and groaned when Pinpan bobbed twice.

XVI

Freet only agreed to let Garrett go ahead without him because of the yantz guard. He, Gunian, and Garrett all felt that whatever was brewing had not yet reached the point of being a challenge to the yantz, not after the way the crowd had dispersed when one appeared on the verge of them attacking Garrett earlier. They believed there was still time to warn the yantz, but as a precautionary measure, Freet was going to remove Gunian's implant and replace it with audios. Garrett, anxious to get something started, was going to the Phogatres. They recognized the new voice as false, and they could talk to the yantz.

When he overtook Midradina on her way to the common room, he couldn't resist teasing her. "Still have your friend?"

"Wrapped around my ankles," she responded stiffly. "It is either that or it hangs on my skirt."

"Give it a name yet?"

She rolled her eyes to look at him and blushed slightly. "Cute seems appropriate as it is a name you favor for such creatures."

"I did not have anything to do with it," he denied again.

The first scream pierced through his ear, brain, and soul. Garrett knew even before he saw the first yantz fall that it was too late for a warning. The attackers had found a litch. Garrett forced himself to move despite the screams in his head that diminished in split second counts until there was a soul shaking silence. He pushed a shock-frozen Midradina ahead of him, down the corridor and into his quarters as the first hand of the nearest attacker grabbed him to keep him from following. The door closed, locking her safely in, as he turned to fight.

Years before, the army had taught him to kill with his hands. Garrett killed. A crushed larynx, a quick snap of a neck, but Garrett couldn't win. He could make them pay, but not win had he been at full strength. Even as his arms were imprisoned and an arm locked around his neck, Garrett made them pay with his feet. One doubled over, screamed, and held his groin as the weight of several others crushed Garrett to the floor. One more paid as Garrett pulled free one leg and drove his heavy heeled boot into a face. Then only Garrett paid.

There wasn't any pain, but there was weakness and semi-consciousness as they put him on his knees, arms twisted behind him. The same men that held his arms stood on his legs to hold him for Zalano.

While blood dripped from Zalano's chin from split lips and a broken nose, he growled in Garrett's face, "Open the door."

Garrett realized then that it was Midradina they wanted. They hadn't been trying to kill him out of fear he would protect the yantz. They had tried believing that because of his connection to the yantz he would protect her, or that he would protect her on his own volition. Whatever their reasoning, they had been right, but now she was safe and would continue to be so as long as he didn't open the door. Nothing they could do to him would force him.

Garrett had no worry over his ability to hold up under torture. Freet's pill was in control of the pain center in his brain, and he had taken one just that morning. That meant he had forty-seven to forty-eight hours. Zalano and his gang would tire long before then. They would kill him long before the pill wore off.

They began immediately. With a signal from Zalano, one man began on Garrett's left hand. He bent a finger backwards until it snapped. Garrett flinched from the pressure and the sound, but his mind was still on Midradina. She had to get to Freet. Freet was the only one who could be trusted. The Phogatres had warned him not to trust them without asking the yantz. The yantz were gone, leaving a disturbing void. Vo still had the implants as did Mysty and Mord. That left only Freet who wouldn't be influenced, and Freet would give his life for her. Freet was in love with her. That was the reason behind the looks Garrett had seen and Freet's behavior when he had discovered how badly neglected her legs were. Freet would protect her, secrete her away through the portal, rehabilitate her legs, live happily ever after, but first she had to get to Freet. Freet couldn't get to her through that mob.

Garrett called out for her to hear, "Cute will guide to help. Go to Pinpan."

"What does he say?" questioned the men around him.

"It is gibberish," Zalano shouted to quiet them.

It wouldn't be gibberish to the glemm with Dina. She was no longer a Midra. She was Dina, a young woman frightened and alone. She didn't know what Pinpan was, but she knew Cute, and Cute knew Pinpan. It knew anything the other glemms knew.

"It can walk through walls," he shouted. With Dina's help it could walk through walls. She could move any wall as easily as she opened a door. "It will lead you to help."

Zalano realized whom he was really talking to. He dropped to one knee, grabbed Garrett by the throat, and hissed, "She can open the door as easily as you."

He pulled Garrett by the hold of his throat while others raised him by the arms to put him in front of the door. They repositioned him, on his knees, with one arm twisted behind him, the other stretched out on the side, elbow braced against a knee to break.

"If you do not wish..." Zalano said to the door, "...him hurt more, you will open the door."

Garrett jerked free of Zalano's hold of his throat to shout, "Don't do it!" He hoped she had already gone, but he fought to avoid Zalano's hand in case she hadn't. "They're going to kill me anyway." A hand from behind clamped over his mouth. Garrett bit. "Follow Cute."

His struggles threw him and the man holding him to the floor and snapped his arm. Zalano dropped his knee on Garrett's chest. His hand clamped over Garrett's mouth, and the objective of Garrett's struggle changed. Men held his legs, men held his arms, Zalano's weight was on his chest, and Garrett still fought. Another set of hands clamped down on his head, one hand under his chin, forcing it up. Garrett fought in desperation to keep the needlepoint of that knife from penetrating his larynx. He didn't need Zalano's hissed words to know what Zalano was going to do.

Zalano leaned down, his face inches from Garrett's. "You do not need your voice to open the door."

Garrett stopped fighting. He couldn't stop them from destroying his voice. Once done, he couldn't warn or guide Dina in what to do if she was still there. He could make sure she had no reason to do what they wanted. As he ceased to struggle holds loosened in reflex. As the thin blade penetrated his flesh, Garrett reared into the blade and twisted his body.

Zalano was too fast. The blade cut, but not deep enough to reach the spine or sever the jugular. And damn Zalano. He drew the knife back with a laugh.

"Bastard," Garrett said, but it was only a gargle.

"You would rather die?" Zalano laughed again. The knife came back, touching lightly at Garrett's temple, and the hands holding him tightened. "With one quick thrust there will be no more concern that the cold-hearted bitch would sacrifice herself to save you."

The point pressed, enough to break the skin, enough to cause a trickle of blood, but not enough to kill. Too many hands kept Garrett from driving the knife in. Zalano had no intention of killing him, not yet, or of allowing Garrett to kill himself. He enjoyed inflicting pain too much. The knifepoint cut a thin, bloody line to Garrett's ear.

"Or here, just a thrust," Zalano tormented.

The knifepoint flicked the translator plug out, the point penetrated the ear canal. Zalano eased it in slowly until there was a pop, and Garrett's ear flooded with the liquid warmth. The knife moved again to cut a thin line to the corner of Garrett's eye.

"Here as well," he taunted and raised the knife straight up. "Are you not going to try for it, Earthling?"

Garrett glared back. He wouldn't give Zalano the satisfaction of seeing him struggle uselessly.

Zalano teetered the razor-sharp knifepoint on the bone edge of the eye socket with enough pressure to pierce to the bone. "I could end this quickly. Open the door." The door didn't open, the knife slipped, entered the eyeball, and Garrett felt another gush of warmth.

"Why do you protect her?" Zalano asked while the knife cut a line across Garrett's forehead, around the temple to his other ear. "Does she rush forward to save you?"

The knifepoint traced slowly around Garrett's ear. He could barely see for the watering of his remaining eye, but still glared back. He refused to flinch as the knifepoint moved to the corner of his second eye, but he couldn't prevent a jerk. Zalano didn't hesitate or taunt. One quick jab and Garrett was completely blind.

"You do not need to see to know what I am going to do." Zalano pushed up off of Garrett's chest. "I am going to mangle you, Earthling, pet of the Midra, limb by limb."

He did just as he promised. Methodically and coldly he had Garrett's arms and legs broken, but Zalano wasn't done. Neither Dina nor Garrett had opened the door though Zalano knew Garrett was still conscious. Zalano committed his last vicious act. He whispered in Garrett's ear. "It is your brain that must live, Earthling. That is what is important, and there are worse things than death now that the yantz no longer live to treat you and Mord can do no more than keep you alive."

With a flick the translator was gone. Zalano's laughter needed no translation. The last sound Garrett would ever hear was Zalano's laughter and a pop. The hands that held him disappeared, and the horror of Zalano's words became clear.

###

Even though Dina had started her desperate run the moment Garrett had told her to follow Cute, she had not reached Freet and Gunian soon enough. Even with the men knowing something desperate was happening because of Pinpan's behavior before the back wall opened to reveal a hysterical Dina, they were unable to cover the distance in time. They had run as fast as they were able through walls she opened. Still they were too late in fighting off the attackers and dragging Garrett inside his quarters. Nothing could be done for Garrett except give him the release he asked for.

Tears burned at Freet's eyes. He would never forgive himself for letting Garrett go alone. Freet clamped his jaw against the sobs that choked him as he watched Garrett's feeble, torturous movements to fold two fingers under, the only way he could ask for three pills. While Dina gently cleansed the blood from Garrett's face, Garrett concentrated every bit of strength and will to manipulate two fingers, forcing the message from his traumatized brain through his mutilated arm to leave three fingers straight.

The quick eyes of Gunian saw it. He saw where Freet's eyes were fixed and asked in a bare whisper, "It is a signal?"

"A way to death," Freet whispered back huskily.

"Understand…able."

The slight break in Gunian's voice was his only show of emotion, unless one considered the absence of his normal insolence. He deliberately looked away as Freet pulled the leather pouch from beneath his belt, and Freet's hands trembled to open it. His hand clinched tight around the three yellow pills he separated from the others. As soon as he slipped them into Garrett's mouth, Garrett would be totally gone from them, but to stay as he was…

"I should not have done as he said," Dina wept. "I should have gone out to them."

Freet shook his head, not trusting himself to speak, and knelt beside Garrett. In his left hand he clenched the pills, knuckles white. His hand shook.

Gunian answered for Freet. "They would have done the same."

Freet moved his hand forward while Gunian talked to hold Dina's attention. She would never understand what he was going to do. He had to act while she didn't see, while she didn't suspect.

"He knew this," Gunian went on. "Had you done as they wished, they would still have done this."

The pills were gripped in the tips of Freet's fingers. As one they would enter Garrett's mouth. In seconds it would be over.

With his fingertips two inches from Garrett's mouth, Freet hesitated. There would be no reversal of what he was going to do. Garrett would be gone forever. While there was life—no, there was no hope, not there, not with the yantz gone, not with the inadequate medical facilities. Nothing could release Garrett from a world of dark and silence.

A quarter of an inch from Garrett's lips the agonizing decision was taken from Freet. Two thin, black arms knocked Freet's hand away. The three pills flew from Freet's fingers. One was caught in the air, and Cute scrambled into Dina's lap to lean out and slip a single pill into Garrett's mouth.

The prevention of his actions did not relieve Freet of anguish, not when Dina realized what Freet had been about to do and gathered Garrett protectively in her arms. She pulled him to her chest and looked at both men accusingly.

"You want him dead!" she cried.

"No!" Freet shouted no longer able to control his own tears. They filled his eyes and rolled down his cheeks. He shot to his feet, drew a deep breath in a vain effort for control and released it in jerks. "It is..."

He couldn't continue. He turned his back to her, hands clenched.

"It was," Gunian supplied, "Garrett's request." He held up one hand, the thumb and forefinger tucked under. "The only way he could ask."

"He is," Freet forced out, "in agony."

"There is no pain," she countered furiously. "Your pill stops the pain. They told me, the yantz told me, your pills stop the pain."

With his back to her, Freet didn't see what Gunian watched in stunned silence. Dina held Garrett to her chest and stroked his hair. Blood from his wounds smeared her gown where he laid limply against her. More amazing she rose straight up from the floor with Garrett locked in her arms. Garrett was unaware of it; deep in sleep, just as he had been unaware the first time, when paralyzed with hunter's drug and his eyes closed of how she had carried him onto the ship. She rose until her own feet and gown edge were high above the floor to prevent his feet from dragging and drifted backwards. As the back wall slid open, she told them, "He must not die."

"To live…like this," Freet answered brokenly, "…is worse…than death."

"He must not die, Chief."

Freet jerked. The first time she had ever spoken his name hit him like a blow. She would never understand and would hate him forever for what he had to do, no matter the personal cost. A deep breath and a set jaw prepared him. He took the pouch from his belt again and turned, unprepared for what he saw.

"He must not die," she repeated as the wall closed to shut them away from her and Garrett.

XVII

It was unsafe to walk the corridors. Dina traveled the back halls behind the quarter cubes. Freet was not difficult to find. He was in the first place she looked, though it was only luck she found him at rest, not on the hunt.

Freet had withdrawn deep inside himself. To control his grief and anguish he had buried them along with the love he had begun to allow himself to feel for her. He was what the hunters were supposed to be, a man who lived only to kill. He no longer wore the shirt to conceal the knives strapped to his forearms, and he carried his crossbow with the quiver strapped to his thigh to prowl the halls in search of prey. He had seen enough faces when he and Gunian had burst through the door of Garrett's quarters into the corridor to drag Garrett inside. Freet had identified many quarries. In three days, six of those had died. Many more would. He was patient and had an eternity to hunt. Garrett had an eternity to suffer. Freet would eat to retain strength. He would sleep to maintain stamina and clearness of mind. He would not feel anything more than the hate that drove him, and any feelings he had once harbored for Dina were as buried as the tears he had shed.

"He will not take substance," she said timidly after opening the back wall to his quarters.

Freet rolled off the bed. "If you will give me command of the walls, it will be useful to me."

"I need assistance in his care."

"No."

She moved towards him and cried, "He must not die."

Freet moved away. "For whom must he live?" he asked coldly. "If it is for him, let him die. If it is for you, continue to prolong his suffering."

"It is for us all. He is—"

"He is in agony."

"There is no pain."

"Not of the body," he agreed and strapped on the quiver.

"They are such small wounds. They will heal quickly."

"Small wounds well placed to do exactly what was done," he told her brutally. "The Garrett we know is gone. The body is useless. He is crippled, blind, deaf, and mute." His voice hardened even more. "He can not walk, he can not move his arms to touch or hold, he can not see, hear, or speak. He is imprisoned in darkness and silence. There is no pill to cure that."

He snatched up the crossbow. Sleep was no longer what he wanted. He wanted revenge. Zalano still eluded him. "Will you give me the command for the walls?"

"Will you help me care for Garrett?"

Freet answered by exiting through the door. He could help. He could insert a feeding tube, by-passing Garrett's refusal to eat. It would keep him alive, and Garrett would hate him for it. He would hate himself for it, for giving into the part of him selfish enough to wish to keep Garrett alive. If he was absent, Garrett would know he had no part of what was being done, and Freet was not certain he could again force himself to move the quick and painless death to Garrett's lips. As long as there was life—no. He could not allow that faint hope. The yantz. were no more. There was no hope of repairing the devastating wounds. Mord would not suddenly become gifted with miraculous techniques needed to perform the delicate type of surgery that would repair severed vocal cords, reconstruct eardrums and fragile inner ear bones, or make new eyes. Freet couldn't do it, and his abilities as a physician were far superior to Mord's. Even if Garrett's senses could be restored, the damage to his knees and elbows would leave Garrett more helpless than the paralysis that had been so abhorrent to him. To be crippled, deaf, mute, and blind was— no, he would not think of it. He could not. Just as he knew he could not cope with seeing it. Yet the fates were against him. He was forced to go to Garrett when Dina found him again.

Despite the danger of the halls, Dina came. Without guards or protection, she hunted him down in panic. "He is gone," she cried hysterically. "I was gone so short a time. They could not open the doors, but he is gone."

Freet's first instinct was to run in the same panic she had. The second was to do nothing. They could do no worse to Garrett than they had already. He quickly realized that they could. They could add pain by holding Garrett until the medication wore off.

"Take me the shortest way," he ordered.

She took him through the walls, back to where she had hidden Garrett away, afraid to trust any of them. Not even Mystaleah or Mord had been allowed more than visits from a safe distance once Mord had finished with stitches, casts, and bandaging. No one was allowed close enough to touch him she so feared they also would attempt to give Garrett what they considered a merciful death. She alone, with only Cute, cared for him.

"I left Cute with him. It is gone as well," she told Freet tearfully, drawing a nod from him while he stared at the large bed, oblivious to the feminine and plush furnishings of Dina's private quarters. When he didn't move she grabbed him by the arm with both hands. "You must go after them."

Freet shook her hands away. "I will while you go to Vo and Gunian for help to search."

She held her head in her hands and headed for the wall they had entered from. "I did not think. I have wasted…"

"You must open the doors," Freet reminded her.

The doors opened; she disappeared through the wall, and Freet still stared at the bed, at the way the soft, shiny cover stretched out across the floor towards the wall. Garrett hadn't been taken. Garrett had rolled out of the bed, crawled to the wall, and down the wall, using it for guidance to find the door. Without sight, without equilibrium it would have been a monumental task for a man with arms and legs. Yet Garrett had done it as well as open a door he should not have been able to open and found his way around a second large room where he bumped into and upset a delicately carved table on the way. There was blood on the soft, deep piled floor covering where Garrett had dragged himself through a small, shattered glass vase. It gave Freet an easy trail to follow into the hall.

Garrett hadn't gotten much further. The sight wrenched at Freet's insides. Garrett pulled himself up on the elbows held rigid by the casts on his arms and dragged his body, weighted down by the heavy casts on his legs. His bandage-shrouded head was against the wall for balance and direction. If Dina had any concept of Garrett's strength and determination, she would never have left him alone even for a minute. He had somehow sensed when she left and had taken advantage.

Freet didn't rush to him. He couldn't let go of his roiling emotions in even so slight a manner. He moved slowly, knelt beside Garrett as he came up on his elbows again, rolling him gently up on his arm. He quickly pressed his medicine pouch against Garrett's fingers, all that were exposed from beneath the cast, so Garrett would know who it was. Garrett stopped struggling, and his fingers hooked to grasp the pouch.

Freet damned Mord's stupidity in those casts. They were twice as thick as they needed to be and extended much further than necessary, which added to their weight. Both legs were encased from the toes to the top of Garrett's thighs, chafing the skin in his genital area. Both arms were encased from his arm pits, where they were chafing his sides raw, covering the ends of the broken left fingers and to his knuckles on his right where the pouch laid, trapped between fingertips and cast. The thickness prevented Garrett from even bending his fingers and thumbs properly, making him feel even more crippled and helpless. He wouldn't have any strength in his hand, but he would have been able to hold to Freet's arm instead of clawing for a hold with his fingertips while still clinging to the pouch with two fingers.

Freet knew what he would do. More than once Garrett had called that ship a gray tomb. It would not be Garrett's, not if Freet could prevent it.

###

The glemms were on the green planet. Their ability to transmit information from one to the other would lead Dina to them. Freet took Garrett instead to the poison planet for a quiet time to sit together and silently say good-bye.

Being hauled around on Freet's shoulders had not been easy on Garrett, neither had his elbow and belly journey. He was asleep with exhaustion long before Freet reached the meadow that closely resembled the mural Garrett had created on one common room wall. Garrett wouldn't be able to see the green grass, but he could feel it on his back. He couldn't hear the water of the small creek babbling over rocks, but he could feel the water with his fingertips. Enough, Freet was sure, to bring mind images of the scene Garrett had painted. Far better than the last thing his eyes had seen to be in his mind when the final sleep came.

There was no longer any rush. Freet could sense that in the way Garrett held to him as Freet lowered him to the ground. It was hard at first. Garrett suffered disorientation from his lack of equilibrium. His grasp eased to just a touch to keep contact as the dizziness passed. There was no panicked tightening as Freet transferred his hold from one arm to the other and moved Garrett's left arm to touch his fingers to the stream. Garrett felt the water and relaxed even more. Only his mouth and chin were visible in the swabs of bandages on his head and throat. It was enough to see he was at peace. There was an end to his imprisonment. He even smiled slightly as he raised his other arm to lift the pouch towards Freet.

Freet wasn't at peace. His instinct as a physician to preserve life as long as there was life was in conflict with what Garrett wanted, what he would want if it were him. And, of course, he would lose a friend, the first he had had in too long a time to count. He was as reluctant as he was willing when he took the pouch and shook out the pills. He was as grateful as he was furious when Dina came from nowhere and knocked him over in her haste to stop him. She dropped beside Garrett, and Cute materialized beside her, no doubt how she had found them. When she touched him, Garrett's jaw set, his teeth clamped together.

"He must not die," she shouted at Freet.

"Why do you forbid him the choice of death?" Freet shouted back. "You never have any other."

"He is not like any other."

With his eyes cold and hard and a slight curl to his lip he reminded her cruelly, "He is a hunter"

"He is not!" she screamed shrilly.

His voice was strained with his efforts at control, and he wanted to punish her. "You were told that. I told you, Mysty told you. Had you listened this would not have happened."

"They would have found him anywhere. He is too much a threat to them. Had we realized we would never have—"

She broke off abruptly, leaving Freet to finish for her. "Taken him to the ship?"

Sobered, she told him, "I brought him. The fault is mine."

Freet took quick advantage. "Why were you on Earth?"

"I...I..." Her hand moved to her chest, just below her throat. Her fingers moved as if feeling for something, and the thumb rubbed against her fingertips as if she held something between them. "I don't know. Something—something drew me." She sighed and dropped her hand. "I could never find it. It was wrong of me to go even before the Karoz—"

"Why did you not send him back?" he asked miserably.

"None can return," she stated flatly.

"You did."

"Not to stay and not where there were people. It was selfish of me to indulge myself, but not so much so that I would condemn any world to destruction." Freet grew silent, listening. "The moment Garrett was touched by the Karoz he was infected. If he were to return, the disease would incubate. He would have contaminated others who would then contaminate others. This is why none can return. It is a horrible disease that destroys the body and drives the mind to insanity. Only being on the ship prevents it from advancing."

He didn't know what disease she spoke of and at that moment didn't want those details. He asked curtly, "We are all infected?"

"All, perhaps all, we've never known for certain, but Mord believes so. We could not simply release all, allowing those who are not to suffer the insane and inhuman cruelties of those who are. Do you not understand? The purpose of the yantz was never to cause unhappiness, but they did not know what to do with beings so different from themselves. All these years they have attempted to find one who could communicate with them, teach them how to create happiness within the safe environment of the ship."

"That was what they wanted of Garrett, to be their teacher? That is why they treated him?"

Her chin went up and her shoulders back. "He would not have lived without treatment," she said defensively. "They would have treated him even had they not heard him, but because they heard him; they knew they could learn from him."

"They heard him?" He shook his head. "He is not telepathic. He has said so many times."

"He did not know." She touched her fingertips to Garrett's ear, his hand to her chest, and then her fingertip to his temple. The message was clear, hear me here. Garrett didn't respond. He lay rigid and passive. Tears flooded her eyes. "He refuses me entry."

Freet's hand lifted a few inches towards her in compassion and dropped again in hopelessness. "It is not enough."

"They are such small wounds," she cried. "Can he not tolerate this until they heal?"

"They will not heal."

"You can not know until—"

"I know!" He shot up to his feet. "I know, he knows. Without the yantz they will not heal. He will forever be—"

"No one knows until—" she began stubbornly.

"They will..." He clamped his teeth for an instant to calm himself. "If he can not see, hear, or speak when the wounds heal, will you then allow him his own choice?"

"Yes."

Her answer came too quickly. The phrase where there is life there is hope ran through Freet's mind. Hope of what? "What are you hiding? Why have you kept him hidden in your quarters where no others could see him?" He pulled her up by the arm. "The yantz? How many yantz were killed? How many? Is that why he can't die? Have they bonded again?"

Her chin went up again. "You are hurting my arm."

Freet released her, but demanded, "Answer me."

"Something has been done."

"By the yantz?"

"The yantz are gone."

"Then how?"

"You must trust me. I can not tell you what has been done; only that it has, and Garrett will heal." She touched Freet's arm in urgency. "You can not tell any other. He must be kept safe. He will heal. You must believe me."

Freet wanted to. More than anything in his entire being, he wanted to believe. Would she have agreed to allow Garrett his own choice, once the healing was complete, unless she was certain? If she was, how could she be? With the yantz dead, how could those injuries heal?

She interrupted his thoughts. "He will heal, I swear to you."

With his eyes on Garrett he rubbed the back of his neck. "If that is true, how will he know?"

"I can not tell him," she cried. "He will not listen."

"The Phogatres?"

"He has forbidden them. They will not trespass."

"For something so important...."

Dina shook her head. "They did attempt. He refused them angrily. It is as if he believes we attempt to have him accept it as a substitute. You see why you must help me. We can not allow him to weaken or starve before the healing is complete."

Freet could understand. Would Garrett?

###

Freet carried Garrett back to the ship only far enough to reset the portal. They returned to the green planet, to the house for shelter, and the glemms. The glemms because Dina still did not completely trust Freet. Mischief did not trust Freet at all and took its guarding assignment seriously. There was no carefree romping. It perched on the end of the bed, inches from Garrett's head, one hand on his cheek, and stayed there. The only time it moved was to watch everything Freet did.

Garrett withdrew even further. Unable to respond to sight or sound, he stopped responding to touch as well. His jaw was closed; teeth clenched together. Freet inserted a feeding tube through his nostril, straight to his stomach. Garrett didn't fight it. Whatever position Freet put him in, he stayed until Freet moved him again.

"He is gone from us," Freet told Dina the evening of the first day.

"He is there." She stroked the glemm in her arms. "He sleeps."

"He is comatose," he corrected though he hated to say it.

"He will wake when he has healed. It will take longer I think than bonding, but he will heal." Her eyes fixed as she gazed at Garrett's bandaged face. Her fingers stroked automatically in Cute's hair until they stilled as well, her body immobile and her features lax.

"Dina?" Freet said softly. "Dina," he repeated louder.

Her eyes shifted to Freet's face. Her hand went to her chest, just below her throat. As the thumb and forefinger rubbed together she said faintly, "Something reaches out to me, something I can not grasp." With a sigh her hand dropped. "He has always done this to me. There seems to be a bond where there is none."

"You are in love with him," he stated, half in reluctant question.

"Love?"

"A special feeling between a man and woman."

"A desire for mating?"

Coloring slightly, Freet explained awkwardly, "There is a physical desire as well, but..."

Dina shook her head. "I do not feel a desire to mate with him." She looked at Freet again. "When he smiles at me a certain way, I feel a warmth spread through me that lifts my spirits, and I feel a closeness to him."

"Do you know what physical love is?" he asked awkwardly.

She colored slightly at the question. "Yes," she answered and quickly changed the subject. "It is perhaps the cray that makes me feel a bond."

"What is cray?"

"Telepathy, though he rejects it, it is still within him. The first day I heard him, and the yantz heard him. It led us to him. He is very strong, but does not use it."

"He says he can not."

"He did not know anymore than you do now."

That gave Freet a start. "Me?"

"All have cray to varying degrees. You can learn to use yours as he will." Her gaze shifted back to Garrett's face. "He has taught us so much. We began to understand what it is that all need, even the Phogatres who thought they needed nothing. Yet he has received so little in return. This now, but even before when he realized he would not be crippled, we could not sense a lightening in his inner spirits." She looked back at Freet. "We sensed a great sorrow within him." When she received no comment, she went on with, "Beneath his smiles of warmth, or cold, or mocking, I have sensed sadness." When Freet still made no comment, she asked bluntly, "Do you know the cause?"

"He does not discuss his feelings," he said evasively.

"I do not wish to intrude on his privacy," she told him sincerely. "I only wish to understand emotions I have never experienced. Have we taken him from someone of special affection for him?"

"He said not."

"Do you sense otherwise?"

"He was alone," he snapped in frustration. He would not divulge a confidence. "You have never known love. How can you understand it? Or a man who would deny himself love to protect others from grief at his passing?"

"You will explain to me."

"No, it is something you must feel for yourself."

"You have love for him," she commented and absently stroked Cute again.

"There are many kinds of love, that of a friend, that of a parent for a child, the way Mysty loves you, between mates, even for a pet."

Dina gazed at him thoughtfully. Her fingers stroked Cute's thick hair with her gaze unwaveringly on his face making Freet uncomfortable. To distract her he asked, "How are things on the ship?"

"Quiet," she answered, her mind still on other things.

"You have been among them?" he asked in concern.

"No." She dropped Cute to the floor, "They come to the intermediary section to complain over the cancelled hunts." She began to drift off, Cute taking its place under her gown as she moved. "Attempt to speak to him. He must understand he will soon be well."

###

Garrett woke three days later, if jerking up violently to sit and gasp for air could be called waking. He jerked again when Freet caught him by the shoulders. His right arm flew up, nearly knocking Freet out with its cast. Freet caught it at the wrist and pressed Garrett's fingertips to his own mutilated ear for identification and quickly laid Garrett down again. He sat beside him, hands on his shoulders until Garrett's breathing leveled. Freet could not trust himself to speak for that long. Not only was Garrett awake, but he hadn't wavered drunkenly. His equilibrium had been restored.

"Do you hear me, Garrett?"

He was disappointed when Garrett didn't respond. He was deeply hurt when Garrett raised his arm to sweep his hands away. That was only the beginning of Garrett's rejection. It wasn't the same as it had been after the other attacks. The cause wasn't apathy or depression, but then the attack, its ultimate purpose, had not been the same, a fact Freet tried to explain to Dina. The Garrett they had known was gone, replaced by someone cold and mechanical. Everything he did was deliberate and with a single purpose.

Before Freet saw the first slight move of Garrett's head that indicated his ears had caught a sound, Garrett was tensing and relaxing his body, toning muscles while still trapped in the casts. Garrett began flexing his feet and clenched and unclenched his hands to build strength when Freet reduced the length of the casts. When the bandages were removed from his eyes it should have been joyous. Garrett blinked and moved his eyes, but only enough for him to know he could see before he struggled to get to his feet despite the heavy casts. He accepted Freet's help with as much emotion as he would have shown a set of metal parallel bars. They never knew when or if his voice returned. Garrett never spoke to them, either to acknowledge their presence or anything they said. He wouldn't so much as look at them, driving Dina to tears and Freet to anger.

Freet talked to him continually just as Garrett had done when they first met. There were two differences. Freet knew Garrett could understand, and Garrett made no effort to quiet Freet. Freet retaliated with crueler, more cutting remarks until the day he found Garrett clumsily chipping at the edges of the leg cast.

"Want cast off?" he asked bitterly. He heaved Garrett to his shoulders. "You think no need help, no need anyone? Then take cast off alone. Water dissolve."

He carried Garrett to the pool as he had once before. His intention was to toss him in, just as he had before. It didn't happen that way. As Freet threw him off his shoulder Garrett caught Freet at the back of his belt, dragging Freet in with him. And Garrett kept him under with his weight on Freet's back until Freet no longer struggled.

XVIII

Mord was surprised when the door to his private quarters opened. Dina, the only one with the ability to do so, had never before entered without first requesting permission.

"I—I am shocked," he stammered.

"Bet you are," Garrett answered coldly.

His footsteps were silent in the black knee-length moccasins he had at one time created for amusement. He wore the black shirt, vest, and pants. The dark brown of his gun belt and holster stood out in stark contrast with every loop of the belt filled with cartridges. His pistol rested in the holster. His rifle was casually cradled in his arms. His right hand lightly held the guard with one finger hooked against the trigger.

If Garrett's intention had been to appear ominous he had succeeded. Mord hesitated before he said, "This can not be. The yantz..."

"You did succeed in getting a litch into the hands of someone who could figure out how to use it as long as the charge lasted. I was just a little too slow in taking that visual, but at least it kept you from making more when you realized those you had were dead."

"I—I do not understand."

"Sure you do. You knew as soon as you heard about it how to get one. Sneaking through those back halls to get to the create room, shouldn't have been too hard for you. All you had to do was pick a time you knew Dina was busy."

"I believe you are..." Mord started out of his massive chair.

"Stay there, Mord." Garrett emphasized his words with a swing of the rifle. The butt was braced against his hip and the barrel pointed at Mord's chest.

"A weapon?" he asked as he lowered himself back down. "You are threatening me with a weapon? Why?"

"You don't have a glemm."

"For what reason would I want such a stupid creature?"

"Why don't they like you, Mord?" Garrett countered quietly. "Or why doesn't Mysty's Glemm like you? It produced one for Dina, why not you?"

Mord scoffed. "The trauma of your injuries has driven you mad with this ridiculous talk of glemms." He paused slightly and changed his tone. "I do not understand how you recovered with the yantz dead."

Garrett didn't answer. He cut him off instead with a terse, "My 'injuries' gave me a lot of time to think without distractions."

"You make no sense. I will not listen."

Mord pushed up, screamed, and fell back to clinch his thigh with both massive hands. Blood seeped through his fingers, and a tiny wisp of smoke drifted up from the rifle barrel. Garrett levered a fresh shell into the chamber.

"You are mad!" Mord cried. "You must stop this insanity. You can not kill me just because I have no stupid pet!"

"Glemm is the only one who ever saw a mutated Thornn. He's the only one who knows what you are."

"You think I am Thornn!" Mord cried. "That is why you do this? But it can not be." He put one hand on the chair edge, pushing up. "Think, Garrett, think." He held the other hand out imploringly. "How could it be? Am I not a prisoner just as you are, just as all the others? How could I be Thornn?"

Garrett fired a second time. The slug tore into Mord's other leg dropping him back into the chair. Over the moans that followed Garrett levered in a fresh shell and asked, "Why didn't the yantz recognize you as Thornn?"

"I am a prisoner, taken the same as the others," Mord moaned.

"I'm going to take out your elbows next, one at a time and then your eyes. I'll leave your ears and voice while I work on you. The difference is when I get through, I will kill you. I won't leave you the way you left me."

"I did not do those things to you," Mord shrieked. "Zalano did. Has your memory gone as well as your sanity?"

"You really tried to work that sanity thing on me. Along with the depressants you kept slipping into the pain pills, my masks, and oxygen, you had me going pretty good. It took me a while to figure out that's where it was coming from, but then like I said, I had a lot of time to think. And develop my abilities. Like how to open all the doors with thought pictures."

Garrett moved to the side and opened the door to the second half of Mord's quarters. Inside were banks of blinking lights "How does it work? What they hear comes to this; it translates and sends it back with your added message? Or do you just broadcast."

Mord's whole manner changed. He no longer gripped the chair arms in pain. He relaxed with his hands limply on his thighs, which had already ceased to bleed. "How have you arrived at these conclusions?"

"Once I realized where the depression came from the rest kind of fell into place. You're the one who passes out the translators. You're the one who implants them while not showing any other medical skill. There are the ceilings too. High in here and the pen room originally designed for much taller people, and low everywhere else with ramps going up to the second level of quarters, which really are no more than cubes—cages of a different design, adapted for the specimens."

He continued in a cold, conversational voice. "Then there was the first thing I thought when I saw you, that you looked deformed. No one else on this ship ever struck me that way, different, but not deformed."

Mord leaned back in the chair with a smug look on his face. "I should have settled for your death."

"You didn't want me dead. You wanted my brain. You didn't care what else Zalano did as long as—how was it he said it—your brain must live? That was why they didn't kill me the way they did the yantz."

"What a fool you are, Earthling, but you do possess an animal cunning."

"I'm like you were before your disease twisted your body and mind."

"You are microscopic in comparison," Mord said with a snort.

"Not as advanced," Garrett corrected, "but I can open the doors. You lost your ability to do it when your disease started. That's why you need Dina."

"Your disease as well," Mord returned with a particularly odd gleam in his eyes.

"That's one of your lies. It's a Thornn disease."

"Are you so certain?" he asked.

"That's a lie you told Dina to keep her from ever going home."

Mord chuckled. "You know only what she has told you and hope to receive other information from me." He chuckled again. "Know this, Earthling; I will live to see our exodus completed."

"Two things, Mord; while I was trapped in that void you put me in, my mind opened up, and there won't be any exodus. They're all dead."

"You do not know this." Mord shook his massive head in denial. "They live beyond the doors the yantz kept locked to me. I will join them now. They will be grateful for all I have done, and none of your meddling will stop us."

Of all he said, Garrett only questioned one thing. "Meddling?"

"The yantz were content to leave things as they were. They knew no difference."

"Not likely with only this level and the Thornn society for example, but they knew there was more for the specimens than what happened in there." He tipped his head towards the infirmary. "They just didn't know what to do after they saved them from you and changed them to quarters."

"Not until you came. You were making them aware of things I did not wish them aware of." He laughed shortly. "I see now I made a mistake in attempting to keep you for myself. I should have settled for your quick death along with that of the yantz. I took great pleasure in entering the sanctuary to finish them. The charge in the litch lasted just long enough to kill the last."

Mord smiled wickedly. "Had your Freet not been so capable of guarding you, I would have had you from the poison. I would have taken the Freet's cray for compensation, had you not interfered yet again. I still find it very difficult to believe he did not die. His own medicine saved him?"

Garrett was asking questions, not answering. "How do you use it? Cut out the brain?"

A wicked smile broadened and twisted his mutated features even more. "Only a small part of it."

"How many hunters have you slaughtered, claiming you couldn't save them?"

Mord shrugged. "The number is insignificant, only the results matter."

Garrett thought of the thousands of visuals in the create room, many more visuals than there were men on the ship, visuals of the men that had been killed and asked, "Have all those lives been worth it?"

Mord's tone turned ugly. "Do you believe the life of one, a thousand, ten thousand of you inferior creatures is worth the life of one Thornn? While you grovel in the dirt, we soar among the stars. Your technology is but a scratch on the surface. Ours—"

"...destroyed you," Garrett pointed out coldly. "Your entire race."

"They are there, waiting. This is but one level and without the yantz for protection, we will soon have the portal back." Mord told him smugly

"Your people are all dead."

"We will take the portal back." He started up. "Or do you believe your puny weapon will stop me from using your cray to replace mine?"

For the first time, Garrett smiled. "Break my bones?" he taunted.

As soon as the door opened, Mord dropped back in his chair and cried, "See what he has done to me? He is insane, gone mad!"

With her eyes wide, Dina told Garrett, "I must speak—"

Garrett did not take his eyes off of Mord "Get out of here," he told her.

Dina flinched with each word, but she didn't back away. "I can not..."

"Dina," Mord screamed, "You must help me."

"...find Chief," she finished.

"He's on the planet. Go stay with him."

"He is not there." Her voice wavered at the last and she kept her eyes away from Mord.

"Dina!" Mord exclaimed in horror. "He is killing me."

She held out her trembling hand to show Garrett what she held, Freet's medicine bag. "I found it in the corridor."

"Wait outside," Garrett ordered.

"Have I not been your friend?" Mord screamed at Dina. "Have I not protected you and cared for you?" As she backed, he grew frantic. "You can not leave..." The door slid shut, and Mord's manner underwent another drastic change. "I knew you were turning her from me."

He lunged up from the chair. Garrett fired once, side-stepped as Mord fell to his knees and levered a fresh shell in.

Disbelief was on Mord's mutated features. He put his hands to his chest, then held them out and gazed at the blood on them.

Garrett told him, "It just depends on where my puny weapon hits you."

"She did nothing because of fear of you," Mord taunted insanely. "She will hate you for this."

Garrett fired one last time and said softly, "I know."

###

As if to prove Mord's prediction, Dina had not waited for him. "Mischief," he called for he knew how Dina had found him.

Mischief materialized instantly and clutched Garrett's hand. Garrett swung it up into his arms and held it tightly for just an instant, and Mischief's little hands held to both sides of his face. "Okay," He had to clear his throat. "Show me where they are."

Mischief hit the floor in a run. Garrett followed with two objectives, to keep up with the fast moving glemm and to watch the corridors they passed through for potential enemies. When doing both at once became too much, Garrett called Mischief back. He ordered him to watch for anyone coming from behind while he concentrated on the front. He no longer needed guidance. Garrett knew where they were going long before he heard Dina's scream.

"I'm coming, Dina," he thought. *"Stall them if you can."*

"Hurry," came back instantly.

"You lied," Dina screamed. "You would have hurt Garrett even if I had gone out to you, just as you are hurting Freet. You are despicable."

"When I say now, drop flat on the floor." As Garrett neared the door he asked, *"Is Freet down?"*

"Yes."

"Okay, now."

Garrett fired as he went through the common room door. No one had time to react to the shock of seeing him. Men fell. Men screamed. The rifle clicked on empty. Garrett dropped it and drew the pistol. None waited to see if the smaller weapon was as deadly as the first. Those in front crawled on the backs of those who had been behind in terrorized efforts to get out. Over in seconds, bodies sprawled over the benches, tables, and floors as the survivors of the deadly volley fled.

"Make sure they're dead," Garrett told Mischief. He took time only to retrieve his rifle before going to Dina, Freet, and Cute.

Freet was flat on his back and unconscious. Dina was sprawled over him, her arms wrapped around his neck. Cute clung over her back protectively.

"Is he dead?" he asked tonelessly while he spilled spent shells from his revolver. Dina shook her head. "Then maybe you'd better get off of him so he can breathe."

Dina jerked up, bobbing in the air until she got herself balanced with the gravity vest. "Do you not care?" she asked accusingly, shrugging Cute from her back.

Her attitude was what Garrett expected. He turned away without answer to ask Mischief, "Are they all dead?"

Mischief bobbed twice and stood on his back legs to slip cartridges from Garrett's belt.

"Is that all you care for now?" Dina shouted. "To kill?"

He swung the rifle from under his arm to Mischief. "You and the yantz wanted a snake stomper. You got it."

She rose straight up. "You think we brought you here to kill for us?"

Garrett didn't answer again. He handed Mischief a handful of shells from his vest pocket and watched long enough to be sure Mischief could load the rifle correctly. At the same time he continued to replace the cartridges in the pistol.

"It is not true," Dina cried. "We did not wish this. It has changed you."

"It changes everyone. Just hope to hell you don't ever have to..."

Garrett shoved her aside as a new group rushed in behind her. Those in front couldn't turn and run from Garrett's deadly greeting because of those in the back pushing them into Garrett's bullets, but the bullets were no match for the blow to Garrett's back when the survivors of the first group rejoined the battle. He was hurled into the rush. Stunned and disoriented, he could do no more than fight to recover his co-ordination and get free no matter how many times Dina screamed. As both his vision and co-ordination cleared, he realized he wasn't fighting alone. The Gunian pulled a man off of him. Behind them the Phogatres smashed and threw men. Beside them was the mountain-sized chimp man, equally effective, and nearly side-by-side to him was Mysty.

He became aware of more. Dina was gone. In her place Vo stood, arms out to stop any who came near Freet with a charge from his hands. Glemms were everywhere. They caught a hand with a knife, tripped, and pushed, anything to help their people. In a short time only a small, battered and bruised group remained on their feet. The combined attack of hunters had not faired any better than the first. New bodies were sprawled.

"Garrett, it was Zalano. He took Dina," Mysty cried.

"I know. Mischief, is Cute with her?" Mischief bobbed twice. Garrett pointed at the chimp man. "Carry Freet." He told the Phogatres, "Watch our backs." He told Mischief, "Show us where they are."

Mischief led the small band at a run through the corridors. Anybody they saw in front of them quickly disappeared. No doors opened as they passed, and no one followed. Nothing interfered until a voice from behind stopped Garrett in his tracks.

"What?" he demanded.

"I believe he is dying," the mountain of a man repeated.

"From what?" he moved back to Freet.

Garrett hadn't taken the time to examine Freet's injuries, but none of what he saw had looked life threatening. He pressed his fingertips to Freet's throat. His pulse was weak and erratic. His breathing wasn't any better. Garrett could find no open wounds front or back, but when he pulled Freet's shirt open he grimaced at the bruise just under the rib cage.

"He must be bleeding inside." Garrett dug into his pocket with a quick glance at Mischief who showed no signs of distress. "Is she safe?" he asked to be sure.

Mischief bobbed twice at the same time Garrett slipped a pill into Freet's mouth. Within seconds Freet stirred in a struggle to find his way to consciousness. Garrett backed away and asked the chimp man, "What's your name?"

"Tonya."

"Get him to the infirmary." He looked again at Mischief and then all the glemms. They all waited placidly. The urgency was over. He asked Mischief, "Is she hurt?"

The answer that time was an ambiguous sway from side to side. Garrett considered it for a bare second before he swung the rifle into Gunian's hands. "Meet me in the infirmary."

"Garrett?" Gunian exclaimed as Garrett moved away.

From the awkward way Gunian held the weapon, Garrett assumed that was the cause of Gunian's distress. "Pinpan can show you how to use it."

"Should you go alone?" Gunian asked quickly.

Garrett obviously thought so. He left without answer.

###

Dina was not with Garrett when he returned. He told them only that she was safe despite their questioning looks, and he had sent her to her quarters to rest. He went directly to the domed table to look at Freet.

"We have done as much as we have seen Mord do," Lamphin told him. "We have not been able to find Mord to do more."

"Lamphin, you and your friends, guard the hunters' entrance. The rest of you guard the scholars' to be sure they don't get into this, except for you, Tonya."

The last caused a few exchanges of glances, but no one commented. The only one to object was Mischief when Garrett told it to go with Mysty. Garrett told it in a whisper, "You're a snitch." Mischief still didn't move. "Does that mean you won't pass on what you see if I tell you not to?"

After two bobs of assurance, Garrett held his hand down. Mischief instantly raised one of his to be swung up into the cradle of Garrett's arm. Garrett whispered, "Have any of the others transmitted what Dina did?" He let a breath out in relief when the answer was no. "Tell them not to." He waited and then asked, "Do they agree?" Mischief bobbed twice to earn a stroke of gratitude before Garrett returned it to the floor and turned his attention to Freet and Tonya.

"Time to make a decision," he told the big man quietly.

Tonya's shoulders sank. "Midradina told you," he stated in fatalism.

"She didn't." It hadn't been necessary once he had opened himself up. "It wasn't hard to know the cabinets and drawers in here have more to offer than masks and plaster if someone, say a Thornn, knew how to use them."

"Much more," Tonya agreed though he made no move to make use of them. "I went to a great deal of trouble in replacing Mord's casts and bandages to keep any from knowing, but you guessed because of Shama?"

"There had to be a reason Glemm knew to take him to you, and you're the only one as tall as Mord."

"You will kill me even though I saved your life?"

"I don't have any reason to kill you, yet."

Tonya recognized the threat in that single last word. "The others will once they know."

"I won't tell them, but I want something in return, starting with Freet. After you've taken care of him, I want you to teach us how to use what's available, and how to use Mord's broadcasting system to undo some of the damage he's done."

"How can I do these things without the others knowing?" he asked, but he had already activated something on the table. A narrow band of light moved slowly down the dome.

"The glemms won't mind getting credit for it."

Tonya's brow furrowed as he looked at Mischief. "It is obvious they have become much more for you than they ever were for us."

Garrett eyes followed the band as it passed over Freet's body. Areas of injury showed as flickers of darker color. At Freet's head and abdomen it flickered darkly, nearly black, the abdomen the darkest and largest area. The band returned there and held.

Tonya talked as he opened and closed cabinet doors and drawers. "For us they were children's pets, growing away from the child as it reached maturity, going on to another child. I see we greatly underestimated them."

"Too insignificant to warrant your notice," Garrett said in bitter sarcasm.

"I believe arrogance was a deciding factor in our destruction." He turned with a loaded tray in his hands. "But we were not cruel people. It was the sickness that turned us."

"You weren't sick when you slaughtered the glemm's Hankians and how many other races?"

"That was centuries before I was even born, when we were a savage, primitive race." Tonya returned to the table, shifted the tray to one arm and pulled out a shelf on the side of the table. He said indifferently, "I do not know who told you these things, but they are distortions."

"Mischief showed me." Tonya's head snapped around. "Keep working." Tonya turned back, and Garrett talked. "After your superior race slaughtered the glemms' humans, they hid their abilities from you. They could tolerate your children, but not your adults. They are highly intelligent beings, telepathic between themselves. They can also transmit what they've seen and heard in minute detail in mind pictures, to us, even to a non-telepath, usually in what we think are dreams."

Garrett looked down at Mischief, thinking of what he had thought were dreams to begin, starting after Dina had stopped Freet the second time from giving him the death he so desperately wanted. Once they began, while locked into darkness and silence he had remembered Mysty's dreams. It had not been a giant leap then to realize Mischief, hand on his face, was showing him things his ancestors had observed. He had seen the Thornn through those dreams, seen their degeneration, and knew what Mord was. He had already realized Mord was the cause of his unexplained depressions, but he couldn't think of a reason for it, believing only that Mord had been influenced too until then. Mischief had given the real reason to him, and everything else slipped into place along with what he had to do despite how he knew Dina would feel about it.

"I know what happened to your people," Garrett stated, though he didn't know the cause of it and wanted to.

"Our foolish bid for immortality on a planet as well as on the ship." Tonya reached through the dome and with a thin light from a pencil-thin instrument cut through Freet's abdominal wall. Blood splattered from the ruptured organ beneath. A suction tube appeared in Tonya's hand from somewhere under the table. He cleared the wound while the dome absorbed the splatters and continued to talk while he worked. "The disease appeared shortly after our arrival here. We first suspected that an infection from the planet had eluded our inherent immunities. We concentrated on identifying the infection while the disease progressed rapidly. More and more became infected to such extreme mutations of flesh and mind we could only contain them in quarantine until they began to die. With autopsies I was able to identify the true cause. Others wished to dispute my findings, but the evidence could not be denied. The Myraid gene we had added to our D.N.A. had mutated in the third generation, and it continued to mature on board ship."

Tonya's hands stilled, and his gaze went inward. "Had it matured to a stage three before we arrived here so much time would not have been lost searching the planet for the origin of the disease. Too many of the great minds had been infected before we knew the cause."

Garrett stated, "You don't seem to be infected."

"I am not a true third generation." His eyes flickered up and back down. He paused and changed the suction tube for a hose from under the table and a stick, looking like a gray tongue depressor. He filled the wound from the hose and shaped the bonding with the stick. "I was considered inferior as my mother was of the second generation and my father of the first."

"Lucky you," Garrett said caustically and asked, "What stage was Mord in?"

"Was? Is he dead?"

"I killed him."

Tonya nodded slowly. "He was in the fourth stage. Though he too was not a true third generation and was infected differently. He was imprisoned, not quarantined, when it was discovered he sacrificed those of our own that he considered expendable to implement the cure for those of more importance."

"While the rest used specimens?"

"Yes, though they were taken first for study of their cultures."

Garrett told him in hate filled accusation. "You meant to use them as slaves, and the only reason you kept such accurate records and translated the languages was because you intended to invade their worlds for more once you had established the new colony here. Don't try lying to me."

Tonya's eyes shifted to Mischief again. "I do not wish for you to hate me for what my people did."

"Whether you sink or swim will be based on what you do now," Garrett told him coldly. "Why didn't the yantz recognize Mord as Thornn?"

"I do not believe they ever saw any of us in a mutated stage to be able to recognize him. To my knowledge they never went beyond this level of the ship."

"So he was put in here to assist with the extractions from the brains of the specimens?" Garrett asked for confirmation.

Tonya answered with a tip of his head.

"He continued to use them when the yantz mistook him for another prisoner?"

"I have always suspected he did, though the treatment is only temporary and with inferior contributions, even more so."

"We're really no more to you than a cockroach," Garrett stated in disgust.

"You are much higher on the evolutionary scale," Tonya answered impassively. "You would perhaps be equal to the seventeenth century of our world."

"Just short of idiot?" Garrett asked.

"You are capable—"

"It was a rhetorical question," Garrett cut him off.

"But incorrect."

"Maybe, but what does matter is that our deaths are immaterial to you. Why did you end up in a specimen cage?"

"I proposed controlled breeding to eliminate the gene to save our race when breeding onboard was forbidden. Those in control had reached an unreasonable level. They considered my proposal to be treasonous and imprisoned me."

Garrett grunted at that. "Where did the yantz come from?" That was something he still did not understand.

"They were a hobby of Qranun. He wished to develop a biological unit capable of independent movement and decision to provide settlers with medical care in remote regions. Qranun succumbed to the second stage before their maturity."

"Lost his cray?" Garrett scoffed slightly. "So they came into existence without knowing what they were supposed to do with their claws and bonding abilities."

"Yes." Tonya withdrew his hands and adjusted the light band to shine on Freet's head. "They were considered a folly. I have often wondered..." His voice faded away, and his gaze fixed again.

"All of you lost your telepathic ability?"

"In the second stage of the disease, but I have not lost my cray."

"Then why didn't Mord go after you?"

"I was imprisoned after he was, and I made certain I never came here after hearing who the physician was."

"So he didn't know about you at all?"

Tonya nodded again and repositioned Freet's head, turning the mutilated ear upward. "I did not think all of my people would have died so soon, but I knew something had happened when I was moved from my cell to quarters and Dina appeared with a yantz at her shoulder."

"Why didn't you ask the yantz what happened?"

"I did not wish them to know I was here either. I was unaware they or Midradina knew of me until she came for me to treat you."

"The yantz didn't tell her; the glemms did. If she had known it before, you would have been in here, treating the hunters instead of leaving them for Mord to scavenge."

Tonya looked at Mischief. "I did not know about them."

Garrett had more questions to ask, but he didn't want to stay around once Dina came in. He had become what she accused him of being in the beginning, a cold-blooded and savage killer that she could not bear to look at. She went straight to the domed table. Her face was pale, and her hands were clasped tightly together. "How is he?" she asked of Tonya.

"He will live." He pointed briefly at the darkened area in the band of light at Freet's head. "That must be observed. Should it enlarge, aggressive procedures must be used to stop the hemorrhaging if auto-assimilation does not."

He went back to cutting away the scar tissue on the lower part of Freet's ear and she asked, "What is auto-assimilation?"

"Accelerated regeneration of tissue stimulated by the molding being absorbed into the blood," Tonya explained.

Garrett backed away and waved for Mischief to stay. When he had realized Mord had to be questioned and killed for all of their sakes, he had also known Dina would never be able to accept the brutality it would take. His one gift to Freet, though he was sure Freet would never forgive him, had been to keep Freet from helping.

XIX

Garrett walked the ship for days, peering into rooms empty of occupants, climbing through stacks and stacks of supplies and building materials that filled colossal holds. He slept whenever he could walk no more, and went without food when he ran out of the dried food he had stuffed into his pockets. Even if he could have accessed the substance dispensers he wouldn't because of the abhorrence he had developed for substance and what it did to his mind. The missed meals may have been reason enough to be dizzy, he thought, but he shouldn't be having hallucinations. Although the one he saw when he walked into the portal room was certainly in good taste.

Tall and slim, she had dark hair with a slight tint of red in it. She was dressed for the outdoors in jeans, sturdy hiking boots, a lightweight, long sleeved shirt open over a tank top, and a small pack hanging on her back.

"I don't suppose you could tell me where I am?" she said in a dry tone, but her hazel eyes were dilated in fear until only a small ring of color showed around the iris,

Garrett realized she wasn't a hallucination and shouted, "Go back where you came from!"

Narrowing her eyes, she told him, "I tried that." She pointed to the back wall. "I know I came in from that direction, but..."

Garrett rushed towards the wall. He had to pull up short when it was the wall he reached, not a portal. "Damn them, what are they doing?" he asked in agitation and shouted as well as thought, "Dina?"

"What?" the woman asked.

Distracted, Garrett grunted, "Huh?"

"Why are—"

"Never mind," Garrett retorted. He rushed to where the control panel should have been. "Stand still. Don't touch anything." The wall where the control panel had been was blank, so he again shouted, "Dina!"

"What?" the woman exclaimed in exasperation.

"Why do you keep yelling what?'" he asked in frustration.

"Why," she returned coolly, "do you keep shouting my name?"

"I don't. What's—?"

He broke off when someone other than Dina entered the room. Freet went straight for Garrett. His fist swung, and Garrett staggered as he blocked the blow with his arms.

"We don't have—" Garrett tried to tell him.

Freet swung again. The blow jarred Garrett, but still didn't connect with anything more than Garrett's arms.

"Damn it, Chief, we don't—"

Both hands, palms flat, stuck Garrett in the chest. He went backwards from the force of it, through an opened portal where there had been a solid wall moments before and down when he tripped over a clump of grass.

He scrambled back to his feet as Freet jumped out after him. Garrett shouted, "Stop it."

"You fight," Freet growled. "No yantz shield protects you now."

"You either, you asshole, your head's—" Garrett ducked and danced back. "Stop it. Your head's—"

Freet swung again. "Head healed."

Garrett blocked that swing, caught the next one by the wrist and spun Freet around, twisting his arm behind his back. His other arm held Freet around the neck. "Stop it, Chief," he pleaded, "before you—oomph."

Freet hit with an elbow in the ribs and accented his words with another one. "No call Chief. Chief name friend. No friend drown, tie up, leave."

Garrett grunted with each blow, but he didn't let go. Freet shoved backwards and slammed his head into Garrett's nose. They both went over backwards, Garrett on the bottom, and he lost his hold. He shoved Freet away and got to his feet with a swipe at his watering eyes.

He backed to stay out of Freet's reach. "Do you want her terrified of you the way she is of me?"

Freet lunged. Garrett danced off to the side. Dina was suddenly there, between them. She lunged for Garrett's neck.

"No," she cried, "his injuries are not healed."

"Tell him that. He's..." Garrett pushed with both hands and ducked at the same time when Freet swung around her at his face. "...the one that won't quit."

Dina did a neat turn in the air to lock her arms around Freet's chest. "No, Chief, he will hurt you."

Garrett straightened stiffly at her words, jerking when they were reminded that someone else was there.

"It looks the other way around to me," the woman said in bright-eyed curiosity.

Garrett was grateful for her defense, but shook his head. She didn't know everything, and he still had to get her back to wherever she came from, regretfully. He liked her instantly. He admired her quiet control of the fear she had to be experiencing and her curiosity that pushed fear to the side.

"Come with me," he told her.

"Wait." She held her hand out to delay him, and Garrett shied away.

"Don't touch any of us," he told her sharply. He didn't want to take any chances on the disease not being strictly Thornn.

Puzzled, but still calm, she said, "Okay, but I have to talk to you before you do anything about sending me back." Her composure shattered to open-mouthed disbelief when movement caught her eye, and she saw Peggy and Boss across the meadow watching them.

"Inside," Garrett told her sharply making her jump. "Now!"

"But…but…" she breathed out and pointed.

"Now!"

Dina was weeping, and Garrett wanted to get away from her as badly as he wanted to get the woman back where she belonged. At least Freet was occupied in an awkward attempt to comfort Dina with that helpless look most men get when a woman is in tears.

"But…" the woman said again as Garrett stormed by her. She looked from him to the two equines, to Dina and Freet, and to his receding back.

"Wait, I've got to talk to you." She stumbled to a stop when she suddenly arrived back in the bleak gray of the ship and stared at him for a moment before she could marshal her thoughts. "I'm Nadine Forester." When that information didn't elicit any particular response, she asked, "Carolyn hasn't mentioned me?"

"Carolyn who?" Garrett asked while he experienced a twist to his gut. There was only one Carolyn who came to mind, a little blond-haired, blue-eyed girl.

"Isn't she here, Garrett?" she asked, giving Garrett a double start.

"Do I know you?" How could he have forgotten her if he did?

"No, but I feel like I know you very well through Carolyn."

"Look," He moved away in agitation, "the only Carolyn I know doesn't know me—won't ever know me." He took a deep breath and let it out slowly. "Maybe we ought to start over. We seem to have our wires crossed some way."

"I'm sorry. I just assumed you'd have as close a bond to her as she does to you. It's obvious I was mistaken."

"Who?"

"Carolyn," she exclaimed in frustration. "Your daughter."

"Carolyn," he retorted, "is with her mother."

"She disappeared a week ago."

Garrett shook his head. "Don't—don't do this to me," he told her and walked away again.

She followed. "I'm not trying to do anything to you. I'm just trying to find her, and I know she went looking for you. She's always been in touch, sensing you, even seeing and hearing you, worrying about her, wondering, loving—"

Garrett spun to face her. "I can't go back," he shouted. "Don't tell me now that she needs me. I can't go back."

Nadine shouted in return, "Then do whatever you have to do to get me back, because something is wrong, terribly wrong!"

Her voice broke and her slim body began to tremble. She moved away and took deep breaths for control. Garrett followed, demanding roughly, "What's wrong?"

"I don't know. I just felt as if something terrible had happened. It disappeared when I stepped in here, wherever the hell here is. I thought it was because she had found you, that you had taken care of whatever was frightening her. Hell," She laughed unsteadily, "the way I was yelling, I thought maybe I was heard by the powers that be. I should have stuck with yelling for her, I guess." She gave him a twisted smile and half a shrug. "She wasn't answering though." She tipped her head towards the air in back of Garrett. "Should I be afraid of that?"

"No," he said and turned. The yantz moved forward an inch, hesitated, moved forward a few inches, and hesitated again. *"Hi, Bud."*

Bud dropped several inches as if giving a tremendous sigh. *"You are not angry,"* Bud questioned, *"that we withdrew and hid as cowards?"*

"No, but—"

"We could not tolerate it," Bud interrupted anxiously. *"We had never experienced death among ourselves and your anguish was—"*

"It's okay."

"We were frenzied and fearful of controlling our actions. We could not trust ourselves even to help you."

"Easy, Bud. It's okay."

Bud dropped in height again and sped forward, front hands extended to grip Garrett's raised hand. It gripped Garrett's thumb and little finger and pushed up against his palm with its head.

Creature, man, and woman all jumped when Freet shouted furiously, "You say dead!"

"I did not!" Garrett shouted back.

"They had me seal them in the bowels of the ship!" Dina shouted and broke into fresh tears. She raged at Garrett. "You can forgive them and not me. It is not fair."

She spun and dove into Freet's arm, sobbing wildly and leaving Garrett totally lost. "What is she talking about?" he asked Freet.

Freet glared in answer while he awkwardly patted Dina on the shoulder. Nadine looked at Garrett with a cocked eyebrow as if to ask how he could be so cruel.

"I didn't do anything," Garrett protested.

Dina sobbed. "You won't talk to me. You leave whenever I come in."

"How can I talk to you, when you won't even look at me?" he implored. "I did what I had to do. I understand why you're afraid of me, but..."

Dina spun around to stare at him. "That is what you think?"

"Aren't you?" he asked dumbly.

She answered by shooting across the space between them throwing her arms around his neck. The yantz barely escaped being caught between them by backing up quickly while Dina laughed and cried at the same time she hugged Garrett fiercely. Laughter gained dominance when she swung from Garrett back into Freet's arms.

"I can see," Nadine commented dryly with her eyes riveted on Dina, "things are never dull around here, and I'm sure they are very interesting, but—"

"Dina, we've got to get her back," Garrett interrupted.

"Back?" She twisted to face him. "She does not please you?"

Garrett's mouth dropped open. "You can't…can't just…just snatch people…"

"She called for you."

"She doesn't even know me. She was calling me to find someone else. You shouldn't have brought her here."

"I did not."

They both looked at Bud. Bud asked, *"There is a difficulty?"*

Garrett threw his hands in the air. "You explain it."

"But I do not understand," Dina told him. "If she wishes to be with you, what—"

"She doesn't! She was looking for someone else, and she has to get back to find her."

"She can not return."

"She hasn't touched anyone. There's no—"

"The portal has closed."

"Open it!" he shouted in frustration.

"I can not." She turned to Nadine. "We are sorry if we have misunderstood. The Earth portal is open for what would be four months of your time. We have heard you calling each time it was open, but did not until this last know the name—"

"Damn it, I haven't been here four months," Garrett cried.

"Their time is not the same as ours," Dina answered patiently. "It was not until this time we knew it was you she called for." She told Garrett, "We have learned more while you were gone. The ship no longer moves through space. That is why none of the others can be returned, not the disease Mord lied to us of. We no longer have access to any but the planets of the hunts and Earth." She turned to Nadine. "The next opening will occur in one hundred and forty-seven of your months at approximately the same Earth time. You will not have aged, and you may return then, if you so insist." She turned back to Garrett. "You as well—what is wrong?" She rushed to him. "Are you ill?"

Chalk white, his eyes glued to Dina's face, he reached out to Nadine, and he had to force the words out. "Picture, do you have a picture?"

Bud shifted around, laying a tiny hand on Garrett's shoulder. *"You are greatly distressed. We have done something terribly wrong?"*

Garrett shook his head numbly and still stared at Dina. Nadine stared at Dina as well. She had to shake herself to slip the pack off her back. As she knelt and leaned forward, the locket she wore swung from her neck. The movement caught Dina's eye. She snatched the circle of gold and nearly pulled Nadine off-balance before the chain snapped. She backed off, clutching it to her chest with both hands with her eyes wild.

"No one is going to take it," Nadine said quietly and laid a restraining hand on Garrett's arm.

The gesture was unnecessary. Garrett couldn't move.

"It's mine." Dina's voice trembled. "It's—it's my..." She closed her eyes, gripping the small oval of gold until her knuckles turned white. "It's my..." She sank to the floor, and her words ripped from her throat in a nerve shattering scream. "Daddy, help me!"

XX

The locket had opened a dam in Dina's—Carolyn's—memory that nearly swept her away and Garrett with her. He had held her, rocked her, talked to her, and listened. Bit by bit he had pieced together his daughter's life. He had told her he was sorry until his throat was raw, damned himself, damned her mother, and thanked God for Nadine Forester. Nadine was who he sought when his daughter finally quieted and fell asleep with Freet sitting with her.

Nadine pointed to one of the chairs in Dina's front room. "You look exhausted."

Garrett had regained his color, but, yes, he was exhausted, emotionally as well as physically. He sank down gratefully. "I'm going to have to get used to calling her Carolyn now."

"I wouldn't worry about it if she's comfortable with Dina, but I am curious as to how she ended up with my nickname."

"I'll ask the yantz if it's important, but just guessing, I'd say she called for you at some point, and they mistook it for her name."

Nadine shuddered. "And called for Daddy when that man was beating her."

The fact that Garrett's stomach heaved at the thought showed on his face, and his voice was strained. "She had gone to the ranch looking for me. He…he told her he would take her to me."

He had to take a deep breath and let it out slowly. He couldn't talk about how wrong he had been about the dream when the yantz had shown him what happened to her. They hadn't just projected the sense of a villain for which his mind had provided a face. It had been Peters who attacked her.

"They kept going back at different points during the time span to find the Daddy she called for. She didn't remember who or what Daddy was so they didn't know they'd found who they were searching for when they found me." He took a deep breath and let it out slowly. "And I didn't know her."

She asked, "How many cycles ago?"

Garrett shrugged. "Has to be least two." He grimaced. "From what I could get they took her in the first cycle at a time after they took me during the second, and you at a time after both of us during the same one they took me from earlier. What happened to her was during the first cycle, but after I was taken the second so to me, there, it hadn't happened yet."

He grimaced and laughed tightly. "It's confusing, but explains why I never sensed any threat to her. One stretch of one hundred forty seven months was enough for her to grow up." He waved his hand in bewilderment. "The time thing here doesn't stop natural growth, just aging. No one mentioned they kept going back to Earth in the same span of time. Chief knew, and he probably would have put it together if I hadn't called her a baby the only time I mentioned her. He did think the yantz went back looking for me, but I told him there wasn't any reason. Hell, I didn't know of any reason."

She gave him a sympathetic smile. "Be thankful for that locket."

"I sent it to Marsha before Carolyn was born, not with any picture in it though."

"Carolyn put the picture in the same day she found it in a box, along with other pictures, and divorce and adoption papers, the past all neatly stored away. She had it for years before Marsha even knew. It nearly drove Marsha crazy when she found out, but then everything Carolyn did nearly drove that bitch crazy. She wanted her to be a doll she could dress pretty and sit in a corner. Don't get dirty, don't spill anything, don't make a mess, don't make noise, don't cry, don't laugh, and whatever you do don't act different. I tried to tell her it's normal for children to get dirty, cry occasionally, make noise, and that her connection to you wasn't abnormal, just unusual. Carolyn shouldn't have been institutionalized or even in therapy, but Marsha wouldn't listen. She kept on about what she called Carolyn's obsession with you and deliberate taunting of her by saying you needed her. Her problem, not Carolyn's, was classic guilt. She knew the condition you were in when she walked out on you."

"She had good reason."

"Bullshit!" Nadine exclaimed and shot to her feet to pace. "Life does not stop because of a handicap, and you wouldn't have set yourself on an isolationist course that excluded any relationships if it hadn't been for the premise of rejection she set when she deserted you. You didn't have any family left to show you that love—real love—exists without limitations. With your mind, you could have gone on, handicapped or not, with a full, complete life, not off into obscurity to await a final end."

She broke off abruptly, realized what she said and that Garrett stared at her. She sank back into a chair. "I'm sorry. I didn't mean to go off like that."

Garrett asked quietly, "Is there anything you don't know about me?"

"Not much," she admitted faintly. "I had to know if Carolyn was really seeing you, imagining, or even making it up. Marsha wasn't much help. As far as she was concerned Carolyn was just plain lying. The only information she grudgingly gave me on you was that you had been permanently paralyzed before Carolyn was born. Carolyn said you weren't. It didn't take me long to find out Carolyn was the one who was right, and I knew she did need you. You would have loved her without thinking she was either crazy or a freak because of her abilities. You know why you kept denying yours, don't you?"

"I—well, I haven't really…"

She answered for him. "If you had acknowledged them here, it would mean you had ignored them—her—there. Hell of a guilt trip."

"Gee, I thought it was just because it freaked me out," he told her drolly, but the thought had occurred to him more than once that if he had paid attention to his dreams during all of those years, he would have saved Carolyn a lot of anguish.

"That too probably," she said with a smile to ease his slight withdrawal. "Does it still?"

Garrett relaxed again. "No, once I started doing it, it was no different than talking, but how did you know all that? Been talking to Chief?"

"Mysty," she corrected. "That Chief is too uptight."

Garrett smiled slightly, making her point at his face. "You should do that more often, with more feeling," she told him.

"It's been a little hard to be my frivolous self lately."

"You'll bounce back. You're too much of a realist to let what you know had to be done stop you. What did Carolyn do she thought you couldn't forgive her for?"

"What she knew had to be done," he answered tonelessly, but the answer wasn't as brief in his mind.

The memory of Dina, blood splattered and dazed, being dragged down the hall by Cute wouldn't just go away, no more than the memory of how close Dina had come to joining the men she walked to their deaths in a hall full of crazed yantz. He suddenly found himself talking about it. She was a psychologist.

"You might want to talk to her about it after things calm down. Mord wanted the doors opened to the rest of the ship. Zalano was still following those orders even though Mord was dead. She opened them, but first she called the yantz from hiding and led those men into them. They were slashed to death." He shivered as a chill swept over him. "Damn Mord. If he wasn't already dead, I'd kill him for what his actions forced her to do."

"You think you should have done it instead of her?" Nadine asked. "How can one man think so highly of himself and so little? What is it, you think since you don't matter, you'll sacrifice yourself to save those who do? Was that why you tied Chief up before you came back?"

"Are you going to psycho-analyze me every minute we're together?" he asked in frustrated embarrassment.

"I hope not," she responded with a meaningful flip of her eyebrows.

The message that flip carried hit Garrett below the belt, literally, with a sensation he hadn't felt for over a decade. The tightening in his groin was one hell of a reminder he'd been off of substance. Startled and embarrassed by the unexpected onslaught to his body, he wanted to squirm. He quickly changed the subject.

"Do you think she will be all right?" he asked.

"She's her father's daughter, and she has you and Chief now. Do you think he's right for her? He seems pretty cold and violent."

"He's a good man."

"A lot like you?"

"Cold and violent?" Garrett countered tightly.

Nadine ignored his terseness and the insinuation. "That's the way he appears, but if he's like you, he's a decent man, kind, considerate, a little misguided in his intentions at times, but strong when he has to be."

"Chief," He emphasized that word, "will be once he's had the chance."

"How much of a chance is he going to get? What is going to happen now?"

"Good question." She raised an eyebrow and waited for more until he told her, "I don't know."

"Sure you do, you just don't want to be the one to take the responsibility of organizing these people into a normal life. Well, as normal as can be. A society without women is— "

"There are women," he stated with a pained expression and pointed towards the ceiling with his thumb. "Next level up. They're separated the same way the men are, hunters and scholars." He grimaced again. "Integrating them with men that haven't seen any woman except Dina for decades and who haven't..." He felt himself blush. "They haven't been able to because of the substance, but once they go off of it..." And he knew how quickly that ablility returned from his own discomfort. He was fighting the urge to get up to hide his physical reaction to her.

When his voice trailed off she asked, "They'll be able to have sex?"

He skidded away from the subject and where his own thoughts were going in regards to her. "I've done enough," he said bitterly. "They don't need what I'm good at anymore. There's been enough killing."

"That isn't what you're best at, and there will be more killing, especially if you don't help them. Or do you intend to take off and let them just stay as they are?"

"You know they can't stay like this, and I didn't say I wouldn't help," he snapped, flustered again.

"But you won't lead."

"No."

"But you do it so well."

"Mysty again?" he queried sarcastically. "He forgets a few things like the yantz and glemms."

"You've had help," she agreed, "but you're the one who brought them together. That's what's needed now, together with organization."

"I was a catalyst to bring one small group together. There's a damned sight more than them."

"A small group that will be the nucleus. You'll need an enforcing unit. The yantz—"

"No!" Garrett exclaimed in alarm. He laughed slightly over the way he startled her. "You don't turn a baby loose with lethal weapons."

"If my math is right, they have to be at least thirty-five years old."

"Some of them are a lot older than that, but none of them are more than a few months old emotionally."

"I don't understand."

Garrett blew a breath out. "I don't know if I can explain. They were designed as a non-emotional, mobile first-aid station for use in remote areas on the planet. No one knows if their designer gave them the capacity for compassion along with empathy, but they were never intended to live long enough to become self-aware, evolve into a new species, or reason the need for or to find a way on their own to reproduce into the hundreds necessary to provide at least one for each of us, something Mord was unaware of when he thought he had killed them all. They were to be used and then disposed of."

"That's cold."

"The Thornn were cold. Any life other than theirs was dispensable. The problem was that by the time the first yantz matured in the lab, their creator had lost his ability to communicate with them. They had an ingrained compulsion to bond, but had no idea their claws were surgical instruments, or that they were capable of treating more than open wounds. With their lack of experience, the claws became weapons to protect the one they had bonded with. Dina was the first they heard outside of themselves, even though they didn't understand her words."

What had happened then hadn't been a pretty picture. The Thornn who had attempted to take her away from the yantz for her cray had been slashed to ribbons with the yantz awakening to fill their compulsion to bond and protect within a matter of hours. Mord, kept caged because they feared his insanity when they weren't using him, and Mysty, he in his cage brought in for the next extraction, were released to care for her.

"They have emotions then?" Nadine prompted when he grew quiet.

"They're learning them," he told her, drawing himself out of thought. "Not actually learning emotion, but learning what those emotions are." He took a frustrated swipe at his hair. "They needed help understanding them, but Dina was in an emotional void. The Phogatres are pragmatic souls and transmit on a different level. They could communicate with words, but not emotions or mental images. After the other two attempts with hunters ended so badly, the yantz gave up."

"Then you came along?"

"They heard me." He gave her a strained smile. "And you—they misunderstood what they felt from you."

"Oh," she asked with a minxy grin, "they thought if I had such strong feelings for you, you should have strong feelings for me?"

"Something like that. I did say they're emotionally immature. They aren't very good at distinguishing one intense feeling from another yet."

"I'd say they're doing pretty good. They recognized love and panic."

"They thought it was for me, not Dina."

"They didn't misunderstand, Garrett," she told him bluntly. "You have no idea how terrified I was when I discovered you were missing too. All they found was where your horse had gone into the wire. They assumed you had gotten hurt, wandered off, and died. I thought I had lost you both."

"You don't even know me," he said in disbelief.

"I've known you for years through Carolyn and believe me, more than once I have wanted to break every sanction of my profession to find you and shake you until your head rattled for all your misplaced noble sacrifices and selfishness."

"Selfishness?" he asked in astonishment.

"Yes, selfishness. As long as you weren't attached to anyone, you wouldn't have to continue when things got rough."

Garrett's voice rose. "If you think it was any damned picnic, you're— "

"You were doing what you wanted. You had no responsibilities, and you didn't want any. You'd have to face up to being a cripple if you did, so every time you heard Carolyn— "

"I wasn't going to have anyone crying over me the way I cried when they died!"

Both were stunned into silence, Garrett by an outburst over something he never spoken of to anyone and her by his rage. She broke the quiet with a soft, "The war?"

He shook his head and lunched up to his feet. He still didn't want to talk about the mangled bodies and the dead friends. He had sworn then he would never care enough about anyone to suffer that kind of grief again or let anyone feel that way about him. The betrayal and abandonment when he returned home, being crippled, conquering it only to learn that in time he would be crippled again had only strengthened that resolve. In a way it was selfishness, but his daughter was one person he could never shut out.

"I didn't know that what I was seeing was real." He began to pace and his voice rose in agitation. "If I had, I would have gone after her. How the hell was I supposed to know what Marsha would do to her?"

Nadine went to her feet. Her temperament shifted right along with his, and her voice rose as well. "You had to have seen what a cold-hearted bitch she was when she walked out on you, leaving you flat on your back in a hospital bed."

"To me, not her own daughter."

"Half yours." She emphasized her words with a stab of a finger at him. "And in her mind it was your fault she walked out on you. You got hurt."

Garrett's voice dropped back to normal in perplexity. "What the hell kind of sense does that make?"

"None," Her voice dropped back to normal as well, "to anyone willing to accept their own failings. You should have seen her when I verified Carolyn's claim that you weren't paralyzed. She about came unglued."

"Unglued?" he questioned in amused perplexity. "That doesn't sound very professional."

"It wasn't. It was purely personal." She gave him a half-shrug. "She had attacked Carolyn the day before, tore the locket off her neck, and threw it in the waste basket, ranting about me being a quack before she dragged Carolyn home. I retrieved the locket, and as soon as I heard that Carolyn was gone, I knew where she was going. I was going to help her find you, even if I never worked again so I went to the house, stuck it to Marsha, and twisted her self-centered guts." She smiled at him, and her eyes sparkled. "I enjoyed every minute of it."

Garrett smiled back despite the unpleasantness of the subject, his inner turmoil, and his fatigue. Maybe it wasn't fair to Nadine. Maybe she could take everything all as calmly as she seemed to because she had yet to realize what it all meant. Maybe she would soon damn the day the yantz had interfered in her life, but he was glad they had.

XXI

Nadine stepped up behind Garrett where he stood in the breezeway and wrapped her arms around him, her baby-swollen belly pressed against his back. Together they watched Peggy unfurl her wings and nuzzle Boss's nose in the field a couple of hundred yards away before she asked softly, "What are you thinking about so seriously?"

"She'll drop her foal in a week or two," Garrett answered evasively.

Nadine knew him too well. "That's no reason for melancholia. What's bothering you?"

"A miracle." He turned to face her, folding his arms around her. "That Boss's missing testicles regenerated is a miracle to us. To the Thornn it was nothing more than an everyday occurrence, an effect of their substance and something they just took for granted and wasted."

"You're worried that we're too dependent on the things from the ship," she stated.

"Too much makes it too easy," he agreed. "They take too much for granted. If Tonya and the others that stayed on the ship…"

Nadine put her fingertips over his lips. "We don't need the ship or anything on it any longer to survive. Your little nucleus has seen to that, especially you and Chief. We're established enough to be independent so stop worrying and enjoy." She tipped her head, replaced her fingertips with a light kiss and turned him to look at the valley below. "This past year has proved it. It's time to celebrate."

The last year had been filled with hard labor and tension. Those who choose to move from the ship to the green planet had to adjust to the radical changes in their lives as well as learning to live in harmony with those of so many different cultures. The three hundred sets of rules Garrett had been expected to learn when he joined the hunters had been greatly diminished after the battle. That number had dropped even more so by those like Tonya who chose to stay in the world they knew onboard the ship, much like the animals that wouldn't leave their cages when Glemm had freed them. New, standard rules had to be formed and then enforced.

Below them the fruits of their labor sprawled out in a small settlement. The building materials from the vast holds that the Thornn had never been able to use had become their homes. Livestock, also from the Thornn holds, roamed the pastures of small farms. Fields seeded from bins onboard the ship dotted the valley and hillsides. More importantly people, men and women, were miniature figures all moving towards the largest building to attend the celebration of their first year on the planet.

Nadine chuckled with the memory of the look of dread on Garrett's face when he'd told her of the women. There had been the problems he had anticipated, of course, but the wills of the many had solved the worst of them and resulted in a baby boom. In the past year, their population had increased dramatically.

Garrett's hand slipped down to find hers. "Guess we ought to go. They're waiting for us."

They walked together hand in hand with Mischief loping in front of them down the hill to the largest of the buildings. Inside half the area was filled with mess hall style tables. The sight was reminiscent for Garrett of the first time he had walked into the common room onboard the ship. Men of all shades from white to green sat there, each with two eyes, two ears, two legs, and one head, each different, but each also in many ways the same. Women sat with them, many holding babies. They all rose to greet Garrett and Nadine. Vo and his mate, Gunian with the woman he was courting, the Phogatres and Mysty, all were smiling. Yantz, in pairs and singularly, hovered, and glemms were scattered about. Through the mass, Carolyn tugged the new, smiling Chief by the hand, her belly swollen with child. Her gait was a little uneven, but after Chief's loving care she was able to walk, and her smile was brilliant.

In private, Nadine asked Garrett, *"Has it all been worth it?"*

There was no hesitation as one arm tightened around her baby thickened waist and he held out his hand to take his daughter's. *"Absolutely."*

The End

About the Author

Larriane Wills also writes as Larion Wills (same pronunciation, different spelling). Her interests in reading are as varied as her genres, that interest beginning as soon as she was able to pick up a book and expanded to putting her own stories to paper.

She invites you to visit her web site, check out the blurbs on upcoming publications, and just say hi at: http://www.larriane.com or by email at larriane@larriane.com

Printed in the United States
79245LV00004B/31-60

9 781934 041185